"RACE. THE COLOUR OF SHAME"

"Ms MacLean's debut novel illuminates the difficulty of racial identity and the chaos it can create. The narrative deftly investigates racism beyond simple black and white figures. This astutely delicate dramatisation of race relations dotted with ghosts, sex scenes and rambling in New Orleans and abroad can be thrilling .The story provides a worthwhile glimpse at how startling the answers to questions of heredity can be."

Kirkus review

"With a fluid and truly elegant style, and the controversial subjects of race as well as reincarnation,the talented Marie-Madeleine MacLean has brilliantly created a sinfully entertaining novel with the full force of intelligence behind a frightening drama. This is indeed a brilliant debut novel and certainly an instant classic…"

Literary and creative Artists

"Race" is a thrilling, thought-provoking and highly imaginative novel which succeeds at feeling original due to its heady mixture of reincarnation, ghosts, family secrets, violence and sensuality, in the disparate worlds of London and New Orleans. Even more impressive is that all these elements unite into a coherent whole, anchored by deep themes and a set of colorful, compelling characters. Combining Christian angels with Voodoo Gods, makes for an interesting and truly original supernatural cocktail which helps recast familiar Christian iconography in a fresh way, that makes readers look and think about the world in a different way"

Hollywood Coverage

"This exceptional debut novel brilliantly defines the unique style, exceptional descriptions and the superb punctuation of its undeniably stylish French author. Crisp, thought-provoking, as well as richly detailed with a undeniable designer's eye, the seemingly aloof Marie-Madeleine MacLean has certainly achieved a brilliant and absolutely seductive novel; certainly as brilliant as its stylish and beautiful author."

Jacques Bruyas. Author

"Race is a truly surprising, inspiring and engrossing story by which the reader will see his horizon of thoughts certainly enlarged, and will realised that his heart is capable of beating for all human beings; irrespective of skin's color and race. Simply luminous."

Brenda Lee Eager. International award winning singer, songwriter

"The truly gifted Marie-Madeleine MacLean is indeed a sheer literary revelation with this fascinating, original and sometimes deeply frightening debut novel, which has been written with great clarity, sincere conviction and an undeniable French charm. 'Race. The colour of shame' is not only an exceptionally brilliant story; but also a truly meaningful thriller. A 'literarity' which can truly be called inspired…"

Diana Rose Hartman. Author.

RACE. THE COLOUR OF SHAME

by

Marie-Madeleine MacLean

authorHOUSE®

AuthorHouse™ UK Ltd.
1663 Liberty Drive
Bloomington, IN 47403 USA
www.authorhouse.co.uk
Phone: 0800.197.4150

Published by AuthorHouse 11/26/2013

ISBN: 978-1-4772-4978-9 (sc)
ISBN: 978-1-4772-4979-6 (hc)
ISBN: 978-1-4772-4980-2 (e)

To the great spirit and soul of the following...

The late civil rights activist, Reverend Martin Luther King, for his supreme dedication to end racial discrimination in the United States of America; and for the matchless eloquence of his exceptional "I Have A Dream" speech, which put to shame the advocates of segregation and argued that racial justice and equality is in accord with God's will, and continues to inspire the conscience of America today...

The exceptional and talented Ms. Oprah Winfrey, whose media presence has not only raised public awareness of the immense human suffering caused by racial prejudice and social inequality; but whose empathy and grace reminds us all to look beyond the superficial and strive for empathy. Ms. Winfrey is also the living proof that greatness doesn't come from a specific gender, genes nor race; and even less by one's family entitlements. Her strength and natural generosity has inspired my constant respect and sincere admiration.

My late father-in-law, the extremely talented best selling Scottish novelist Alistair Maclean; for his advice and generosity. I can still sense your shadow...

My first literary agent, the late Mr. Jay S. Garon, formerly with "Pinder Lane & Garon Brooke", New York, NY. I truly thank him for his priceless advice and counsel, and for the most invaluable advice "to always stick to my guns and to listen first to my inner voice; instead of the confusing advice of others who would have preferred I do formula books..."

And finally, a huge thank you from the bottom of my heart to the Almighty, as well as my incredibly efficient 'Guardian Angel', for having protected me against myself during my 'sweet journey through hell', while I was suffering the terrible lost of my loving sisters, Jaqueline-Edwige and Monica, their children Stephane and Paola, as well as my adorable brother Jean-Pierre.

In addition, shortly prior, I had the painful lost of three of my best friends; the sweet and beautiful Josée, Evelyne and Kookie; all of whom died of cancer...

I also thank the Lord again for giving me the strength during the last two years to cope, on a daily basis, with the painful mental decline of my beloved mother, the beautiful, sweet and generous Yvonne-Marguerite, who recently passed away with Alzheimer's. She was pure, constant undiluted love, and her nurturing strength and faith made me who I am... I miss you terribly, maman.

May God bless their loving souls...
Amen.

"We all live on the same planet;
but not in the same world…"

Prologue

"New Orleans. Louisiana"

La Rêveuse

A fluffy whitish thing, soft as a cloud slowly hovered above the new-born's face...

The infant wanted to reach out and grab it, but something sinister in the metallic blue eyes of the man who held the pillow seemed to paralyse her. The tiny baby girl exhibited neither terror nor tears; instead, she mimicked the expression of her killer, as if she was little more than a mirror, as if she hadn't lived long enough to cultivate a will of her own. Yet, if the man had looked a little bit closer, had cared to gaze beyond the infant's fleshly eyes and into the window of her soul, he would've seen the discouragement; sensed the rage that waited behind that silent mask of resignation...

After all, the soul had barely begun to remember itself. It had breathed the stale air of the palatial birthing room of the Hoxworth Castle for less than an hour, and already knew that it would not be allowed to fulfil its destiny. Not at this time; not in this particular body...

When the little head of the infant crowned between her mother's legs, the soul felt blessed that it had been given another chance to live. Attentively, it registered each utterance that echoed throughout the room. Several people had gathered around the princely bed, nervously awaiting the new Hoxworth heir, and they'd softly cooed, whispering their warm welcomes.

The soul had felt its tiny lips curve into a natural smile, as the blue-eyed doctor carefully wiped away the blood that smeared her little face and carefully proceeded to inspect her skin. Counting each finger and toe, his trained eyes had lingered on the soft flesh of her belly, perhaps a bit too cautiously...

"A perfectly proportioned baby girl," the family doctor proudly announced, handing the infant to her mother. "You must be thrilled, my dear!"

The young mother had breathed a sigh of relief. "She is more beautiful than the summer sunrise... I will call her Angelica Aurora Maria," she announced, beaming.

Her husband proudly smiled, accepting the congratulations from the family and the elite members of the household staff; but his mother, Theresa, did not stop staring at the infant, scrutinising her, as if searching for a defect.

"Look! Her skin is darkening!" The matron snarled a moment later, snatching the baby from her mother's arms before handing it to the doctor.

Seconds later, a deadly silence slid over the room, like a cold shadow...

"She is not white!" The elderly woman's words crackled with disgust; then she shrugged her shoulders, shucking off any responsibility for events that would inevitably follow.

"Joy and celebration" had given way to fear; voices had become high-pitched and accusatory. The soul prayed for a compassionate servant, like the young black maidservant who stood in the corner, weeping as she wrung out the bloodied cloth the doctor had used to clean the baby.

In a blink of an eye and without a single word, like so many times before, the death sentence had been pronounced...

"How can it be?" Reginald Hoxworth, the father lamented, as he nervously watched the infant's skin slowly losing its pinkish cast and becoming more alike to a "café au lait". His expressive grey eyes darted anxiously from his new-born daughter to his young beautiful wife, not knowing who to blame, before he mouthed silent curses to both God and the devil, casting a particularly wrathful stare at the handsome black butler, the brother of the young maid servant who wept.

"This is hardly unusual," the family doctor said, in a matter-of-fact way. "After all, sir, such a misfortune was not completely unexpected..." He added while lowering his eyes.

"Take it away!" The matron ordered with great disgust, dismissing the baby with a wave of her bejewelled hand. "And give my daughter-in-law something to calm her nerves. She's hysterical,

3

can't you see?" Disdainfully, she shot a wicked glance towards the baby's mother, who'd curled up in the foetal position, her body shaking convulsively, her grief settling into her heart like a viper.

Fervently, the soul prayed…

The grandmother's demands were executed without further discussion.

The doctor motioned for one of the oldest black maids to remove the mulatto infant from sight, before swiftly injecting a previously prepared hypodermic needle into the ivory flesh of the now screaming mother.

"No! Please, I beg you, Theresa," the mother pleaded. "Don't do it! Have mercy on my child! We could give her away… Nobody needs to know! Have mercy, please; pleeease Theresa!"

The eyes of the birthing party sunk to the floor…

They all knew too well what had to be done, and despite the desperate moans of the broken-hearted mother, they all silently told themselves that it was for the best...

If such a thing had happened in Paris, Rome, or even New York, it would have been different; but this was New Orleans in the South and, more importantly, these were the Hoxworths.

One mulatto infant was enough to bring down the entire house of cards and force the matron and her son to forever abdicate their positions as the undisputed "King and Queen" of New Orleans' high society.

No! That wayward colour gene - the same one that had found its way into the Hoxworth dynasty one drunken night and many generations ago - must be cast out, with little thought to the soul which had tried, again and again, to be born and speak its truth.

One day I will live, the soul promised itself, as its assassin lowered the white lace pillow, while the young black maid made the sign of the cross, her eyes wide and terrified, but unable to look away.

The doctor's face was grim as he firmly pushed the pillow down.

"What a pity. Despite the tone of her skin, she would've been a beauty," he sadly remarked.

The mulatto infant didn't struggle; the soul was too proud...

It was only a moment before the baby surrendered to the darkness and became still as a doll; then the soul rushed back to whence it came, but the pain of being discarded like the contents of a full chamber pot would follow it into its next incarnation, like a spectral tail of a comet. The sour memory of betrayal and abandonment had latched onto its core, as a reminder that it would not find peace, nor restore its innocence, until its murder was revenged.

Wandering through the ethers between death and life again, the soul would wait for the opportunity to return to the earthly world; but the soul was patient by nature, as time was merely a human construct, and knew that one day it would take its revenge. Soon enough, the soul would be reborn again...

Amen.

Chapter One

"New Orleans"

Present Day

It was barely eight in the morning and the air was already stifling...

André Boivin, a gentle man with a broken heart, folded the pale blue blanket that covered his wife's frail body and carefully smoothed the white cotton sheet around her; then he lovingly caressed the familiar creases of her wrinkled face, before placing a soft kiss on her forehead. Futilely, he prayed that her voice would fill their home with life like it did before she fell ill; but he knew that it was only a question of days before Josephine would take her place in the small cemetery, alongside five generations of her kin...

Holding her bony hand, André lingered, wishing for the impossible. If only God would grant his beloved Josephine one more month, they could celebrate their Golden Wedding Anniversary; but it was a month that could as well be an eternity...

Since the day that André fell in love with Josephine, he'd selfishly prayed that he would die first. Not because he feared sorrow, but because he feared going insane with grief, and also because he feared for his beloved daughter; Angela...

André couldn't understand his wife's stubbornness, and no matter how hard he often tried to convince her to change her mind, Josephine remained adamant in her decision that before she died, Angela would be told the terrible truth.

Thirty-two years ago, Josephine had given "Madame" her word; but now she refused to enter the world of the dead with a broken promise tainting her soul.

Age had made Josephine terribly superstitious, and she'd told André that she'd be cast into the fire of hell if her soul didn't come clean before the Lord.

André shivered when he imagined how his youngest daughter would react when she found out that her life was built on a lie...

Given Angela's love of justice, she would no doubt confront the remaining players in the tragic family saga and fight to uproot the motives behind the repeated atrocities committed in the name of "honour".

Yes, my golden child would fight, André sadly thought.

It was that upcoming battle, and the inevitable repercussions it would have on their family, which caused his bones to ache.

André raised his tired eyes to the ceiling, questioning the mind of the Almighty. Shaking his head in dismay, he crossed himself. If he were to accomplish the task at hand, he would need to ignore his worries about the future and simply focus on the present.

He parted the faded rose-printed chintz draperies, before summoning all his remaining strength, so that he could push the heavy paned windows open.

The outermost branch of an ancient magnolia tree sprang gracefully into the room, as if it had been waiting for the last chance to offer sweet Josephine a fragrant pink blossom. André hoped its sweet scent would bring her solace from the pain. More than once, he had caught his wife whispering to that tree with a beatific smile brightening her face. She told him often that the old magnolia tree was the guardian of their secret; more likely, it helped to carry the burden of her lie, a verdant confessor that helped to alleviate the shame that crawled into her belly, whenever she'd slid over Angela's questions...

"Why must we tell her?" André asked his sleeping wife. How could Josephine - how could he? - admit something that they didn't even dare to whisper about in the dark because they were too afraid that their beloved golden child would hear them through the thin walls? But André knew there was no use in arguing the issue any further, because Josephine was a headstrong woman and she wasn't going to turn into a mouse just because she was dying.

He tiredly closed the bedroom door and silently made his way down the old wooden stairs. They seemed to creak and moan with more complaint than usual; or perhaps the house was too quiet, already in mourning...

As André picked up the phone in the living room, the furrows on his brow suddenly deepened.

How do you tell your child that her mother is dying?

How do you keep your voice from trembling?

How do you tell your child to hurry home in time to give her mother a final embrace, knowing that she will find out that everything she believed in was, in fact, based on a lie?

Angela would not be able to bear Josephine's death, let alone face the terrible battles that lie ahead of her.

Even the width of the Atlantic Ocean wouldn't suffice to hide André's own weaknesses, his guilt and his shame; and yet, it had to be done.

After all, it was Josephine's dying wish…

Finally, with trembling fingers, André succeeded in ignoring the conflicting voices in his head and tiredly dialled the number. Across the pond, a woman with a decisively British accent picked up:

"Hello. This is the Royal Ballet School. How might I help you?"

"This is Mister Boivin speakin'. I'm Angela Boivin's father. Can I please talk to my daughter, ma'am?" He struggled to keep his voice from faltering.

"Well, I'm sorry, sir, but Miss Boivin is in rehearsal at the moment. Might I take a message for her?"

"No. This can't wait no longer, not a moment. You see… her Mama's dyin'," André said, almost apologetically.

"Oh, Blessed Mary," the woman whispered, her cheery English reserve giving way to panic. "Of course, I'll fetch her immediately! Don't go anywhere, sir, please." She put him on hold and the music of Schubert floated sombrely through the airwaves.

"Thank you, ma'am," André sadly said, feeling his throat tightening. Although he had rehearsed a speech, now he couldn't remember a word of it; instead, a parade of images marched through his mind…

It had been five years since he'd seen his golden child. Angela had come home to introduce her husband, a handsome and wealthy well-bred English attorney. He and Josephine were very happy that their youngest daughter had found love, but her siblings had had a more difficult time accepting her choice of a husband. The three of them acted as if Angela had committed high treason, but as usual, Josephine kept calm, trying her best to keep peace in the family.

Angela was always a good girl and a clever one, André told himself, smiling as he remembered her twirling under the shade of that old magnolia tree.

By the time Angela was six, she had already set her sight on the heavens.

"I'm going to be a ballerina, daddy-pie," she proudly told him, with more assurance and determination than any of her siblings. From that day forward, André never doubted that his adorable "little poodle," as he affectionately called her, would be a star.

Angela exceeded in everything she set her mind to, even catching the eye of the haughty Miss Lili Wing, a former prima ballerina who had an uncanny ability to sight and mentor future stars. Miss Wing had obtained a grant for Angela that allowed her to study at the Classical Dance Academy in the city, and soon afterwards had convinced her parents to send her to London, where she would rapidly blossom under the tutelage of the famed "Elyse Veloso", at the Royal Ballet School.

In less than a decade, the beautiful Angela Boivin became one of the brightest stars to light up the international ballet scene; yet, she never forgot her common roots, or the harsh reality of the poverty from which she came.

From the day Angela began earning a decent salary, she gratefully sent her family as much money as she could; and within a couple of years, she had paid off the mortgage of their New Orleans home, enabling her father to quit his job at the slaughterhouse, where for over forty years, he had inhaled the foul stench of death…

The memory of standing amidst a room of bloody sow carcasses catapulted André back into the present. He was about to hang up when Angela's lovely voice broke the silence.

"Hello, Daddy. What is it?"

For a few moments, they silently listened to the rhythm of each other's breath. Angela was too afraid to ask what was wrong, and André didn't want to break the sad news.

"Is it Mama?" She finally asked. "It is Mama, isn't it? Is she…?"

"Your Mama is… No, poodle, she's not well-," André said with a broken voice, holding back his tears.

Angela suddenly felt a sharp pain in her abdomen, as if an invisible hand seemed to claw her intestines. Deep down, she already knew what her father was going to say. Her dreams of late had been more foreboding than usual. The strange steel blue eyes and the motionless angels floated in and out of her dreams, but the shadows were becoming more pronounced, much more frightening than before. She often awoke drenched in sweat, unable to breathe, grasping for air, choking as if the white downy wings of the angels were suffocating her in her dreams.

By the time her father finally mustered up the courage to explain, Angela didn't want to hear the bad news anymore.

"It's her heart, honey... You know your Mama, always working hard and giving all she had to everyone, but her own self." André was mumbling, his own sorrow paralysing his tongue.

"But can't you find a better doctor? I'll pay any price, daddy, you know that! It's way too soon!" She almost shouted.

"I know, Poodle, I know... But there's nothing that can be fixed anymore. It's your Mama's time, that's all; it comes to all of us..." He sadly said, refraining from crying.

"Not Mama, not Mama!" Angela cried. "Not now!"

"It's gonna be alright, honey... Your Mama is ready. And she's sufferin' too much for the life to stay in her."

Angela angrily wiped away her tears. "It's not fair! How long until...?" She slowly began, feeling revolted.

"Just a few days... A week at best," André almost whispered, guiltily wishing that he'd called his daughter sooner; but he had hoped that the stubborn Josephine would reconsider telling her about old "madam Elisabeth"...

"I'm... I'm really sorry, Poodle," he finally said, before he broke down and wept.

Hearing her father sob took Angela by surprise. She had never heard him crying before. Now it was her turn to be strong.

"Yes daddy... I understand," she said sadly. "I'll catch the next flight... Tell Mama that I'll be home soon... I love you, daddy-pie; and please, please, don't cry."

Chapter Two

"London"

England

Angela hung up the phone and clutched the desk, futilely trying to keep herself from spiralling downwards into a vortex of despair...

Feeling the burning tears, Angela closed her eyes and wrapped her arms around her shoulders, and then she slowly began to rock back and forth, pretending that she was in her mother's loving arms. Suddenly, the melody of an old lullaby that had soothed her when she was a child and when the summer sky was full of lightning and the air crackled with thunders began to play in her mind:

> *Don't be afraid, my golden child,*
> *Don't be afraid of wind nor thunder light.*
> *Don't be afraid, my golden child,*
> *Mama is here and all is right.*
> *Hush, hush, sleep now, and close your eyes,*

Don't be afraid of night
Close your eyes, my golden child.
As long as Mama is here, then all will be right...

But now Mama will be gone and nothing will be right anymore, Angela sadly thought, rocking more rapidly, before briskly shaking her head, to force herself back to sanity. *Mama's still alive and it is not the time to give in to grief; not yet anyway...*

Angela called home and asked her chambermaid to pack a suitcase for the trip to New Orleans before phoning her husband.

"Law Firm of Haddington and Haddington. Mr. Pierce Haddington's office. This is Mrs. Dobson speaking. How may I help you?"

Angela hesitated. "Hello Mrs. Dobson. May I speak to my husband, please?"

"Oh, hello Mrs. Haddington. What a lovely surprise," the receptionist softly said. "I wanted to thank you for the tickets to the ballet... You were absolutely divine, but I must say that your new partner wowed me. Who is that gorgeous Russian blond? My husband was a wee bit jealous, I think. He..."

"I'm truly sorry Mrs. Dobson, but I need to speak to my husband now. It's quite urgent."

"Oh, I apologise for going on and on," the receptionist said, taken somewhat aback by Angela's strange tone of voice. "It's not often that I get a chance to speak with you. Your husband is in conference at the moment, but he shouldn't be more than half an hour.

You could leave a message perhaps. He's with some rather upscale clients - petrodollars, you know…" She said, lowering her voice.

"That won't do. It's imperative I speak with him now. My mother is dying, and I'll be catching the next plane to Louisiana, where my family lives."

"Oh my Jesus! In that case, I'll fetch him… I'm so sorry," Mrs. Dobson nervously said. As she rose from her chair, she noticed the dark blond well-mannered elegant woman in her mid-sixties approaching her desk, her pencil-thin eyebrows raised with obvious interest; she'd obviously been eavesdropping…

"Is that my sister-in-law on the line?" The woman asked, an insecure smile brightening her alabaster powdered face.

"No, Mrs. Haddington. It's your nephew's wife, Angela. She needs to speak to him."

Gail Haddington's superficial smile fell from her face like a brick and was rapidly replaced with an expression of undiluted contempt.

"Oh, I see… Doesn't she understand that we don't interrupt important meetings each time we need to whine about our aching Prima Donna feet?" As if she were marking her territory, Gail Haddington firmly placed her terribly expensive Hermès 'Kelly' brown crocodile handbag on the secretary's desk.

Mrs. Dobson's heart raced as she stood up for Angela. "But she rarely - if ever - phones the office, Madam. This is an emergency!"

"Well... let me be the judge of that, Margaret, will you? What's exactly the problem?" Gail dryly asked, swiftly moving her waffle thin body to the left, blocking the secretary's way.

Mrs. Dobson firmly placed her hands on her waist. "For God's sake, Mrs. Haddington, her mother is dying! Now let me pass, would you please?" She demanded, fully aware that speaking in such a manner to the highly irritable Gail Haddington could cost her the job.

A slick smile crept over Gail's face as she nervously toyed with the large triple strand of priceless 'Mikimoto' white south sea pearls that hung around her slender neck.

"Well, I just can't imagine my nephew mingling with those people again," she finally said before raising her eyes. Gail could feel her facial muscles straining to frown and was extremely glad that she'd taken her dermatologist's advice to receive some Botox injections last week...

"Well then, I suppose that this little funeral will be quite a folkloric event, if nothing else..." She dryly added, grabbing her expensive handbag and gingerly stepping out of the way. "What are you waiting for? Go... go!" She dismissively waved her taupe-gloved hand. "And while you're in there, Margaret, tell my husband not to keep me waiting much longer; and also, my dear, bring me a cup of Earl Grey with lemon, as well as some of those delicious watercress and salmon sandwiches... I'll be in the salon."

Mrs. Dobson shrugged. It wasn't her job to cater to the culinary desires of the insufferable Gail Haddington, but knowing how bitchy the woman could get, the secretary decided to do as she was told. After all, Pierce Haddington was a kind employer, and jobs were hard to get lately. *But first things first,* she told herself, as she walked passing in front of the senior Mrs. Haddington. She softly knocked on the double mahogany doors of the conference room. A moment later, Pierce picked up the line, his voice worried.

"Darling, what's wrong?"

"My father just phoned. My mother is dying..." Pain coursed through Angela's body as she painfully spoke the words again.

"Oh, good grief! I can't tell you how sorry I am. Well, give me two hours to pack. And don't worry, darling. I'll take care of everything!"

Angela's mind flooded with a familiar embarrassment. "No, my darling, please... It's not necessary, but thanks for the thought. I prefer to go alone... You'll be out of place there, you know that," she softly said, feeling sorry for him.

"But darling, that would be highly unethical and just plain rude!" He firmly protested.

"Please, try to understand. My mother is so ill that she won't notice your absence anyway..."

"But the rest of your family will," he insisted.

"Please, Pierce... It's better this way. They've already made up their minds about you." She sadly said, feeling ashamed.

"All right, all right then." His tone was a mixture of reluctance, anger and resignation. "At least, let me take care of the expenses. Tell your father to choose only the best of everything.'

"Thank you, my darling. I truly appreciate the gesture. I need to go now. I'm on standby for the next flight. Pray that I get a seat."

"Absolutely not! The firm's travel agency can accommodate you, and my father's chauffeur will meet you at the house in an hour to take you to the airport. Is there anything else you need, my love?"

"No. Thank you, darling. You're a lifesaver! I love you; I really do..." Angela lovingly whispered, her eyes filling with tears again. Suddenly, the old lullaby started to play in her head again.

Don't be afraid, my golden child. As long as Mama is here, then all will be right...

"No, nothing will be right again without Mama in my life; nothing..." Angela sadly thought, crying.

Chapter Three

As soon as Angela hung up the phone, she heard the choreographer's voice wafting through the hallway...

"What is going on, Angela?" Veronika cooed, practically flying towards her. Veronika Valiskaia was still as light on her feet as she was when she danced for the world famous "Bolshoi" in her youth; but her Russian accent, although diffused by the years living in England, was still quite audible. Her doll-like lavender eyes darted back and forth as she spoke.

"For God's sake, my dear, we've been waiting for you over ten frigging minutes, and it won't be much longer before Boris loses his patience! I certainly don't want to put up with another one of his moody tantrums. So, Angela, would you please hurry back so we can finish rehearsing this last scene and call it a day? My feet are killing me... Chop, chop! Let's get on with the show!" She spun on her heel, her movement just harsh enough to show her irritation.

"I'm dreadfully sorry, Veronika, but I'm done for the day. My mother is dying. I've to fly to New Orleans immediately."

The choreographer performed a graceful half pirouette, turning to face Angela again. This time her expression was stern and fraught with worry...

"When? Now? New Orleans? Today? But we have work to do! Can't it be postponed?" Her tone was shrill and staccato, and she flitted about like a hummingbird; an annoying hummingbird...

Angela put her hands to her ears in irritation. "No, it can't! My father said it is only days until..."

"How awful, chérie, but still? How will we manage here? My poor Boris won't like this a bit, not a bit!" She nervously said, hyperventilating. "And there are fittings scheduled and even photos haven't been taken for the press release yet. The tour's less than a month away! Dear God, please! Don't tell me that..." The pupils of her eyes dilated with fear. "But you will make the opening in Monte Carlo?" She asked nervously. "Angela, no matter what happens, you must think like the magnificent artist you are! You have an obligation to your public, my child, an obligation to your art! The dance must go on. The..."

"Please, pleeease Veronika. Spare me! This is not a scene from a play. My mother is dying, do you hear me? Dying!!!" Angela exclaimed before she snapped her fingers in front of the choreographer's eyes. "Where is your heart? How would you feel if your mother was dying?"

"Well, she died when I was five, so I don't remember much," Veronika candidly answered.

"It's not a wonder," Angela sadly replied, turning to leave.

The choreographer followed her down the hallway, prancing after her as nervously as a Chihuahua on speed.

"Angela, my dear, please! Let me handle this. At least allow me to tell Boris that you're leaving. I know how to calm him down."

"You might've had the heart to calm me down, Veronika… A simple 'I'm sorry' would've been nice!" Angela snapped. "But you do what you want," she coolly added. "And make sure to tell your dear Boris that I apologise for the "inconvenience" that my mother's death is causing him today." She icily said before turning around.

"Of course my dear… Yes, I'll do just that," the choreographer sweetly answered, ignoring the sarcasm. "I know exactly what I'll tell him. Boris is such a sensitive man… But just promise to be back in time for the opening in Monte Carlo, "ma chérie". Please, pleeease!" She begged, now looking really sad…

Without another word, Angela firmly closed the door of her dressing room.

As she changed into her street clothes, she heard Boris shouting in his Russian tongue, while Veronika futilely attempted to placate him. Then she heard a hard thud against her door. Angrily, she opened it and realised that the enraged six-foot-three blond had thrown his ballet shoes and was now pacing up and down the hallway like a spoiled child. Veronika was scurrying about him, trying her best to calm him down.

If the scene were not so appalling, it would be comical…

When Boris saw Angela, he thrust out his muscular chest. "So, Lady, how long must I wait for your return? When will your mother die?" He almost shouted with his thick Russian accent, as hard as gravel.

"I refuse to answer that!" Angela exclaimed, groping in her bag for her car keys.

"You'd better start thinking about it now! No matter how good you are, my dear Angela, you are not near to being prepared. Be warned! I will not be known as an object of ridicule on account of your failure! I am "Boris Parchenko", and no one ridicules me! You understand? No one! You must understand that!" Boris finally shouted, visibly beside himself.

"My dear Boris, if you're the subject of any ridicule, it certainly won't be on my behalf... Now, if you please excuse me, I have a plane to catch!"

In her rush, Angela had forgotten to latch her burgundy 'Escada' shoulder bag, and her wallet fell to the wooden floor. The photo holder had slipped out and lay wide open for all eyes to see...

"Your wallet!" Veronika hollered, picking it up before suspiciously eyeing the photographs. Angela sharply turned around; but before she could snatch her belongings from Veronika's hands, she saw the all-too-familiar expression of surprise...

"But... but who are these... these people?" Boris peered over the choreographer's shoulders. A mixture of confusion and disgust appeared upon his face, and he vainly tried to stifle a laugh.

"That is my family,' Angela calmly answered, gracefully stooping down to pick up her wallet.

"Really?" Veronika said, visibly surprised. Her powdered face flushed the exact colour of the Cosmopolitan cocktails she often drank. "Your family? You don't say?" Her voice twittered with uneasiness.

"Yes Veronika, this is my family. This is my mother, Josephine; and this is my father, André," Angela finally said, nervously pointing them out. "And if you wish, you can flip the pocket and gawk at my sisters, Blanche and Aimée... As for this handsome fellow, he's my brother, John." She said again while looking straight into her eyes.

The choreographer traded knowing glances with Boris, making sure that he could get a good look at the family's photos, before handing them to Angela.

"So, Veronika, what did you expect, Aryans?" Angela defiantly asked, as she reinserted the photo cover into her wallet.

"Angela, chérie..." The choreographer slowly said lowering her eyes, visibly embarrassed... "We all knew you were of some sort of... exotic ancestry, but it never occurred to me that your family would be quite so, uh; quite so... un-exotic I suppose... They're just... well, they're just black!" She flatly said, still avoiding Angela's eyes. "Certainly the press doesn't know of your humble origins, otherwise someone would've taken pains to acknowledge you as a "black" dancer! Looking at you, my dear, I assumed you may have had some Latino or Middle Eastern blood; or perhaps even some Oriental influence," Veronika painfully explained, looking somewhat puzzled and quite worried; even sorry...

Since Angela was a child, she had been studied and categorised as if she were a cell under a microscope, awaiting a label of identification. As far as she could remember she was always pointed at, separated, chastised and even often alienated. At the age of seven, she realised that she was a "hybrid", as beautiful as a rare orchid perhaps; but a hybrid nonetheless…

"Sorry to deceive you, my dear Veronika," Angela sweetly said with pronounced sarcasm. "However, that's just what I am: "a mulatto". And God as my witness, I'm quite proud of it!" She finally exclaimed with a smile.

Before the waiting tears could fall from her beautiful greenish eyes, Angela rushed down the hallway; but she wasn't quick enough to save herself from the sting of Veronika's stern warning to Boris…

"This is not good, my dear Boris; not good at all! She's going to give you a hard time. I can feel it and I'm never wrong about these things… I know she is a great dancer, but you may be better off if you demand a more appropriate partner for the upcoming tour in Monte Carlo. And sweetheart, if it's ridicule that you fear, you'll have the intelligence to keep this chunk of gossip hush-hush. Promise me that, darling… Of all the surprising things I can't believe Angela is a Negro…" Veronika added, joyfully clicking her tongue.

An angel passed and the devil smiled; again…

Chapter Four

After masterfully fighting his way through heavy rain and London's endemic traffic, the impeccably Ronald McGee smoothly parked the classic "1958 MY" burgundy Bentley Continental at Heathrow departures, not heeding the "Do Not Park" signs.

After checking Angela's 'Louis Vuitton' luggage, the stylish chauffeur promptly escorted her inside the large airport, where a kaleidoscope of humans in all shapes, sizes and skin colours rushed to catch planes to Paris, Rome, New York, Sydney, Kuala Lumpur, Beijing, Dakar, Tahiti, Bora Bora or the Caribbean, all of them travelling for business or pleasure, or tiredly returning to where they truly belong; those places that they call "home"...

Angela wondered how many among them were on their way to pay their last respects to a dying loved one, as she glanced at her platinum and diamond 'Patek Philippe' watch; she realized she had just sixteen minutes to reach the gate before her plane departed. As she gracefully sprinted through the long and crowded corridors of Heathrow, she cursed herself for donning a black cashmere turtleneck and a superb ankle length black mink coat. Not only was her body already soaked with perspiration, but she also realised that she'd have little need for such heavy clothing in New Orleans. As for her high-heeled 'Jimmy Choo' black crocodile boots, they were suddenly unbearable, and she couldn't help thinking about the plight of those noble Chinese women who were forced to bind their feet in the name of beauty. Her wrists also ached from hauling a heavy vanity case, but she didn't dare check it; too often, the low pressure of the baggage compartment had caused the jars that held her expensive creams and perfumes to explode.

What was I thinking? She nervously thought, while trying to stay calm.

It wasn't as if Angela was going on tour; and yet, here she was, travelling with her normal accoutrements. Perhaps she was in denial, wanting to pretend that she wasn't on her way to watch her mother die. Anyway, it was not as if she could throw on a pair of jeans and a simple white sweatshirt. Paparazzi always lurked about, just waiting to snap away at celebrities unmasked, and Angela was too much of a perfectionist and too professional to damage her polished public image or dishonour her highly respected ballet troupe by letting the tabloids catch her looking down and out. Keeping up appearances, she knew, had always its price…

As Angela nervously presented her boarding pass to the gate attendant, she felt the eyes of a tall man in his forties, fall sensually upon her. Such predatory behaviour was to be expected at airports, she had long ago concluded. Perhaps it was instinctual, a sort of "genetic urge" that afflicted men with a desire to plant their seed in foreign soil...

Angela did her best to ignore the man's come-on and calmly walked through the telescopic passage towards the jumbo jet; but she sensed his strong masculine aura behind her and could almost feel him sniffing her scent like a tomcat on the prowl...

Fortunately, as always, the firm's travel agency had managed to procure her a first class ticket, which usually served to segregate her from most of the horny males on the make. Most of the men in first class were much too busy preparing for business meetings and money to think about sex - or so it seemed - and besides, they would have boarded by now.

"Welcome back, Mrs. Haddington. Nice to have you with us again! Number eight is the window seat," the lovely redheaded stewardess said, gesturing to the right.

"Bingo! I'm lucky number seven!" Hollered the man behind her.

Angela took a deep breath and tried to imagine herself in a bubble of light, a trick she had learned from a savvy yoga teacher. Certainly, this man could not be worse than the annoying jerk that was sitting next to her on a flight between Rome and Sydney a few months back. For twenty extremely long hours, that one kept feigning sleep; just so he could let his head sometimes fall upon her breast...

Angela nervously looked around, searching for an empty seat. Unfortunately, the flight was oversold.

"Mrs. Haddington, I'll take your cosmetic case and your coat. Please let me know if you need anything else. My name is

Frances," the stewardess said with a slight Scottish accent. When Angela handed her things to her, the Texan intervened.

"Don't bother, Miss. I'll take care of this mighty-fine little lady. It's the duty of a gentleman; and I'm nothing if not one of them!" He donned a big stupid smile, and snatched Angela's "Louis Vuitton' vanity case and 'Fendi' mink coat from her grasp; then he hoisted the case into the overhead compartment and stuffed her coat on top of it, as if it were a cheap bomber jacket...

Angela cringed as she watched the man slamming the door shut, crushing the delicate pelts. But today, she didn't have the energy to reprimand him.

"Let me help you," the stewardess offered, exchanging a knowing glance with Angela. She opened the bin, swiftly removed the beautiful coat and carefully smoothed the fur. "I'll hang this up in the closet, Mrs. Haddington," she said sympathetically, smiling like an angel.

"Thank you, Frances," Angela softly replied, with a deep sigh of relief.

"That's what I like to see... Good old-fashioned service!" The Texan boomed. "While you're up there, bring me a double whiskey, would ya, baby?"

"Sorry, but that's not possible prior to take off, sir."

"So, sweet heart, bring me two doubles as soon as we reach cruising level then," he smoothly ordered, cockily evaluating the redhead's body. "A seven on the nose," he mumbled.

Angela closed her eyes, doing her best to ignore his crassness, unwittingly giving him the opportunity to judge her.

A nine on the dot, he nonetheless decided. Angela had legs up to her ears and a curvaceous little ass tight enough to crush a peanut. *All this beauty needs is a pair of 500 cc implants and she'd be a perfect ten!* He grinned. *Just a few thousand bucks and she'd be on par with the hot strippers back home. Man, oh, man, I can't wait to get home... We grow them big in Texas.*

They grew everything big there...

"Ever been to the Lone Star state, sugar?" He sensually asked Angela, flashing his large gold and diamond studded Rolex 'President'.

Indifferently, she turned to the window and listened as the pilot welcomed the passengers aboard and described the weather conditions in Miami, where they had a stopover, and in New Orleans; but the mention of her hometown immediately caused a familiar uneasiness to creep into her body...

Painful echoes of the past suddenly reverberated in her mind; she strangely heard the voices of friends and siblings, and was again attacked by the name-calling and labelling.

Whoever said that words can never hurt you was dead wrong, she sadly thought, her heart pounding as she remembered being tagged with nicknames like "the Zebra" and "Café au Lait". Often, she was told that she was as "faded" as a worn out shirt; and once, her history teacher - a disturbed middle age widow with ebony skin

- openly accused Angela of bleaching her skin. The woman went so far to tell the entire class that Angela was indeed a living disgrace to her African ancestors...

The profound cruelty of such words lingered in Angela's subconscious. Some things are never forgotten, no matter how hard one try.

When the stewardess handed out the eye masks, Angela donned hers immediately, hoping that the 'Xanax' she took en route to the airport would help quiet her tormented mind.

The sleazy Texan continued to chatter, becoming increasingly drunk by the minute; yet, soon his words mingled with the hum of the plane, and the chronic drone succeeded in ferrying Angela into the land of dreams; or more aptly in her case: nightmares...

Chapter Five

Louisiana

After an uneventful landing in New Orleans, Angela carefully slid by the Texan, who had passed out in his seat; thankfully, it had been a smooth flight...

She silently retrieved her belongings and rapidly made her way to baggage claim, her body aching after the long trip. All of a sudden, her senses were inundated with the pungent smell of whiskey and sweat. Just behind her, the Texan's swarthy face lit up like a Christmas tree...

"If it ain't the pretty little lady... I thought you'd got off in Miami, sugar. What a nice surprise!" He exclaimed with a grin. "You fell asleep so fast I never had the chance to ask you what your business is here in Orleans, sweet heart?"

"I... I was raised here. I'm visiting my family. My mother, she's..." He didn't deserve an explanation. "If you don't mind, Sir, I'm in a hurry," she dryly said before walking faster.

"Hey, honey, at least let me give you my number; in case you get lonely…" The Texan winked with confidence, but by the time he'd reached into his pocket for his card, Angela had turned on her heels and was rushing across the arrival room towards two tall black men.

"Still a sight for sore eyes, ain't she daddy?" John sweetly remarked.

"Damn right she is, my boy!" André Boivin proudly replied. Warm tears of joy welled up into his tired eyes as his golden child fell into his arms and relaxed into his love; but abruptly, André nervously pulled back and Angela deeply sighed; again…

Even in this day and age, she noticed that a few people still stared at the family reunion, discretely pointing, nodding and nudging each other, their eyes quite surprised and questioning. Angela could almost hear their thoughts: What was such a gorgeous and elegant wealthy beautiful woman doing embracing two obviously poor black men?

Hypocrites!!!

Lowering his eyes, John nervously steered the baggage cart out of the terminal and into the parking lot where his father's old red Dodge waited.

Angela glanced behind her and saw the Texan gawking as he stepped into a fancy black Lincoln limousine. "God ain't happy about this, ma'am. You need a good talking to! Goddamn negro-loving bitch!" He viciously shouted before slamming his door.

As the Texan's words painfully sunk in, Angela felt shame rise around her like burning flames. Speechless, she turned her eyes to the ground, unable to look at him anymore. She felt as if she had been transported into the past again, then a deep anger filled her, and she abruptly kicked the sidewalk. *It's not me!* She nervously reminded herself, raising her head and glaring at him, her eyes alit with fire.

"You jealous pompous ass," she hissed under her breath.

"Let's get goin', Poodle," her father calmly said, placing a protective arm around her shoulder. "Let's get you home where you belong."

André hurried his pace, walking as briskly as his old legs would carry him, while keeping his arm protectively around his precious daughter; but deep down the poor André Boivin felt insulted and ashamed. Terribly ashamed; again…

Chapter Six

New Orleans

Forty-five minutes later, the old Dodge was passing through the northwest section of New Orleans; a rundown black working class area known as the "Faubourg Marigny".

"Home" was a two-story clapboard bungalow that had been built during the Great Depression. Unlike many of the little cheap bungalows that were located near it, the Boivin's house radiated serenity and freshness. The white picket fence was newly painted, as were the dark green window boxes that spilled over with white geraniums and English ivy. The well-tended garden softly imbued the air with the lush scent of paradise. The colours spoke of "Manet", playing off one another as if they were in a French countryside, rather than a working class Louisiana black neighbourhood. Rows of delicate fuchsia and pink cyclamen, drifts of pale lavender "forget-me-nots", regal amethyst columbines, and multi-coloured Welsh poppies, created a romantic tapestry worthy of heaven…

Mama always had a green thumb, Angela sadly remembered, a loving smile floating on her face.

On the long shaded veranda stood the familiar green light wicker furniture. The many romantic cushions were a patchwork masterpiece, lovingly hand sewn by Josephine with colourful flowered printed remnants of cloth that she found for pennies at a yard sale. A spectacular lavender blue wisteria draped languorously over the sides of the peaceful veranda, overflowing and luxurious, while the soothing serenade of Josephine's beloved canaries melodiously echoed from each of the large two cages, which stood on black ironwork pedestals on opposite ends of the porch.

There are far fewer birds than there were five years ago, Angela sadly thought; the dozen were now only five…

Deep down, Angela mourned for the lovely birds, for herself, and for her beloved mother.

As her tears haplessly streamed down her cheeks, she tiredly opened the screen door and stepped inside the little living room, amazed that the old ceiling fan was still humming as unevenly as always.

The room hadn't changed a bit; Angela could have walked through it blindfolded, without so much as touching a piece of furniture; the couches were still covered with the same bright floral cotton slip covers, and the tables and chairs still smelled like lemon wax…

The favourite photographs of her family had been carefully arranged by her mother on the hand-crocheted doily that covered an end table. A yellowed wedding portrait of her parents as well as a few photos of her grandparents were placed in a semi-circle around an oversized picture of herself - costumed in an ethereal white tutu, satin shoes, and a sparkling tiara - frozen in the act of dancing "Swan Lake". It was the first time that she'd starred in Tchaikovsky's masterpiece. The performance took place a decade ago in Vienna.

Grade school portraits of her sisters and her brother, as well as herself, had been lovingly arranged on another little end table. Angela remembered the day those pictures were taken. Aimée, her eldest sister, had thrown a temper tantrum. She was angry and terribly jealous that she didn't look at all like Angela; that her Negro hair was full of kinks and wouldn't grow below her shoulders; that her big eyes were deep brown rather than golden; and above all, that her skin was the colour of bittersweet chocolate instead of a light golden glow, like a loving kiss from the sun...

Aimée had once overheard her parents refer to Angela as their "golden child," and since that day, she had hated everything about herself; and everything about her beautiful youngest sister...

Angela never felt particularly pretty, let alone "golden". Until she discovered the ballet, she simply felt alone...

Only when Angela danced on the small school stage, she found real peace; it was as if she became part of something grander and larger than herself - the music - and she was lofted into a strange heavenly state of grace. When the audience showed delight by granting her the first of many standing ovations, she was more than just proud: she felt liberated from all the racial prejudices that plagued her throughout her tormented childhood; her skin could have been green or blue, and the audience would have cheered all the same...

Angela lovingly smiled as her eyes locked onto her mother's beloved old rocking chair, which swayed slightly in the breeze, as if Josephine's spirit had already taken its place on it. She could almost see her mother rocking steadily, while busily mending holes in her children's socks, or listening to them telling tall tales, or squabbling with one another. But unfortunately now, the room felt empty, as if its loving soul – the gentle Josephine - had already taken its leave...

Overcome by a sudden sense of doom, Angela ran out of the room and into her little bedroom. As she slowly opened the door, she was quite amazed that it remained so true to itself; a monument to her past, a shrine to her childhood...

Strangely enough, everything was situated exactly as it was when Angela left her home at the age of seventeen to study ballet in London.

The little white iron canopy bed with its pale pink sheer fabric; the faithful wooden desk that her father gave her for her eleventh birthday; the white wicker armchair, and the beloved books and objects of her childhood; everything, without exception, was exactly as she had left it...

Angela delicately picked up one of the many Caucasian porcelain dolls that waited on the shelves to greet her like old friends. She remembered a time when those special dolls - so beautiful with their fine hand-stitched English clothing and lily-white porcelain faces - were the only friends she had.

How jealous my sisters were of those dolls... She sadly thought, shivering.

The precious dolls had been gifts; mysterious gifts that were delivered by the postman in shiny boxes on Christmas and her birthday. Her parents never told her where the expensive dolls came from, or whom they were from, and somehow Angela tamed her profound curiosity. It was as if, deep down, she unconsciously knew that asking too many questions would jinx her good fortune and so she kept silent. She preferred to believe in the magic of life, in goodness, fairies and Santa Claus; she simply preferred not to open wide Pandora's box, as not to unleash the demons of her past; again...

With a trembling hand, Angela was reaching to pick up a particularly finely dressed doll, when her father came in with her belongings; within a second his eyes widened, darting nervously from his daughter's face to the doll...

Is that fear in daddy's eyes? No, it can't be, she thought; yet she knew enough to lower her arm. André smiled with relief, before carefully hanging her expensive mink coat in the tiny closet, stroking the fur as if it were the belly of a kitten.

"Your ma was always so careful to clean this room without disturbing it, honey," he softly said, moving his eyes to the doll again. "An' I like to keep it that way. So you be careful, young lady. An' just in case you notice, I repainted the walls one day when yer ma were out. I made sure to replace all the furniture and knick-knacks right where they be before, but don't you dare an' tell yer Mama that I did anything of the sort." He said with a sad little smile.

"You really think Mama didn't notice, daddy-pie?" Angela softly teased, while lovingly taking her father's arm. "You still act like teenagers in love." She added before tenderly kissing his cheek.

A crimson blush spread over André's dark skin. "D'ya wanna freshen up b'fore ya see yer Mama, Poodle?" He asked, visibly embarrassed.

"No, Daddy, I prefer to see Mama now."

Angela noticed her father's face fall, but without a word he tiredly led the way up the creaky old stairs, bracing himself.

When he opened the door of the bedroom, the acrid odour of medication hit Angela as solid as a punch to the stomach. The familiar scent of violet and amber that always exuded from her mother's pores had been disgustingly replaced by the foul stench of death...

There was no more humming of hymns; another habit of Josephine that Angela cursed herself for taking for granted. The only sound in the little room was the laborious breathing of a dying woman and the afternoon breeze hissing through the branches of the old magnolia tree...

Trembling, Angela looked down at her mother. She silently stood there, staring, in awe of her Mama's natural born saintliness, but she was shocked by the hollow greyness that infected her face. Even in the dim light, Angela could feel death hovering about, heavily and clumsily. She had expected it to be graceful, a macabre dance perhaps, but a dance. *There should be some poetry to dying*, she sadly thought; instead, death was imperfect and limping, a gimp of a thing...

41

Patches of Josephine's scalp as large as plums shone between the sparse white hair on her head; a chestnut coloured wig lay on the nightstand, like some kind of strange road kill...

It was extremely hard to believe that the sick old woman was her beautiful beloved mother. If Angela had seen this fragile old woman on the street, she wouldn't have recognised her...

The scorching pain was way too much to bear, and Angela bit her lip so she wouldn't scream out "no!!!" from the top of her lungs.

The shock made her dizzy. She sat on the edge of the bed and delicately took her mother's bony hand in her own, trying her best to keep herself together. Josephine's skin was cool to the touch and thin as rice paper, and her fingers were now bent and crooked. She slowly opened her eyes. For a moment, Angela feared that her mother wouldn't recognise her; but as soon as her vision adjusted to the light, Josephine lovingly smiled.

"My baby... my sweet, sweet baby... It is you, isn't it? I must've been in heaven with the Almighty already."

"Yes, Mama, it's really me, in the flesh. I came to see you," Angela lovingly said, trying to sound cheerful, as if it was just a visit, while refraining from crying.

"Why you come now, baby?" Her mother asked, beaming, with a tender and childlike voice.

"Because I missed you a lot, Mama, and I wanted to be near you."

Josephine lifted her thin arm and grasped at her daughter's straight shiny auburn hair. "What a sweet, sweet baby... You missed your Mama, my angel. Your Mama missed you so much too, my love..."

"But I'm home now, Mama; I'm home... And this time I'm going to stay," Angela said softly, trying to ignore the voice in her head that added "until you die, that is..."

"You're goin' to stay, my sweet love? You making a promise to your old Mama?" Josephine softly asked, and instantly, the brilliant force of her heart inspired her being. It was as if suddenly her eyes had begun to sing.

"Yes, Mama. It's a promise," Angela assured, wiping away her tears.

"Oh, my sweet baby... You make your Mama so... happy," Josephine tiredly whispered, as her arm fell weakly onto the bed.

"D'ya want sumpin', hon? Can I get ya some water?" André asked.

Josephine slowly shook her head. "No... I don't need nuttin', papa. Not now that my baby is here." As André delicately put his hand on her forehead, she closed her eyes, her body shuddering from the strain of talking.

"Honey, I think it is better if we let ya Mama sleeps... Ya see, Poodle, she ain't sleeping too well and needs all the rest she can get." André said while taking Angela by the hand.

Before reluctantly leaving the room, Angela softly kissed her mother on the forehead. When her father slowly closed the door behind them, she suddenly felt as if she were being suffocated in her own skin, and perturbing images from her recurring nightmares overtook her; the cloudlike thing, floating slowly downward towards her face, smothering her until the soft whiteness faded into black nothingness…

"Daddy?" She asked, her voice worried, looking suddenly afraid.

Her father took her hand and Angela could breathe again. Little by little, she relaxed and she then let him lead her back down the wooden stairs and into her little bedroom, as if she were a little girl again.

"Daddy pie, I just need a few minutes," she murmured, apologising as she closed the door before she collapsed on the bed. Finally alone, Angela let herself go, her body convulsing in waves of deep sobbing, knowing full well that it would only be days before the invisible umbilical cord that bonded mother and child would be severed; again…

Only days before Josephine's loving soul would be free; again…

Only days before the wheel of life would turn one more time; again…

Again.

Chapter Seven

"The House of Angels"

The enormous burgundy walled room was populated with a silent army of strange angels...

The Holy Angels were gazing heavenward beyond the large vaulted ceilings, their painted eyes radiating compassion, beauty and truth. Each angel was similar in its holiness, yet unique in its complexity; each one a representative of a different human race...

Some angels were truly statuesque, their faces creamy white, with roses blushing on their cheeks, their hair golden, their eyes as blue as the Grecian sky in the summertime, their features delicate and childlike, reminiscent of the ideal Caucasian European beauty depicted by great Italian and Dutch Renaissance masters.

Other angels were less elongated, with eyes as dark as fertile soil. The wood from which they were carved was stained in olive tones, their bodies thick and their hair coarse. Some of those exotic angels exemplified honesty and laughter, while others possessed an earthy majesty as imposing as the Andes; but when studied more closely, a notable fear was evident in their expressions. Perhaps their Indian faces reflected the horrors they had witnessed during the dark days, when "Christianity" triumphed over the Pagan cultures of North and South America...

Then, there were the other "exotic angels"...

These were "dark angels", carved from precious ebony wood, their shiny black forms shone in the light, their bellies sometimes extended and pregnant, and their intriguing eyes glistening with the primordial wisdom of mankind.

Those exotic angels had been crafted by artisans for the white masters of the vast plantations, who then gave them to their African slaves, in order to tame them and keep them in line...

There were others angels, of course, originating from all corners of the world, in all shapes and all sizes: little cherubs, seraphims, and even beautiful archangels.

In spite of their "differences", all the angels that sat, stood, or reclined in the nooks and crannies of the large churchlike room, whether they were tall or squat, brown or yellow, black or white, happy or sad, had a common purpose; they all had been created to protect, to guide, to appease, but above all, to listen to the pleas of the mere unhappy mortals who often fervently prayed to them.

Gloriously, today the angels were alive...

Passing through the room, one could feel their probing eyes following one's every movement, beaming with compassion and love, their prayerful hands pointing upward towards heaven, their faces breathtakingly luminous.

This strange place was an otherworldly sanctuary that beckoned one to take leave of the mundane sensibility of the real world, as to give way to that heightened awareness that was the privilege of Caucasian priests and great Oriental mystics.

At the end of the large room, beside a life-size statue of "Saint George" slaying the dragon, stood a slender ink black woman dressed in an immaculate white robe, her head crowned by a blazing white lace turban, part of which trailed down her back like a beam of moonlight. She exuded a natural grace, a divine gift that is given only to those who possess a natural faith in both "Gods and Goddesses" that is beyond question. It was obvious that her pious gift was not something that could be achieved; not in a single lifetime, anyway...

The luminous black priestess lovingly acknowledged all the silent angels with a regal nod, curving her full lips into a blest smile. She was truly beautiful, despite the fact that she had no eyes. On either side of the bridge of her little nose were two dark holes, seemingly fathomless; but so strangely alive...

From these strange empty pits, the black priestess could see far beyond one's flesh into the depths of one's soul, and she could immediately know what each person was really made of; despite the well carved mask of appearance...

Her name was Mambha, which meant "Ray of Light" in the dialect of her ancient African tribe.

In the close Voodoo community of New Orleans, Mambha was known as "Sister Light" by hundreds of devoted followers and patrons, who often came to seek her advice.

It had been many years since her eyes were violently stolen from her; but she had forgiven her abuser before she'd even regained consciousness, simply because she instinctively knew that her loss was a blessing in disguise...

It was simple. When Mambha lost her ability to see the world with the aid of cones and rods, her gift of sight - the "shining" sight that was her birthright - was divinely perfected beyond her wildest dreams.

Mambha was truly blessed, she knew, for when she gazed at someone with those black holes, she could also see the colours of their aura with her inner eye. With uncanny precision, the black priestess would diagnose subtle changes, discrepancies and breakages that were symptomatic of illnesses; she also could see with great precision where the mental anguish - rage, grief, heartbreak, betrayal or pain - accumulated...

Sometimes, if a devotee came to her soon enough, she could prevent an emotional illness from manifesting as cancer, or a heart attack, or a lingering disease.

Mambha could clearly see evil as well; for evil was an arrogant force too prideful and lazy to disguise itself...

"Evil" was the only thing in life that Mambha truly feared; that she truly despised...

In the on-going "battle for the soul", the black priestess knew that for the first time in the history of humankind, evil was becoming inbred; a fact of life, a necessity of survival...

The auras that the priestess passed on the overpopulated streets of New Orleans were becoming duller, their colours mingling, as if an artist had mixed too many colours on the palette.

Evil is a muddy demon, Mambha sadly thought. Evil lacked the clarity of wisdom and the clear light of primordial love; the most important element of life...

True love was the core of the black priestess' spirituality.

Without discrimination, Mambha fervently prayed to the Christian saints, as well as the African loas and blurred the boundaries of rigid religious dogmas. Mambha joyfully danced into the esoteric realm of spirit, where only pure, undiluted love, held reign...

As each saint in the Catholic pantheon has a specific function, so each deity in the African Voodoo culture has its innate purpose; but the primary difference is that the Catholics believe in a supreme being, a "God Almighty" who is omniscient, all-powerful; a being in Himself, as well as a part of the mystical Trinity.

The loving Virgin Mary, as co-redemptory of humanity, as well as mother of God Jesus Christ, is about the closest that one could get in the Judeo-Christian world to a Goddess, Mambha sadly thought.

"Mary" was a woman with a room of her own, as Virginia Woolf would say; and yet, Mambha felt deeply sorry for the sweet Madonna, simply because she was terribly overworked...

As the Good Book promised, the "Mother of Christ" never ignored the prayer of any faithful devotee; although the waiting list was long, and certainly would never end...

Still, Mambha took pity on the Good Virgin and, unless it was an absolute necessity, she often invoked and petitioned lesser-known Christian saints who were more than happy to have some work.

Mambha also knew that fervent prayer benefited both the petitioner and the spirit whose favours were sought: if a spirit - a saint or a deity - was not called upon, "he" or "she" would eventually be forgotten; perhaps even lose its place in the celestial hierarchy, thus be forced to incarnate again before it had attained liberation from the karmic wheel. Even worse, some pure souls would simply dissipate, like a lonely cloud melting into a hot cerulean sky...

The Christian church knew full well what irrevocable damage it was doing when it dug up and burnt the bones of heretics, before casting them into the wind; making sure to kill each and every one of their spirits in addition to the flesh, so that they would not be remembered. When the name was forgotten, their identities would be lost forever...

In the ancient African Voodoo culture, it was standard practice to prepare an altar four weeks prior to All Soul's Day and place personal photographs, artefacts or hand-drawn memories of one's ancestors on a white altar cloth; along with white chrysanthemums, purifying herbs, and white votive candles.

Once a week, the person would lay a sampling of the dearly departed's favourite foods on a white dish and simply listen; listen carefully...

If one knew how to really listen with his heart, one could hear the dead speak through dreams, signs, and ancient symbols. The dead were extremely useful. They aided the sick; sometimes they offered blessings; sometimes they merely told stories; sometimes they revealed secrets long ago buried in closets, secrets that protected one in the eye of a hurricane.

In other words, sometimes for better; sometimes for worse...

For the black priestess, invoking a name of a thing - whether it is a god or a goddess, saint or sinner, peasant or prince, folk or fairy, always kept the soul of that thing truly alive.

Mambha deeply believed that the greater number of people fervently praying, invoking, or simply believing in any particular spirit; the more powerful that spirit would become. She instinctively knew all too well that no soul really wanted to spend eternity loafing upon a cloud...

Luckily, souls and their names, as well as their truth, are stubborn things; and a soul betrayed will not rest until its truth is told, Mambha sadly thought, before throwing forth a light laugh.

Today, Mambha was invoking a deity known as 'Elegua'; an old African god ruling the crossroads, passages, and matters of death, as well as the return of the soul into incarnated life and of all the dangers in between...

After lighting two beeswax candles on which she had rubbed an herbal infusion concocted during the last new moon, she lit a round of charcoal and placed it in the large bronze censer. It scattered before a half-circle of intricately carved wooden representations of the nine lesser African gods and goddesses, who worked as "liaisons" between Elegua and the black priestess.

Mambha had personally sewn clothing for the tiny dolls and decorated them with precious conch shells and coloured crystal beaded necklaces.

When the inside of the charcoal round had turned hot red, Mambha dipped her hand into an roughly woven embroidered bag and strew a handful of mystical resins of frankincense, myrrh, sandalwood, mugwort, lavender, wormwood and other herbs, a magical blend known to "lift the veil" between the living and the dead...

Mambha delicately picked up the censer and waved it around herself, delineating a magic circle, cleansing and purifying the sacred space in preparation for her old ritual; then she deeply inhaled the incense and was momentarily taken aback. She knew the scent as one knows a good friend, but there was definitely something distinctly unusual this time...

A man's smell, Mambha thought, smiling and sensing the rich tobacco aroma. *Yes! And vetiver, a fine cologne...* She heartily laughed. *It had been too long since she had had a man*, she sadly thought; and now a "man's spirit" has chosen to join her "party". *Well, so be it!*

Mambha sensed no negativity in this male soul; only a deep sadness. It was so strong that it was almost palpable... Perhaps he had come to heal himself; if that were the case, she had no intention of casting him out of her circle.

Mambha elegantly nodded her head in a gesture of welcome, as a thin spiral of sweet white smoke slowly snaked its way around the dolls, bringing their spirits to life. She proudly knelt down on the shiny black wooden floor and began chanting a prayer in an old Senegalese dialect that had been passed down by her ancestors; all of them blessed, or "burdened", with the gift of foresight; all of them being the daughters of Eve...

As the black priestess continued to softly chant, her breath became rhythmic and her body began to sway from side to side, slowly moving in a languorous wave, her long slender arms overhead, her multitudinous silver and gold bracelets chiming like bells, until the elusive "Elegua" entered her body and possessed her.

Today, the ancient African deity was in a "pleasant mood", talkative and charming; yet, the black priestess saw through his banter and felt his loneliness, that he was all but forgotten by most of those who honoured him. Unfortunately, gods and goddesses were not totally immune to the pains of loneliness; as the black priestess fully knew...

Mambha let the deity speak for a moment, but before her body was completely exhausted from being in the trance state, she asked her question.

Elegua's answer was crystal clear: Death!!!

The "Dark Angels" will shed their blood once again. There was no doubt about it; her time too, would soon come to an end...

Mambha slowly eased out of her trance, releasing the arrogant Elegua and brushing away the protective circle with a wave of her bejewelled hand, as protocol required, before settling down on a purple silken pillow, as to fully contemplate her vision.

The black priestess deeply shuddered with horror when she realised that the soul that she had been watching over and praying for since it was reborn, was now fully awakened...

Lately the soul's pain was so potent that the consciousness of the human body that harboured it was now beginning to crack under the strain, trying to drown out its tormented voice with compulsions and obsessions, with disciplines; with dance, perhaps...

The poor soul was soon to be completely aware of itself; thus would fulfil its destiny and take its revenge.

Soon, a woman's life would be forever changed... Mambha thought, shuddering again.

Yes, the soul was ready to act, the black priestess sadly thought; and those who crossed its dangerous path - innocent or guilty, men or women - could die in the violent tsunami of its awakened will...

Mambha would be one of those returning to the comforting arms of the divine light; but for the first time in her life, she wasn't shuddering in fear or horror. Long ago, in a particular vision, she had seen her killer, seen his enormous and skilful hands; her own death, she knew, would be quick and painless...

No matter. The black priestess looked forward to release her luminous soul from the old cage of a body that hung now on her, with her skin sagging like a chicken's throat. Mambha giggled girlishly when she thought of the pleasures of being reborn into a freshly wrought new body. However, it was the death of others that concerned her now, for she had cultivated a great heart throughout her many human incarnations; and her profound compassion was such, that she always felt the sorrow of each soul, and always did her best to become the loving guardians of those poor souls who sometimes crossed her path…

Mambha fervently prayed for the tormented souls of those poor humans who clung hard to this world; those lonely souls that would experience the transition to the Other World as a harsh trauma. For those particular souls, her prayers were a melodic mixture of African Voodoo and Latinate Catholic litanies. The black priestess also gave special consideration to those poor souls who would inevitably wander into hell, simply because they could not see the light; for those hapless sinners who lived their entire little life without thought of the afterlife, or any faith in goodness; nor for the plight that awaited such unfortunate people, because "life" had always been given to them for a particular reason.

Yes, Mambha fully knew that "death", as it was called by humans, was in most cases no tragedy; but a life lived without any thought of death, or the lifetimes to come, truly was…

Chapter Eight

"New Orleans"

The wet blinding heat of the New Orleans morning roused Angela from a restless night's sleep; then her inner demons slowly faded away...

Lately, the recurring nightmare that had haunted her since her childhood was becoming increasingly vivid. A cold shiver coursed through her body when she remembered how she had awoken at dawn, drenched in sweat, her arms clutching a pillow; not knowing why she had been pushing it down onto her own face again...

Had she actually tried to suffocate herself???

Gathering her wits, Angela took a deep breath and attempted to focus on her daily routine, trying her best not to dwell upon the horrific vivid images of her nightmare.

She rapidly showered and moisturised her face and body with her precious 'Estee Lauder' creams. She neatly tied her hair at the nape of her neck with a black velvet ribbon, dabbed some coral lipstick on her cheeks and lips, and brushed a coat of black mascara on her long curly lashes. Using a soft feathery puff, she finished up with a light coat of "re-nutritive" translucent powder, hoping that the make-up would mask her troubled emotions...

Angela dressed without much care, donning a pair of 'Ralph Lauren' black velvet jeans, a white silk shirt, and her 'Jimmy Choo' crocodile boots. She sprayed a few clouds of her beloved 'Eternity' perfume above her head, before looking at herself in the full-length mirror. Her waistline had shrunk in the past few weeks, she noticed, as she pulled the black crocodile belt to the last notch. If she kept losing weight, she'd have to get the shoemaker to punch more holes in it, no doubt pleasing Veronika, who liked her troupe reed thin, but worrying Pierce.

Dear Pierce...

How Angela wished she were "home" with her beloved husband; and how strongly she prayed that her mother's death was as illusory as the nightmares that constantly plagued her...

Shortly after, Angela found her father scuttling about in the kitchen, frying eggs, baking biscuits, and brewing French coffee.

"If it ain't my beautiful Poodle!" André joyfully exclaimed in his slow lackadaisical manner, his dark eyes full of tenderness. "How'd you sleep, honey?"

"Just fine, daddy-pie, just fine," she lied. She could still feel the weight of the pillow on her face, so she tried hard to push back the rest of the nightmare - the angels, scores of them, strangely, silently surrounding her; some of them resembling prey birds more than heavenly figures...

The worst part were the eyes: a pair of strange hypnotic steel blue eyes that always bored into her very soul; and there was another set of eyes, or rather "empty sockets", where eyes should've been…

"Now, young lady, you go take a seat right there an' wait for your breakfast," her father said, feigning cheerfulness.

André had brought out the beautiful red and gold 'Royal Worchester' china that Angela had given her mother for Christmas, fifteen years ago, when she had just begun to make a good living and wanted to share her good fortune with her family; but the sweet Josephine rarely used the elegant service, thinking that it was stuff for "kings and queens" and not for the like of common folk…

Angela's father was obviously taking extra measures to ensure that his "golden child" would feel at home.

André had also exceptionally cut fragrant pale roses, as well as white lilies, and carefully arranged them in a precious middle size 'Waterford' crystal vase; another of Angela's expensive gifts. The windows were wide open, the white lacy curtains slowly dancing with the soft breeze, while the canaries happily chirped their first songs of the day.

Angela sat upon one of the old wooden chairs taking in the delicious smells, slowly sipping the excellent coffee, while remembering how her family would lovingly gather together around that same old table, when her beloved Mama and adorable Grandmamma Lili happily cooked a storm of wonderful Creole "soul food", that was well-known to charm the belly and also cure the soul…

Mama's kitchen was the true heart of our home... She lovingly thought, sadly smiling.

Angela wondered where the heart of her home in London would be.

Our bedroom? It has had its moments to be sure, but it certainly lacks the soul-warming presence of Mama's kitchen... Maybe some houses lack hearts; or maybe Mama's heart was so large and strong, and her spirit so pure, that her small body was not enough to contain it... She sadly thought.

Suddenly, Angela felt terribly guilty. Only now she deeply regretted that she had never invited her parents to visit her and Pierce in London. After her mother's heart-breaking final departure, she would ask her father to stay with them for a while, she suddenly decided.

"That's what I like to see, Poodle," André said, sliding two large eggs done over easy on each of their plates. "That bright-toothed smile ya do so well." He laid a wicker basket full of golden corn biscuits on the table, alongside a tub of fresh butter.

"Daddy, how is Mama feeling?" Angela suddenly asked, her smile washed away by guilt. For an instant, she'd almost forgotten that her mother lay upstairs, at the threshold of death's door...

André poured himself some coffee, took a hot biscuit and heavily buttered it. "Last I checked, she was sleeping, honey. And a good thing for that." He softly said with a sad little smile.

"I won't wake her then." Angela looked into her father's eyes, with a knowing. "There's something Mama wants to tell me, isn't there, daddy?" She nervously asked. "I had such strange dreams last night… What's happening, daddy pie?"

André slowly reached for her aristocratic hand, hoping to ease her anxiety; but deep down, he continued to pray that his sweet Josephine would take the secret to the grave with her…

"Better to let her sleep, honey. Mama's resting now and that's a gift of the Lord," he softly said again, without further elaboration, but with a strange expression in his eyes.

They sat in silence, listening to the peaceful song of the canaries, thinking about their life, while picking at their food as they had little appetite…

A moment later, they heard a hard knock at the front door, followed by the clamouring of feet and bodies. Angela smiled, happy to see her brother and his family, until she saw the disapproving frown on her sister-in-law's face…

"Marquesha" was not a pretty sight; particularly when she was in a foul mood, and Angela's presence was more than enough to elicit that state.

A squat obese, dark black skinned woman who must've spent as much money weaving, straightening and colouring her hair as a rich African-American pop diva, the perfidious Marquesha possessed a set of ferret like eyes that were as sharp as the ones of a Spanish Inquisitor. Her two teen-aged daughters, Kenya and Sahara, passively followed her into the kitchen.

The two girls immediately smiled when they saw the beautiful Angela, and Marquesha shot each of them a glance straight from hell. They then looked at one another, rolling their eyes...

John gently jabbed his wife in the ribs with his elbow and whispered something into her ear. It must've done the trick: suddenly, a toothy grin covered Marquesha's round face.

"Angela! Been a long time, girl! I'm thrilled to see you," Marquesha crooned as she ignored Angela's open arms, turning her large back to give her father-in-law a kiss instead; then she took a few steps backward and gave her a good looking over. "Mmmmmhmmmm," was all she said...

Her elder daughter, Sahara, ran forward to hug Angela. "Ya are so pretty, aunty," she exclaimed, sincere and loving as a puppy dog.

"Don't she now?" Kenya agreed, petting Angela's cheek. "Yer skin's so soft; so white..."

"Well, my darlings, it's one of the benefits of living in England," Angela gently explained. "The dampness and lack of sun does wonders for the complexion..."

Kenya pricked up her ears. Her skin was coarse and dark and covered with blemishes. "Hell, if I move to England, would my skin 'come soft and light like yours, Aunty?" She asked, smiling.

Marquesha's fake smile vanished like a stolen jewel. "What the hell you want skin like that for, child?" She yanked Kenya away from Angela, and placed her fat little hands akimbo on her large hips. "Kenya! You should be proud of your own colour! England my ass! That's a place for white ghosts!" She nervously exclaimed, visibly disgusted, before she heavily sat down, while throwing Angela a wicked glare; then she nervously tapped her inch long Flamingo pink acrylic fingernails on the table. "My Lord, Sister!" Marquesha exclaimed again, her eyes viciously screaming. "You do look strange… What you been doing, girl? Bleaching yer skin? You whiter each time we see you…" She perfidiously said with great disgust. "You ashamed of yer roots or what? You ashamed of yer black Mama who's dying up there? What's wrong with you, girl? Get to a tanning booth! You practically white these days... You a shame to all of us!" She almost shouted, as she shook her long hair extensions in dismay.

"A shame?" Angela defensively asked. "I was born with my colour, just as you were born with yours, Marquesha! I wouldn't bleach my skin or roast in a tanning bed; and I've certainly never been ashamed of my parents!" She proudly declared, looking straight into her ferret eyes while slightly raising the tone of her voice.

At this precise instant, Angela couldn't help thinking about how she had felt when Veronika and Boris saw the photographs of her family. *Am I ashamed?*

"Yah sister? Ya think ya a real soul sister? Growing lighter by the year, marrying a white man, and living in the white man's world and all… Everything you do, girl, is a slap to our people and our race!" Marquesha viciously exclaimed while dangerously locking eyes with Angela. "Now, you becoming some kind of freak, sister, like that Michael Jackson, the good Lord bless his soul; a freak… Yes, you are!"

"Pleeease, stop now! This is neither the time, nor the place," Angela nervously said, revolted, as well as deeply annoyed. This was an old and tired argument...

Marquesha always criticised everything about Angela: the way she spoke, the way she moved, the elegant clothes she wore; even criticised her neatly coiffed lustrous natural hair. The "sweet" Marquesha saw her beautiful and famous sister-in-law as a heretic - a Judas to her noble race - and Angela knew full well that there was absolutely nothing she could do, or say, that would change Marquesha's twisted mind...

Even if she divorced Pierce, spent an hour a day at a tanning salon, and donned a pair of black contact lenses, as well as a large Afro wig, "Marquesha the snake" would discover something that would prove that the divine Angela was indeed a traitor to the great African-American community.

Perhaps if I left the ballet and studied African tribal dance... Perish the thought! Angela thought, visibly perturbed by this quite strange idea...

"I'm just talking truth, sister!" Marquesha viciously exclaimed again, before spooning a few tablespoons of sugar into her coffee. "So, how's Mama Josephine, papa?" She sweetly asked, finally changing the subject.

"Sleepin', I'm hoping." André nervously said, visibly annoyed by her behaviour.

"Good! Building her strength. And talkin' bout strength, we got a treat for ya!" Marquesha said with a little smile, before she slapped her daughter on the arm. "Go git that box from the car, girl!" She dryly ordered.

Kenya sprinted out of the kitchen and returned less than a minute later, laden with a large pink box full of extra sweet assorted donuts. Ravenously, Marquesha grabbed the only jelly donut and rapidly stuffed it in her big red painted mouth...

"Ummmm." She sensually said, before she threw one on Angela's plate, as if she were a dog.

"Maybe if you'd had some meat on ya backside, sister, you would've landed ya self a good black man, instead of that white waif-loving honky of yours..." She grinned, before she heartily laughed. "Why ain't he here, anyway? Your little "white man" too good to stand by his pale skinned wife, while her poor black Mama's dying; or is your white man already tired of ya skinny ass, sister?" She viciously said, before laughing like a little devil.

"Marquesha!" John shouted. "That's enough for one day, woman!"

"For your information, Marquesha, I asked my husband not to come," Angela calmly stated. "I didn't want to put him through this... This abuse!" She politely said, visibly revolted.

"Well, too bad girl! A real man would've come, whether ya told him to or not, sister! What? You ashamed of him too? Or is he ashamed of the fact that ya is really a nigger in disguise?" Marquesha viciously laughed again, visibly enjoying the moment.

"Marquesha, the only thing I'm truly ashamed of, right now, is you!" Angela nervously exclaimed, before she regally left the room...

"Damn it, woman! You got a big mouth on you straight out of hell!!!" John shouted.

"You know I'm only telling the truth 'bout your sister. Plain an' simple... Even a birdbrain like you can see the writing on the wall." Marquesha candidly said with a disarming smile before blowing a kiss to her husband.

Angrily, André stood up. "Marquesha, I'm saying this once. There'll be no more insultin' my daughter in my house, or you'll be out on ya big fat rear!" Then angrily, he pointed towards the door.

Sadly, Kenya and Sahara hung their heads, while their dragon-tongue mother grabbed another heavily coated sugar donut; then donned an expression of perfect innocence...

"I think we best are going," John reluctantly said, lowering his eyes.

"I reckon you should, son... Ya Mama's asleep and there ain't much to do here anyhow," André sadly said. *The truth hasn't even come out yet, and already my family is splitting at the seams.* He sadly thought, while refraining from crying.

Marquesha indifferently snatched the box of donuts and gestured at Kenya and Sahara.

"Come on, girls! We not good 'nough now that the lil' 'princess' be home," she dryly said with a sour laugh. A clap of thunder shook the air. "Don't want to get stuck in a downpour," she advised, acting as if nothing had happened.

As far as Marquesha was concerned, she was the "voice of reason", and Angela was a Nigger traitor; a Nigger traitor, as well as a monster...

Without a shadow of a doubt, this was going to be a long, unpleasant day for the Boivins; yes indeed...

Chapter Nine

"New Orleans"

Desperately in need of some peace, Angela rapidly retreated into her little bedroom, beaten and totally drained by the unpleasant morning's argument...

Pierce had left a message on her cell phone, pleading that she reconsider her decision and allow him to fly to New Orleans so he could be with her during her time of need. Yet, as much as she craved her husband's love, Angela knew full well that his presence would simply complicate an already overly complex situation; Pierce would be about as welcome as a skunk in a kitchen...

Despite their genuine love for one another, and no matter how hard they tried to ignore it, Marquesha would surely do her best to provoke and ridicule him more than once; again...

A deep sadness rapidly fell over Angela, and her mind was suddenly besieged with unanswerable questions: Who would she cling to for solace when her mother had passed from this imperfect world? Who would lend her the necessary strength to keep going? Would she ever be happy?

As successful as Angela might seem to the eyes of others; in spite of her great beauty, her obvious talent and her "fabulous international career", as well as her extraordinary marriage to a very desirable man who had been one of the most eligible bachelors in all England, she nevertheless felt deeply unfulfilled and she didn't know why...

Why are the nightmares getting worse lately? She shuddered. But somewhere, deep within her soul, she knew that the key to her happiness was to be found in those strange demonic dreams. Whatever haunted her now was simply trying to tell her something. Lately, it spoke in vivid images: calm, but sad steel blue eyes; black angels; blood; so much blood... Whatever it was, that "thing" patiently waited in the core of her being, in the marrow of her bones. Yes, it was waiting now to tell her something; but what?

Angela hadn't noticed that there were tears streaming down her cheeks, until she heard the soft knocking on her door. Quickly, she jumped up out of her bed, wiping her face, before covering the redness with powder.

"Come in," she nervously said, putting on a brave smile.

Blanche's expression was solemn. She must've already heard what happened in the kitchen...

"Hiya, sis," she said, before tenderly kissing Angela's cheeks. "Don't be crying now on account of that fucking bitch. Stirring shit's her specialty, sweet heart!"

"Ohhh, it's not just Marquesha, Blanche... Mama's dying and everyone is acting so... so normal! The same bickering as always... It never stops! I'm so tired of it all. Sometimes I think I can't take it one more day." Angela tiredly said, refraining from crying.

"Awww, girl. People deal with sorrow in all kinds of ways... An' it ain't the same for that bitch Marquesha. It's our Mama, not hers, honey." Blanche's dark eyes were brimming with tears.

"I'm really sorry," Angela sadly said. "I'm sorry for both of us."

The sisters lovingly hugged then softly cried, taking solace in each other, just as they did when they were little girls. As the burning tears finally receded, Angela said again, "How are you, my darling? God, I've missed you so much."

"I'm fine, just fine..." Blanche nervously said, suddenly pulling back. "How's your Pierce doing?"

"Wonderful," Angela awkwardly said while trying hard to smile.

"Good for you! Poor Aimée can't say the same 'bout her good-for-nothing husband... The bastard's spends his time blowing his money on booze and women. I hoped that the years would calm him down, but 'stead them doing the opposite... Her boys dropped out of school, too; but what can she expect with a good-for-nothing husband like that?" She nervously said while raising her eyes.

"Ohhh Blanche, my darling, I'm really sorry to hear that." The loneliness hit Angela again as she guiltily realised that her perfect "upscale world" was so far apart from her sisters. "And you? How are you?"

"Well, you know, George is a good man. Works his butt off. He just got promoted to supervisor, so we had ourselves a lil' celebration. And my boys made the honours list in school... Can you believe that? I got no complaints, girl, none." Blanche said with a bitter smile.

"That's nice to hear, my darling. And your daughter?"

"Well, she's on the verge of marrying, and I'm not so happy about that... The guy's not a prize - got himself three kids from a former marriage and pays a big chunk of child support; not to mention that he's fifteen years older than her and has a reputation for womanising... Pig! My Karen's pretty enough to be a model and she's settling for a brother who's just not good enough!" Blanche bitterly said, avoiding her eyes.

Angela thought for a moment. "Why don't you ask Karen if she'd like to visit Pierce and me in London for a few weeks; even a few months? Maybe she'll find out she's not as much in love with this man as she thinks." Angela softly said, before taking her sister's hand.

"Yeah, nice of you to offer, Sis, but with you almost passin' for white and your rich hubby being one, don't ya think my Karen will feel a bit "out of place" in that fancy world of yours." Blanche said with a little grin.

"Blanche! You sound just like Marquesha! I'm your sister, remember? We've got the same parents, the same grandparents, and the same blood flowing through our veins. What kind of talk is that?"

Angela sweetly reproached, while lovingly wrapping her arm around her sister's shoulders.

"Yeah, yeah, honey, but you're different... I don't know what happened, but there's no denying the truth of it, sweet heart. Just look at you!" Blanche nervously said, with a little smile. "I don't have nothing against white folk anyway, 'cept I don't want my girl marrying one of them pasty white Englishmen neither!" She dryly said, avoiding her eyes again.

"Please, Blanche!" Angela finally exclaimed, visibly revolted. "London's also got West Indians, Jamaicans, Barbadians, Nigerians, South Africans or Gabonians... Name a culture and we have it! Believe it or not, my darling, there are people from all races and all cultures living in peace there; and Pierce and I will truly do everything we can to make Karen feel at home; I hope that you know this..."

"Nahhh... nope! Thanks anyway, Sis, but I want my daughter to marry a nice African American man; not some dark skinned nigger from Gabon! I've heard those Niggas fresh off the boat don't have a chance to make a mark in this world. In America, it's different... Our people have been here for a long time." Sadly enough, her expression was deadly serious.

"Blanche! Listen to yourself! You sound positively racist!"

"I'm no racist, Sis. Nah, not me! I just don't want my daughter so far away from home. That's all," Blanche calmly said, feeling that she had said enough.

"Well, Karen can come to visit for a couple of weeks if that's what's bothering you. Just to take in some culture. The English countryside is beautiful this time of year, and we'd love her company."

"Look, Sis. I just don't want her there, 'kay? And I don't want my Karen thinkin' any strange ideas to follow in the footsteps of her famous aunt and think it's okay to marry a white man either... In fact, I thought it might be good that you didn't bring your white guy along..."

"I see," Angela sadly said, with a tinge of coldness in her voice, as she slowly rose from the bed. "Well, so you know, Blanche. I refused to let Pierce come with me to spare him from our family's stupid prejudice against him; but not to spare you, or anyone else for that matter." She firmly said, while looking deep into Blanche's eyes.

Angela was quite surprised that Blanche's resentment hadn't subsided at all in the past five years; instead, the violent volcanic forces of racial prejudice seemed to be growing stronger...

Marquesha's racial fury was manageable, but Blanche was her sister, and that was breaking her heart.

The strong ground of their family was quickly turning into quicksand.

After Blanche left, Angela crawled under the covers and sobbed until she fell merrily into the arms of Morpheus, the jet lag finally catching up with her; but again, her nightmare had just begun...

Chapter Ten

"New Orleans"

It was just after midnight when Angela's father gently shook her awake, his face grave as he informed her that her mother's time had finally come...

Hurriedly, Angela threw on her long ivory satin robe. Holding back her tears, she raced upstairs and nervously opened the door of her parents' bedroom. Strangely, Josephine was wide-awake, propped up in the bed, her head resting on two large white cotton pillows; her mother was waiting for her...

When she saw Angela, Josephine widely opened her arms and beckoned her with a loving smile; a loving smile that only a mother could give to her child...

Like a somnambulist, Angela slowly walked towards her beloved mother, noticing that several white candles had already been placed on each of the bedside tables, their soft light lending a warm glow to Josephine's emaciated face. The window was open and the curtains were pulled aside.

Daddy did it so that Mama's soul could easily fly up to heaven...

"Come here, come my baby," Josephine almost whispered. Angela simply obeyed, sitting down on the bed, indulging herself in the pleasure of their last closeness.

"Please, please, don't cry, my lil' one. I'm goin' to see the Lawd and this is a time for rejoicing... All my family comes tomorrow." Her mother lovingly smiled. "Life ain't permanent, my sweet love; and believe me, it's a blessing for that, child."

As Josephine softly spoke, it seemed as if the cold hands of death had already claimed her; and yet, her words were kind caresses. Strangely, Josephine looked younger than she had in years; in fact decades younger than she did just yesterday...

"No, I don't want you to go, Mama; not yet..." Angela sobbed like a child, desperately clutching onto her mother's sleeve.

How Angela wished that she could share her mother's faith; how she wished she were stronger...

"Hush now, my lil' angel. I got something to tell ya." Josephine took a deep breath, summoning all her strength, so she could speak. "My sweet lil' heart, please go to the closet and get me that black shoebox from the top shelf." She tried to lift her arm to point to it, but was way too weak.

With great apprehension, Angela quickly did what she was told.

"Now open it, my child. No wastin' time anymore! I won't have it. My good Lawd is waiting." Josephine softly said, while lovingly smiling.

"Yes Mama, your good Lord is waiting…" Angela sadly said before nervously opening the shoebox, while a little voice inside her head was telling her not to do so.

Inside the box were countless newspaper clippings and old photographs…

With her hand slightly shaking, Angela picked up what was obviously a professionally photographed portrait of a young and elegant pale blond woman standing next to a young blond boy with piercing blue eyes, who looked about ten years old. The two of them regally stood in front of an impressive white colonial mansion…

A yellowed clipping from what must've been a society column showed the same woman in a gorgeous lavender silk evening dress, dripping with expensive jewels, her silky lustrous blond hair elegantly falling in waves to one side of her face.

The caption read, "Adding a touch of grace from across the Atlantic, the ethereal presence of Mrs. Elisabeth Mary Hoxworth alone, certainly was enough to charm money from even the most miserly of New Orleans' wealthy gentlemen; yet, as always, the kind-hearted wife of the distinguished Mr. Jonathan Hoxworth was more than just a presence. Mrs Hoxworth shocked her less gregarious peers by approaching each and every man in her mansion's ball room and personally asking for a generous donation to the charity that she had personally founded; still, the "Negro hospital" she hopes to raise more funds for, may need more than just charm…"

"That beautiful lady seems like a very nice woman, Mama," Angela observed, while her hands strangely started to shake even more.

"Don't you remember her, child?" Josephine softly asked, while scanning Angela's beautiful greenish golden eyes.

That question hit Angela like a thunderbolt. How many times had she seen those beautiful blue eyes gazing upon her, always filled with a strange and quiet sorrow?

"Ohhh, Mama. Now I remember... This nice lady gave me all those beautiful dolls, didn't she? The fine porcelain ones with the pretty clothes and the long blond hair..." Angela said, softly smiling. "They're still sitting on the shelf of my room. I remember you telling me to hide those dolls from Blanche and Aimée, so they wouldn't be upset."

"That's right, my sweet baby, because I never wanted any trouble," Josephine softly said, before lovingly reaching for Angela's hand. "Elisabeth Hoxworth was such a gentle soul that she couldn't understand that ya sisters would be so jealous... Ma'am Elisabeth brought those dolls all the way from England jus' fer ya, my angel." Josephine sweetly said while intensely scanning Angela's eyes again.

"But who is she, Mama? And why was this lady giving me such expensive gifts? Who was I to her, Mama? I... I don't understand..." Angela worriedly said, her hands shaking again.

"Oh, my sweet, sweet angel, it's a very long story... Unfortunately, my love, I don't have time for it all... What's important is that you know that ma'am Elisabeth truly loved you, my sweet Angela; she loved you more than you ever knew, my child... I know now that the good Lawd only kept me alive so long, so I could tell ya the truth, my love." Josephine said before tiredly closing her eyes.

At this precise instant, Angela's head strangely began to ache. "I... I don't understand, Mama... Tell me what?" She said with a broken voice, and then her lips started trembling.

Josephine clutched Angela's hand tightly. "My dear child, you listen carefully now... Ma'am Elisabeth Mary Hoxworth is your real Mama, my child. That's the truth of it... I'm so sorry for waitin' so long to tell ya, my love, but it's time for you to know the truth." Josephine sadly said, refraining from crying.

"No Mama! Stop it. You're delirious! You're my mother!" Angela almost shouted, hoping to drown out the words that her soul told her was true. "It's a lie! A lie!!! That woman is white, Mama! White!!!" She finally shouted, her body shaking now like a leaf.

Strange deformed images suddenly bombarded her mind - zebras, white lace pillows that smelled of expensive French perfume, angels black as ebony; and blood, so much blood, red as blood can be, everywhere...

Stop it!!! A voice hysterically shouted in her head.

Angela's head started to dangerously spin. The air became so dry that the room felt like the Sahara Desert at mid-day. Her throat was not so parched, but had a bitter taste. For an instant which felt like eternity, Angela looked long into Josephine's warm brown eyes, her "mother's eyes"; eyes that couldn't tell a lie; wouldn't tell a lie; but obviously had done just that; repeatedly...

Suddenly, Angela felt an incredible surge of raw anger rising like a lethal hungry snake from the pit of her belly. "Mama, why are you telling me this now? It can't be true!" She shouted again, feeling now as if she were dying inside.

Looking terribly sad, Josephine sighed heavily. "I wouldn't lie 'bout something like this, my angel; but that woman is who really brought you into this cruel world... Me and yer papa, well, we just were blessed to been the ones who raised ya, my love..." She said with burning tears in her eyes.

"So... So daddy's not..." Angela stopped herself from asking the foolishly hopeful question. "Then, who is my real father? Did this woman give me away because she had an affair with a black man? Was she ashamed of me?" Suddenly, her tone turned terribly bitter and her eyes lost their softness...

"All I know, my angel, is that Ma'am Elisabeth told me that yer daddy was her husband. And if that were so my love, Mister Hoxworth was white as any white man can be; whiter even..." Josephine sadly said, before wiping some tears.

"But... but that's totally ridiculous! Obviously, someone is lying! If that were the case, I'd have blond hair and blue eyes and my skin would be white as snow, not tawny!"

"Well, ma'am Elisabeth swore to it and I weren't one to ask too many questions, my child..." Josephine sadly said, lowering her eyes.

"Maybe you should have, Mama!" Angela harshly reproached, wringing her hands in anger. "God! No wonder I never fit in! My whole life has been a sham!" *A shame and a sham...* "Why did you and daddy take me, Mama? You certainly couldn't afford another child."

Josephine softly squeezed Angela's hand again. "I was Elisabeth Hoxworth's chambermaid. Worked right there in that monster of a house for many years... The missus was a good woman. She treated me right, my child, which was more than I can say for the others in that place..." She sadly said, her eyes filling with tears again, as she remembered. "Three days after ya were born, ma'am Elisabeth came to me with her eyes all rimmed and red, and pleaded for me to take you in... I don't want to think what might've happen'd to ya if I didn't." Josephine closed her eyes again and shuddered.

"And her husband? He didn't want me either? Were they so ashamed of my skin colour that they tossed me out like if I was garbage?" Angela nervously asked, visibly revolted.

"Mister Jonathan? I don't know what went on in that man's head after you were born, my child, but God bless his poor soul," Josephine sadly said, before piously crossing herself. "Poor man lost his mind and shot himself in the head the day before I take you away..." She added as tears fell along her emaciated cheeks.

"But that doesn't make sense, Mama; no sense at all!" Angela incredulously said. "If this man wanted to get rid of me and succeeded in doing so, why would he shoot himself? Why???"

"Well... Embarrassment, I suppose... You see, child, Mister Jonathan was the son of the great Sir Reginald Henry Hoxworth, the former governor of Louisiana... This proud man was the heir to an old and prestigious American family and blue-blooded to the core. At the time you were born, he was campaigning to win the governorship himself and follow in his famous daddy's footsteps, and he was well-placed to win; I guess when Mister Jonathan saw that you were of darker skin than him, and people began talking, he committed suicide rather than live with the shame…" Josephine said with a broken voice while avoiding Angela's eyes.

"So, what happened to my mother then?"

"The poor ma'am Elisabeth was made a pariah… Ma'am Eileen Mackenzie-Hoxworth, "the grand dame of New Orleans" herself, took her precious only grandson from his poor momma, and raised him. She's still living there in that old French castle, like the queen she thinks she is, your strange grandmother… She's very, very rich you know; but she's got the heart of a cold blooded snake, or the devil in her, some say… Everyone that really knows her, fears her… Ma'am Eileen, soon after her only son killed himself, made sure that Ma'am Elisabeth was disgraced and thrown penniless out of her big mansion on the street… The poor ma'am Elisabeth had to sell some of her jewellery, in order to get herself 'nough money to buy her passage back to England, a place called "Ashington" was where she bore from; an' she gave me quite a bit to help with your raising, too, my angel. She was generous people. After that, she called once a month, wantin' to know how you were… Sometimes she spoke 'bout takin' you to England, but I think she was too scared. Those days, it weren't like it is now, my child; believe me…"

"But it wasn't that long ago, Mama. Just 32 years! And come to think about it, I don't see much has changed in the past three decades," Angela remarked bitterly, thinking of how she'd also been treated by the Haddingtons after she'd married their son…

"But why didn't you tell me all this earlier, Mama? Why???" Angela furiously asked.

"Well, my child, when you were little, we thought it for the best that you had some kind of stability in ya life; but later on, we just... Well, I don't know. Forgive me, my angel. I really hated keeping that lie for so long and I hope the good Lawd forgive me," Josephine sadly said, repentantly, before caressing Angela's face. "And poor Ma'am Elisabeth came to see you three times in all. She stayed at a discreet hotel in town, just long 'nough ta make sure ya were blossomin' into the beautiful flower you are." She lovingly said, while wiping some of her tears.

"So, Mama, what am I supposed to do with this information now? Tell me!"

"I... I don't know... Maybe I'm selfish, my child, but I just couldn't die with that lie circling round my old head like a vulture out of hell. But you are a strong woman now and too young to be without a Mama at all." Josephine tiredly said while lowering her eyes. "My dying wish is for ya to find now Ma'am Elisabeth... There's something she knows that she never told me and maybe she'll tell you. I could always feel it, lurking 'bout in that castle; something truly evil going on in there... I was glad to be able to leave that sad place and that wouldn't have been possible if things didn't go as they did... Please, my child, don't blame Ma'am Elisabeth for givin' ya up to me. You must understand that she was young and scared when her husband killed himself." Josephine sadly said while silently crying.

"I'm not blaming anyone, Mama; and I am not blaming you." Angela uttered, her voice harsh and cold.

"I know it don't help now, my angel, but I'm truly sorry that ya got this burden now... All I know is that some truths are like too stubborn seeds to give up searching for a place to plant themselves and grow... I also know that time has come now," Josephine said with a deep sight. "I take the blame for not thinkin' bout this sooner, my child, but now ya need to face the truth and find out who you came from... Like I said, the Hoxworths still live here in Orleans, an' ol Dame Hoxworth is still a force to be reckoned with... This lady must be seventy, or eighty years old by now, but you wouldn't know if she were older than forty-five... I think she's trying to cheat death; and if anyone could, it's her!"

Josephine gave a short-lived smile before reopening the shoebox again and pulling out a headshot of Elisabeth. "Look here, child. See her face, her nose... Don't ya see that ya look like her?" She pointed out with a bony finger.

Reluctantly, Angela finally studied the old photography. Clearly, she'd inherited many of Elisabeth's finely chiselled Caucasian features; the same high cheekbones, the elegant aquiline nose, the delicate lips...

"But my eyes aren't like hers, Mama. Do I have my father's eyes?"

"Oh, it's more than that, child; much more... I remember telling myself from the first I saw you. I said 'this baby's got the eyes of an old soul.' You had a particular shine to them that weren't just from that light green and amber colouring… No, my angel, there were always something more special about ya eyes; somethin' so strange that they often come to me in my dreams and make me know that I had to tell all the truth to you before I pass. Always I saw yer eyes in my dreams; always…" Josephine said sadly, before crying again.

"I see strange eyes in my dreams, too, Mama; but they're not mine, nor yours, nor anyone I know." Angela blurted out. She never mentioned her nightmares to Josephine; not even when they first began coming to her when she was just a child…

"Sweet dreams I hope, baby." Josephine softly asked.

"No, Mama, terrible ones, but nothing for you to think about now," Angela nervously said, looking away. *Perhaps there was a reason for the truth to be told…* A strange shudder overcame her, as if a living cold - an icy thing with a life of its own - was crawling through her bones and chilling her heart, turning it into stone…

"Just remember I love you, Mama," she softly added, with eyes like limpid mountain lakes. But Josephine had already fallen into a peaceful sleep, the last sleep of her life. She was lovingly holding the picture of Elisabeth Hoxworth in her hand, and close to her heart…

Angela whispered a last final goodbye then she slowly walked down the creaky old stairs, her eyes downcast, while feeling the weight of the entire planet upon her shoulders. As if on cue, Blanche got up from the old living room's sofa, where she had sat in silence with the rest of the Boivin family, each awaiting his or her turn to say a last goodbye…

"Are you okay, hon?" Blanche asked Angela.

"Fine," Angela softly replied. *What am I supposed to say? That I've just found out that I'm not just losing my mother, but my entire family?* She sadly thought, while refraining from crying.

To continue to act as if she were bonded to Blanche, Aimée and John by "familial love" seemed now like a farce; it wasn't as if they were closely knit by friendship or common interests. She smiled wanly and silently retreated to her little room, purposefully isolating herself, already cutting the invisible ties that linked her to her adopted sisters and her brother. When she sat upon her bed, Angela sadly realised that she was alone now, really alone...

Shortly before dawn, Josephine Boivin let forth a sigh as she reached her Creator in Heaven. It was a sound of peace, a sound of joy; the sound of a freed soul experiencing its final release from the slavery of that terrestrial burden called "the body"; in fact, it was a cage...

When Angela entered the silent room that morning, she saw that a tender smile was etched on Josephine's face. Her expression was that of a woman who'd achieved her goal; her mission among the living had been successfully accomplished. Indeed, Josephine's loving soul had spoken to Angela's and the truth had finally been passed down. Just enough of the truth to set the wheels of fate spinning once again; just enough to change Angela's entire life...

Amen!

Chapter Eleven

"La Rêveuse"

The vast "de Montpezat" estate was more than a mansion; it was in fact an authentic French castle...

Built in the Eighteenth Century, it was a regal retreat for a French nobleman, "Count Eugéne Armand Gérôme de Montpezat", who required an escape from the incessant complications of the extravagant Louis XV's court, at Versailles...

Too many jealous husbands had challenged Count Eugéne to duels, and he had run out of excuses to postpone the fights. Frankly, his age was catching up to him and he feared for his life. He had grown bored of sporting with death, and for the first time in his life, the French Count had fallen in love.

Yes, the consummate "blue blooded bachelor" had finally given his precious noble heart away, although it was not to some enchanting white-wigged French courtesan whose plunging "décolleté" was capable of jolting his regal penis into a high salute... No, not even close! The lucky recipient of the Count's sincere love was 150,000 acres of virgin Indian land set on the bank of the mighty Mississippi River, just an hour's ride from the newly built city of "La Nouvelle Orleans". The refined French Count had finally found a lush and beautiful regal sanctuary in the New World; America...

The design of his elegant house began modestly enough; at least in comparison to the de Montpezat's family castle, which loomed majestically over the French region of "Dordogne". However, since a tender age, the Count was accustomed to extreme luxury; and so he bribed several of France's finest court artisans and greatest architects, offering them five times their normal salary, if they would sail across the sea and build his new castle in the "barbarian" new colony...

The Count imported expensive red marble columns, precious silk damask draperies, gilded Louis XIV and XV furnishings, exquisite needle point "Aubusson" rugs, and priceless "Gobelins" tapestries. The pantry was stocked with a large mix of the aromatic "herbs de Provence" as well as delicious French "Cochonailles" and the vast cellar overflowed with the most delectable wines, champagnes and rare cognacs that the refined kingdom of France had to offer; Count de Montpezat simply wanted the best...

Flush with trainloads of gold that he'd made from the vast crops of tobacco, cotton and indigo that flourished in his newfound American land, and blissfully content with the 70,000 square foot French palace that he'd christened "La Rêveuse" - the "Lady Dreamer" - the extremely refined Count only needed one more accoutrement; an heir. And so he married the most beautiful courtesan of the royal

French court; a virginal seventeen-year-old blue-eyed duchess with an hourglass figure and a prestigious bloodline; as well as a body to damn a saint...

Unfortunately, for all the Count's hard work, "La Rêveuse" only remained in the de Montpezat family until 1886... That year, the sole surviving heir, Count Ferdinand Etiénne Louis Philipe de Montpezat, bored by the drudgery of his highly hedonistic life, stupidly attempted to impress his noble friends on his thirty-second birthday by playing Russian roulette. Every tragedy however has its upside...

And so it was that the noble magnificent French estate was snatched up for a tenth of its worth by "Stiles T. Hoxworth", a third generation American patriarch, born of dirt poor Irish immigrants who'd found their good fortune by squatting on Indian territory and mercilessly exploiting the land; decimating Indians, flora, and fauna...

The Hoxworths used the indecent amount of money they'd received by plundering, to acquire several huge plantations and investing in the highly profitable American business of Negro slave trading...

The cunning Stiles T. Hoxworth bought the de Montpezat estate, "La Rêveuse", as an expensive present for his lovely new bride "Callista". Both Stiles and Callista were truly transformed by the regal purchase. The moment they took residence in the beautiful French castle, they felt that their Irish blood was cleansed of its lowly immigrant platelets; they not only felt entitled to the 'de Montpezat' land, but also to the ancient noble French lineage!

From that day forward, the Hoxworths, as well as their spoiled offspring, walked, talked, acted and simply demanded to be treated like true European royalty…

The present "ladyship of the house", the extremely elegant, beautiful and ageless Dame "Eileen Patricia Rose Mackenzie-Hoxworth" - who chose to occupy a mere 5000 square foot Master Suite in the heart of "La Revêuse" - was accessorising her spectacular 'Carolina Herrera' ivory hued silk shantung gown, with an accessory that she hoped would catch the envious eye of every woman: a sumptuous 1930's platinum 'Cartier' brooch, richly emblazoned with a large 22 carat cushion shaped Mandarin garnet and rose cut diamond. Her carefully selected dinner guests would be arriving at any moment now; the old-moneyed gentlemen would arrive with their pretty new wives, while the senators and politicians, with their older ones; as custom dictated…

Dame Mackenzie-Hoxworth took a deep breath; inhaling the antediluvian scent of rich Cuban tobacco, fine French perfume, old sherry, and decadent "necessary luxury" which permeated from the richly panelled Louis XV study of palatial proportion that elegantly surrounded her.

From the day of her societal "début", the always-divine Eileen Mackenzie-Hoxworth had made it her duty to uphold the old-fashioned social mores and complex "etiquette" that she'd learned perfectly from her extremely refined mother and grandmother. Such behaviour was sometimes a slap in the face of feminism;

but of course, the old-moneyed men of the South truly loved her attitude...

The artful Eileen let those gentlemen always think that they were "in control", and always took great pains to constrain her 'ladies in waiting' from discussing anything more substantial than charity balls, rare orchids, fine art; and even sometimes "Parisian haute couture", as to appear more frivolous...

However, beneath this "impeccable refined façade" was a streetwise lady who wasn't to be toyed with: in fact, the lovely Dame Hoxworth ruled the "crème de la crème" of New Orleans with silk velvet gloves. She had the power to make or break anyone; and indeed, everyone who was "someone" simply knew it...

The "poor" did not interest Eileen at all; although she was often quite amused by the bravado exhibited by those poor fools who childishly attempted to rise above the class they were unfortunately born into...

As Eileen elegantly often said to her wealthy friends: "little people with big dreams make me laugh!" In fact, the "grand dame of New Orleans" adamantly believed in entitlement, particularly her own, but she was not a fool and knew that "great privilege" received by birth right often brought with it many constant obligations; as well as an army of jealous enemies...

Fortunately, most of Eileen's enemies could be tamed, or simply made to "disappear", with the help of the mighty dollar, ahhh, the magical power of money...

One more task. To make a call, Eileen stately sat behind a priceless rosewood desk which had once belonged to the Queen "Marie Antoinette"; the same one that Stiles Hoxworth had bought for a ludicrously low price, shortly after the poor French royal lost her regal head…

"Mrs. Hoxworth! What a pleasure. I've been thinking about you. I couldn't imagine a more pleasant voice interrupting my dinner," Stephen Montgomery, her young investment banker, said joyfully before he swallowed a bite of a delicious "filet mignon", seasoned with a dash of fresh green pepper.

"That's lovely, Stephen. However, I'm in a terrible rush, dear." Eileen impatiently said, already annoyed…

"Well, my dear Mrs. Hoxworth, I think it's time we take a more aggressive approach to your portfolio… It is time we buy out those down-trodden dotcoms," he joyously went on. "The reason I'm at the top, my dear Mrs. Hoxworth, is that I look at the market in a, uh, well, for lack of a better word; a perverse way… You see, Madam, I invest my money - which means "your money" - into the dogs!" The investment banker said with a little laugh. "I always say to myself 'what the fuck am I doing buying this shit company out of the gutter?' Yet, as you know, my dear Mrs. Hoxworth, it always pays off at the end…" He loudly laughed, this time while salivating looking at the succulent meat.

"That's nice, Stephen, very nice…" Eileen uttered impatiently, before she admired herself in a large intricately carved Louis XIV gilded mirror, while Montgomery droned on about the ever-rising Euro and Yen...

True, Eileen's cerulean eyes sometimes told of a long and experienced life, but the society columnists couldn't even begin to estimate her true age...

The fresh cell injections that Eileen regularly received in Switzerland, at the world famous Clinique "La Prairie" in Clarens-Montreux, along with the artistry of her highly skilled Beverly Hills plastic surgeon, the handsome doctor "Jason Diamond" took good care of that! Not that the exquisitely elegant Dame Eileen Mackenzie-Hoxworth was totally immune to the burden of her years, or of each passing day. In fact, her vertiginous emerald green silk-embroidered 'Manolo Blahnik' stiletto pumps were already killing her delicate little feet, something that was highly annoying...

"What I'm proposing is that we invest a million or so in Compustat.com. What do you think, my dear Mrs. Hoxworth? Trust me on this one," Montgomery finally said, inwardly smiling, while thinking about his juicy commission...

"Bravo, Stephen, Bravo! Once again, you've convinced me that you are the best man for the job... I must say that you're almost as good as your daddy was, God Bless his soul," Eileen softly crooned, rearranging her criminally expensive large pendulous diamond earrings; then, like a skilled matador, she remained silent for an appropriate moment before she got to the point of her call...

"Well, my dear Stephen, to make this conversation short, I need ten million dollars immediately... The funds must be withdrawn from my international portfolio - nothing American – and the transaction must be done with the utmost discretion," she added in a hushed whisper, almost blushing with the thought.

Why would Dame Eileen Mackenzie-Hoxworth need an anonymous 10 mil? Montgomery wondered, while sucking his finger seasoned with a little bit of the sinful French creamy sauce.

Even when his shrewd father had told him never to ask a rich client to divulge what he is doing with his - or her – money, the curiosity was now truly killing him...

"On which particular account, Mrs. Hoxworth? Cayman or Switzerland?" He sweetly asked, deeply puzzled.

"The latter, dear; the latter..." She softly said while rearranging her hair. "As I said, my dear Stephen, get the funds as soon as possible, please. I know that we'll probably be penalised for one thing or another, but just do your best; you know what I mean..." Eileen said lowering her voice, before she laughed coquettishly, while reaching for her solid rose gold 'Cartier's' minaudière...

"Well, Madam, I'll do my best." He nervously said. In fact Montgomery was shocked; for Eileen Mackenzie-Hoxworth to need money so badly that she was willing to take a big loss, was completely out of character. "But, may I ask you a question?" He meekly asked. *Screw my father's respect for the privacy of the filthy rich!*

"Of course, my dear Stephen," Eileen cautiously answered, becoming a bit tense.

"You certainly know that you have other liquid funds available to you at any time, madam; so what's so hush-hush that you require such a complicated transaction?" He sweetly asked, raising an eyebrow.

"Well, dear, let's say... that is none of your business!' She firmly clipped. "And all of mine, if you understand what I mean!"

"I'm... I'm truly sorry, Mrs. Hoxworth," Montgomery apologised, before just biting his tongue. "You know that I'm only trying to protect your interests, and..."

"Of course you are, dear, you are... But this is my business, my boy, not yours!" She icily said. "By the way, Stephen darling, would you like to know why I gave my money to your daddy, even though I was courted by at least ten other eligible investment firms; some that might've been more experienced in finance?" Eileen softly asked, speaking as sweetly as if she were simply talking to a stupid child.

"Well, don't bother thinking too hard, dear," she snipped, before the investment banker could answer. "I chose your daddy, my boy, simply because he perfectly knew who the boss was; and above all, my dear, because your daddy always knew when to keep his mouth shut!" She dryly exclaimed, truly delighted by her stockade.

If there was anything Dame Eileen truly hated, it was a stupid employee who didn't know his or her place. If that impertinent Negro chambermaid of hers had kept her big trap shut, or if Eileen had had the foresight to hire someone to cut off Josephine's fat Negro tongue, she wouldn't be in such an awkward position now...

If poor Montgomery believed in ghosts, he would've sworn that his father had just slapped his face; he could practically feel his cheek sting...

"Be sure to let me know when you've done your job, my dear. Be a good boy now. Ta-ta, Stephen," Eileen sweetly said, hanging up before the poor man had the chance to make amends. *Let him live with his mistake...* Eileen thought while smiling devilishly. At this precise instant, it gave her great pleasure to know that Montgomery had lost at least one good night's sleep...

A moment later, Eileen's stylish black butler informed "Madame" that the first guest had arrived. She graciously acknowledged the information with a quarter of a smile, before dismissing him with a wave of her well-manicured hand.

The divine Dame Eileen Mackenzie-Hoxworth took a last satisfying look in the monumental golden mirror before spraying a flowery cloud of 'Balanciaga' perfume high above her regal head; then she elegantly adjusted her large diamond earrings, so they would capture the light when she gracefully glided down the castle's spectacular white marble staircase. *My grand entrance must be impeccable...* She thought, smiling like an Egyptian cat, while trying to eliminate Angela from her mind. After all, dinner for thirty would be served soon. The political gossip would be, as always, extremely useful and new lucrative deals would certainly be made; then once again, the extremely well chosen guests of "La Rêveuse" would remember the experience as one of the highlights of their lives...

It feels good to be so rich, Eileen happily thought as she regally strode down the spectacular marble staircase, while leaving behind her elegant statuesque silhouette a trail of expensive French perfume.

Eileen Mackenzie-Hoxworth was indeed born with a solid platinum spoon in her pretty mouth, and in spite of what some poor idiots had sometimes thought, she had never once, during her entire life, become tired of all the great privileges that being filthy rich constantly offered; never!

Ahhh, it feels so good to be Queen; yes indeed...

Chapter Twelve

"New Orleans"

On a pale sunny morning, more than one hundred people squeezed into the little wooden chapel, where the funeral of Josephine Beatrice Boivin was being held...

The service was conducted by the Reverend Thomas Brown, a tall and handsome black man who spoke so eloquently that even those well wishers who'd never met Josephine were almost moved to tears. A black choir of twenty, wearing satin robes of purple and gold, fervently sang old Negro spiritual hymns from the south.

"Sister, sister, rise in the light and feel the love of our Lord Jesus! Sister, sister, when you were born, you cried and the world rejoiced! Sister, sister, when you died, you rejoiced and the world cried!"

"Amen! Amen! Amen!" the African-American congregation sang, raising their arms and shaking their hands in rhythm with the music.

"Sister, sister, be with the Lord in Heaven for all eternity!" The chorus chanted.

Wearing an extremely well-cut sleeveless black silk velvet 'Lanvin' dress, with a spectacular matching wide-brimmed straw hat that she found in London, Angela stood elegantly in the front pew, her aristocratic ballerina's body stiff and unmoving, while her gleaming tears were falling, like drops of dew, on the old wooden floor...

Even though Angela tried to hold on to her faith in "God and heaven", she couldn't rejoice in her Mama's passing; in fact, she was too bitter to even grieve her own loss, still reeling from what her beloved Josephine had told her while she laid on her death bed...

For God sake, why? Why did Mama leave me with such a heavy burden to bear? Why did she have to tell me the damned truth? Why couldn't she take it to the grave with her? Why??? She bitterly thought, while trying to hold her tears.

Angela was so confused now that she didn't know whether to grieve, bite someone, or simply scream...

After the choir finished the hymn, she tiredly sat down and tried her best to lose herself in the tenor magnificence of Reverend Brown. His well-practiced pitch filled the vaulted room, and Angela noticed that the black middle class audience was entranced and seemingly immune to his arrogance. The man spoke as if he and God were comrades; both of them carrying an equal load of responsibility for their flocks...

A self-proclaimed authority on the subject of "eschatology" - life after death - his favourite topic was by far the dramatic battle between God and the devil for the so precious human soul; the prize of all prizes!

On, and on, and on, the Reverend prattled, gesticulating with such undiluted passion, that one would think he was a mad conductor of a grand philharmonic. Skilled in the use of precise repetition and subtle inflection of tone, he truly mesmerised his audience. Brown was nothing if not the consummate confidence man, both extraordinaire showman and salesman... *God he was good!*

Angela nervously turned around and looked with compassion on the spellbound audience. She was no stranger to the smooth-talking Reverend's sermons, and she almost smiled as she sadly remembered sitting on her Mama's soft lap, listening to those sermons on Sundays when she was a child. The sweet Josephine would always be dressed in her Sunday finery, wearing hand-knitted white gloves and a pretty dress she'd sewn for herself of lavender, pink, or mint green cotton fabric - her favourite colours - always with a lace collar and a little hat that was dyed to match.

Angela fully knew that her adorable mother never quite bought into the reverend's fearful speeches or the grim reality of "fire and brimstone". The sweet Josephine would simply stare at the large wooden crucifix and mouth her prayers to the poor "lil' Jesus" and his "poor Mama", the good and beautiful Madonna. But at the end of each prayer, Josephine would close her soft brown eyes and whisper the words "mea culpa" three times; something that always surprised Angela...

Angela also recalled that whenever her mother fervently prayed, a wonderful scent would exude from her skin: violets and amber. Her mother, most of the time, wore no perfume, because she couldn't afford such a luxury, but she always smelled better than any woman in the world.

When Josephine was dying, the peculiar smell had vanished; but now, strangely, it softly filled Angela's nostrils and soothed her heart, like a balm from heaven...

Angela wondered if anyone else noticed the wonderful scent, or if it was just her imagination. She discretely looked around, before she stared again at her Mama's casket, until she sadly realised that all the numerous prayers that were whispered petitioned the all mighty for one thing: that her beloved Josephine would be forgiven for lying during all her life to her, and that her sweet loving soul would be completely absolved of the stain of that sin...

Josephine's life seemed to most like an open book, each chapter describing the life of a model Christian; and yet, she had lived for those last three decades in the cold shadow of a lie...

How could she? Angela wondered if her adopted mother was being judged for her sin. Josephine had taught her children to believe in a God of Love, but Angela always had her doubts; especially now...

Now, Angela silently sat in the pew, nervously twisting a strand of hair that had fallen from beneath her hat, while she tried her best to mentally pray. She asked "God", or whoever was up there, to help her forgive her dear Josephine for lying to her. Angela also prayed to the sweet Madonna and asked her to help her forgive Elisabeth Mary Hoxworth for abandoning her; something which was even more difficult...

How could I ever forgive a woman who threw me away, because my skin was a few shades darker than she thought fitting? She bitterly thought while closing her eyes.

Still, Angela tried to let go some of her destructive anger. After all, who was she to cast stones? What child isn't burdened with the sins of her father, or her mother's? The fact was that on this imperfect little planet, nobody was totally innocent from primordial sins…

As the black choir began the closing hymn, the pallbearers silently took their places then slowly lifted the heavy mahogany coffin. It was time to say a last goodbye; time to place Josephine's remains in the hearse waiting outside the little church.

The large procession would follow in line; headlights turned on, as the hearse slowly drove to the nearby old cemetery; to Josephine's final resting place…

Angela, André, and the rest of the family sadly followed the pallbearers in utter silence; with the exception of "Marquesha", who, as usual, was gossiping about something or another…

The casket was covered with flowers from their neighbours' gardens, as well as expensive wreathes. Angela watched sadly as a sudden gust of wind, a strange chill of a wind that contrasted with the late-morning heat, grabbed a bunch of yellow daisies tied with a pink satin ribbon - a gift from one of Josephine's poorer friends, no doubt, and then wildly blew it onto the street. The yellow bundle scuttled away like the hat of an unlucky man on a blustery London day.

André was sprinting to catch the flowers before they were lost, when Angela noticed the elegant black and silver 'Maybach' Mercedes-Benz, parked directly across from the hearse. Strangely enough, a black chauffeur wearing white gloves and an impeccably tailored dark blue suit, stepped out from behind the vehicle and commenced to exhume a large funeral wreathe from the front passenger seat...

The middle-aged stylish chauffeur nodded courteously to someone in the limo - presumably his passenger, then, carefully holding the expensive wreath with both of his gloved hands, he solemnly walked towards the hearse.

The black tinted window of the passenger compartment had been lowered just enough for Angela to see a pair of woman eyes peering at her - Wedgwood blue eyes that seemed vaguely familiar... Angela shivered, fully aware that the person in the limousine was watching her; studying her as if she were a wild animal...

Those eyes... Angela instinctively feared them; and yet, she sensed that whoever possessed them feared her just as much as she feared her; maybe even more...

André picked up the daisies and rapidly re-joined the procession; while the eyes behind the tinted glass followed Angela's every move...

The chauffeur placed the wreath on top of those that already lay on the casket, then rapidly returned to the limousine and sped off.

Only then was the window raised...

Angela made a note of the license plate "EMH # 3" then silently watched as the quarter million dollar German limousine disappeared from her view. When she looked at the newly added expensive wreath, she was surprised to find it was even more impressive than she'd imagined. Immaculate and powerfully fragrant, that wreath was exclusively comprised of rare white South African camellias; those were Josephine's favourite flowers...

A lavender moiré banner was elegantly wrapped around it. Three golden words had been embroidered on it: "Rest in Peace".

Ohhh yes; indeed...

Chapter Thirteen

"New Orleans"

Death...

Most people try to avoid death as if it was contagious, but this natural aversion did not pertain to "Grande".

Death, and its accompanying rituals, gave Grande a thrill; the same kind of thrill that a peeping Tom got, when spying on a beautiful woman undressing...

Whenever Grande smelled the sweet scent of death, there he would go; there he would patiently wait; there he would watch; as delighted as a child watching a clown at a circus...

As the black mourners sadly exited the little chapel and then silently gathered behind the hearse, Grande suddenly stopped his nervous pacing. He ceased to plead with the devil to take the deceased straight to hell, before he found a nice shady place underneath a large poplar tree, where he could relax and enjoy "the show".

From his ideal observation point, Grande rapidly scanned the crowd and tried to guess the gender of the "dead meat in the box"; this was one of his favourite funeral parlour games…

It must've been a black bitch and a well-off one at that, he deduced, taking note of the excessive snivelling that was going on.

As always, Grande took great pleasure in watching the sorrow of others. His thick lips parted in a miserly smile; he opened his mouth only wide enough to reveal the perfectly chiselled points of his fourteen carat gold canines. This was a well-practiced smile.

Judging by the quality of the mahogany casket and those gold plated handles, someone has dropped a good deal of cash on the dead black bitch… He thought, smiling again.

"Negritos con dinero! Bastardos!" He viciously hissed in Spanish, before extracting a toothpick from the pocket of the red floral embroidered Texan shirt he wore; then he methodically scraped some barbeque beef meat from between his carnivorous teeth.

Grande was about to find a better use for his day off, when he saw the divine Angela…

No doubt that nice little bitch has a body that would drive a man to murder. He thought with a smile, before he slid his hand into the bottomless pocket of his jeans. As he firmly grabbed his growing erection, he sensually chanted: "puta! puta! puta!" while imagining the beautiful Angela on her hands and knees, wiggling her tight little ass in his face, begging him to fill her tight little cunt with his huge throbbing member…

Yes, she has a very nice ass, but it's not as perfect as Lupe's, he concluded; still, this "little ass" was sexy enough to keep him good and hard for quite a long time, but Grande had yet to meet a woman whose ass could compare with the voluptuous ass of his mother...

His mother "Lupe" wasn't the most intelligent woman in the world, but what a behind! It was as prominent as the hump on a camel's back, and moved like it had a life of its own.

Ever since Lupe was thirteen years old, she had intelligently used that particular part of her anatomy, to keep each of her nine bastard children well fed. Grande was number five and his real name was 'Cuauhtémoc', after a great Inca warrior prince; but people in his country called him "Grande" because of his tall and imposing stature.

Grande had inherited his exotic genes from his father, a giant Samoan who worked on a cruise ship and met his mother on a one-day layover in Acapulco. Grande was the tallest and cleverest of all Lupe's bastards; and the most vicious too...

His tiny sensual Mexican mother never found out the name of the sailor that fathered him, but she fondly held his memory in her heart. In spite of his size and the fact that he was half drunk, the huge Samoan made love to Lupe with a certain tenderness that she'd never experienced before; and hadn't experienced since...

Because Grande reminded her of a solitary "romantic moment" in an otherwise harsh life, Lupe always favoured him over all her other children and took him wherever she went; she even brought him to her day job at the mortuary in "San Miguel de Allende", their native town. It was there that Grande became infatuated with death and all its mysteries...

Like her son, Lupe was prone to eccentric forms of amusements. She had great fun pretending that Grande was a dead infant, whenever her boss, "Don Felipe", would leave her alone. Lupe would gleefully place Grande inside the most luxurious child's casket, where, like an angel, he would quickly fall asleep...

Almost inevitably, a grief stricken customer would notice Grande sleeping in the casket and let go a loud scream; then Lupe would tickle her son until he woke up, and both of them would laugh so loudly that the customer would run out of the mortuary in terror...

As Grande grew older, he took his "naps" in larger caskets, and soon, the very thought of death triggered a rush of endorphins, euphoria, and great relaxation equivalent to sex.

By the time Grande was fifteen, he'd seen his mother washing hundreds of dead bodies in all shapes and sizes, preparing them for the embalmer. The dead were rich or poor, ugly or beautiful, young or old, but all of them were quiet; nice and wonderfully quiet...

Above all, it was the appealing calmness of the dead that always soothed Grande.

Several times in his youth, he tested the calm of the dead by brutally kicking them, trying to wake them from their eternal sleep; but nothing he could do or say would make them utter a word, nor a single cry, nor a single sound; in fact it was simply wonderful...

Sometimes, Grande would lift the rigid eyelids of the dead, wondering where the life that had once animated them had gone. Although he'd read a few books on religion, he hadn't found any proof; at least not enough to fully satisfy him. Grande became obsessed and he wanted to know what happened at the precise moment that the so-called "soul" left the body; and above all, where the mysterious soul really went...

It wasn't long before Grande's insane curiosity became a full-blown obsession.

At 15 years of age, Grande decided that he would witness the soul's journey, no matter what he had to do...

Grande had it all figured out: he would need to be present when the soul departed the body; then he would know whether the soul went to heaven or hell; or merely disappeared...

Grande began experimenting with animals, taking a certain pleasure in swiftly twisting the neck of the chickens his mother raised, but he soon grew extremely bored; *chickens don't have souls like humans do.* He sadly thought one day, thus they would never give him the answers that he ultimately sought. Grande also realised that he would discover nothing from the eyes of a person who died in a state of fear. Fear, he knew, was a strong, opaque emotion, and he was convinced that it would act like a veil, preventing him from seeing the truth, and thus spoiling his experiments. Grande decided then that he would figure out a way to trick his future victims.

His well-chosen victims must believe that they would live to tell their tales, even as his powerful hands slid softly around their necks; even as they heard the sound of their own necks breaking...

Lustily and greedily, Grande stared at Angela's graceful neck, slowly stroking himself and fantasizing about the secrets that her beautiful golden eyes would reveal when he killed her. *What a neck! So elegant; so delicate; so fragile... Puta!!!*

As Grande imagined his large hands on her swan neck - twisting, snapping, and cracking - his hand moved faster and faster around his penis. "Puta! Puta! Puta!" He sensually groaned again. Just a moment more and he would release his load; or would have, if he hadn't seen the elegant black and silver 'Maybach' limousine...

At the sight of the expensive German limousine, his large member deflated as fast as a helium balloon stuck with a pin.

Nervously, Grande quickly removed his hand from his pants, feeling guilty as a child stealing candy, then he rapidly reached for his cowboy hat and he tipped it respectfully, wondering why the well-known passenger inside the 'Maybach' would take interest in a funeral for a Negrita. But he knew best that he shouldn't dare to ask such a question to the passenger in question, simply because he was not a fool.

Yes, Grande always took great pleasure in playing with death, granted, but the man wasn't stupid enough to play with fire; and even less to play with his own life...

Chapter Fourteen

"London"

Impeccably clad in a 'Alexander Wang' burgundy jersey dress, but without so much as a souvenir to declare Angela could pass easily through the customs checkpoint at Heathrow International Airport, wanting nothing but to collapse into the loving comfort of her husband's arms...

With his ravishing smile and boyish good looks in his bespoken tailored dark blue suit, Pierce Haddington was easy to spot.

Angela joyously waved as the handsome Pierce ran towards her; then, with an air of chivalry, he lovingly took her chin in his hand and deeply kissed her.

Angela might've melted then and there, if Pierce's uncle, the honourable "Stuart Haddington", hadn't wedged himself between them. Much to Angela's dismay, Stuart gave her a sloppy, drunken kiss hello...

"Uncle Stuart," she softly said, before politely pushing him away. "What a delightful surprise to see you..."

"Yes, well my dear, I had a sudden impulse. I ran into your better half at the St. James Club earlier on, and it occurred to me that I hadn't the pleasure of seeing your lovely face for some time... so I thought I'd just string along." He joyously said, beaming like a child; an annoying child...

"Well, it's nice to see you," Angela lied, while trying her best to keep her distance.

Stuart's breath was so potent with Scottish whiskey, that she almost felt nauseous; but his Wedgwood blue eyes were mellowed by drink and his pink apple cheeks were flushed to such a bright cherry red, that it was impossible to be completely annoyed with him.

Stuart often reminded her of Santa Claus; a drunken Santa Claus...

Suddenly, his expression sobered. "Please, my dear child, accept my sincere condolences," he solemnly said, before lovingly taking her hand. "I remember when I lost my own mother. I was devastated. And my father suffered a nervous breakdown... He had to go away for a rest; yes he did. Poor chap..." He ruefully said, his big blue eyes softly wandering to Angela's breasts as if he could find some maternal comfort there...

"But eventually, the old man got over dear mum," he slowly continued. "Time cures all things, my dear child. What I remember is the funeral procession... Everyone in London was there; everyone! Even some of the royal family..." He proudly said with a little smile.

To Angela's relief, Pierce interrupted his uncle's reverie, "Ready, darling? Shall we go?" Angela nodded, lovingly taking his arm. "By all means, my darling!"

The three of them left the well-heated building and emerged into the familiar cold dampness, where Stuart Haddington's superb forest green and gold Daimler Regency 'Empress Saloon' regally awaited them. Stuart's chauffeur removed his cap; then he respectfully opened the doors for his passengers, before loading Angela's suitcase in the large trunk.

Back to the good life, she thought, gratefully…

Having been raised in poverty, Angela had felt somewhat awkward around the well mannered English-Caucasian staff at first, but she quickly got used to it; and that particular night, she was so exhausted by the pain of life that she wondered how people who never had such wonderful privilege manage to go on living during times of crisis. Only now, the sweet Angela could almost understand why some people might be pushed to the extreme for money…

Pouring himself a generous amount of brandy from a large crystal decanter located in the built in cocktail cabinet, Stuart asked with a mellow smile, "would either of you care for a drink?"

In unison, Pierce and Angela shook their heads.

"Suit yourself," Stuart said, a hint of contempt souring his voice.

Pierce studied Angela's face; there was definitely something wrong…

"You said on the phone there was something I should know, darling," he whispered to her. "What is it?"

"Let's wait until we get home," Angela nervously replied. She sighed deeply before she softly rested her head on his shoulder in a futile attempt to shut out the world as they drove towards the heart of London.

How complex my life has become lately... How is Pierce going to react when I tell him what Mama told me?

"Will you be going on tour again soon, dear; or are you going to take a break?" Stuart asked while discretely observing her.

"I don't think that the latter is an option, Uncle Stuart. I have to work. Perhaps after Monte Carlo, though... My father isn't doing so well, and I'd like him to stay with us for a while... He's already agreed, although it took quite a bit of convincing on my part."

Stuart raised one of his thick reddish brown eyebrows. "Wouldn't the old bloke be out of place in your world, my dear?" He bluntly asked, while searching for her eyes.

"Why, uncle Stuart? Because he's black?" Angela defensively said, while for the first time, locking eyes with him...

"Well, my dear child... I wouldn't have stated it quite so insensitively; but now that you mention it, yes... As you know, your colour barely shows, my dear; but, from what I've seen in your family's photographs, your father is as black as a chimney sweeper, and you perfectly know how prejudiced people can be; especially among the upper classes..." Stuart softly said, with a condescending little smile.

Angela dangerously narrowed her gaze. "Uncle Stuart, I don't care what people might think or say! I simply intend to give my father an open-armed welcome, whether we 'upper crust' folk like it or not!" She nervously exclaimed, raising her voice for the first time.

"Then, by all means, my dear, welcome him..." Obviously, the smooth Stuart Haddington had acquired a wicked sense of diplomacy in the many decades he'd spent practicing law, so he simply smiled, before saying again "I'm just taking a proverbial walk in his shoes, that's all... If I were him, my dear child, I'd feel downright 'uncomfortable' alongside all of us pasty faced Brits; but of course he's your blood, and you have the right to do as you wish, dear." He softly said again, smiling even more.

There's no point waiting. He'll know the truth soon enough anyway... Angela thought.

"I might as well tell you now, Uncle Stuart. André and I are not related by blood," she almost whispered, suddenly lowering her eyes.

Pierce abruptly let go of her hand. "What are you saying, darling? I... I don't understand."

Stuart's bushy eyebrows shot up an inch higher than seemed possible. "Yes, this is quite new... So, by all means, tell us, my dear!" He rapidly downed the rest of his brandy and generously poured himself another. When he handed Pierce a glass and tipped the bottle over it, this time his nephew did not refuse it...

"Would you like a drink now?" He softly asked Angela, as if alcohol was a panacea for the world's problems. She did not respond, but instead she inhaled deeply and slowly began to tell the confusing tale of her roots.

"Before she died, Josephine told me that my real mother is in fact a Caucasian-English woman named Elisabeth Mary

Hoxworth…" Angela softly said, visibly embarrassed. "She was married to a certain Jonathan Hoxworth, the only son of an extremely rich and powerful Louisiana family. Jonathan Hoxworth committed suicide two days after my birth… I guess this man was ashamed that I was not white enough…" She hesitantly said, as she felt a twang of guilt. "Elisabeth swore that I was Jonathan's legitimate daughter, but no one believed her…" She hesitantly continued before lowering her eyes. "As you said, uncle Stuart, prejudice is still alive and well. Anyway, my estranged mother must've had an affair with a black man and lied to her husband; otherwise I'd have been white… But I guess that I'll never know who my real father is." Angela sadly concluded while she felt the heat rise into her face; but she painfully went ahead and told the rest of her incredible story…

"Well, well, well," Stuart jovially remarked, while generously refilling his large glass. Unbidden, he clinked the precious crystal with Pierce's, if as celebrating the occasion. "So, my dear child, you're one of us, after all!" He added with a cocky smile. "Half of you, at least…"

"Uncle Stuart, pleeease!" Angela grumpily interjected. "I can assure you that this news was not something that I enjoyed hearing." She icily said, before she nervously stared out the window; the headlights of the vehicles on the opposing side of the highway took on a ghostly cast. *Like frenzied souls rushing around in search of a home*, she sadly thought, wondering where she truly belonged now; where her "home" really was…

"Daaarling," Pierce compassionately said, lovingly taking her hand. "You must be devastated, my love!"

"Well… That would be an understatement," she sadly said, removing the large manila envelope containing the photograph of Elisabeth from her stylish 'Gucci' burgundy handbag, before nervously handing it to him.

"I can see the resemblance…" Pierce awkwardly said, passing the photo to his uncle.

"Well, she's a beauty, your mother!" Stuart exclaimed, his admiration evident as he looked from the photo to Angela and back again. "How old was she when this was taken, my dear?"

Angela frowned at the old lecher. "Twenty-two… I was born two years later."

"Ahhh, so she'd be approximately 56 now," he proudly replied. No matter how much alcohol the refined Stuart Haddington consumed, his mathematical prowess never failed him…

"You know, my dear. This may not be such a tragedy… You've obviously found your true roots, and they're nothing to be ashamed of; on the contrary… possibly, you've gained a sibling and of course, a lovely English mother; I can't see that this is all that bad." He said while tenderly smiling.

Angela could see what Stuart was trying and she took a deep breath to calm herself.

"Perhaps, Uncle Stuart, perhaps; but if you don't mind, I'd rather not discuss the matter any further… My nerves can't take it, anymore!" Exhausted from battling her conflicting emotions, Angela shut her eyes and decided that oysters were enviable in their innate ability to protect their vulnerable parts, as easily as she could most of the time zip up her dress...

Pierce and Stuart filled the embarrassing silence with innocuous chatter concerning business, as well as the latest tennis match, and soon they had cruised into the upscale suburb of "Chelsea". Five minutes later, they smoothly pulled in front of their stately four-storied Edwardian town home, on Fulbright Street. Angela was practically out the door before the Daimler stopped...

"Why were you so short with Uncle Stuart, darling?" Pierce asked as he rapidly followed Angela up the black marble steps.

"I'm just irritated, that's all! And as you know, your dear uncle can be highly irritating; even when I'm not irritated." She nervously said while avoiding his eyes.

"Well, the poor man is only doing his best, darling," Pierce said gently, before tenderly caressing her lovely face. Feeling stupid, Angela looked into her husband deep ocean-blue eyes and fell into him.

Pierce's protective arms closed around Angela and she felt as if she were ensconced in a loving and extremely secure cage; a cage that kept the world, and its terrible madness, out; a protective cage that she desperately wished to never leave...

Shortly after, as their reunion slowly turned to passion, their mouths found solace in a tender kiss, and she slowly melted into him, surrendering to his love.

That night, Angela gave herself to Pierce in a way that she hadn't for a long time, because she truly wanted to feel alive; but above all, to forget what Josephine told her. She urgently wanted to escape this unbearable new reality and simply be a woman.

That particular night, more than ever, Angela wanted Pierce's love; that unforgettable night, Angela desperately needed it…

Amen.

Chapter Fifteen

"London"

Fifteen minutes later, Stuart Haddington's forest green and gold Daimler Regency arrived into the high-end neighbourhood of "Mayfair", coming to a smooth stop in front of an imposing 17th century town home.

Unfortunately, most of the surrounding homes had been bought by foreigners, as well as the Russian nouveau riche, and instead of the lavishly draped windows and carefully groomed hedges, these newly acquired expensive homes had a quirky edge to them. For a quarter of those houses, the windows were almost naked, giving passers-by the opportunity to look into their goldfish bowl lives, which were now decorated by unusual, over-priced, modern "objects d'art"…

"Will you need my services later, Sir?" Stuart's chauffeur asked.

"No, my dear Clive," Stuart tiredly said, finally parting with the brandy he'd been lovingly clutched. "That will be all for today… I'll see you tomorrow at 7:30 as usual. Thank you, my boy!"

The chauffeur respectfully nodded. "In which case, I bid you a good evening, Sir."

Stuart grabbed his brown ostrich attaché case and his black hat, before briskly walking up the large white marble steps that led to an impressive massive carved door. He patted his dark blue coat, searching for the pocket that held his keys, and when he finally found them, he fumbled a bit before opening the massive door. As quietly as possible, he stepped onto the extremely spacious foyer's black and white marble chequered floor, shaking his head as he trudged quickly under the huge three tiered Italian crystal chandelier, praying again that the enormous thing wouldn't fall on him...

The scale of the entrance dwarfed him to the point that he often felt like he entered a room designed by the unforgettable Lewis Carroll in "Alice in Wonderland"; but there was no sense in arguing with his lovely wife about interior decoration. Gail's fashion sense was heralded by London's greatest and gayest, and who was he to deny her the simple, if costly, luxuries?

After all, which high society English lady could live without a criminally expensive chandelier as tall and as big as a Christmas tree hanging in the foyer???

Stuart took a deep breath, then strode towards the 'petit salon' - which was nothing near to being *"petit"*, where his dear wife, the extremely poised and always aloof Gail, and their lovely daughter, the sweet pale blond Annabelle, were sitting on a stylish overstuffed red leather 'Chesterfield' sofa, opposite a monumentally 18th century carved red marble fireplace; a fireplace that was a pure replica of the one that warmed the "Blair Drummond Castle" in Scotland. The luminous flames of the blazing fire cast a warm glow on the pale skinned women's faces and softly lit up the large 'Van Dyke' portrait of 'Charles I', which regally hung above the spectacular mantel. As always, Gail and Annabelle Haddington, were tastefully clad; an extraordinarily stylish red and green tartan dress from 'Vivienne Westwood', for the daughter; and an emerald green draped jersey dress from 'Dior'; for the mother. The scene was worthy of a Christmas cover in *"Town and Country"* or *"Architectural Digest"*.

"Hello, daddy," Annabelle lovingly said in the sweet girlish voice she reserved exclusively for her beloved father.

"Hello, sweet heart!" Stuart joyfully said before he handed his Cashmere coat, hat, and attaché case to a young pretty maid whose name he couldn't remember. His wife's temper assured a high turnover rate when it came to the staff...

"Stuart!" Gail flatly exclaimed in her usual high-pitched voice.

"Gail!" Stuart almost shouted, mimicking her enthusiasm.

Even though Gail was much too thin, Stuart didn't find his uptight wife unattractive; in fact, Gail could be quite naughty in bed. And today Stuart had brought her a treat: a tasty titbit of gossip...

Perhaps I'll get lucky... Stuart thought with a smile, as he poured himself another generous drink. He comfortably sat down on a plush 'Chesterfield' armchair that matched the sofa, facing his aloof wife and well mannered daughter, and he softly smoothed the pleat of his dark blue 'Burton' slacks, before he neatly crossed his legs; then finally settled in...

"I have quite some news, dear..." Stuart joyfully said with a mysterious smile, not looking like Santa Claus anymore. "It seems that our dear Pierce's little "black bird" is rather alike to that famous canary that got caught in a coalmine," he said proudly, literally beaming.

"Well, get to the point, Stuart!" Gail stifled a yawn, already annoyed.

"Well, what I am trying to say, daaarling, is that Angela's real mother is as white as you, dear! And, her blood might even run bluer than yours... What a hoot!" Stuart broadly grinned, visibly satisfied.

"What???" Gail asked excitedly, before nervously ringing for the maid. "Melanie! I need a Martini now! Dry, two olives. Use the Grey Goose!" She dryly demanded, before turning back to rigidly face her annoying husband.

"Now, my dear; tell me all the details... Everything you know; and please, pleeease Stuart, stop drinking so much! Your eyes, my dear, would impress a cocker spaniel. Disgusting!" Gail nervously exclaimed, before raising her eyes.

Somehow, Stuart Haddington enjoyed the obvious delight in his wife's well-powdered face.

Gail is certainly a beautiful woman, but she just isn't really my type; not enough meat on that bird... He sadly thought, before finishing his story.

"Ah well," Gail said when he'd finished telling the story. "So her mother is a white British tramp, instead of a black servant. So what! It's not such a big deal... Frankly, my dear Stuart, I don't believe that our dear Angela could be related to this Hoxworth family... I truly think that the poor girl is nothing, but a mulatto bastard!" She disdainfully declared, while fingering her triple strand of fine South Sea 'Mikimoto' golden pearls.

"Stranger things can happen, dear... I saw a program on the telly once; it was about 'wayward genes', genetic traits that pop up seemingly out of the blue... Generations after copulation, they somehow infect one's DNA sequencing and -"

"Wayward genes, my ass!" Gail snarled, as she looked at her daughter, whose wide-open eyes were transfixed on her father. "Heavens!" She shouted. "If Annabelle's future in-laws hear about this, they're likely to have a collective coronary... You know how class conscious those Bainbridges are, Stuart. Angela's status as a prima ballerina has helped them overlook the fact that her skin is not as light as ours, my dear; but if word gets out that on the top of this she's a bastard, it might just be too much for them!" She lamented, looking truly terrified.

Instantly, an ocean of burning tears formed in Annabelle's lovely blue eyes.

"Mother, Phillip isn't like his stodgy parents." She painfully said before lowering her eyes.

"Oh pleeease, my darling, don't be so naïve! Phillip is the heir to a large fortune and he's not a saint, for heaven's sake! If his fortune is at stake, Annabelle, your dear Phillip will choose money over love, my darling. You can be sure of that!" Gail dryly said before nervously fingering her priceless pearls again.

"I must say that you're right, dear," Stuart nervously said. "I hadn't thought of that... This could very well put a spanner in the works."

"Ohhh, father! Whatever shall we do?" Annabelle lamented. "The Bainbridges are bound to find out."

"Not if we keep this hush-hush, my darling." Gail rapidly suggested before taking her daughter's hand.

"Yes, perhaps so," Stuart agreed, visibly thinking.

"Please, Stuart, have a serious talk with Pierce," Gail urged. "And remind him how important this marriage is for our family; and how vital it is that we keep this to ourselves... What was he thinking when he married that coloured girl? His first wife was certainly a much more desirable property." Gail sighed heavily before nervously reaching for her Martini.

"Even so, dear, one must give Angela her due. The woman is quite a success." Stuart mildly said, avoiding his wife's eyes.

"Ohhh pleeease, my dear, spare me; she's nevertheless a mulatto bastard!" Gail adamantly stressed. "Oh Stuart, if there was only some way we could convince this stupid Pierce to divorce this coloured girl... to dump this inconvenient woman once and for all!" She exclaimed, with fire in her eyes.

"That, my dear Gail, would prove to be extremely difficult... His love is rock solid!" Stuart said, avoiding her cold eyes again.

"Love, my foot! It's only sex, that's all it is! I should have a serious talk with that stupid Pierce. Convince him once and for all of the harm he is really doing to our extremely respectable family name… It's truly disgraceful! That coloured woman is a liability! It's just a question of getting it through his thick head. Pierce's English after all!" Gail almost shouted, visibly revolted.

"Gail, dear, I think you're running up against a brick wall," Stuart calmly said.

Stuart was disappointed; he thought that his wife would be thrilled with the news.

Forget about getting lucky… He sadly thought, before reaching for the alcohol bottle again.

"That we shall see!" Gail icily said, before pinching her face. "Yes, we shall see…" She hissed again.

Without another word, the hot tempered Gail left the large study and regally made her way to the mahogany panelled elevator; then she pressed the button of the third floor, to her private bedroom suite.

As Gail silently rode the elevator, she admired herself in the gold Venetian framed mirror and raked her well-manicured pale pink nails through her efficient hair-do, pondering whether or not to dye her naturally greying curly hair; after all, she was English, and she always liked the Queen's look…

Still, it is time for a change… Gail sadly noticed that while her alabaster skin was still translucent and virtually wrinkle-free, her pale grey eyes - her best feature - had somehow lately lost their sparkle. As for her lips, they seemed thinner too, despite her attempts to add some fullness with an extra coat of gloss. At fifty-nine, despite her criminally expensive 'La Prairie' Swiss beauty creams, as well as nine hours of religious sleep and an extremely comfortable life, the elegant Gail Haddington looked like a frustrated post-menopausal woman...

Gail forced a smile to lift her drooping cheeks, but with little success.

What do they expect? She nervously thought, feeling tired of it all. She had lost her *"joie de vivre"* a long time ago and a lifetime of forever had passed since she felt true enthusiastic bubbles inside her...

When the elevator smoothly stopped, Gail was suddenly overwhelmed with undiluted panic, an eerie feeling, as if she were trapped inside a giant pyramid with only her poor lost dreams as company.

The click of her stylish 'Walter Steiger' black patent high heel pumps, upon the immaculate white Carrera marble floor strangely reverberated as she nervously strode down the long corridor, and the clacking seemed to echo her nerve-wracking thoughts.

I must do something, but what? She lamented, ready to explode.

The only gift that God granted Gail, was the ability to wag her tongue as gracefully as a miniature French poodle to manipulate her family and friends; as well as society with the best of English manners. Gail Haddington was in fact a master of intrigue; and so she set to work...

Gail's own life may not be moving towards the "happy ending" she'd long ago imagined, in her childhood dreams, but the life of her only daughter was an entirely different book; one that Gail would definitely lend a masterful hand in writing...

Chapter Sixteen

"London"

The next morning, Angela struggled to push herself from her intricately carved canopy bed.

Although Angela had managed to sleep until almost eight o'clock, she restrained the urge to dive back under the protective down comforter, when she slowly opened the silk mango coloured draperies and saw the famous grey London mist looming everywhere...

Perhaps the weather sat well with the natives of Britain, as well as the frogs and snails that made the Isles their home; but that morning, Angela terribly missed the warm sunshine of her native town of New Orleans.

Angela grimaced as a gust of rain pummelled against the leaden windowpanes, then she noticed that the recent series of late summer storms had already stripped most of the trees bare of leaves. *Winter would come early this year... I hate the cold.* She thought before sadly turning away, shivering, preferring the comfort of her inviting room.

Angela's cosy bedroom had become her sanctuary, a precious interior secret garden in which she displayed all her favourite furnishings; antiques that she'd lovingly collected over the years during her numerous travels with the royal ballet company.

She remembered that she bought the beautiful Italianate 18th century pale green canopy bed, as well as the large gilded oval mirror, in Venice, the evening she'd met Pierce…

From the eternal city of Florence, came the 14th century hand-painted Italian bombé commode, along with its accompanying bedside tables. A large needlepoint carpet festooned with bright roses had called out to her in Lisbon; reminding her so much of the floral printed cushions her beloved Josephine loved, that she couldn't resist purchasing it…

Above the beautiful Italian commode hung a 18th century French painting of a young shepherdess wearing a pale-blue dress; a gift from a Lyonnais chef, who'd had it sent backstage as a token of his great admiration. In the French city of Lyon, she'd also found a pair of precious tufted red silk velvet Napoleon III armchairs, as well as a black lacquered coffee table from the same period delicately inlaid with precious mother-of-pearl.

Angela gazed at the large hand-painted Bavarian desk, which had been one of the rare expensive gifts from Cecilia, her distant mother-in-law…

A photo of Josephine, with a beatific smile on her face, predominantly sat on the left-hand corner of the desk. It was here that Angela took pleasure in writing weekly letters to her beloved mother.

I wish I had relished those hours more… She thought guiltily, as she remembered being so overwhelmed in her own concerns that she barely thought about the words that she wrote. Now her heart ached with remorse, grief, and bewilderment…

Why did I not ask more questions? If I'd paid more attention, Mama might've told me that she was sick. She sadly thought, feeling terribly guilty and terrible alone as well.

Now Angela had a quest to fulfil; an unhappy one…

"Oh Mama… Mama!" Her fingers stroking the cold silver frame that elegantly framed Josephine's portrait. "Why!" For an instant, Angela hoped that her mother would answer her from beyond the grave; but she wasn't the type to believe in ghosts, so she quickly buried the idea, washing it away with a long hot shower.

Once Angela had dressed in a well cut 'Donna Karan' black wool jersey jumpsuit, she rapidly walked down to the kitchen, where her Irish cook, Millie, was preparing her breakfast.

"I'm so sorry about your mother, Madam. I lost my own mum fifteen years ago and my heart still aches for her," the cook emotionally said before respectfully lowering her eyes.

Angela's eyes suddenly grew misty. "One never completely heals from the death of a mother, it seems," she softly said, before taking a seat at the yellow velvet banquette, beside the large bay window.

"Yes Madam! It seems to be so… Nevertheless, time heals the worst of it and lets us get on with this business of life; for all it is worth anyway. I sometimes wonder…" The cook sadly said.

"So do I, Millie." Angela said, while gazing out at a cherry tree and watching as a little grey bird flew towards the stone fountain for a drink. "So do I…"

"Will you be having your usual for breakfast, Madam?"

"No offence to your porridge, Millie, but just coffee this morning." Angela said while watching the bird.

"I understand your lack of appetite, Madam, but paring yourself down to skin and bones won't get you closer to your poor mum… If you don't mind me saying so, Madam, you've already lost too much weight…" The cook said with a little embarrassed smile.

"Thanks for your concern, my dear Millie."

"You'll be home for lunch, Madam?"

Angela almost smiled, grateful for her cook's maternal nagging. "No Millie, I've got to get back to work." She flatly said, sadly smiling.

"But you really need to rest, Madam. Grieving takes a toll; and a big one at that," the cook softly said, continuing to stir a pot of porridge large enough to feed a family of six. "I almost went crazy myself," she softly confessed, reaching for her white lace apron to dry her eyes.

"To tell you the truth, I wish I could disappear for a month, Millie; but I've a tour commencing in three weeks and an entire dance company depending on me." Angela sadly said. Anxiously, she recalled her last encounter with the arrogant Boris Parchenko and her thoughts suddenly turned as dark as the black coffee that she drank. She realised that she was in no mood to deal with the Russian dancer's erratic temper and extremely rude manners. For the first time in her life, Angela considered taking a sabbatical from the ballet; but soon after, she quickly pushed the idea away...

The show must go on, she sadly thought.

Yes indeed...

Chapter Seventeen

"Ashington"

Many miles from London, in the large silent nave of a 12th century church near the River Thames, Elisabeth Hoxworth fervently prayed for her beloved daughter; prayed for Angela...

As usual, Elisabeth knelt on the cold stone floor with her eyes closed and her palms piously pressed together, alone; except for the life size antique paintings of the many martyrs and saints that had been frescoed on the ancient earthen brick walls...

The pale blond frail woman breathed deeply, inhaling the stale scent of the dwarfing holy place, of frankincense and myrrh, strangely mingled with the smell of humanity; people who, much like herself, were pleading with their maker for whatever they believed would ease their pain, dry their tears, or above all, ensure them entrance into the next world; a mysterious world, which, they hoped, was much better than this one...

"My sweet Lord," Elisabeth slowly began. "Please grant me the serenity to accept the things I cannot change, the courage to change the things I can, and the wisdom to know the difference… I am always grateful for the silent inspiration of your Holy Spirit and the assistance that was granted to aid my human weakness… My beloved Father in Heaven, I implore your gracious help in my present need. Please, God Almighty, protect my beloved Angela in the days, months, and years to come… Overlook my unworthiness and grant my request, as I rely so entirely on your mercy, my sweet Lord." Elisabeth softly said before she took a deep breath and piously continued.

"I implore you my Lord, in the name of Christ, your beloved Son, and his Blessed Mother, to protect my daughter Angela from the forces of evil… Please, my Lord, release me from the lies that I have been forced to carry; and when my time comes, lead my poor soul to my beloved Jonathan and let us be together in peace in your light for all eternity… I know that I am a merely a sinner and mostly a pagan woman, my Lord; but even so my heart is pure. Spare our beloved daughter the misery that we endured, and grant her the strength to go on with her life; but let her not judge me too harshly, my Lord, as she does not know the truth… Though the favour I seek is great, make my faith in Christ your Son even greater, so that you may grant what I so trustfully ask you in His name. Amen!" Elisabeth emotionally said while refraining from crying.

With her eyes still shut, Elisabeth slowly made the sign of the cross before solemnly kissing her fingers. When she tiredly stood up, large rows of votive candles cast her frail shadow on the stone floor and she felt dwarfed again by the giant stone columns that surrounded her; terribly small and so, so insignificant…

To the ancient church, Elisabeth Mary Hoxworth was just another poor shadow passing through its giant nave; another lost poor soul in search of the "eternal light", yet frightened away by the shadow that such light sometimes creates...

Before leaving, Elisabeth randomly opened her old Bible and read from the Gospel of John: "you will cry and weep, but the world will be glad; you will be sad, but your sadness will turn to joy." Her lips trembled and the beating of her heart slightly accelerated. Tears of peace falling, Elisabeth slowly crossed herself again and whispered a final amen. An angel smiled...

I know you will help me, my good Lord, she lovingly thought, smiling for the first time, *because you know my heart is pure and you cannot let me suffer forever for a sin I did not commit... Now you know that too, Jonathan, my dear love...*

With that last happy thought, Elisabeth raised the fur collar of her brown coat; then she silently left the great house of the Lord, bracing herself for a new unhappy day.

Outside the massive church, the pale sun slowly moved behind a thick blanket of clouds, hiding itself from Elisabeth's vision; hiding again...

Amen.

Chapter Eighteen

"New Orleans"

While Elisabeth Hoxworth found solace within the thick walls of the Old Catholic church; in the sunny city of New Orleans, the black priestess meditated in the mysterious House of Angels...

Mambha was in a deep trance; one that she had induced by drinking a potion of sugar cane alcohol that had been infused with powerful African herbs and Amazonian hypnotic mushrooms. In the past few days, some spirits had been aggressively pursuing her, and in her vivid visions she saw so many souls, so many tears; and so much pain...

Now the black priestess knew that the soul of the mulatto baby, who was murdered long ago, was becoming a force so strong that she could see the angry red light of it; Mambha could feel the constant pain of the soul, as well as the profound pain and extreme confusion of the woman who harboured it now. Yes, she knew, a young woman was on the verge of remembering herself in her previous life and would soon realise the purpose of her present incarnation. Such an occurrence was rare - and so fraught with danger - that it was both a great privilege, but also a curse; this, the black priestess fully knew...

The innocent eyes of the dark angels that were scattered about the large red room sometimes seemed to flicker, so Mambha cast a strong aura of protection around this young woman. Mambha could also anticipate the tragic events that were to come and she fully knew that if, in her present incarnation, the young woman did not survive, the inevitable would be postponed yet once again...

Mambha would not allow that to happen again; not to this poor soul, for she felt she was somehow bonded to it by destiny.

The black priestess intensely invoked an ancient and powerful African deity of protection, before she intoned a lengthy incantation to ward off the dark vicious spirits, lighting a black candle to empower the spell; then she burned a bundle of dried mugwort, which she had tied together with a white cotton ribbon, and she slowly waved her wand to create a protective magical circle. The pungent white smoke hesitantly spiralled upwards, towards the large vaulted ceiling; spiralled towards the light...

With a small straw fan, Mambha dispersed the heavy smoke and began to softly chant: "Ummmm - b baloulelelee aiyoo, ummmbuloulelele aiyooo ghandigileee aiyoo - ummmmm..." Soon, her own luminous soul had expanded beyond the boundaries of her fragile human body, her vision now crystal clear. She suddenly became both the centre of the universe and the circumference of it; the black priestess was now a pure, undiluted loving light...

Mambha lovingly reached into the ethers and firmly withdrew a strong shield of protection and this she carefully wrapped around the vengeful soul and its current keeper; the fragile mulatto ballerina...

Mambha was about to reach into the mystical beyond for an "athame" - a magical dagger that she'd used to draw a protective shield around the young woman, as to protect her from muddy evil forces - when she sensed a strange and strong presence...

Mambha softly smiled, for it was not the first time that this particular spirit had visited her; she remembered the distinct scent of fine sweet tobacco and pleasant French vetiver cologne; along with a trace of the familiar scent of absinthe...

Mambha slowly turned around her and sensed that in the left corner of the red walled room, amongst a group of tall pale porcelain skinned angels, the male spirit was taking form.

Today, his tormented soul was restless as well as stricken with profound guilt, great shame, and grief; so much grief...

Tell me your name, my friend... Who are you and why have you come to me? Mambha asked without speaking.

The voice was inaudible at first, but as the male spirit gained strength from the herbs and from the black priestess's own psychic energy, so it became clearer; much, much clearer...

"I... am... I am... Jonathan Hoxworth", the ghost hesitantly said *"and I want you to save Mary-Elisabeth".*

Who is she to you, Jonathan? Mambha asked, smiling.

Mary-Elisabeth... is... my daughter! The ghost forcefully exclaimed, his voice now as strong as a lion's.

Angela... Mary-Elisabeth... The mulatto ballerina... The vengeful soul... The murdered mulatto child...

At the speed of light, and with the lucid precision that only the great mystics could experience with the ancient knowledge of their blessed soul, the black priestess' spirit went back to the moment when the tiny "Angelica Aurora Maria" was murdered in the Hoxworth castle birthing room; to the precise moment of her murder and the final struggle of her suffering soul...

The black priestess deeply shivered. The cold breathe of death was now freezing her bones...

The mulatto ballerina would soon discover the horrible truth about her birth, and soon after this, someone will want to take her life again. The old curse was not over yet, and the supernatural forces of demons and angels will have to battle again; again...

Please, please, priestess, help my poor Mary-Elisabeth. Someone I love is going to kill my daughter... The ghost of Jonathan Hoxworth forcefully said, before slowly dissolving in millions of brilliant particles, in the stale air of Mambha's private sanctuary.

As a thunderbolt, a surge of violent energy touched the black priestess head and she immediately lost consciousness. While the priestess' body was motionlessly lying on the shiny wooden floor, all the angels in the room were silently crying; crying again...

Chapter Nineteen

"La Rêveuse"

"Madam" Eileen Mackenzie-Hoxworth was mad as hell, as she nervously dialled the Royal Ballet School in London...

The always so refined and "apparently calm" Eileen, had just discovered that the stupid Josephine Boivin had revealed all the truth to Angela, even though Eileen had paid a large amount of money for her secrecy; but strangely enough, Angela had not contacted Eileen yet, which made her think that that latter would want her share of the large Hoxworth fortune...

Wasting no time with sweet "hellos" or extremely polite "how-do-you-do's", Eileen, like a true American, got right to the point...

"So, Angela, what do you have in mind, exactly?" She dryly asked, ready to fight.

"I don't understand what you mean, Mrs. Hoxworth; and I have no idea why you are calling me... I'm at rehearsal, you know. I have a tour coming up." Angela flatly said.

"Ohhh, come now, Angela! I have no time for your little games; and please, don't play dumb with me! Now that my former maid, Josephine, your adopted mother, has spilled the beans, I'm certain that a smart girl such as yourself has at least a few schemes brewing on the back burners of your mind... hmmmm?" Eileen's voice was as smooth as a snake's skin; but lethal as a butcher's knife...

"Truly sorry to disappoint you, Mrs. Hoxworth, but I have no idea what you expect me to think; let alone say!" Angela calmly responded; feeling puzzled.

"Really?" Eileen nervously smiled. *Perhaps the girl isn't as conniving as I'd presumed, after all...*

"Well, my dear Angela," she slowly began, while trying to remain calm. "Let's just put it this way. Unfortunately for everyone, you now certainly know that you are the bastard child of Elisabeth, my stupid former daughter-in-law; and this means that you are somewhat related to my family by that unfortunate marriage... It was a huge mistake for Josephine to tell you who and what you are, my child; but as she did, I advise you to simply forget it; for your own sake, of course... Leave me, as well as my grandson alone and you'll be fine, my dear; but if you try to cause any sort of problems, I promise that you will regret that you ever heard the name Hoxworth." Eileen pronounced each word like someone carefully pulling scarves from a drawer, with great emphasis on each and every syllable...

"Problems? But what kind of problems?" Angela nervously reiterated. "I'm afraid I don't understand, madam. In fact, you've totally lost me… If you think for even a minute that I'm interested in you or your precious Edmond, you are truly mistaken!" Angela said coldly, starting to feel deeply irritated.

Eileen let forth a little groan. "I see you already know my grandson's name… Again, I repeat, Angela: if you have any intentions of soiling Edmond's good reputation by insinuating that you were born of the same father as he, you will deeply regret it, my dear… Your mother was nothing, but a two bit whore!" Eileen coldly said with great disgust, before slightly raising her refined voice. "If you know what's good for you, Angela, keep your distance; then stay in London, where you truly belong; and let the ghosts of the past remain buried." She said lowering her voice before she paused; then, with a charming voice, she softly added "my dear child, I am not at all angry at you, but I'm simply a protective grandmother who truly loves her only grandson… Again, my dear Angela, I have no idea why that poor Josephine would want to hurt you by telling you the ugly truth… There is no sense in it, really. But because I am a compassionate woman, and understand that you aren't responsible for either Josephine's or Elisabeth's terrible error, I will give to you the one thing I can…" She softly said. "I have opened a Swiss account in your name, Angela, and there you will find a large sum of money; much more than you should ever need…" She paused. "I truly hope that this gesture will lessen your pain, my child, and that any strange thoughts you may have had to blackmail me, or my dear Edmond, will be once and forever definitely eradicated…" She firmly said. The information will be sent to you… anonymously, of course; but I think you will be pleased, my dear child, by the amount of zeros…" Eileen softly said; her voice now as sweet as orange blossom honey…

Angela was aghast. "Mrs. Hoxworth! I am absolutely not interested in you or your dear grandchild; and even less in your money! Do you understand me?" Angela dangerously said raising her voice, while refraining from shouting.

"Ohhh, a girl with principles; so uncommon… So refreshing! Come now, Angela, it's just money; and you perfectly know that I do have lots of it…" She coldly said. "Let's say that it's just a token of goodwill, my dear. You don't harm me; and I don't harm you. N'est ce pas? Just think of the gesture as a little gift!" Eileen sweetly said again, her voice becoming strangely velvety. "You may donate it to your favourite charity if you please."

"Sorry, Madam, but I don't want your money!" Angela said icily, suddenly feeling extremely cheap.

"Well, have it your way, my child," Eileen calmly said. "But listen to my advice on this one thing: do not believe what Elisabeth tells you… This despicable English woman is a liar and should go straight to hell for what she did to my poor son. To think that, because of her, my son killed himself, you know!" She said raising her voice, as if ready to fight again.

"Yes, madam, I'm fully aware of that and I'm truly sorry… Sorry that the colour of my skin was the reason for your son's death!" Angela's voice was sincere, but cold; extremely cold…

"Well, I hope my dear Jonathan is at peace now…" Eileen softly said with misty eyes. "Every day, I still live with the terrible image of him lying there, in that pool of blood; so you understand why I don't want you to start snooping around. My poor Edmond couldn't tolerate it; my dear grandson, who is such a sensitive man… Edmond was just a young boy when his father committed suicide; I hope he has forgotten about the whole bloody tragedy…" Eileen said with a dash of emotion in her voice. "So, my dear Angela, let the past be and simply take the money, and have a great life... I must leave you now, so pleeease, do me a favour, Angela; and for your own safety, my child, never contact me, ever!" Eileen icily said, sounding strangely lethal.

With that simple phrase, the "ohhh so chic" Eileen Mackenzie-Hoxworth firmly hung up, and a strange chill rapidly enveloped Angela; a deadly chill, again…

Chapter Twenty

"London"

After a gruelling twelve-hour rehearsal, Angela went directly home and took a long shower, hoping that the hot water would relieve some of her tension...

She'd had a hard time focusing all day; she couldn't stop thinking about what the arrogant Eileen Hoxworth had said. *How could this woman make such assumptions?* Angela was revolted by the woman's gall, knowing full well that she was no blackmailer.

Angela was drying herself off, when Pierce opened the door and stepped inside the large bathroom, startling her.

"Ah, there you are!" He said with a big boyish smile, his dark blue eyes appraising her half-naked superb body; his eyes lingering on her firm perky breasts and gleaming black pubis. For some strange reason, at this particular instant, Angela felt uncomfortable and wrapped the white towel around her body, before Pierce stepped closer then lovingly held her by her waist.

"You haven't kissed me yet, my love," he softly whispered in her ear, tightening his aroused body against hers. He tried to pry open her lovely mouth with his tongue, but as much as Angela needed to feel his love, she involuntary felt her lips tighten...

"What's wrong, my darling?" Pierce softly asked, visibly surprised.

"Nothing... It's... It's my mother," she said, tears forming in her eyes. *My mother and the fact that my entire life is now falling apart...* She sadly thought, feeling sorry for her husband.

Before reluctantly releasing her, Pierce smiled gently and lovingly kissed her forehead.

"How bloody inconsiderate of me, darling," he said, taking her hand. "Come on into the kitchen; let's have some supper..." He added with a tender boyish smile.

"No, my love. I'm too tired to eat." She sadly said while avoiding his eyes.

"In that case, I could ask Millie to serve you a tray in bed if you'd like?"

"Thank you, darling, but all I simply want is a glass of hot milk with a spoon of honey." She softly said while caressing his cheek.

"Be right back, then, my love." He tenderly said before softly kissing her on the lips.

By the time Pierce returned with the hot milk, Angela was already asleep...

He tucked the soft cotton sheets around her splendid naked body, longingly staring at her.

It had been more than a fortnight since he had made love to her. He slipped into bed beside her, spooning her, but his strong erection woke her from her slumber and she rapidly moved away from him, leaving him deeply frustrated. It took him more than an hour to fall asleep; and even then, he turned and tossed all night...

Pierce awoke at dawn, still as sexually frustrated as he was the night before.

He looked at Angela, who was sleeping soundly, and despite his longing for her, he quietly rose from the bed and walked into the large bathroom, hoping that a hot shower would help relieve his stress. As he felt the water gently running over his tense body, he immediately got a strong erection and began to slowly masturbate. As he stroked himself, he was inundated with sexual images...

A beautiful procession of young women's bodies, in all shapes and forms, wildly paraded through his mind. The first was a new brunette waitress who worked at the deli near his office, where he sometimes stopped in to grab a quite good roast beef sandwich. He didn't know her name, but there was something about that girl that was extremely arousing. Pierce pictured her luscious mouth, painted carmine red with lipstick, and her even more luscious breasts, as well as tight little behind...

His penis became hard like a bamboo cane and he began to masturbate more and more vigorously; then, shortly after, another pretty face appeared...

It was the angelic face of that lovely redhead he had seen two weeks ago, sensually coming out of a cab. He saw her sultry body with her long slender legs that were exceptionally beautiful; almost as beautiful as Angela's...

Pierce masturbated even faster, as the new image of an Italian girl who he had seen yesterday at the tearoom at "Harrods" suddenly strutted into his mind. Her breasts were large, voluptuous and magnificent; and her behind, in the black leather skirt she wore, was a vision of perfection ...

Pierce sensually groaned as a plethora of pretty female faces and splendid young bodies rapidly appeared, one after another; each more tantalizing than her predecessor, in a festival of flesh and undiluted primordial lust.

It only took a few more vigorous strokes of his firm hand upon his large steel-hard manhood, for him to come. For one supreme ecstatic moment, his eyes still closed, Pierce was totally submerged in the feeling of his cataclysmic orgasm, suddenly released from all tension; until a few seconds later, he heard Angela scream...

Pierce had barely recovered from his sexual ecstasy and he almost stumbled on the slick white marble floor, as he rushed naked and wet into the spacious bedroom. Once in the bedroom, he couldn't believe his eyes. A strange man stood directly above Angela, holding a large pillow over her face. Pierce let forth a shout, partially out of fear and partially because the room was suddenly as cold as ice. "Get away from her!" He screamed. "Get away!!!"

The man slowly turned around to face him, but his expression was so vacant of emotion that Pierce blinked a few times. *I must be dreaming... What kind of man is that?*

When he reopened his eyes, the man had simply vanished, and Angela was sitting up, screaming and pointing above her, where a large greyish cloudlike mass hovered a short moment, before it slowly moved towards the door and was rapidly sucked out into the hallway...

Outside the bedroom, Pierce heard a woman's piercing scream. He quickly draped Angela's satin robe around his naked torso and nervously opened the door, ready to fight. Amidst pieces of broken porcelain, spilled coffee, and croissants, one of the chambermaids sat, hysterically crying, her eyes showing great fear.

When the girl regained her senses, she told Pierce what she had seen: a kind of man had seemingly "popped out" from the middle of the bedroom door and went on to glide down the hallway. His expression was blank, "but his eyes were full of sadness", the chambermaid said. When the strange man looked at her, she felt strangely paralysed with an intense unnatural cold...

"I'm really sorry I dropped the tray, Sir, but it was horrid! When that thing passed through me, I saw my own death, Sir. I swear it! I'm to be hit by a drunk driver on a rainy day... I saw it all! The windshield exploding in my face! My head hitting the wheel! Then a strange silence... I was dead; I knew it, Sir, dead!" Suddenly, the chambermaid turned her mind to practical matters. "I must get insurance, so my children will be safe... I must do it now, Sir!" She nervously exclaimed, before she slowly began to clear the debris of breakfast, incessantly mumbling, like an old woman who had lost her mind...

Pierce helped her collect the shards of the teacups and urged her to forget what she saw. "There must be a rational explanation, Anna," he flatly said while trying to stay calm. "There was no ghost. It was an intruder; a burglar of sorts... I'll have the locks changed and the security system inspected today, I promise!" He firmly said, visibly confused, trying his best to look normal. But the chambermaid pointed to the stairs, her hand still trembling.

"No, Mister Haddington. I know it was a ghost, I swear; a real ghost! I heard the flapping of wings and then it turned into a sort of viscous cloud and was sucked out the window..." She nervously said, with an expression of great fear painted upon her rosy face.

Resigned, Pierce gave her the day off and went back to tend to his wife.

Angela was still in bed, nervously clutching onto her pillow, obviously traumatised...

"No, it's not just a nightmare, Pierce; it's a ghost!" Great fear spilled from her eyes. "I felt it in my bones... I saw it with my own eyes... Please, pleeease Pierce, believe me!" She finally shouted, visibly out of control.

"My darling, I believe that you saw something, but it wasn't a ghost! You've been under so much stress lately, that your imagination is going a bit wild... There was simply a man in the room. An intruder," he tried to assure her, not knowing what to think anymore, and doubting his own words.

"No Pierce, it began first as a nightmare," Angela insisted, terrorized. "But then I woke up and I realised that I'd been trying to suffocate myself in my sleep... It's happened before, but now it's become more than a dream; it's become reality! He's here, I know it... What is happening? Oh my God, what is happening to me???" She hysterically cried, while looking lost and totally exhausted by her mixed emotions, while burning tears were falling like little rivers down her pale cheeks.

Pierce nervously took a deep breath and finally took Angela in his arms, before softly stroking her hair as if she were a child; then he held her for a long time, until she became calmer.

An hour later, Pierce was late for work, knowing that an important Arab client was waiting for him; and he hated nothing more than making a rich client wait. He deeply sighed and he nervously glanced at his 'Omega' Sea Master watch again, before he turned the ignition of his sleek silver 'Aston-Martin'.

As much as Pierce loved Angela, he couldn't help but be terribly annoyed by her behaviour lately; women, he thought, could be so irrational sometimes...

The devil smiled; again...

Chapter Twenty-One

"London"

Without the slightest hesitation, Angela phoned her beloved André in the middle of the night, simply because she badly needed his loving reassurance...

Ohhh, why can't things return to the way they were before Mama died? Why? She sadly thought; feeling terribly exhausted.

"Daddy?" Her voice became small and girlish, as she tried to hide her pain.

"Hello, Poodle," André said somewhat drowsily, but there was something in his tone that worried Angela; something was off. "I was waiting for your call, honey... Your Mama told me that I would hear from ya tonight." He tiredly said before sitting on the bed.

"Daddy pie, are you taking your medication?"

"Don't worry about that none, I am fine my love." He firmly said, softly smiling.

"Daddy, I know that you're tired, but I think that it would be a good idea to come to live with Pierce and me for a few months... Have you thought about it?" She softly asked.

"About what, poodle?" His head was terribly fuzzy.

Angela deeply sighed, as she knew that older people often struggled with short-term memory loss and more so when stricken by grief or great despair; but she had a feeling that André's strange behaviour was caused by something more serious. She prayed it was not Alzheimer's...

"About coming to London to live with me for a while, daddy; we talked about it when I was there, remember?" She gently reminded, as if she were talking to a child.

"Oh, yeah... Sure thing you did, poodle... And I thought about it plenty, but I don't think yer Mama would 'preciate me leavin' her." André said smiling tenderly while closing his tired eyes.

"Daddy, Mama's in heaven, so you wouldn't be leaving anyone... You'd be coming to stay with me, to keep me company." Angela softly said again, refraining from crying.

"I know, poodle, I know... But I can still smell your Mama 'round here... An' she likes me to read to her... I sit on the grass near her lil' grave an' bring her a good cup of joe, just like she liked it, dark and sweet; and I read to her from the Good Book." He sadly laughed before adding, "You know how your Mama is. She loves to let me talk, while busying herself with sumpin' else... But you know your Mama honey; she can't stand it if I'm not there!" André tenderly said while picturing his beloved Josephine in his mind.

"Daddy, please! You have to let her go! Mama is not there anymore, remember?" Angela suddenly said, raising her voice.

"Jus 'cause you can't see it with yer eyes, don't mean it don't exist, my love... I can feel yer Mama's spirit, just like before... She's here all right! Not all the time, but she sticks by me as close as ever." He smiled. "And when I bring her flowers, I feel her wrap herself around me like I were a king... Your Mama always loved flowers, ya know." André lovingly said, as his tired eyes were becoming misty again.

Angela's throat tightened. Lately she was often frightened for her own sanity; and the fact that her beloved father seemed to be losing his grip, was the last thing she needed now in her life. Yet, she was even more frightened of what might happen when André finally grasped that Josephine was truly dead...

Deep in her heart, Angela knew that once the poor André fully realised that his beloved wife was gone forever, it wouldn't be long before he joined her; wherever she was...

Deep down, Angela knew that André's tired body would simply wither away.

Yes, papa would surrender his life to the promised peacefulness of the hereafter and the dream of reuniting with Mama... She shuddered, as a single tear slowly fell from her cheek.

"Sorry, but I hear her callin' me now, poodle. Ya know Mama's not a patient woman... And ya got to phone ma'am Elisabeth; because I can't tell you how many times yer Mama has told me to remind you... I gotta go now, my child. I love you, poodle." Then, after those simple words, the line was dead.

153

While refraining to cry, Angela tiredly gazed at the silver-framed portrait of her beloved André and Josephine that she'd prominently placed on her writing desk. She couldn't believe now how assured she used to be, before Josephine's final revelation; thinking that she knew who she really was and where her life would lead. What a fool...

In the past, Angela had always felt so blessed to have her parents' constant love; so fortunate to have made a good marriage and to have an exceptional international career. Usually, Angela felt almost guilty at having found so much contentment in her life; but now, she wasn't sure of anything anymore...

It was as if not knowing why, a terrible curse had suddenly befallen her, and now she felt deeply cheated, betrayed, as well as terribly alone; as if fate had suddenly decided that she had it too good for too long and it was time to destroy her 'fairy tale' life...

Even Angela's constant struggle with her origins and the colour of her skin suddenly seemed so petty now. At this precise moment, it seemed that she had become powerless, as if strange events were about to unfold and she had no control over things anymore; as if suddenly, Pandora's box had been wildly opened...

Lately, Angela's horrific nightmares were becoming more vivid, as well as more vicious, and had moved from the realm of the dream, to a muddy reality.

What were once sheer illusions, were now real enemies, which were constantly pursuing her, night and day.

Bizarre frightening deformed faces were beginning to show themselves much more often, still mute, but moving their dark mouths as if they were trying to reveal something terrible; as for the strange large red room where the motionless angels lived, it was lately changing too. The viscous red walls were becoming deeper in tone; as red as the colour of fresh blood. Newborn naked babies were motionlessly lying in the protective arms of faceless pale skinned women, who continuously wept and endlessly wandered; as if in search of the primordial light...

In Angela's recent vivid nightmares, there was also that strange sad man who had finally shown himself in her bedroom. Pierce had insisted that the sad man was holding a pillow above her face; but what Pierce saw, and thought, was a "strange man", was in fact a ghost. Angela was certain about that now; and she also knew that the ghost's intentions were not to suffocate her, but in fact, to save her from herself...

Strangely, when Angela looked at the ghost's sad face, she wasn't really afraid; rather, she felt somehow bonded to it and almost pitying the poor thing, as if she could feel, or even understand, his profound pain. But what disturbed her the most; was that this strange ghost had finally found a voice. Before Pierce heard her scream, Angela remembered the sad ghost urging her to "wake up." While he kept repeating "wake up, Mary-Elisabeth, wake up!" As much as she would've liked to believe that it was all a mistake and that the ghost had somehow confused her with a certain "Mary-Elisabeth", the whole thing didn't make any sense to her. However, Angela had the strange feeling that whether she wanted or not, she would soon find out the answers...

Lately, it was as if Angela was being harshly pulled, forced, or guided to acknowledge something; something that she wasn't sure that she really wanted to know; something that the arrogant Eileen Mackenzie-Hoxworth certainly didn't want her to know...

What could be so horrible? Why was Angela so terrified lately?

Tiredly, shaking and sobbing, Angela fell back into her bed, wondering how she could bear that entire awful secret, as well as the painful loss of the loving Josephine. And now her beloved daddy - her rock of Gibraltar - who was slowly, but surely, losing his mind; all those burdens were more than she could bear...

Was there anything else more terrible that could happen? Did anything make sense?

If, at this point of her life, Angela only knew one thing for certain, it was that she wasn't sure of anything anymore; and even less sure of whom she really was...

Chapter Twenty-Two

"New Orleans"

The pleasant sight of the warm golden sun, shining brightly in the cloudless Louisiana sky this morning pleased Edmond Hoxworth, and once again convinced him that his power was so strong that he could control the weather, and that God and all His saints truly loved him...

Just yesterday, it was down pouring, and the forecasters had predicted even more rain for today; which just wouldn't do. Not when Edmond had planned to enjoy himself on the golf course with the rich and powerful Senator Goodman...

Just as Edmond was about to open his mansion's massive front door, his well mannered black butler, "Princeton", respectfully told him that Mister Stephen Montgomery, his investment banker, was now on the line...

After the required "how do you do... very well, thank you," Edmond politely urged Montgomery to get to the point, while nervously glancing at his platinum 'Rolex President'. Quick as a tattling child, Montgomery told Edmond that his "sweet" grandmother was mysteriously siphoning a large amount of money from the family's international account. At this particular point, Edmond listened extremely carefully as the investment banker explained that he was quite concerned about the sudden recklessness on Eileen's part...

"The only reason I called, was because I always admired your grandmother's financial savvy so much; and this is just so unlike her, my dear Edmond... With you being the sole heir, I thought you should know," Montgomery softly, but firmly said, hoping that by overriding Eileen's authority, he would have her only heir eating out of his hand when the rich old bitch would be gone...

"Well, thank you Stephen... You did an excellent job in calling me. I will remember this," Edmond sweetly said, trying his best not to let his intense irritation show in his voice. He was definitely not pleased with his grandmother's action; not pleased at all. Nor was Edmond pleased that Montgomery betrayed his grandmother's trust, so he made a mental note to find a new investment banker as soon as Eileen passed away; but until then, the man had his purpose...

"No problem... You're the man, Ed," Montgomery sweetly said, beaming, while dreaming about his future juicy commissions.

En route to play golf with the Senator, Edmond made a call to a private eye known for his great discretion. Following a hunch, he asked him to find out everything he could about one "Angela Boivin-Haddington"; a character and a name that he now truly despised...

In the middle of the ninth tee, the private eye called Edmond's mobile and provided him with a list of important information concerning Angela's upbringing and life; from the date of her birth; to the fact that she'd been in New Orleans just a week ago to attend her mother's funeral...

A little red light suddenly flashed in Edmond's brain, when he heard that Angela's mother was a black woman named "Josephine", for the name was somehow familiar to him. In fact, it was the name of one of his mother's favourite black chambermaids; a particularly sweet woman who was kind to him when he was a child...

After Edmond's father killed himself, the sweet black woman suddenly left. There was no explanation for her dismissal. Edmond had begged his aloof grandmother to tell him what had become of the "sweet Josephine", but Eileen's carmine lips, as always, were sealed as an oyster...

An eerie feeling of "déjà vu" suddenly overcame Edmond, like an icy fog over the Rocky Mountains. Angela's date of birth correlated with both his father's death and the black maid's sudden departure: could the two events be related? Hummm...

Even as a child, Edmond had understood what had happened, because he had heard the harsh arguments between his mother and his grandmother; as well as the words "coloured bastard baby".

Edmond did have a sister, he now remembered. Somehow, he'd assumed that his sister had left with his mother, because one morning, he no longer heard the sound of the infant cries...

In fact, thinking about it now, it was as if the baby girl disappeared from their family's mansion on the same day that the sweet Josephine did...

Edmond didn't need any more proof; the intense feeling in his gut confirmed his assumptions; and that by itself, was more than enough for him.

After making his sincere apologies to the senator, Edmond left after the ninth tee. He was too upset to concentrate anymore; Edmond hated to lose...

That fucking coloured bitch... She's blackmailing my grandmother!

Usually, Eileen told Edmond everything; especially when it came to money...

Edmond's blood was simmering and his facial muscles were dangerously tightening; as for his eyes, they were as cold now as the white-blue glaciers of Patagonia...

So, the little mulatto bastard bitch wants to make money on our backs!

Edmond nervously cracked his knuckles, one after another. "If this woman shows her dirty face in this city again, she'll have a big surprise coming!" Edmond viciously said under his breath, while rapidly elaborating a plan.

Once comfortably seated on the back passenger seat of his white "LS600H" 'Lexus' limousine, the hot blooded Edmond Hoxworth rapidly raised the thick black glass privacy panel and then called his "cleaning man", a strange Mexican-Samoan with large lethal hands, better known, for his wealthy clients, as "Grande". The man was huge, efficient and vicious; very, very vicious.

The devil smiled; again...

160

Chapter Twenty-Three

"London"

A week later, Angela and Pierce had a dinner "tête à tête" at Stefano's, a wonderful Tuscan restaurant located in Knightsbridge, which they frequented often.

It was the first time that Angela had gone out with her husband since her return from her mother's funeral in New Orleans, and she felt as nervous as if they were on a first date. Tonight, Angela truly wanted to open up to Pierce, but she didn't want to mention the increase in her nightmares; nor to mention the sad ghost, or whatever it was, or Pierce might think she had totally lost her senses; she didn't need any more complications...

Pierce ordered an excellent bottle of old Chianti and their favourite wild mushroom risotto. Angela tried her best to smile and relax, but even the warm familiar atmosphere of the place seemed somehow threatening...

At the small bar, there were two beautiful young women sitting together, which were staring at her and talking rather loudly.

Angela was sure that she heard one of them mention her name; not that this was unusual, since she was a celebrity. People often pointed at her and spoke about her, as if she was immune to their comments; but somehow, this was different, and the whole scene had a negative feel to it…

Pretending that everything was alright, Angela nervously smiled at her husband, and she quickly excused herself; then she regally wove her way through the crowded restaurant, turning many heads. She was clad in a superb glove fitting 'Hervè Léger' black satin sleeveless dress and was walking like a feline towards the powder room, in the hope to find some momentary relief and solitude.

When Angela returned, she was surprised to find that one of the women from the bar, a curvaceous brunette in a tight red dress, was sitting at her table, conversing with her husband. *I am not going to get paranoid over this,* Angela nervously told herself, while trying to stay calm.

"Ohhh, it's quite an honour to meet you, Miss Boivin," the woman warmly said, before sensually standing up and giving Angela a cheek-kiss, as if she were an old friend. "You are simply exquisite, Miss Boivin. On stage and off!" She warmly smiled, seemingly truly delighted.

Angela attempted a polite smile, but she wasn't in the mood to deal with fans. Besides, there was something peculiar about this woman that she didn't trust. It might've been the spectacular red dress she wore; expensive as it looked, the wisps of material barely covered her nipples, and they thrust forward as prominently as two ten carat diamonds beneath the thin silk...

Angela took a deep breath, trying harder to calm herself.

Pierce is not the cheating type, she reassured herself; but then, until a few weeks ago, Josephine was her genetic mother, and ghosts were something that children pretended to be when they played dress-up on Halloween...

Why can't I shut my mind off? She nervously thought, while suddenly feeling extremely tired.

"Nice to meet you," Angela politely said, with a weak smile, backing up a bit. As an artist, she could force politeness, but she certainly wouldn't return the woman's friendly kiss...

"Miss Boivin, when will you be performing in London again?" The woman softly asked, with a disarming lovely smile, while fluttering her lovely eyes.

"Two months from now, the company will be performing 'Giselle'," Angela calmly said, before sitting closer to her husband and putting a proprietary hand on his firm lap...

The woman slowly turned towards him. "Please, my dear Pierce, do not forget to remind me." Her smile was radiant and her voice was as sensual as the air in the tropics. "I'll make a point of being there!" She joyfully exclaimed, suddenly happy as a child.

"I will definitely remind you," he politely answered, slightly avoiding her lovely eyes.

"But it is so far away," the woman said with a pout, her inquisitive eyes back on Angela.

"Next week I dance in Monte Carlo; then Milan and Rome." Angela flatly said.

"Really?" The woman said, widening her feline jade green eyes. "And how long will you be gone?"

"It's a short tour... More or less ten days," Angela softly replied, her stomach was in knots.

"But my dear Angela, how can you possibly stay away for so long? Won't your handsome husband miss you terribly?" The woman said before she sensually turned again to face Pierce. "Isn't it difficult for you to remain alone, my dear Pierce? She softly asked, ten days is a long time for a man..." She sensually added with a little ironic smile.

"Well, it's not as bad as it sounds," Pierce nervously responded, suddenly embarrassed. "I'll be flying down to see my wife on the weekends, you know..."

"Ohhh, I see..." The woman slowly nodded, before tossing Pierce a knowing smile. "But aren't you just a tad jealous? Come on? Beautiful as your wife is, she must have admirers by the dozen, arms filled with roses, waiting at the door of her dressing room, just to catch a glimpse of her, no?" She softly said before she slid her gaze from Pierce to Angela and slyly winked...

"No, I don't worry about that," Pierce firmly said, before taking Angela's hand to kiss it.

"My husband has no need to worry," Angela calmly stated, while her dislike for this irritating woman was exponentially growing; then she nervously squeezed Pierce's hand, hoping he would find a way to banish the ravishing bitch from their table; but unfortunately for Angela, the woman had her own agenda...

"Well, my dear Angela, woman to woman, you must worry a little bit about leaving your handsome husband alone while you're away, no?" She softly asked while sliding her eyes like a wild cat.

"No, not really... You see Miss, I trust my husband!" Angela firmly responded, with a cold smile.

"Then, you're a rare couple, indeed... Faithfulness is a quite unusual thing these days... I must say that when I take into account my own experiences with men - whether they're single, married, or don't know the difference." The woman slowly said with a little ironic smile. "I have good reason not to trust them, my dear. I'd be a fool to think any other way... Nonetheless, it is quite refreshing to see a couple that still believes in such old-fashioned values," she added doubtfully, looking back and forth at the two of them.

"Well my dear, I'm truly sorry to hear that you've been so unfortunate in your choices," Angela dryly said, as she inched closer to her husband.

"And for how long have you two been married?" The woman calmly asked, ignoring her visible change of attitude.

"For almost five happy years," Pierce quickly answered, while Angela threw him an angry look. *It's none of her business!*

"Oh, my God! That's a lifetime and a half, in marriage years..." She exclaimed before raising her lovely eyes as if she was surprised. "And here you are, still in love..." She added with a little ironic smile.

She is condescending and awful, Angela thought, having had more than enough by this time. "I don't think I caught your name," she abruptly said, standing up and extending her hand, hoping that the woman would get the hint and leave.

"How terrible of me not to introduce myself... Rose-Mary is the name. Rose-Mary Bernhart." The woman said with a ravishing fake smile.

"Miss Bernhart is one of my clients," Pierce quite nervously explained. "She owns an antique gallery in Bond Street."

"I've the best antiques in London," the woman boasted. "French, Italian, Spanish and Portuguese are my specialty; but I also have quite a large collection of great 17th century Dutch paintings... Please, come see me, Angela..." She hypocritically said with a little annoying grin.

"Sorry, but I only purchase my antiques when I travel!" Angela coldly said as she sat back down on the red velvet banquette; then she deeply sighed, giving up for the moment.

The woman beamed like a girl who'd just won a competition. "Well, I best be off... Do have a wonderful dinner, my friends... And I hope you both continue to have success in your marriage. It would be nice if someone would finally prove all of us cynics wrong..." She punctuated every word with a sensuous gesture, and Pierce's gaze discretely followed her every languorous move...

"Thank you, Miss Bernhart," Pierce said innocently before slightly bowing his head.

"I'll be seeing you soon, Pierce. Right?" The woman sweetly asked before she flashed her winning smile again, then she sensually leaned back just enough to give him a glimpse of her voluptuous breast; her arrogant nipples dangerously pointing straight at his eyes...

Angela nervously noticed her husband blush.

"Most definitely," Pierce said a little bit embarrassed, before stupidly lowering his eyes.

"Well, goodbye, my dear Angela... It was truly a pleasure meeting you. Love your dress!"

"Likewise," Angela indifferently said. *You slut!*

Tightly packed in her stylish 'Dolce & Gabbana' sexy red dress and swinging her tight little behind like a Brazilian girl, the "sweet" Rose-Mary Bernhart sensually returned to the bar, while turning her beautiful torso sinuously, before throwing a little nod to Pierce and Angela as she slinked away.

The heavy scent of the woman lingered over their table, spoiling the taste of the food. Angela immediately recognised the unmistakable scent of Christian Dior's 'Poison'; an expensive, but lethal perfume; that the sweet Rose-Mary obviously overindulged in...

"Who is that woman?" Angela nervously asked, frowning.

"I told you, darling, she's a client." Pierce sweetly said, visibly embarrassed.

"But all those questions? What kind of a "client" makes such assumptions without knowing a person? Tell me!" Angela asked again, while scanning his eyes.

"Well, my darling, I don't know... But I guess she's just exceptionally friendly, that's all." Pierce calmly said, pouring her some Chianti. He certainly didn't intend for their romantic evening to be interrupted in such a way; especially not by a beautiful woman like Rose-Mary Bernhart; he could perfectly see that she was the type of woman who purposefully made other women uncomfortable...

And Angela doesn't need that tonight... I don't need it either. Pierce nervously thought while drinking some wine.

"And for how long has she been a client?" Angela suspiciously asked, scanning his eyes again while searching for the truth.

"Well, just recently... She was referred to me by my Aunt Gail. She seemed quite taken by Miss Bernhart." Pierce uncomfortably said while avoiding her eyes.

"Really?" *Gail obviously didn't want that beautiful slut making moves on her own husband, so she dumped her on mine!* Angela frowned. "Even so, Pierce. She's already talking to you on a first name basis! Did you invite her to be so... familiar?" Angela coldly asked.

"Of course not, darling. None of my clients calls me by my first name. That's an American custom, isn't it?" He sweetly asked with a disarming boyish smile.

"Whatever!" Angela mumbled, pursing her lips with dissatisfaction. "This woman is English and should know better... So, I just hope that her extreme `friendliness' doesn't extend beyond words!" She coldly said before she bit the inside of her cheek. What was she saying? It wasn't like her to give Pierce the third degree. Angela trusted him, didn't she?

"Oh, come on, darling," Pierce softly said, laughing nervously as he raised his wine glass for a toast. "You're not the jealous type, no? Although, I must say that I'm a bit flattered... I mean, who would want to hit on an old married guy like me?" He grinned.

Angela's frown deepened. "Pierce, pleeease! If you're an old man, then I'm an old married hag! Plus the woman was practically naked! A dress like that isn't decent; it even would be daring to wear for the Academy Awards!" She quite seriously exclaimed.

"Well, my love, I must admit that it was something of an outfit, wasn't it?" Pierce warmly laughed before he tenderly put his protective arm around her shoulders and sensually kissed her on her lovely neck.

"Ohhh, stop it! I didn't like at all the way this woman was eyeing you... Is she in heat or what?"

"Darling, I can't believe it, you're really jealous!" He finally laughed, visibly delighted.

"Of course I am!" Angela said nervously. "Who wouldn't be with a woman like that hovering around her husband?"

"But she's just a client, my love; nothing more, nothing less... So please, don't worry so much, my darling. You perfectly know that I only love you! And why in Heaven's name would I fool around with another woman who isn't half as good-looking as you are? Please, my love, you have enough on your plate right now, without adding infidelity..." He said more seriously, before tenderly kissing her hand.

If you only knew... Angela nervously thought, suddenly thinking that she'd received a statement from the Swiss bank.

The extremely rich Eileen Mackenzie-Hoxworth had recently deposited the incredible amount of ten million dollars in an account under Angela's name. All that money just to keep Angela's curiosity at bay and to keep her mouth shut. *Why???*

Angela sadly looked at her handsome husband. "Well Pierce, there is something to what that woman said regarding trust... It was the one thing she said that she was right about; you are indeed a man, not a saint, my love... and there's always that first time." She calmly, but seriously said, while looking deep into his eyes, as if searching for something.

"Not as far as I'm concerned, my darling... And having established that I am faithful, and yours, sincerely and truly, may I now have a real kiss from the most beautiful woman in the world; my adorable wife, Mrs. Angela Haddington?" Pierce softly grinned, before he devilishly flashed his dark blue eyes. God, he was charming!

"Yes, you may, Mr. Haddington," Angela softly acquiesced, before she lovingly gazed at his beautiful eyes, and then tenderly kissed his sensual lips.

The excitement that stirred in her body was immediate and intense, so she allowed his hungry tongue to play with hers for just a moment.

Pierce sensually smiled, and then he discretely glanced around the restaurant, before he sported an impish smile and let his hand slowly migrate to Angela's crotch. Her hand was suddenly shaking as she fed him a forkful of creamy wild mushrooms risotto, and she couldn't help but give in to his magical touch. She blushed, then she subtly covered his hand with the red linen napkin, finally allowing him to do as he pleased; after all, her dear husband was just a man...

Pierce was truly irresistible when it came to getting what he wanted from a woman; a wonderful trait that, in lieu of the recent interaction, caused Angela to feel quite insecure. *That woman had better behave! Ditto for my handsome husband... Double-ditto even!* Then, as Pierce's inquisitive fingers entered her silk panties, Angela let forth an unintentional moan, and she melted into nothingness; again...

Chapter Twenty-Four

"Monaco"

When the giant red curtain silently closed upon the magnificent stage of the Opera of "Monte Carlo", Angela rushed to her dressing room, her arms laden with large bouquets of red roses...

The dresser took the roses from her arms and placed them in the expectant vases, already filled with water.

"Hello, hello, hello... You were truly exquisite, madam! And that's a firm understatement! Now take a load off your feet. Sit! Sit! Oh, before I forget, your husband phoned five minutes ago," announced "Claudine", her personal dresser. Claudine Calmette was an efficient pixie-like woman with short straight grey hair, who could have easily passed for a gay man.

"I would've caught the call if the ovation hadn't been so long," Angela said, undressing.

"Mon Dieu, Madame!!! Never say such things! You should enjoy your ovation. It was well-deserved," the dresser enthused.

"Thank you, Claudine. That is quite a compliment coming from you, since you're a veritable connoisseur of ballet." Angela warmly said, before she affectionately kissed her on the cheek.

"Thank you, madam. It has been for me thirty-five years behind the scene, and I've never regretted one day. Now sit, sit," she said, pulling out a golden chair for Angela before handing her a red phone.

Angela rapidly dialled her home number in London, but after four rings the answering machine picked up. *The butler must've had the night off... But why isn't Pierce answering at this time of night?*

"Well, Claudine, I think that my husband must've gone to sleep..." Angela said softly, not believing a word that came out of her mouth. It had been only four days since she left London and she already missed him terribly. Since she saw that outrageously sexy "new client" of his, Angela's thoughts of him were now tainted with a tinge of jealousy; she truly hated this new feeling...

"You need to get dressed and get to the party, Madame. Prince Albert and his wife will be there," Claudine said with a slight French accent, her nimble hands helping Angela out of her pale blue diaphanous costume.

"The party..." At this point, Angela didn't really care, and even the thrill of her standing ovation had been overshadowed by anxiety. *Where could he be? I don't understand...* She nervously thought while starting to remove her stage make up.

Later on, when Angela finally returned to the regal hotel suite at the magnificent "Hotel de Paris", it was past three in the morning, and she was totally exhausted. Exhausted from making chit-chat with fans and strangers; exhausted from dancing; exhausted from smiling when all she wanted to do now was cry…

Why do I feel this way…? Why? Lately, not even the dance seemed to work to ease the constant torment of her mind. It was as if all the ghosts of her past had finally caught up with her. Lately, Angela had the unpleasant feeling that she had almost lost her sense of self, her real identity: *who am I? Certainly not a great dancer in the same vein as Boris…* And yet, now she deeply envied the arrogant Russian ballet dancer for his focused passion like never before. Before her beloved Josephine died and left her with the burden of the truth, Angela bitterly recalled that she had always been able to completely lose herself in the dance. So, what had happened lately? Why didn't the magic work anymore?

As every ballet aficionado knew, performing 'Petruska' was extremely demanding, even for the most disciplined dancer, and Angela was more than just tired; she was extremely insecure now.

Angela tiredly crossed her suite with its white marble vestibule and beautiful gold-leafed console, ignoring the spectacular white rose bouquet that the concierge had sent up, and then she took a deep breath and absently looked around her. Exquisitely decorated with Louis XVI furnishings, the extremely spacious suite was fit for a princess; and yet, Angela felt like a mongrel, a misfit, and an imposter…

Angela was practically sleepwalking, her sore ballerina feet caged in vertiginous red satin 'Louboutin' pumps, dragged behind her when she tiredly passed through the elegant French double doors before she stepped outside onto the large balcony. Taking a deep breath of the salty Mediterranean fragrance, she leaned over the intricately carved iron railing; then she looked up at the stars gleaming on the velvety dark blue canvas of space, and at the stunning opalescent moon, which that night seemed to speak to her. Full and nurturing, the moon strangely reminded her of her mother...

The breathless beauty of Monte Carlo by night, its dazzling little port filled with the most beautiful yachts in the world, as well as the romantic stone castle of the 'Grimaldi' family, which was far away framed by softly curved mountains, was transformative and restorative. That night, Angela genuinely smiled for the first time; but she longed again for her beloved mother, as well as her husband's loving touch...

With the thought of Pierce, the events of the past weeks flooded back into her mind; along with the knowledge that soon she would have to contact Elisabeth Hoxworth. In the last two days, her father had left several messages on her voicemail, insisting that Josephine was growing impatient...

Lately, Angela constantly worried about André. More and more, he seemed to retreat into another world; Josephine's world. In the last month, he spent most of his afternoons at her grave, reading her the newspaper and "talking" with her. It was becoming obvious that since the love of his life was gone, the world of the living seemed to hold little interest for him now...

Her brother John had phoned her with great concern a week ago. André had been arrested, mistakenly believed to be a homeless vagrant. The police found him spooning gruel into the bowl that he had placed on the still fresh mound of earth that covered Josephine's grave...

The next day, André was taken to a neurologist and a psychiatrist, but there were no signs of Alzheimer's or any other degenerative diseases. Still, Angela knew that André deeply longed to join his beloved Josephine, wherever she was. The spirit world, whether real or imagined, seemed to have claimed him for its own, and it became clear that André's troubled spirit was preparing to depart from this little miserable world, for an infinite place made to free the soul from its cage...

Angela took one more look at the glorious moon and at the billion dollar magnificent vista, wishing that it could give her the answers she searched. She thought of calling her husband, but it was late and she did not feel comfortable confiding in him anymore. She hadn't even told him yet about Eileen Hoxworth, or her bribe. Somehow, it was becoming clear to Angela that she didn't want to tell Pierce about money, simply because it would just complicate things...

It was enough that Pierce had to deal with her recurring nightmares, or whatever they were, but the fact that he never mentioned the "ghost" episode again, as if he didn't really believe what he saw with his own eyes, somehow deeply perturbed Angela; so she did not bring it up...

Daddy would certainly understand, but telling him about my own otherworldly experience might push him into Mama's world for good... She sadly thought, suddenly shivering.

Angela turned her back to the opalescent moon, crossed the elegant salon, and tiredly walked into her large bedroom. Although it was as grand as the rest of the suite, Angela did not fully appreciate the opulent French décor. At this precise instant, her tormented mind was far, far away, in the little clapboard bungalow in New Orleans where she grew up, and for the first time she realised that she truly missed her life; the one she knew...

As hard as it was sometimes being ridiculed by her black classmates, somehow, she had felt safe there; safe and truly loved...

The ground she walked on was the ground of poverty, granted, but the ground was solid and firm. Strangely enough, she knew now that she would give all the money she had for the comforting security that she once felt; for the knowledge that the next step she took would not be off a lethal precipice...

Tiredly, Angela unzipped her spectacular 'Yves Saint Laurent' white silk taffeta gown printed with large black roses; and let it fall like an exotic flower upon the beautiful 'Aubusson' needlepoint carpet. She motionlessly stood in the centre of her exquisite French haute couture gown, in front of the large gold-framed mirror and sadly stared at her beautiful reflection, before coldly studying herself as if she were a stranger, noting the grace of her slim arms and elegant hands, her swanlike neck and her softly muscled back, as taut and sensuous as a panther's; then she took a good look at her exceptional beautiful long legs; legs that were insured for a million pounds a piece...

What a joke! Here she was, a "mulatto bastard" standing in a palatial suite of a five star palace in Monte Carlo, quietly losing her mind; she, the pathetic daughter of a beautiful pale blond English woman with innocent blue eyes and of an unknown Negro...

When Angela finally slipped beneath the covers of the large canopied bed, sleep took her fast, but her dreams stole the chance of real rest. As always, the strange man with the cold steel blue eyes was silently waiting for her, holding the lace pillow.

Soon, like a cold shroud; darkness and primordial fear would fall upon Angela.

Soon, she could not outrun the dark shadows that lived within her soul...

Soon, she could not escape anymore her inner demons.

Soon... soon...soon; again!

Chapter Twenty-Five

"Monaco"

With horrific images of her vivid nightmare lingering in her mind, Angela awoke at dawn, drenched with sweat and bruised...

Each day, the fine line between her dream and waking lives became more blurred, more confused. The surreal characters were also becoming more real, the images more cohesive, as if the once chaotic chapters were slowly piecing themselves together into a linear plot...

But the ideas had not yet solidified into a full-fledged horror novel; the main element, "the motive", the core that drove the entire action, was still shadowy and vague, although the pieces were intact...

Angela saw the now familiar mysterious red room which, as usual, was filled with an army of silent angels; but now, an intriguing black eyeless woman dressed in an immaculate white robe - a nimbus of light circling her head - stood in the centre of the room. She was chanting a strange foreign litany; a prayer of some kind that seemed to sooth the chaos.

Am I going insane? Is my brain playing strange tricks on me???

Greatly disturbed, Angela also noticed that her olfactory sense had become as acute as that of a pregnant woman. Even after she awoke, she was certain that the smell of vetiver and sweet tobacco lingered in the room. *How could it be just a dream?*

Like Alice in Wonderland, Angela was being led into frightening unknown places; but this time, she was led by the black eyeless woman into a temple of some kind, and an impressive bronze door menacingly stood before her.

Angela felt as if she were entering a forbidden place that resembled an ancient European mausoleum in its grandeur; yet, the massive bronze door remained locked and bolted, and the large key was far out of reach.

Angela felt as if she had entered a strange fairy-tale; but nothing akin to Disneyland…

Unable to find any kind of peace in her bed, she took a hot shower and dressed quickly in a 'Chanel' pale green tweed ensemble with assorted handbag and pumps, then she spent the morning pensively roaming around Monte Carlo's enchanting port, where an impressive display of multimillion dollars yachts sporting international flags caught her eye and reminded her of the great power of money.

I have come a long way… She sighed. *But where am I really going now? Will my next journey take me to an asylum?*

Angela sadly sat on the quiet terrace of a little café, her beautiful eyes hidden behind large black 'Chanel' sunglasses, and sipped a cappuccino as she watched the changing moody sky. For the first time in her life, in these picture perfect surroundings, Angela felt alone; so terribly alone...

Later that day, browsing through the luxurious boutiques in the "Boulevard des Italiens" that had once pleased her, she felt completely apathetic. It was as if she could not see beauty anymore.

Perhaps the black eyeless woman is just a symbol of who I will become if I don't fulfil my quest. No! That's just crazy! She nervously thought.

That afternoon, when Angela returned to her suite at the famous "Hotel de Paris", she found a telephone number on her bedroom desk. It was written in her handwriting; and yet, she was almost certain that she'd left the number at home...

Like a haunting song that she couldn't turn off, the name written on the paper resonated in her head: Elisabeth Hoxworth... Elisabeth Hoxworth... Elisabeth Hoxworth...

The now familiar name kept repeating itself again and again, whispered by a disembodied voice.

Elisabeth Hoxworth... Elisabeth Hoxworth... Elisabeth Hoxworth...

It was time.

Tiredly and reluctantly, Angela dialled the number, her heart pounding; then she closed her eyes.

"Bainbridge residence," a young female voice announced.

"Is this Ashington 45689?" Angela asked hesitantly.

"Yes, it is. How may I help you?"

Suddenly, Angela felt her throat tighten. "I… uh… I was hoping to speak to Elisabeth Hoxworth."

"Elisabeth Hoxworth? You mean Elisabeth Addlesby, don't you?"

"Uh, I don't know… I just know this person under the name of Hoxworth," Angela nervously explained. "Maybe she remarried? I'm the daughter of Mr. and Mrs. André Boivin, from New Orleans…"

"Oh, I see… Hold on a moment then, and I'll go and fetch her." The young woman softly said. "Aunt Elisabeth, Aunt Elisabeth!" She shouted.

Elisabeth was in the garden, pruning a cluster of white Japanese chrysanthemums.

"A woman's on the phone for you. She says she's the daughter of the Boivins?"

At once, the blood drained from Elisabeth's rosy face. Then she could hardly get off the little gardening bench she sat on. As if she could feel her aunt's suffering, Jennifer grimaced and offered her arm. *The arthritis is a curse; one that such a kind woman certainly doesn't deserve,* she sadly thought, before she handed Elisabeth her cane and gently helped her into the big house.

In the kitchen, Elisabeth's eyes moved to the photograph of her late husband. It had been hanging on the wall for so long that the stripped mint green wallpaper beneath it was a different hue altogether. *My dear Jonathan,* she lovingly whispered as she nervously picked up the phone, *could it be?* At this precise instant, she thought she saw Jonathan smile, in that impish way he had, and her breathing became somehow easier.

"Hello?" Elisabeth hesitantly said, while putting her hand against her heart.

Angela felt her heart race as well, like a trip hammer. "Hello... This is awkward, I know. I'm the daughter of Josephine and André Boivin..." Angela uncomfortably said. "My mother passed away a few weeks ago, and before she did, she made me promise to call you, madam; she also explained things to me before she died..."

"Ohhh, my poor and dear Josephine... I'm so sorry to hear that. You poor child... Josephine was a gem, a true gem." Elisabeth sadly gazed at the photo again and wondered what Josephine had exactly said...

The last time Elisabeth had seen Angela, she was just a child wearing a pink and white polka dotted dress and she'd longed to take her back to England that day, to steal her from Josephine; but she couldn't do that to either the sweet Josephine or André. In fact, she hadn't the heart...

"Thank you for your consolation, madam, but I think we need to talk..." Angela nervously said. "My mother thought it was important. I must say that I only vaguely remember you, but I remember the dolls... Just before my mother died, she showed me a clipping of you from an old magazine and explained many things; too many things in fact, and I can't say that I'm happy about this... It was difficult enough growing up as a mulatto in a dark-skinned neighbourhood, but it's even worse knowing now that I am a bastard as well; and an unwanted one at that!" She coldly said while raising her voice.

Like a dagger, Angela's harsh words pierced through Elisabeth's fragile heart. Immediately, she felt a sharp pain in her chest; then she gazed at the photo of Jonathan, her eyes full of pleading.

"Please, my child, please don't say that... You are certainly not a bastard and you were not unwanted! Believe me Angela; I never wanted to give you up." Elisabeth tiredly said with a broken voice.

"Well madam, as far as I'm concerned, I only have one mother; and she's dead now! No one can replace Josephine. Do you understand me? No one!" Angela coldly spoke, each word a bullet.

"Please," Elisabeth said in a weak voice. "Pleeease, Angela, you must believe me, my child. What did Josephine say when she asked you to contact me? Was she angry at me?" She was now feeling extremely confused, and a sharp pain slowly began to spread from her left arm into her chest.

"No, Madam. She wasn't angry with you, but I am! As far as I'm concerned, you're just an adulterous woman who abandoned me after having an affair with a Negro!"

"No, it's not true, Angela. I am not an adulterous, and your father was not a Negro!" Elisabeth cried, while her entire body started to tremble. The blue veins of her hand became more pronounced as she raised her arm to caress her husband's face. *Jonathan, my love,* she painfully whispered. *Why is our daughter being so harsh with me? Could you help her to understand, my darling; please...*

"Angela, my child. I truly love you with all my heart, as I always have... My husband, Jonathan Hoxworth, was indeed your father. Please, my child, believe me..."

Angela nervously laughed at Elisabeth's words. "Ohhh, I see..." She dryly said, her tone full of irony. "Why did he kill himself, then? And why did his mother throw you out of his mansion and take your son to bring him up as her own?" She viciously said, feeling full of hatred.

"Because it was all a mistake, my child, believe me... I don't understand why you were born with a darker skin than us, but all I know now is that it wasn't the first time... There's something off with that Hoxworth family." Elisabeth anxiously said, lowering her voice. "Jonathan's mother didn't tell me what it was when I married her son, but there's nevertheless a family secret... You must believe me, my child. It was not my fault." She finally said with a broken voice.

"Ohhh, come on, Elisabeth... get real, will you? You're not talking to an idiot anymore! If I'd been Jonathan Hoxworth's daughter, then I would have been white like you and your beloved husband, so please stop with the excuses; I've had enough!" Angela icily said, raising her voice again. Suddenly, she was overcome with a strange feeling that someone, "or something", was watching her... Then she smelled the scent of tobacco and vetiver again...

Angela stood nervously staring at her frozen reflection in the mirror, while holding the receiver in her hand, wondering now what else to say. At this precise moment, her face was ashen; so pale that she probably would be mistaken for a Caucasian. It seemed as if all her blood had been leeched from her body; as if she almost expected to see a pool of red blood on the floor, surrounding her...

As Angela motionlessly stared into the mirror, she realised that the eyes that looked back at her were not her own anymore. Her eyes were as pale as the moon, yet a certain brightness and clarity shone through them; an otherworldly brightness...

Those strange eyes were the eyes of the ghost!

Angela and the ghost had simply merged; they were becoming one now.

In fact, those strange eyes were extremely sad, filled with remorse and little else and Angela watched as her mirror image slowly moved, even though she stood stock-still.

Suddenly, it was not her voice that eschewed from her tongue; instead, she heard a man's voice saying, "Forgive me, please... Forgive me, Mary-Elisabeth. I didn't know the truth back then; I was a fool..." Then, her mirror image slowly returned to normal, and the tobacco and vetiver scent left as quickly as it came.

I am losing my mind... God, please, help me!

"Angela, Angela?" Elisabeth desperately intoned. "Please, my child, don't talk to me that way... You've no idea how it hurt me to watch you being raised by another woman." Her voice seemed old and broken, and she was certainly crying.

"Oh, I see... Now I'm the one who made you suffer?" Angela brutally replied, as if the woman's palpable pain angered her even more. Now she decided she would not let this unfaithful woman get under her skin, and she would never let her in her heart; never!

"Madam, you're absolutely nothing to me! Nothing!" Angela almost shouted, full of undiluted rage. "Josephine raised me, and she will always be my mother, my one and only mother; so there's no place for you in my life because it's way too late now..." She coldly said. "As long as I live, Madam, I'll never forgive you for abandoning me; never! In fact, you could die right now and I couldn't care less!" She finally shouted, while wishing Elisabeth's death.

Angela was amazed at the amount of rage that boiled now inside her. It seemed as if she was truly possessed by an intense force that she couldn't control anymore; possessed by a vicious and lethal demonic force...

Elisabeth's hand tightened around the receiver and she tried to speak, to defend herself; but she couldn't emit a single word. A sharp pain seared through her chest before the world violently spun around her. She grasped at a nearby table, causing a crystal vase full of freshly cut flowers to fall to the wooden floor and shatter; then, like a broken porcelain doll, Elisabeth fell heavily to the floor...

What have I done? Did I actually tell that woman that I couldn't care less if she died! A sudden dread filled Angela.

"Elisabeth?! Hello? Are you there?" After what seemed an eternity passed, the deadly silence was interrupted by a loud scream.

"Oh God! Oh God! Aunt Elisabeth!" Jennifer shouted hysterically. "God no!"

"Hello?! Hellooo??! Can anyone hear me?!" Angela desperately asked, her lips trembling. Jennifer picked the phone up from the floor and breathlessly explained: "For God's sake, what did you say to her! My aunt has collapsed! I need to call the hospital now."

Without another word, Jennifer hung up, leaving Angela anxiously holding the phone, the dial tone humming like an angry wasp. Slowly, Angela sat down; then closed her eyes. Her heart felt heavy with guilt.

What is happening to me? What have I done? Mama, please; pleeease help me...

Next to Angela, but invisible to her eyes, the poor Josephine was crying.

Chapter Twenty-Six

"London"

In the full-length mirror of her large dressing room, Gail Haddington impatiently contemplated her poised image...

Not bad; not bad at all... If I were a man, I would certainly screw myself! She thought smiling, before she girlishly laughed.

The "little" black dress from 'Escada' that she wore today was expertly tailored and exceptionally flattering. Gail gathered a spectacular, but scandalously expensive 'Helen Yarmak' golden sable fur coat that she had recently bought during a trip to Moscow with her husband; then she carefully closed the large glass door of her immense refrigerated closet full of beautiful furs, before she let her eyes wander on the many black lacquered shelves of her spacious dressing room, displaying an incredible choice of luxurious handbags, mostly made of rare exotic skins. For an instant, Gail hesitated between a red crocodile 'Kelly' handbag, made for the respectable French house of 'Hermès'; or a pink fuchsia 'Lady Diana' handbag, from the non-less respectable house of 'Christian Dior'...

Today, Gail wanted to look picture perfect for the discerning eye of her top-notch personal shopper, the always impeccably chic 'Suzanne Tabak', whom was expressly arriving from New York for a luxurious shopping spree in London, Paris and Rome.

Hating herself when she was hesitant, Gail deeply sighed, dropped the thought, then went directly towards today's 'objet du désire': a ravishing bright violet crocodile handbag masterfully designed by the "American Queen" of precious handbags: the oh so chic, 'Lana Marks'...

Having been born with a platinum spoon in her mouth, to Gail, real elegance was in the minute details; but a truly intelligent fashion statement was always assured by donning expensive classical garments. In her particular case, Gail preferred to look elegant and expensive at all times, simply because she had no taste for the casual.

Even when Gail slept alone - which was most of the time - she always wrapped her body in the finest silk and always perfumed her nightgown with her beloved florist's "Edwardian Bouquet".

Gail Haddington always lived by two simple mottos: "life is too short to be sloppy or average" and "a woman over 40 should never look back; particularly if she's trying on a bathing suit..."

Gail made use of the latter motto every morning when she pushed herself from the tub. She was still pleased with her frontal appearance, but lately, her once "boyish" behind seemed to be migrating southward, cursed by gravity...

When the ivory phone rang, Gail was glad to be distracted, and when she heard who was on the line, her red painted lips curled in a wicked smile.

God, that woman sounds like a bedroom goddess, if there ever was one... "How are things progressing with my nephew?" She softly asked, in an elegant contralto voice.

"Very well, my dear, extremely well indeed! At our last meeting, this poor Pierce was ready to fall... When he stood up from behind his desk to walk me out, the poor man was so embarrassed by the spontaneous reaction my sexy dress had created, that he quickly closed his tweed jacket to hide his eager manhood." The woman sensually said before laughing. "But he wasn't quick enough, my dear. What a big boy! Whoever said that lawyers aren't sexy? This one calls for a complete rethinking of the profession..." She giggled this time, in a teasing girlish way.

God, she is good! Gail thought before she elegantly laughed along with the woman, while continuing to scrutinise herself in the mirror, internally debating what precious jewellery should she wear today to spice up her little outfit.

"Good; Very good, darling... I see that you keep your promises. Soon I will keep mine," Gail softly said, regretfully thinking about all the money she'll have to give that refined slut. "So, when will you be giving the Estacada, dear?" She asked with a honeyed voice, smiling like a sphinx.

"Any day now; or should I say any night now... This isn't something I want to get over within an hour, my dear Gail. You see,

I intend to enjoy it again, and again, and again…" The woman purred like a cat, visualising Pierce's attractive naked body in her wicked mind.

"Well, I see that you really like what you do, my dear." Gail dryly remarked. "Do you always mix business with pleasure?" She coldly asked, while raising a perfectly arched eyebrow.

"Of course I do; and as often as I can… It's what makes my life worth living, my dear Gail..." The woman's voice was now a sensual purr.

Slut! Slut! Slut! "Well, that's the spirit daaarling! But please, my dear, make sure that the pictures are clear as water."

"Don't worry, my friend, they always are… But this time, I think I'll keep a double of the most interesting ones for myself; because sometimes, a single girl can get lonely at night…" She sighed.

"Lonely? Coming from someone like you, I find that quite surprising," Gail said with a dash of disdain.

"Well, you should know better, my dear... At one time or another, we all sleep alone… Don't you, darling?" With that simple question, the woman hung up.

For a moment, Gail Haddington bitterly thought about that last remark.

"At one time or another, we all sleep alone." Unfortunately yes, indeed…

Chapter Twenty-Seven

"Monaco"

As the reddish sun finally sank into the calm Mediterranean Sea, Angela called the home of her genetic mother, hoping to hear that she was alright...

This time, it was Elisabeth's sister, Jillian Bainbridge, who answered the phone.

So I have an aunt as well... Angela nervously thought.

Jillian was as soft-spoken as Elisabeth, who was now recuperating in the hospital.

"It is not so strange that my sister had a heart attack," Jillian calmly explained. "Her heart was already weak, and I'm certain that hearing from you was quite unexpected... She loves you very much Angela, you know." She paused for a moment, before adding; "We are very close... So I will tell you that your anger towards her is highly inappropriate and completely misdirected; after all, you know too little of the saga of your real family to cast stones! You wouldn't even allow her a word edgewise, so that she could explain... Elisabeth could've died, you know!" Jillian nervously exclaimed.

"Well, Madam, I'm truly sorry; but I only called to fulfil my mother's dying wish... I'm referring to Josephine, not Elisabeth," Angela cautiously remarked. "Truthfully, I don't want to patch things up with your sister; and it's true that I am extremely angry! Wouldn't you be? To me, the facts are clear enough... Elisabeth had an extramarital affair with a black man and gave me away to Josephine, as easily as if I were a piece of trash!" Angela tried to keep her voice calm, but the feeling of anger inside her was overwhelming now.

"I know that's what you think, my dear child, but you are wrong," Jillian calmly stated. "You should, at least, hear her side of the story before you judge her, don't you think? My dear Elisabeth has dealt with enough pain for a lifetime, believe me, Angela. Since the day she came back from New Orleans, she's lived her life as a recluse; even though she was quite a beauty, she only leaves our home to attend mass. Despite numerous offers of marriage, she remained true to her husband."

"I'm sure your sister became pathologically depressed," Angela nervously said. "After all, her husband killed himself because of what she did..." She firmly added.

"The poor Jonathan overreacted, because he didn't know all the truth! His mother didn't tell him the story of his ancestry; so he didn't know that a coloured wayward gene was part of his biological inheritance. To protect her famous name, his mother let him believe that Elisabeth was unfaithful; but by destroying my poor sister, in fact she killed her own son... Eileen Hoxworth can be as cold-hearted as the serpent that caused the Great Fall." Jillian's voice was filled with bitterness.

Like a lioness, Angela paced around the room. "I don't understand where you're going, Mrs. Bainbridge! Have I lived my entire life in a house of cards? Oh, pleeease, please; will you get to the point!" She harshly said, dangerously raising her voice.

But Jillian would not be hurried. Her voice remained soft, even, and slow. "Angela, your resemblance to Jonathan Hoxworth is uncanny. Strip away the skin colour and there would be no mistake that you are a product of his seed, my child... Have you seen his photograph?" She calmly asked.

"No, never." Angela tiredly said, before closing her eyes.

"But you are aware of the resemblance to your mother? Now you will be in for more surprises... Elisabeth has many photographs of you that she has cut out of celebrity magazines, and do you know that Jonathan had a beauty mark in the exact same place as yours; right above the left corner of his lip? It's quite becoming... When you see a photo of him, you'll certainly stop accusing my poor sister of adultery; and above all, stop wondering who your real father was; you'll also see the resemblance in your brother, Edmond, too." She firmly said, slightly raising her voice.

Now, Angela was silent; deadly silent...

Certainly, Eileen Hoxworth's ten million dollar bribe would make a lot more sense if Angela were indeed related to her son; and if that was the case, Angela would be a rightful heir to the large Hoxworth fortune and their highly coveted name; but she also would be an inconvenient bi-racial Hoxworth heir...

The implications were truly staggering.

People will kill just to keep their reputations clean, a voice warned from the far recess of her mind. Eileen Hoxworth's paranoia might not only be plausible; it might be necessary...

"Could you prove that?" Angela defiantly asked.

"Prior to your birth, my child, when Eileen would indulge a bit too much in the sherry; well, she would talk sometimes... She never really said anything that would incriminate her, but it seemed that she needed to relieve herself of her own burdens, since her only son killed himself. Eileen built a wall of stone around her heart, I suppose... Perhaps she even believes the strange story she invented to keep her sanity."

"Yes, and..." Angela said, growing more impatient with every word. She didn't really care about Eileen or Elisabeth. She just wanted the truth, and she was angry; extremely angry...

What you want is revenge, the voice urged. Lately, it seemed to be getting stronger.

"And... From what your mother and I have been able to piece together, we've come to the conclusion that your skin colour was caused by what geneticists call a 'wayward gene'. What this means is that, six or seven generations ago, one of the Hoxworths had a child with a black woman; probably a slave... One can only imagine how the Hoxworths kept this hidden throughout six or seven generations;

but obviously, they managed… The Negro gene, however, still lives in their family's DNA, and you are certainly the living proof of it, my dear child." Jillian calmly explained.

"But that's absolutely crazy! You mean that in six generations, I was the only mulatto child? It's simply impossible!" Angela strongly argued; her mind racing.

"Unfortunately, Angela, I doubt you were the only one… I'd rather not think about that at this time, but consider a child who is born with blue eyes, even if both parents have brown eyes; and blue eyes are one of the most recessive genes… The Negroid gene is always dominant when mixed with other races, my child; so it will certainly last longer in a Caucasian gene pool and will continue to pop up for generations." Jillian very seriously said.

Angela didn't know what to believe anymore; in fact, she was totally lost…

Her head throbbed so much that she was overwhelmed by nausea and felt like vomiting. She wished she could wash her skin away - the black, the white, the grey; everything! At this point of her life, Angela would simply prefer being colourless; even transparent, if she could...

"It's a difficult truth to accept, my dear child, isn't it? I know…" Jillian softly, but firmly said again. "It would be so much easier to curse my poor sister for her presumed infidelity and shoot her with the spears of unresolved anger of the past... So much betrayal and deceit; so much pain..." Jillian tiredly said, sadly remembering the past.

"And why should I believe you? Why?" Angela calmly asked, even though she was on the verge of shouting again.

"Just come here, my child, and have a good look at the photographs of Jonathan. It's not a question of faith, Angela. You will know, believe me; if you don't already," Jillian stated with confidence, while refraining from crying.

"If this theory about a wayward gene is true, I certainly wouldn't have been the first mulatto baby; so, where are my sisters and brothers in colour? My aunts, uncles and grandparents? Where are all of us who inherited this damned coloured gene?" Angela coldly asked, while feeling extremely drained by the deranging subject.

A heavy embarrassing silence fell between them...

"Well, Angela, we looked into it when my sister returned to England," Jillian finally said. "We even hired a private detective in New Orleans, but he couldn't find anything... Whatever happened to your kindred relations, one thing was certain, my child; they weren't anywhere to be found; not even a trace..." She sadly said, while thinking about the horrific implications...

After Jillian's words sank to her heart, Angela felt like she was suddenly suffocating...

She would've probably taken those millions that Eileen Hoxworth offered in a split second, if she were living in the black ghettos of New Orleans. No doubt, her "mulatto relations" were bought off. What else?

"I still want tangible proof, Jillian! I also want to know what became of my kindred, as you call them; and if I have a coloured aunt or uncle out there who has survived this… This, ordeal; this I really want to know!"

"I understand, Angela... It's your right, after all; and I'm more than willing to give you some advice on how to go about it, if you'd like to come and visit us first…"

"Really? Well, I'd appreciate that." Angela said surprised.

"To tell you the truth, Angela, I'd like to know myself…" Jillian said with great sincerity. "As my sister's life has been totally destroyed by this old family secret, I'd like nothing else than to see justice meted out; besides, my dear child, I'm a fan of 'an eye for an eye'," she firmly added, her voice suddenly hardening. "You have now in your favour the miracle of modern technology; something that we, unfortunately, didn't have at our hands thirty-two years ago; but it'll take some work on your part… First, you'll have to convince Eileen or Edmond Hoxworth to exhume Jonathan's remains, to test his DNA; then, you'll need to compare his with yours… A post-mortem paternity test and voila! We have proof!"

"Sounds like a piece of cake!" Angela nervously exclaimed, shuddering at the thought.

"Technically speaking, my child, it should be; but I sincerely doubt that the Hoxworths will simply give you access to their magnificent family crypt… There is not only their reputation at stake, my child, but an enormous sum of money as well; I'm sure you're aware… Jonathan bequeathed all of his vast fortune to your brother Edmond, and you'd be entitled to half of it, if you could irrevocably prove that you are his rightful heir; and that doesn't even count the large fortune you'd inherit when his mother died... Eileen had her own estate, you know."

Angela nervously blinked a few times. "I'll tell Edmond Hoxworth that I'm absolutely not interested in his money... I can understand his grandmother's fear of tarnishing the great family name, but this is the new millennium, and I am almost sure that Edmond can't be that prejudiced; nor that he won't keep me from learning the truth," she firmly said, while trying her best to convince herself.

"Perhaps Angela, perhaps..." Jillian said pensively, unconvinced. "I think I would pray for a judge and a good jury who are not influenced by the old racial prejudices of the South; nor by the Hoxworth name..."

"Court... Oh my God, the media will be all over this!" Angela almost shouted.

"Much to the chagrin of the great Eileen Mackenzie-Hoxworth, 'Louisiana's grand dame'. But in the end, my child, won't it be worth it?" Jillian said with a small laugh.

"Well, I suppose," Angela nervously said, shuddering at the idea of standing before a jury for the colour of her skin; for her real identity; her very soul. Then she sadly realised that she would be crudely exposed, scrutinised, analysed and judged again, for the world to see...

"Tell me something, Jillian," Angela slowly began. "What makes you so sure that this wayward gene came from the Hoxworths, and not from your side of the family?" She coldly asked, even though she somehow knew that she was climbing up the wrong tree...

The fact that Eileen Hoxworth had rapidly attempted to buy Angela's silence, was enough to convince her that the Hoxworths were privy to a costly family secret.

Even an extremely wealthy woman like Eileen Mackenzie-Hoxworth wouldn't throw around ten million dollars, if the fault was in Elisabeth's ancestry; and to think of it, the Bainbridges never owned black slaves in England, so the chance that the Negro wayward gene came from the English side of the family was extremely remote...

"Please, Angela, now that Josephine opened the door, it's your obligation to finish this and find out the whole truth; if not for yourself, then do it for the sake of your real mother! Her life was totally destroyed when she lost her husband, you, and Edmond. Two years after my poor Elisabeth was banned from the Hoxworths, I found her working in a hospice in North Carolina... She was extremely frail and emaciated, and lived in a tiny room fit only for saints or martyrs". Jillian said with a broken voice. "Her only possessions, besides the old dress she wore and the silver crucifix that hung above the excuse for a bed she slept on, were photos of her dear Jonathan and her children... My dear Angela, Elisabeth had many photographs of you as a baby." Jillian softly said. "I suppose that she kept in touch with Josephine, but she was too ashamed to seek out her own family... Like a saint, my poor sister felt the need to live a life of poverty and suffering, and she constantly blamed herself for what happened to you, my child; as well as for Jonathan's death." Jillian paused to catch her breath, to hold back her tears. "Believe me, Angela; my sister has suffered enough... Now that you understand, I hope you'll cease to judge her unfairly; and now that you know her existence, my child, I don't think she could bear losing you again… Elisabeth won't forgive herself, so you must find the strength in your heart to forgive her!" Jillian finally said with a broken voice.

An intense bitterness swelled on Angela's tongue; she could taste it now. She was paralysed, confused, and terribly ashamed. "All right then. I'll meet with Elisabeth," she bravely said, her throat tightening with nerves.

"Thank you… Thank you, Angela. You're a dear heart and I'm proud of you, my child. You'll be happy to know that you have a family with us." Jillian softly said while picturing Angela in her head. "I have my daughter, Jennifer, your cousin, and she has children of her own… In some ways, God has been good to us, Angela." Jillian said, sadly smiling. "God has given us a chance to meet one another on this earth, as well as to make amends and find the truth before it is too late. As you know, your mother is not well; and…"

"Then I will see you soon," Angela interrupted. She didn't want to hear what Jillian had to say. *God can't expect me to deal with the loss of two mothers at the same time, as well as the dark mystery of the Hoxworths…*

When Angela hung up the phone, all the violent anger and profound hatred that she'd been harbouring since her beloved Josephine told her the truth about her birth, had finally dissipated like a single cloud of mist in the desert sun. Instead, Angela felt a strange compassion for Elisabeth; a sentiment that she was not really prepared for…

She tiredly fell to the bed and sobbed. She might've stayed there all night if the voice of the ghost didn't shock her out of her devastating grief.

Angela clearly heard the manly voice. Disembodied or not, it was as sad as a mournful violin. "Mary-Elisabeth... Mary-Elisabeth... You must go to Ashington... Your mother needs you." Then the sweet scent of pipe tobacco and vetiver permeated the room; again...

Strangely enough, for the first time since her beloved Josephine died, Angela was not afraid anymore. In fact, a strange feeling of peace enveloped her, like the soft wings of an angel; her guardian angel...

Amen.

Chapter Twenty-Eight

"Ashington"

After Angela finished her third and last performance of "Petruska" in Monte Carlo, she caught the first plane from Nice to London; from there, she would take a shuttle flight to Ashington and finally meet Elisabeth...

At the little airport, Angela was greeted by Jillian and Jennifer, who were excellent representatives of "good English stock". They both had pale pinkish skin as radiant as their Queen's, and their brown, forest green and dark blue clothing left a lot to the imagination; they were definitely very proper and seemingly extremely conservative...

Jillian widely opened her arms and donned a warm smile. "Angela!" She lovingly exclaimed. "I am so happy to finally meet you, my child. We thought this day would never come; and yet, we never gave up praying; and here you are! It's simply incredible... You look so much like my sister. Doesn't she, love?" Her daughter nodded, her dark cobalt blue eyes sparkling. "Yes, mum, she does... Hello, I'm your cousin, Jennifer," She warmly added, before giving Angela a big hug.

With a linen handkerchief, Jillian was dabbing tears from the corners of her eyes and the intensity of the scene was making Angela somewhat embarrassed. It didn't make sense to her that these virtual strangers were overcome with such sincere emotion over her; and to think that they were English...

"Mum, pleeease, you promised not to cry," Jennifer softly said, tenderly wrapping her arm around Jillian's shoulder.

"I know love, I know..." Jillian softly apologised. "But I'm just a sentimental old woman." She said while drying her tears. "Now come, my dear Angela; let's get you home!" She finally exclaimed with a big tender smile.

Home? What a lovely word: home... Angela thought, puzzled.

The three of them briskly walked into the parking lot, where Jillian had parked her brand new red 'Austin Cooper'.

"No, please," Jennifer said, cutting in front of Angela, so she could sit in the back seat. "You sit up front with mum. That way she can point out the high spots of our little town."

"Yes, all five of them!" Jillian exclaimed with a little laugh. "Buckle up and prepare yourself, my child." Jillian drove the little sports car more like one would a sedan, her eyes intensely focused on the road. When they entered the old part of Ashington, she slowed down while driving over the antique cobblestone roads, before sharply turning onto Pembroke Street and parking in front of a lovely building with a wood façade that was lacquered in shiny dark forest green. Two pretty bay windows flanked the heavy front door, and above the large door hung an antique iron sign that read "The Earl Grey Tea Room".

"You live in a tearoom?" Angela asked, visibly surprised, while wondering if they were a bit on the eccentric side...

Jennifer laughed. "Sorry to disappoint you, cousin," she said, with a charming smile. "It would be quite a life-style, wouldn't it, having ones' parlour second as a public tea room... Our house, though, is at the back; but we thought we'd take you the scenic way..."

"I see," Angela said, but she didn't. Although her newfound relations seemed quite nice, she wasn't sure she understood their particular British sense of humour; after all, she was still an American...

"Are you hungry, Angela?" Jillian asked, pushing open the heavy door of the lovely tearoom.

"Not really," Angela replied, even as she was inundated with the tantalising scents coming from the large room.

"Ohhh, what a pity! Are you sure I couldn't tempt you? This is one of the oldest tea rooms in Ashington, and you won't find a better place to enjoy high tea anywhere else, my child... Your great, great, great grandparents opened it more than two centuries ago..." Jillian proudly said. "We try to keep the tradition and stick to the secret recipes of yore; of course we've refurbished and repainted to keep it sanitary, but the spirit of the place is still intact, don't you think?" Jillian joyfully smiled, demonstrating her great pride of ownership with a graceful wave of her alabaster hand that simply said "this is ours!"

"In fact, it does evoke a wonderful sense of the past..." Angela politely answered while looking around. The large wood beamed ceiling was entirely hand-painted, decorated with ivy and colourful birds, and three large brass chandeliers hung from red velvet ropes. Lovely paintings with bucolic scenes of the English countryside of the 18th century were elegantly hung on the dark cherry wood-panelled walls. The original antique long white marble pastry counter and solid oak furnishings of the same period were carved masterpieces of local craftsmanship. The little round tables were clothed in linen that perfectly matched the green carpet, and an antique cranberry red hurricane glass with a candle had been placed at the centre of each. The large cosy room was full of elderly Caucasian English women dressed with care, enjoying little English pastries and sandwiches; and of course, English tea…

"It's absolutely lovely!" Angela sincerely exclaimed while warmly smiling. "All those ladies must be so happy that you've preserved the sanctity of its old world charm."

"Yes, indeed, my dear Angela. I've been blessed to inherit it." Jillian proudly beamed. "I couldn't imagine doing anything else in life… But it is part of your birth right as well, Angela; since it was created by your ancestors; so you'll always be welcome here as one of us, my dear child." By the tone of her voice, it was obvious that she was deadly sincere…

"Well, thank you, Jillian, that's very nice of you to say," Angela softly replied, embarrassed, even though she felt more troubled by the idea than for the fact that, contrary to most places in her native American country, not a single coloured person could be seen in the place…

A pretty middle-aged Venetian blond waitress with a glowing rosy complexion slowly passed in front of Angela, smiling like an angel and smelling like a rose. She was wearing a flowery calf-length dress with a white lace collar, as well as a crisp white apron, and she was holding a large tin tray carrying a white porcelain teapot and a plate displaying an array of extremely appealing English pastries; this time, Angela felt terribly tempted…

"Well, we mustn't dilly-dally… Come, come Angela; let me show you all the rest, my dear child," Jillian warmly said, before leading the way through the large storeroom and into a spectacular country style kitchen that opened into the big house, just behind the tea room.

"This is our little house, Angela," Jillian said with great pride, smiling like a child with her lovely baby blue eyes. "My sister and I were born here… Your grandfather and great grandfather were born here as well." She lovingly said before gently taking her hand.

"Ohhh, it's absolutely lovely!" Angela sincerely exclaimed.

The ancient house had an aura of peacefulness to it, as if the house had its own spirit; as if it was reassuring, benevolent and kind…

"Our house was originally our family's farm… This was once the outskirts of Ashington; now it's the old tourist section." Jillian said with a dash of sadness. "There's a lovely garden at the back. I wouldn't sell this house for all the money in the world, my child… Since I'm too old now, I want Jennifer and William, her husband, to take over the tearoom. The house and the tea room will be theirs, when I die…" Jillian said while lowering her eyes.

"Oh, mum," Jennifer nervously exclaimed. "Stop it! Angela just arrived and you're already talking about retirement and death!"

"Ohhh, I am sorry, Angela," Jillian softly said with a sad little smile. "And you just have lost your adopted mother..." She sighed. "Elisabeth said such wonderful things about her dear Josephine, you know." She paused, letting her gaze fall on her "exotic" beautiful niece, while wondering how life could have been for her if she had been raised in a different world. Even for an instant, Jillian couldn't imagine seeing the well mannered, refined and elegant Angela Haddington living in New Orleans, in an all black neighbourhood...

"My dear Angela, we have a lovely room prepared for you upstairs," Jillian warmly said, before lovingly taking Angela's arm, visibly trying to change the subject.

"But... But I was planning to stay at a hotel," Angela protested.

"Nonsense, my child!" Jillian sweetly countered, energetically waving the thought away with a gesture of her finely tapered hand. "Now, young lady, take your bag and follow me!" It was less of an invitation than an order; an order that Angela had no choice, but to accept...

Without further protest, Angela followed Jillian into the extremely inviting living room.

There was an antique and spectacular large stone fireplace, surrounded on both sides with large crisp flowery chintz couches. They were festooned with an array of large handmade needlepoint pillows, finished with red trimming and adorable little green pompons. Then they passed through the particularly impressive library. A pair of comfortable red velvet lounge chairs had been positioned on either side of an antique sculpted wooden fireplace.

A 17th century English writing desk was tucked near a tall leaded window overlooking a picture perfect classical English garden, in multiple shades of green...

A country style bouquet of freshly cut flowers, as well as several fine books, carefully edged between a pair of lions bronze bookends, had been neatly placed on a round shiny wood table. Hundreds of antique leather-bound books filled the numerous bookcases, which covered all four walls. Each minute detail of the impressive room spoke of great tradition, as well as great respect for the past. But instead of being overwhelming, the beautiful library was peaceful; so very, very peaceful...

"This is my husband, Jeremy's, favourite room," Jillian softly explained with shining eyes. "He spends hours here, smoking his beloved pipe and reading the newspaper; or a good book... My mother; God bless her loving soul, used to tell me that my grandfather loved this room so much, that she often had to use her womanly wiles to keep him from sleeping here." She said with a girlish little laugh. "I'm truly glad that my dear Jeremy likes this room so much, because a man loitering about the house can be quite a nuisance." Jillian warmly said. "But you already know that, don't you, dear?" She softly asked with a little grin, before affectionately taking Angela by the arm again.

At that instant that seemed to last an eternity, Angela thought of Pierce...

They didn't see one another enough to have the luxury of thinking each other a "nuisance". Between her touring and his overtime at the law firm, they were lucky to spend one day a week loitering around their estate...

"By the way, Angela, do you want children?" Jillian softly asked, quite out of the blue.

Angela felt her face slightly flush. "Yes, someday. But my career; well... The right moment has not arrived yet... My husband is in no rush. Pierce has two children from a previous marriage." Angela said with a touch of embarrassment.

"Ohhh, that's wonderful... And do you do see your stepchildren often?"

"No, Jillian, unfortunately... His ex-wife doesn't seem to like sharing her offspring... I know it causes my husband a bit of grief." She said, this time embarrassed, before avoiding Jillian's eyes.

"Ohhh, what a pity, my child. Divorce certainly can leave a mess in its wake... I know that it drives me batty that I have a nephew in New Orleans who is off-limits to me; and without saying, it breaks Elisabeth's poor heart!" Jillian deeply sighed before softly taking Angela's hand again.

Jennifer rolled her eyes at Angela. "Follow me, cousin," she firmly said, turning on her heel and walking briskly down a long corridor that smelled of lemon wax, towards a large spiral wood staircase that looked as if it should be in a Jane Austen novel.

Upstairs, after passing through the third threshold, Jennifer slowly opened a massive antique wood door in a dramatic motion, revealing a beautifully feminine room entirely done in light pink and sage green. The heavy English floral chintz drapes and refined bed-coverings, as well as the celadon green striped wallpaper, were reminiscent of 'Laura Ashley'. A spectacular antique Scottish queen size canopy bed, topped with a puffy down comforter, regally stood between two high leaded windows, which overlooked the peaceful English garden. The beautiful bed faced a massive stone fireplace, flanked by an exquisite pair of multi-coloured needlepoint armchairs with matching fringed ottomans. As a final touch, a colourful Portuguese carpet, designed with garlands of large bright flowers, had been laid on the shiny wooden parquet floor...

The room was simply perfect; pure "English perfection"...

"How do you like your room, my dear child?" Jillian asked with a warm smile.

"Well, it's not only beautiful; it's enormous!" Angela joyously exclaimed, quite impressed.

"Your mother and I were born in this very room, my child... I only changed the wallpaper and linens a few years ago; otherwise, it is exactly how it was when my great-grandmother decorated it... I'm hoping that sleeping in this particular bedroom will give you a sense of your true heritage, my dear Angela." Jillian emotionally said, visibly trying not to cry again.

"If you're lucky, cousin, tonight, you'll be haunted by the family ghosts..." Jennifer chimed. "You wouldn't believe how many Americans come to England, just to stay in old houses like ours, as if a ghost would never enter a modern home equipped with high speed internet!" She laughed, visibly delighted.

Suddenly, Angela's expression became anxious. "Angela," Jennifer said again, bemused at her cousin's reaction. "You know that I'm only joking, right? Surely you aren't afraid of ghosts?"

Jillian shot her daughter a stern look and quickly changed the subject, before walking to the antique bed and pointing to the massive dark wood headboard. "If you look closely, my dear child, you'll see the monogram of our family carved there. It's dated 1732." She proudly said before scrutinising Angela's tormented eyes.

How strange it is to stand in the room where my real mother was born; when only just a few short weeks before, I didn't even know I had a white English mother...

"Let me show you something else," Jillian warmly said, as she walked towards a massive antique Tudor commode that displayed a collection of old photographs in precious English silver frames.

"This is Mary and Charles Addlesby... They are your grandparents, Angela. This picture was taken on their wedding day."

Angela carefully studied the old black and white photo, feeling now quite perturbed...

Mary was dressed in a long straight ivory satin dress, embroidered with seed pearls and little silk flowers. From her head, a long lace veil hung to the floor, secured by a crown of white silk flowers.

Mary was lovingly staring at her husband, an extremely handsome man.

Charles Addlesby had bright and clear intelligent eyes, a sensual mouth that looked as if it smiled easily, and thick wavy sandy hair. Without a doubt, the Addlesbys formed a handsome couple.

Jillian showed Angela the rest of the family portraits, taking the time to explain "who was who", as well as how Angela was related to them. They were all blood relatives; all very pale skinned Caucasian; all very English...

"I hope that seeing this side of your family will help you feel more at home, my child," Jillian warmly said before putting a loving arm around Angela's shoulder.

"Well, I must admit that it feels quite strange..." Angela admitted with an embarrassed little smile, while still avoiding Jillian's inquisitive eyes.

"Well, my dear Angela, I can only imagine... But here is the particular photo I promised to show you; the one of Jonathan Hoxworth; your father..." Jillian pointed out, observing her reaction.

Angela slightly hesitated before looking at the picture.

My father... It was true that Jonathan Hoxworth looked "vaguely familiar"; and yet, she couldn't place him...

What Jillian had told Angela was certainly valid, because the similarities were too many to blame on coincidence. Just as Jillian had said, the shape of Angela's mouth, as well as her eyes, could have been cast from the same mould, and the small beauty mark was situated at exactly the same place as her own.

Could it be? Angela nervously thought, while feeling now the violent beating of her heart.

"So you see, my dear child," Jillian softly, but firmly said. "You will certainly forgive your mother now, won't you? The Hoxworths have borne their share of tragedy almost as if they've been cursed; and I'm quite glad, my dear that my poor Elisabeth finally got away from them... But you, my dear Angela, you are only beginning to find out the truth, and I fear that your journey will lead you to knowledge that you might not want to hear, my child; things that you will not accept... And yet, the truth, they say, sets us free at the end." Jillian emotionally said while now avoiding Angela's eyes.

"What a shame that this handsome man killed himself," Angela sadly said, her eyes still focused on the man who ceased to be, because her skin wasn't pale enough to be logically related to him, or his beautiful wife...

"It was only one drama in a series of them." Jillian sombrely noted "as far as I can remember, my child, your grandfather Hoxworth died while cleaning his gun, and his older brother died when he was just a babe, only a month old; he suffocated himself with his own pillow... Isn't that something?" She sadly said, visibly surprised. "As for Eileen, your rich American grandmother, she lost her only daughter, whose name was "Angelica Aurora Maria", just after the poor girl was born..." She sadly said, lowering her eyes. "The Hoxworths were an interesting family, but wealthy as sin. As for your poor mother, Elisabeth was so young and so naïve, as well as unfortunately totally love struck, that she didn't know what she was marrying into..." Jillian sadly said again, while slowly moving her head...

"Mum?" Jennifer interrupted. She watched as a dark shadow crossed Angela's face, as she nervously listened to the Hoxworth family drama.

It isn't just fear... That woman is angry! Jennifer thought. "Mum, why don't we leave Angela in her room to rest a while, before we head out to the hospital to visit Aunt Elisabeth?" She softly said while firmly taking her mother by the hand.

"I'm fine," Angela mildly protested, even though she was in fact deeply troubled.

"Travelling is hard, my child." Jillian said. "Please, make yourself at home. Unpack your things; and once you're done, we'll treat you to some home made shepherd's pie and a delicious bread pudding." She warmly said with a disarming smile.

"Perhaps a hot bath would be nice," Angela said; feeling suddenly extremely tired.

"Of course it will, dear," Jillian smiled, before giving Angela a warm hug. "If you need anything, just say so; and pleeease, my child, take your time."

Ten minutes later, in the cosy pink and green bathroom, Angela let the warm water soothe her muscles.

Jillian and Jennifer had taken care of everything... She thought while analysing the room, before she closed her eyes, trying to relax for a while.

Twenty minutes later, when she emerged from the tub, she felt renewed and a lot calmer. Cuddling herself in the long plush pink terry cloth robe that was heated by the bathroom furnace, she finally smiled. But when she entered the bedroom, the smell of sweet pipe tobacco and vetiver was again in the air, and she could even see traces of smoke lingering, as if the smoker had just left the room...

Jillian said her husband smoked a pipe... Perhaps he'd arrived home from work and had wandered into this room; but that would be highly inappropriate...

Suddenly ill at ease, Angela cautiously looked around the room. Everything looked somehow normal, just the way she recalled it; the exception was the photo of Jonathan, which had fallen to the floor, but far from the commode.

It couldn't have leaped over there on its own...

Angela shuddered. She felt that strange chill again; the same one she felt when the ghostly apparition appeared to her that morning in London.

I'm not alone in this room... There is something, or someone, in here with me... I can feel it! She thought, frightened.

Being extremely careful, Angela picked up the precious silver frame from the floor, before she anxiously stared at the image; the image of her strange father.

Jonathan's clear eyes seemed to smile; a sad smile, but a smile nonetheless...

Angela delicately returned the old photograph to its rightful place, before she slowly scanned the room, trying to figure out where the scent came from; but she couldn't make heads or tails of it, so she looked back at the picture.

Suddenly, Jonathan's photo seemed strangely alive, his handsome features becoming almost three-dimensional. Angela walked to the left, and his eyes followed her; then she walked to the right, and still, they were trained upon her, those now familiar saddened eyes...

I'm going crazy... I can feel it!

Angela took a deep breath, trying her best to remain calm. It wasn't as if she were afraid of Jonathan, afraid of "her father"...

Angela simply smiled back at the photo, while sending a positive vibration towards the picture; then the scent of the now quite familiar sweet tobacco and vetiver became even stronger, as if someone, or "something", were really in the bedroom with her...

"It's him", Angela calmly thought, for the first time her lips curving into a loving smile *"and he's trying to tell me something. But what?"*

Angela's female instincts told her that it wouldn't be long before she found out the answer; not long at all, then the picture smiled again...

Chapter Twenty-Nine

"Ashington"

It was close to three pm by the time Angela, Jillian and Jennifer arrived at St. Patrick's Hospital...

When they stepped into the aseptic small room, Elisabeth was resting. She was linked to a heart monitor, and a middle age redheaded nurse with a pale translucent skin, was calmly making some notations in her medical file.

While softly caressing Elisabeth's greying hair as she spoke, Jillian lovingly whispered her sister's name. Slowly, Elisabeth opened her pale blue eyes and put on a weak smile, when she recognised her sister and niece; but when her tired gaze fell on the beautiful Angela, she reached out for her hand...

Without hesitation, Angela took Elisabeth's hand and felt her heart melt.

For the first time, Angela truly recognised her own face in Elisabeth's, without being blinded by hate.

"We'll leave you two alone for a while," Jillian softly said. "I'm sure you have some important things to discuss." She added with a loving smile, while taking her daughter by the hand.

Despite her age, Elisabeth's lavender blue eyes still gleamed with a certain intensity; but an ocean of profound pain, as well as a never-ending sorrow, seemed mysteriously trapped in them...

There was a strange ethereal air about Elisabeth Addlesby-Hoxworth, as if she was only holding on to the bonds of the earth by a fragile gossamer thread. Her life was a slow silent death caused by a painful heartbreak; one that only her daughter's love could redeem...

For a while, feeling slightly embarrassed, the two women simply looked at each other in silence, until Elisabeth began to slowly tell Angela her side of the tragic story.

Two years after Edmond's birth, Elisabeth and Jonathan wanted another child, but it wasn't easy to get pregnant the second time. Once before, Elisabeth gave birth to a stillborn son; then many years passed. By the time Elisabeth became pregnant for the third time with Angela, they had lost all hope and thought that it was God's will that Edmond remain an only child...

Elisabeth and Jonathan felt doubly blessed when she made it to term with their new beautiful baby girl.

Like all of the Hoxworth women before her, Elisabeth gave birth in the birthing room of "La Rêveuse", with the family doctor's assistance. A few minutes after Angela was born, the heavy curtains were drawn and the murmuring began; then the black maids became strangely silent; deadly silent...

At first, Elisabeth didn't understand what was really happening, until the nurse opened Angela's swaddling garments and showed her that her baby's skin had slightly darkened; then the doctor's face became grave; extremely grave...

"I can still remember his words," Elisabeth nervously told Angela. "She's not white! She's not white!" The nurse almost shouted. "Then, everyone looked at me as if I'd committed a crime... They all looked at you as if you were a monster, a sort of demon! Even though you were smiling and truly beautiful, my child, nobody wanted to look at you anymore... I remember that Eileen and Jonathan silently left the birthing room, and less than a minute later, I heard them talking loudly through the closed doors... I remember that Eileen screamed 'She's a Negro bastard!' And I cried... If it wasn't for my dear maid, the sweet Josephine, who stayed all the time by my side, holding my hand, I would've been entirely alone..." Elisabeth tiredly said, before she began to silently cry, her hands shaking like the last leaves in a late fall storm.

With each of Elisabeth's painful words, Angela felt her poisonous anger dangerously growing.

How could they?! Monsters!!!

For the first time, Angela was infuriated and appalled to realise that the poor Elisabeth, her mother, wasn't even given an opportunity to prove her innocence. The terrible verdict had been coldly decreed by her mother in law, the rich and powerful Eileen Mackenzie-Hoxworth; and obviously, no one had the courage to argue with her; not even her only son...

221

"Oh, my child, don't be angry at your poor father," Elisabeth softly urged, as if she could read Angela's troubled mind. "He simply believed his dear mother... My dear Jonathan trusted and deeply respected her; Jonathan wasn't a bad man..." She finally said with a loving smile, while picturing him in her troubled mind.

Nervously, Angela nodded and sniffed the air. The tobacco and vetiver scent was there again, and she strangely felt as if she was being watched by someone, from behind her shoulders...

Elisabeth was visibly exhausted from telling the horrible story. She had closed her eyes that were now full of tears, but her hand still clutched Angela's; somehow, there was still strength in the woman...

Angela sadly watched her genetic mother resting, while the story viciously circled about her mind...

The more Angela thought about it; the angrier she became...

In her entire life, Angela had never felt so much poisonous hatred, and it was high time that someone stood up to these pretentious Hoxworths, and stopped them from playing with people's lives, as if they were merely pawns on their chessboard.

In a nano-second of intense lucidity, Angela realised that she would have to meet her strange grandmother, Eileen Mackenzie-Hoxworth "face-to-face" and finally confront her, once and for all; yet, somewhere within the deep recesses of her tormented mind, Angela also felt that there was much more to the story, and also that the whole dirty truth would be life-transforming; as well as deeply frightening...

Chapter Thirty

"Milan"

Italy

At Milan's world famous "La Scala", with more gusto than ever before Angela masterfully danced *"Sleeping Beauty"*, thrilling the audience with an incredibly flawless performance...

That particular evening, it was as if a magical fire was burning inside Angela's being; a strange fire energising her, truly propelling her like a goddess.

When Boris, who played the difficult role of the Prince, kissed Angela's red lips before he took her in his arms, the Russian star dancer could feel the palpable energy emanating from her body like never before. Never, in his entire career, had he felt anything so electrifying; and found it extremely bizarre, as well as quite frightening...

After the "grand finale", the transported Italian audience gave a long-standing ovation, shouting "Brava! Brava! Brava," giving even more energy to Angela with their tangible adoration.

Angela elegantly curtseyed, an ethereal vision in her white ballet skirt that was sparkling like a starry light. As she graciously bowed, again and again, warm tears of joy suddenly blurred her vision; then the air around her strangely became imbued with the scent of amber and violet: Josephine's scent...

That same evening, Pierce had arrived in Milan to spend the weekend with Angela. When he walked into her bedroom suite, she had just finished her shower and was wrapped in a long white terry cloth bath towel, her skin damp, glowing and soft as a newborn baby.

Pierce lovingly took Angela in his arms, and then kissed her with a passion that she hadn't felt for some time.

"What was that for, my darling?" She sensually asked, raising her eyebrows in surprise.

"That was because I've missed you more than I can say, my love." Pierce lovingly said, before kissing her neck.

"Hummm... I can tell!" Angela ironically smiled, then she pulled back a bit as she felt his rock hard erection pressing against her crotch. "Do you want to take a shower and order something to eat, darling?" She asked, before giving him a soft tender kiss.

"Not really, my love... But what do you say we forget it for the time being and get down to what I really want to do?" His eyes wolfishly glinted as he firmly grabbed her extremely thin waist.

"Meaning?" She asked with an adorable smile.

"I want to make love to you now, Angela. Nothing else in the world will satisfy me."

"Well, Mr. Haddington, that sounds fine to me." She softly said before she kissed him again; this time lovingly wrapping her slender arms around his neck.

Pierce grinned and pressed himself against her crotch again...

"In that case, my dear Mrs. Haddington, I demand that you prove to me how much you missed me, too." He sensually said, smiling like a wolf, before kissing her passionately.

Slowly and teasingly, Angela undid the corner of her bath towel, then she tauntingly began to reveal her gleaming body. Pierce admired the striking contrast of her golden skin against the bright white towel, as always amazed at the magnificence of his wife's exceptional body...

With awe, he drank in the vision of her small and firm perky breasts, her smooth straight shoulders, and her incredible long beautifully chiselled legs. Like a repentant sinner in front of a sacred altar, Pierce fell to his knees and lovingly wrapped his arms around her waspish waist, before he laid his head against her toned, soft golden belly...

Again and again, Pierce passionately kissed her sensual tummy; each burning kiss a symbol of his sincere love; then he slowly rose to his feet and gazed into her beautiful gold-flecked greenish eyes, before their lips moved together, as if attracted by powerful magnets. His tongue caught hers, and his large hands sensually caressed her tempting curves.

With total abandon, Pierce fervently kissed the divine Angela, until, unable to wait any longer, he powerfully lifted her impressive body into his arms and proudly carried her to the elegant white king size bed, as if he were a warrior, and she, his prize catch. Then he carefully put Angela on the bed, and he quickly threw off his clothes. Spreading her long slender legs wide open, Pierce laid himself atop Angela; then, looking deep into her loving eyes, he thrust his large manhood deep inside her, to make her his again...

At first, Angela softly moaned, before she lovingly wrapped her chiselled limbs around his muscular torso, as to return Pierce's intense passion. She never needed his love as badly as tonight, and Pierce could tangibly feel her need.

Foreplay could wait; Pierce knew Angela wanted him now!

Within moments, the intense power of their passionate lovemaking seemed to have completely fused their bodies together. Angela and Pierce seemed to have become one being, commingled by the invisible force of their devouring passion, rocking back and forth with the effortless rhythm of their intense love-making; until a few moments later, unable to hold back any longer, they shared one of the most powerful climaxes of their life in an ejaculation of joy.

Total release...

The addictive afterglow deliciously percolated in their minds, enveloping their senses and dissolving the mental and physical tension that had built up in the past weeks.

For a long time, Pierce and Angela remained lovingly entwined in each other's arms, continuing to caress and stroke each other, while whispering sincere loving words.

Only much later, Pierce and Angela reluctantly pulled themselves from the warm comforting bed, to have a romantic dinner in town.

That particular evening, the weather was unusually balmy and Milan had much to offer; yes indeed…

Chapter Thirty-One

"Milan"

The next sunny morning, Angela and Pierce leisurely remained in bed, making love repeatedly, just as they did when they first fell in love...

They didn't get up until almost noon, and after many cups of fine Italian espresso, they finally decided to do some serious shopping in town.

The sky in Milan was exceptionally blue that day, with only one or two lonely clouds that marred the pure monotone canvas. The air was crisp, fresh and gloriously bracing...

Like newlyweds, Pierce and Angela walked arm-in-arm, fully immersed in each other's magical presence. When passers-by saw the handsome couple, they often smiled, perhaps reminding them of times gone past, when they too had experienced the wonderful lightness of love...

Pierce and Angela strolled along the fashionable streets near the imposing church of 'Il Duomo', in the heart of Milan. Along the way, as was their ritual, they purchased expensive gifts for each other. At the 'Hermenegildo Zegna' store, Angela bought for her beloved Pierce, six beautiful pastel cotton shirts with six assorted silk ties; as well as five pairs of gorgeous handmade shoes. Later on, in another elegant store, a stunning multi-coloured 'Missoni' knitted dress caught Pierce's eye…

Half an hour later, they left the store with the dress, as well as three gorgeous designer hand bags, and eight pairs of extremely sexy Italian high heels to show off Angela's spectacular ballerina legs…

Almost three hours and 27.000 Euros later, laden with a large amount of expensive packages, Pierce and Angela finally stopped for a late lunch at 'La Tavola', a picturesque restaurant just behind the monumental church.

The little quaint Italian restaurant was full of life, and as soon as they stepped in; Angela caught the eye of almost every man in the place. A few minutes later, when she sat down, one of the men raised his glass of wine and joyously made a toast. "To the most beautiful woman who brings sunshine to our hearts!" He said in Italian; then another man also raised his glass and toasted Pierce. "You're a lucky man, my friend!" He exclaimed with a big smile. "Your wife is very beautiful," he said, admiringly, as if he were a true connoisseur.

"Well, darling, it would seem that you've created quite an impression today…" Pierce proudly said, beaming while putting his arm in a possessive way around her lovely waist.

Angela blushed and it was obvious that she didn't like attention; in fact, the gawking men always made her feel like prey…

"Pierce, do you think that my dress is too sexy?" She worriedly asked.

Angela was wearing a superb long glove fitting black jersey turtleneck dress, accented with a large silver buckled belt and a pair of extremely stylish high heel black suede boots; all 'Gucci' creations...

"Not at all, my love," Pierce tenderly reassured her, while placing another possessive hand around her fragile shoulder. "Your dress is just fine, my love! It's simply not your fault that it can't entirely hide the shape of that luscious body of yours." He added with a sensual grin, beaming again...

"Ohhh, I shouldn't have worn this dress today... I forgot that we're in Italy. The men here are just so... responsive!" Angela uncomfortably said, blushing, while lowering her lovely eyes.

"Oh come on, darling! You can't wear sweat pants and baggy sweaters simply because you're in Italy; after all, my love, you're with me today!" Pierce exclaimed with an irritating, but quite charming macho smile.

"You're right," Angela softly said, grateful that her husband was by her side.

In some Latin and in most Arabic countries, a beautiful woman has little freedom without a man to protect her... She nervously thought, feeling like prey again; an extremely beautiful prey...

When the Italian waiter arrived, Pierce ordered a large plate of delicious "antipasti", as well as an 'Osso Buco', and a bottle of excellent 'Chianti' wine from Tuscany.

"Do you remember that little restaurant in Venice, where we had that delicious Osso Buco, my love?" Pierce softly asked while lovingly taking her hand in his.

Angela drew a blank...

"Near the 'Piazza San Marco', my love... I think it was called 'La Bussola'." He said with a tender smile, before sensually kissing her hand.

"Oh yes, I remember now... They made the most wonderful 'Risotto ai Frutti di Mare'." Angela said, softly smiling.

"Exactly, my love! We had just made love for hours that morning and you were extremely hungry," he sensually reminded her, before he reached for her knee, the wolf in him glinting again...

"You don't forget anything, do you?" She blushed, embarrassed, lowering her eyes again.

He softly took her hands in his again. "Not when it comes to making love with you, my love... How could I? Have you already forgotten?" His beautiful dark blue sapphire eyes were expectant and full of love.

"No," Angela almost whispered, as the waiter silently brought the bottle of Chianti.

Pierce sensually smiled. "I think we should make a toast, my love."

"To what?" She asked, as she raised an eyebrow.

"But to us! To our five years of blessed marriage and all the many years to come... To that and to all the great happiness you have brought to my life, my love. You have made me a very happy man, Angela; do you know that?" His intriguing eyes shone like the Caribbean Sea under a full moonlight.

"And I'm an extremely happy woman," Angela lovingly whispered, before softly kissing his sensual lips.

"So, my love, let's drink then to our wonderful life together... And to my hopes, that soon, you'll be able to take a break from your career, so that we can have children." He tenderly said, before kissing her hand again.

Angela looked at him in total surprise. "But Pierce... I... I thought you didn't want any more children... You told me that Patricia and Robert were enough, no?" She asked, visibly surprised.

"Well, so I thought, my love..." He softly said, while remembering the visit he had with his Scottish parents just before arriving in Milan. Surprisingly, his ex-wife, the aloof and elegant, ash blonde "Barbara", along with their two beautiful children was there. The crafty Barbara had, little by little, steered the conversation to Angela; then almost blamed her for breaking up their perfect marriage...

Pierce's own children had even confessed that they were somehow ashamed of their famous step-mother, simply because she was not white, but "a mulatto"...

Even after Barbara and their children left, things didn't calm down. Pierce's mother, the extremely refined Cecilia Haddington, told him that although she "quite liked" her new very talented daughter-in-law, it was true that Angela was not of the same class as "dear Barbara"...

To this day, Cecilia had often continued to give her ex-daughter-in-law expensive gifts for her birthday and for Christmas; while presenting Angela with much simpler things, as if she didn't know the difference between "couture quality" and 'K-Mart' supermarket.

"Angela wasn't raised in luxury like we were, my son..." His mother sharply remarked. "She's not the type to wear expensive things, or fine crocodile handbags; in fact, where she comes from, they eat alligator..." Cecilia dryly joked. But Pierce was not amused; not amused at all...

Pierce took a sip of Chianti and tried to push the ugly scene out of his head.

"But I really want to have children with you, my love; in spite of the fact that I may be a grandfather soon." He grinned, before softly kissing her hand again.

"So, you're not worried that our children might end up being near in age to your grandchildren?" Angela seriously asked, while intensely scanning his eyes.

"I guess not... I mean, it's not like they'll be raised in the same house," he said with a little laugh. "So what do you think, darling?" He tenderly asked, while lovingly looking into her tormented eyes.

"Well, you know that I've always dreamed of having children with you, Pierce... But we'll have to postpone it, until I've completed my contract with the royal ballet company... I don't think we want me "pregnant and being sued" simultaneously, do we?"

"I know, darling, I know… I just hope that before you sign a new contract, you'll be kind enough to take a break, to give us our first child." He warmly said with real love in his sparkling eyes.

"I'll be honoured and happy to carry your child, Pierce," Angela almost whispered, before she softly kissed him on the lips. She was melting inside…

"On that day, you'll make me the happiest man in the world, my love!" He exclaimed with a big smile before joyously kissing her hands.

After this, Angela and Pierce kissed so tenderly that it seemed as if all the people in the restaurant had suddenly vanished, and if the chattering of conversation had transformed into "heavenly music"…

"Amore, amore, amore," a young handsome Italian man joyously sang, borrowing the classic melody made famous by the great Italian diva, the divine "Mina".

The waiter came back with a large plate of antipasti; then Pierce and Angela feasted on prosciutto, roasted eggplant, goat cheese in virgin olive oil, large black Italian olives, as well as fresh asparagus with a delicious creamy lemon sauce…

"Pierce, I want to tell you something about my mother," Angela said, after she'd finished eating.

"You mean Josephine?"

"No, my darling; I mean Elisabeth Hoxworth…" She softly said, slightly embarrassed.

"So, what about her?" Pierce hesitantly asked. He'd never heard Angela refer to her genetic mother, as her "mother" before…

"Well, I've misjudged her," she said embarrassed, while lowering her eyes. "I never gave her a chance and I feel truly awful about it; especially now that I know she's telling the truth, no matter how strange it seems."

"Telling the truth about what, darling?" Pierce asked, visibly surprised, while looking deep into her eyes.

"About my birth... As strange as it seems, Pierce, I truly think that my genetic father is Jonathan Hoxworth, and I am sure now that I'm not a bastard; and also that my mother didn't give me away because I was the product of an adulterous affair she had with a black man." Angela seriously said, surprising herself with her own words...

"I'm really sorry, Angela," Pierce calmly said, knowingly. "I know that it's extremely hard for you, my darling; but you need to remember that who your father was, or was not, doesn't really affect who you are now, my love."

"Yes it does, Pierce. But that's not the point. The point is that my genetic mother is not lying! How could Elisabeth lie to me when she really thought that she was dying; so what did she have to gain? She swore before God that I was the legitimate daughter of her husband, and I truly believe her now; especially since I had a closer look at Jonathan Hoxworth's picture." Angela firmly said, while not avoiding his inquisitive eyes.

"Well, I understand, my darling; but nevertheless, it does seem somewhat incredible, no?" He calmly said, visibly unconvinced.

"Nevertheless, Pierce, it could very well be a bad trick that Mother Nature played on me." She seriously said, annoyed.

"You mean "the rogue gene theory"... That the Negro gene actually skipped more than five generations... What are the chances? Really?" He doubtfully asked, opening wide his eyes. It was apparent to Angela that he didn't really believe her story.

"The more I think of it, Pierce; the more I'm convinced... Deep down, I can feel it now!" She firmly countered, even more annoyed.

"I hope for your sake that it's the truth, my love." He softly said, still unconvinced.

"And I hope for my mother's sake that it is... After all, Pierce, she's the one who's had her life devastated by all this tragedy! I've lived a normal life in comparison to her." Angela nervously said feeling deeply revolted.

"If that's what you think, then what this woman has endured is simply awful." He flatly said, feeling slightly annoyed that she was spoiling his romantic mood.

"Exactly! And this is why I'm making it my mission now to clear her name, because I also want to give her the chance to see her son Edmond, so that she can find some kind of peace before she dies... I hope that it's not too late to give her that." Angela sadly said, feeling deeply perturbed by that last thought.

Pierce took Angela's hands in his again, before looking deep again in her tormented eyes. "I hope you succeed, darling. And I also hope that the Hoxworths won't try to prevent you from achieving your goal... They have a lot to lose, you know," he said in his lawyer's voice, thinking of the many important consequences that his wife's

RACE. THE COLOUR OF SHAME

actions might have upon the Hoxworths life and their honourable reputation; as well as the mixed reaction of their extremely upscale American entourage…

"I don't know why, but I think that I'm now much stronger than they are… We're stronger than that, Pierce," she resolutely said, before sadly lowering her eyes again.

As Pierce ordered coffee, Angela excused herself and went to the powder room. She was touching up her light make-up, when her cell phone rang in her little bamboo handle black 'Gucci' handbag.

The call was from London; but it was an unfamiliar number…

"Hello, Angela," the sensual voice of a young woman chimed. "How is your little romantic "tête-à-tête" with your handsome husband coming along? Having a good time, sweetie?"

While Angela was still trying to identify the caller, she suddenly felt taken aback by the strange question…

"Excuse me?" She dryly said, feeling tense again. "Who is this exactly? I don't recall your voice."

"Well, my dear Angela, you can call me your biggest fan if you want to, but for the moment, my name is quite unimportant… What should be of utmost interest to you now is "where" your handsome husband spent the night before he thoughtfully came to visit you in Milan… If you think that your beloved Pierce slept in your marital bed, you are wrong, sweetie; very wrong…" The woman slowly said her voice as sweet as pure sugar cane…

"Who are you and how did you get my number?" Angela worriedly asked.

"Oh, sweetie, pleeease... You're asking all the wrong questions; focus, focus, focus! Now sweetie, who do you think your dear Pierce spent the night with? He is a wonderful lover, you know... Ohhh, silly me; but of course, you're already aware of that!" The woman cackled. "Well, I must be off, sweetie. Ta-ta!"

And with those last stupid words, the line was dead; and so was Angela's heart...

Chapter Thirty-Two

"London"

Quite glad to be back home, the handsome Pierce Haddington quickly paid the cabdriver, giving him a good tip; then he rapidly unlocked the door and went straight upstairs to his bedroom...

Pierce removed his navy blue 'Burberry' raincoat and hat, then quickly undressed and put on a pair of perfectly pressed pale blue cotton pyjamas, while feeling extremely tired. He was just about to get into his comfortable bed, when he noticed a flashing red light on his answering machine; two messages...

Pierce rapidly pressed the button, hoping that it would be Angela; even though he didn't know how many more of her strange nightmares he could bare to listen to. He simply wanted to forget about everything having to do with "otherworldly events" and get their lives back to normal. Hopefully, a baby would do the trick...

But it wasn't Angela; it was the extremely sensual Rose-Mary Bernhart...

"Hello, Pierce. It's ten past eight, and I'm home." She softly said. "I thought you might want to have dinner with me... Somewhere cosy and intimate? Give me a call. I miss you, lover boy!"

As always, Rose Mary's voice was tempting, breathy and languorous. Pierce felt his heart race as he listened to the second message.

"Hello, big boy, it's me again! Quarter after ten and you're still not home... Ohhh, what a pity! I'm here all alone." She said with a girlish voice, "if you come back before midnight, give me a call, lover boy. I miss you, you know." She more seriously said...

It was close to midnight. Pierce thought of going to bed without returning the temptress call, but a little voice told him to do otherwise. He nervously dialled the number, surprised that he'd already memorised it. *Well, it's an easy number...* He thought, trying not to feel guilty.

"Hello, Rose-Mary." He nervously said, as his voice deepened, and his muscles slightly tensed.

"So, there you are; at last! I was worried about you... Was your flight delayed? You didn't answer your cell." She said, slightly displeased.

"Sorry, Rose-Mary, but I forgot to turn it back on... You know how they insist that you turn all electronic devices off, while airborne," he awkwardly explained, wondering why he was suddenly feeling so guilty.

"Well, your mind must've been elsewhere, my dear Pierce," she softly reproached. "But you've been on my mind all day, my darling… I can't seem to stop thinking about what a wonderful time we had, before you left me all alone and traipsed off to Milan…" She forlornly said, while sensually twirling her long lustrous hair around her index finger.

Before Pierce could rationally think, the words slipped off his tongue. "Neither can I, Rose-Mary"; then he bit his tongue…

"Really?" She breathily said. "I'd like to try to repeat it soon, down to each and every minute detail…" She purred.

Feeling embarrassed, Pierce fiddled with his gold wedding ring, too flustered to respond.

"So tell me, lover boy," the tone of her voice was now sultry and extremely confident, "what are you doing at the moment?"

"Well, I'm simply going to bed. I'm beat," he flatly said, before looking at his night stand watch.

"At this early hour? That won't do at all…" Her voice was pure undiluted "femme fatale"; sexy as a siren in hell, and just as hot…

"But I've got to be at work early tomorrow morning and…"

"Well, I know that, silly!" She stopped him in his tracks, "but six hours of sleep is plenty, for a man as virile as you… Come on, big boy; you know that I'm right." She purred again.

"Normally, yes," Pierce defensively said. "But the travelling drained me. Believe me, I'm unusually tired." He flatly said, slightly annoyed.

"Unusually tired? Oh, Pierce, I wonder why? You poor little thing… What you really need in fact, is an emergency house call

from the beautiful woman with the best trained hands in London..."
She sensually said, softening her voice. "I'll remove every kink
from your neck and caress every gorgeous muscle of your back and
legs... But that's not all, my darling; a man like you needs much more
than even the most artful hands..." She purred. "No, hands aren't
enough for a handsome man like you; so I'm going to give you "Rose-
Mary's VIP treatment" and transform my entire gorgeous body into
a pleasure device; just for you..." She purred again. "Every luscious
silky inch of me will be at your entire service, big boy... Just imagine
my big delicious firm breasts springing from my lacy bra and slowly
travelling down the length of your tired back, as my little tongue
licks and dances over your zones of delight," she said with a moan.
"Remember that place you nastily manoeuvred me to the last time
we made love, big boy? My tongue is already beginning to tango..."

Pierce felt all his blood flow to his groin, as he sensually
pictured the temptress' creamy white skin, as well as her firm
buttocks and voluptuous breasts; so soft, so feminine...

In many ways, the beautiful Rose-Mary Bernhart could've
been Angela's polar opposite. His wife was as magnificent as a
wild cat, every muscle toned to perfection; while the voluptuous
Rose-Mary was like a ripe peach, over-flowing and juicy; so soft, so
squeezable, so wicked...

"So, lover boy, what do you think?" She sensually asked.

"It truly sounds wonderful, Rose-Mary; but it won't happen
tonight... I'm sorry, sweet heart, but I'm truly exhausted." He
sincerely said, while putting one hand over his steel hard sex tool...

"Why?" She nervously asked; her annoyance palpable. "After all, you spent the weekend relaxing, didn't you?! Unless, of course, you spent all your energy satisfying your adorable little wife... Is that the case, lover boy?" She dryly asked.

"Oh, come on, Rose-Mary! It's not fair to ask me that type of question." Pierce nervously said, also feeling annoyed.

"Why not? Aren't we "close friends", my dear Pierce?" Her voice was a purr again.

"Yes... Yes, we are; but that's not the type of question that friends ask, my dear." He nervously said.

"Well, let's say then that we're very, very special friends... So tell me, lover boy, how many times did you fuck your lovely wife this weekend?" She coyly asked, firmly waiting for his answer.

"Rose-Mary, pleeease!!! I don't want to talk about that," Pierce said, terribly embarrassed, while slightly raising his voice.

"Why not, lover boy? It's fun, no? But if you're too tired to come over to my place, then you can at least entertain me for a while over the phone, don't you think?" She sensually asked. "Let's compromise... So tell me, lover boy, how many times did you really fuck that pretty bitch? Did you push deep and hard? I want all the juicy details; I'm listening..."

An angel passed, blushing...

Chapter Thirty-Three

"Ashington"

As a sad pale moon slowly rose in the sky, Elisabeth stood happily in her bedroom, engaged in a loving conversation with her beloved deceased husband...

That night, Elisabeth was flushed with excitement, because it had been a long time since she had something special to tell the great love of her life.

"Jonathan, my love, our daughter called me tonight," she slowly began, her voice serene and placid. "Angela has taken the task of being our champion and she is going to find proof that I wasn't unfaithful to you, my love." She paused, as if she were awaiting his answer. "Oh, yes, my sweet love, I know that you know that, but our son doesn't believe it; and neither does your mother... When our dear Edmond finds out, he'll have to forgive the grudge he bears against me, and I hope that I'll finally be accepted by your family and be able to see our son again; and when the time comes, I hope that I'll be buried beside you in the Hoxworth family crypt, my dear love...

I'm thrilled!" Elisabeth exclaimed, as warm tears of joys slowly fell from her tired eyes. "Oh, my love, our daughter is so beautiful and kind..." She softly said, smiling. "So, please, Jonathan, my love, do whatever you can to help her succeed." She paused for a moment. "God has finally answered all my prayers and for the first time since you left me, my love, I have started to feel alive. Now I have real hope, because I can feel that I am no longer alone... Ohhh Jonathan, my love, please help our poor child and stand by her side night and day, because she will need your protection now. With your help, my love, I know that we'll win this battle; and very soon, I'll be finally able to return to New Orleans and see our dear son... He's all grown up now. I wonder if he looks like you?" Elisabeth softly said, but her heart ached once again when she thought of her son...

"Please, my love, protect our dear Edmond, too. Make sure everything goes well for our son. I need the two of them so much, Jonathan; so much..." She finally said with a broken voice.

With a deep sigh, Elisabeth crossed herself, before she fervently prayed on her knees.

"Oh my Lord, please watch again over the soul of my beloved husband, Jonathan Hoxworth. And watch over our beloved children, too... I thank you again, my Lord, for giving me back my daughter, Mary-Elisabeth," Elisabeth whispered, referring to Angela by the name she'd given her when she was born. Why Josephine decided to change Angela's name, was still a mystery to her. "In your mercy, Dear Lord, you have answered my prayers," she finished, feeling deeply moved by mixed emotions.

After crossing herself, she switched off the night table's light and lovingly whispered, "Good night, my dear Jonathan. Good night, my love."

As Elisabeth snuggled under the covers, she beatifically smiled.

Jonathan was in the room with her; she could feel his benevolent presence...

Elisabeth could smell now his fine French vetiver cologne, as well as just the slightest tinge of sweet tobacco.

Elisabeth smiled again, while thinking that her beloved Jonathan always refrained from smoking in their bedroom; out of courtesy to her...

"Sleep well, my love," she whispered again, hugging "his" pillow to her heart. "I love you so, my love. So much..." She lovingly said, while closing her eyes.

Jonathan Hoxworth smiled. "I love you too, my love," he lovingly whispered in her ear, as his wife slowly drifted into a peaceful sleep; a nurturing sleep in which Jonathan will visit his beloved Elisabeth again, until her soul will be freed from her carnal envelope; until their two loving spirits will be reunited again...

Amen.

Chapter Thirty-Four

"Principe de Savoia Hotel, Milan"

It was just past two p.m. in Milan, when Angela called her father...

André was always up early, and today he picked up the phone practically before it rang, as if he had been expecting her call.

"Hello, daddy-pie. How are you this morning? Is everything all right?" She softly asked.

"Yeah, poodle, but ya asked me the same question two days ago... Don't worry so much, honey." André lovingly said, truly happy that Angela still cared so much about him.

"What did you do yesterday?"

"Yer brother and yer nieces came with me to visit yer mama; then we all went to Blanche's house for a cup of joe and to shoot the breeze... Aimée was there, honey, but yer poor sister wasn't doing so good... That no good husband of hers was fired again." He sadly said while sitting on a chair. "I don't know how she does it... Haven't seen that girl buy a thing for herself in years... If it weren't for Blanche giving her hand-me-down clothes, my poor Aimée had been right runnin' round naked!" André lamented, while slowly shaking his head.

Angela felt truly sorry for Aimée, but she had made her own choice when she married that man; she also refused to listen to the advice of Josephine and André and now she was paying the price...

"Don't worry so much, daddy. I'll wire her some money as soon as I get back to London. You know that she can count on me."

"Yer an angel, poodle; ya really are... As always." André sadly said, feeling glad to have such an exceptional person in his life.

"Well, it's nothing, daddy; don't worry about that. But what about you?" Somehow Angela felt awkward calling him "daddy"; especially when the object of her call was to enlist his aid in proving that Jonathan Hoxworth was her real father. "Do you need anything?" She softly asked, while feeling guilty for her last thought.

"I'm fine, poodle, I'm fine... If I need anythin' I'll tell ya." He softly said before closing his tired eyes. A pause breached the conversation, until a deep sigh slipped out before Angela was able to catch it.

"What's wrong, poodle?" André asked worriedly.

"Well, daddy-pie, I need your help," she slowly began. "Now that I've visited Elisabeth and spoken to Eileen Mackenzie-Hoxworth, I've decided that I need to do some serious investigating if I'm ever going to find the truth, once and for all!" Angela firmly said, but with a dash of anxiety in her voice.

An involuntary shudder coursed through André's body. "What you need, my baby? Tell yer daddy." He truly wanted Angela to be happy, but if that meant giving up her roots, he wasn't sure he wanted any part of it. Maybe he was a little jealous, but deep down, he felt like her true father, because God knows that, he and Josephine, were about the best parents that a daughter could ever dream of.

The Boivins weren't perfect, but they were good decent people who'd stood by their beloved "golden child", through thick and thin. Meddling in the muddy past might significantly change Angela's present – André's present included – and he didn't like that idea at all; as for the fact that the Hoxworths were involved now with his daughter's life, just made the matter more difficult...

Angela could almost hear his thoughts. "Daddy, are you listening?" She softly asked.

"Yeah, poodle... I was just thinking'," his voice trailed off.

"Please, daddy, I need you to help me," she meekly said. "Would you find me a private investigator in New Orleans who specialises in ancestry? It would be a great help."

"D' ya think it's a good thing t'chase the ghosts of the past, poodle? Even if that man is yer real father, sweetheart, what good will it do you? Ya don't need a dead man as a father, my love... I love ya, honey, and I'm yer daddy," André's voice was cracking, and his lips trembling, as he closed his eyes again.

"Please, pleeease, daddy-pie. Those are hurtful words! Do you really think that I want proof that Jonathan Hoxworth is my father, so that I can replace you now?" She nervously asked. "No one will ever replace you in my heart, daddy, because I truly love you! You know that, daddy, don't you?" As Angela said those simple words, her eyes harboured a thousand tears.

André remained deadly silent, trying his best not to cry.

"Daddy, did you hear what I just said?" She softly asked, while feeling terribly guilty for his palpable sorrow.

"Yeah, my little poodle; yeah my love, I hear ya. And ya know how much I love ya too... I'm jus' an old fool, who's afraid to lose ya; that's all!" André said with a broken voice, while burning tears started to fill his tired eyes.

"That won't happen, daddy-pie. But I don't want you to be upset with me, for wanting to find out my true origins." She lovingly said, as if she were now talking to a child.

"I ain't upset," André lied, nervously twisting the phone cord. "I'm not upset, my love." He sadly repeated, while silently crying.

"You know daddy-pie; I'm doing this for Elisabeth, too... Don't you think that this poor woman deserves to have the chance to see her son, before she dies...? Don't you think that Edmond should know the truth?" Angela gravely said, while feeling her heart breaking in two.

"Well, I'm sorry, my love... I'm just an ol' fool, poodle." His voice was broken now. "Just an ol' fool." He said again, while feeling terribly ashamed.

"No, daddy, you're not! You're far from being a fool," Angela firmly said, feeling deeply sorry for him. "So, daddy, will you please find me an investigator?" She softly asked again.

"Yeah, poodle, I'll do it today." André nervously said, while wiping away some tears with his hand.

"Thank you... Thank you, daddy-pie. I have to go to the opera house now. I'll call you tonight. I love you, daddy; never forget that." She lovingly said, while terribly missing him.

"I love ya too, my little poodle. I love ya too, my love..." He sadly said while closing his eyes again.

As father and daughter hung up the phone, painful tears fell from André's and Angela's eyes; until an angel passed, crying...

Chapter Thirty-Five

"London"

It was a quarter after seven, when Pierce Haddington left his office and stepped out onto the street below...

The weather was quite chilly, so Pierce hurried towards his car, when he suddenly noticed the familiar dark green Range Rover; it was double-parked...

As Pierce rapidly approached it, the dark window slid down and a woman called his name.

"What are you doing in this part of town?" Pierce asked, quite surprised.

Rose-Mary Bernhart donned a sultry smile that perfectly suited her...

"I had to see a client in the neighbourhood," she lied, "and since I was so close to your office, I thought that I would pop in." She said with a ravishing smile.

"Is that a fact?" Pierce grinned, while getting closer.

"Quite the truth and nothing but, lover boy," She softly said, before crossing her heart.

Rose-Mary was dressed all in black, with a tight turtle neck, a short leather skirt and knee length high heels suede boots; a simple, but deadly ensemble, that wonderfully showcased her amazing figure...

"So tell me, are you doing anything tonight?" Pierce sensually asked, as the distinctive spicy scent of her heady French perfume sensually reached his nostrils.

"Alas, my dear Pierce, my plans currently involve dinner alone... Unless?" She expectantly said, while she raised a perfectly shaped eyebrow.

"And what do you say I get in my car and you follow me? No need for you to dine alone." Pierce warmly said, his eyes wolfishly glinting as he noticed Rose-Mary's nipples hardening under the thin cashmere wool.

"By all means, lover boy," she sensually smiled, visibly satisfied.

Less than fifteen minutes later, they sat cosily at a discreet table at the "Blue Buddha", an excellent gourmet Cantonese restaurant on Dickens Street, near Piccadilly. They feasted on shark fin soup, fried oysters in ginger sauce, abalone in a pungent spicy sauce, and succulent "Scottish lobster", in a sweet and sour sauce that she sensually fed to him with her expert fingers...

When the Chinese waiter arrived with the check and their fortune cookies, Pierce was happy to see that the universe was validating the necessity of his exciting extramarital liaison.

"Pleasure is a central part of your life," he read aloud, grinning.

"Mine says 'never give too much of a good thing...'" Rose-Mary sensually laughed, before reaching for his crotch...

Twenty minutes later, when they arrived at her posh flat in Mayfair, they were in high spirits and ready to party. Rose-Mary poured each of them a cup of hot sake, before leading Pierce into her "inner sanctuary"; her extremely feminine bedroom...

Pierce smiled. The main attraction was the king-size satin-tufted crimson bed, dressed with black satin sheets and impregnated with her beloved 'Poison' by 'Dior' perfume...

This was certainly not a matrimonial bedroom. It smelled of pure undiluted sex as well as permissiveness. Even a refined "English gentleman", could certainly unleash his sexual drives, however animalistic, without worrying about "etiquette", or walls talking. This decadent sex goddess bedroom was simply sinful; simply wonderful...

Pierce grabbed rapidly Rose-Mary by the waist and forced her full red lips apart with his tongue, then she hungrily sucked her tongue deeper into her mouth; a foretaste of something better and "bigger", to come...

First, her turtleneck came off, and Pierce's "nimble fingers" were expertly removing her extremely feminine black satin-and-lace 'La Perla' bra, releasing her voluptuous D-cup breasts. At this point of the action, Pierce's movements were urgent, insistent, and rough. There was no time for lengthy lingering caresses...

In seconds, off came her "Jean-Claude Jitrois" leather skirt and black panties - a diaphanous slip of silk and lace - that effortlessly slid down her voluptuous legs ...

Rose-Mary sensually arched her curvaceous back; then she arrogantly thrust her full large breasts forward, becoming an ivory-fleshed sex goddess, wearing nothing but a black satin-and-lace garter belt from 'La Perla', as well as extremely exciting black silk stockings...

In the filtered reddish light, Rose Mary's smooth alabaster skin seemed to glow, while her long lustrous black hair sensually moved against her sinuous back, as she slowly walked across the room, like a cat. Her dark mount of Venus was glistening, wet, and her nipples were so lush that poor Pierce couldn't help, but think that Satan himself designed those tempted buds for the sole purpose of making men lose their wits...

Without any guilt, Pierce rapidly undressed and leaped onto the sinful bed.

Rose-Mary sensuously danced to the beat of some background exotic Californian Jazz music, before she finally threw herself on him, like a sexy vampire, with the intent of devouring Pierce's appealing body with her own; her very skin hungered for him and her breasts took on a life of their own; squeezing him, caressing him, making him moan in pleasure, again and again.

Smiling like the devil himself, the "sweet" Rose-Mary Bernhart taunted and teased the handsome Pierce Haddington, until he begged for mercy...

When she saw the sculptured "masterpiece" of his exceptional penis, a strong electric bolt shot down her spine, just before her "expert tongue" began to greedily feast. Pierce's penis must have been nine inches, and it was thick and richly veined, with large, delicious heavy balls...

Electricity coursed down Rose-Mary's spine as her tongue fell greedily upon Pierce's rock-hard member.

"I want you, badly," she lovingly whispered. "Take me, hard and rough! Yes, ravage me, lover boy!" She nervously said, before she straddled him teasingly, expertly; then, a few minutes later, she slowly raised herself off of him and sashayed out of the bedroom. A breath later, the devilish Rose-Mary returned with a can of whipped cream, broadly smiling...

She laughed. "There was a reason I passed on dessert, lover boy." She sensually said, and her eyes glinted as she coated his hard penis with the fluffy sweet cream; delicious decadent "French cream", from Normandy...

"Don't you dare come just yet, lover boy..." She purred. "I've got rules! You make me climax three times, before you let go your load," she cooed. "Or else..." Her eyes glimmered with a hint of danger; a sexy danger.

The woman was truly wild...

Rose-Mary sensually pulled her long silky dark hair away from her alabaster Madonna's face, so that Pierce could watch her sensual mouth bob up and down on his beautiful cock; then, when his penis was as hard as a rod of steel, she daintily lifted her chin, slowly rolled over, and spread her sexy legs widely apart...

"My turn!" She suddenly ordered, throwing him a she-devil of a smile. "This is going to be more exciting than screwing the Queen of England, lover boy!" She grinned, before closing her eyes.

Rose-Mary was right! Her intense screams of pleasure, rapidly pushed Pierce over the edge.

One after another, she quivered with orgasmic delight while Pierce ravaged her, moving harder, deeper, panting like an animal, until she shot a warm liquid that bathed him in her intoxicating sexual fluids. Her strong vaginal muscles were intensely pulsating, massaging Pierce's penis until he let himself go, and allowed their sexual juices to combine.

A few minutes later, like a true sex goddess, the divine Rose-Mary Bernhart sensually smiled; then she slowly slid her large breasts down Pierce's smooth sweaty chest, before she placed her sensual mouth on his now deflating member, lapping up the delicious "elixir of love" that they'd created together, just as if she were a starved cat. When Rose-Mary looked back at Pierce again, it was obvious that he was in heaven...

Amen!

Chapter Thirty-Six

"New Orleans"

"The House of Angels"

As a soft volute of aromatic white smoke slowly rose in front of the black voodoo priestess, she softly chanted a death song in an African dialect that was so old, that it had never been written down...

Contrary to the title of the incantation, there was no hint of sorrow in the ancient melody; rather it was as uplifting and as soothing to the soul as a sweet lullaby...

Mambha lovingly dedicated it to the newly dead; to all those "lost souls" who hesitantly lingered between darkness and light, desperately searching for a luminous spiritual porthole; a porthole that would entirely cleanse them of the human's impurities they'd certainly accumulated during their last incarnation, so they would be pure enough to meet with the source of all things; the eternal nurturing light...

Mambha's voice was as clear as the pure crystalline water rushing down Mount Kilimanjaro in springtime; then within minutes, overtaken by internal vivid visions, she fell into a deep trance.

For the first time in months, Mambha's vision was one of joy, rather than horror...

The black priestess silently watched, as the soul of an ebony skinned woman, in the prime of her life, graciously walked on an endless field of pristine cotton clouds. The woman was lovingly smiling, before she was reunited with the man who had been her beloved husband in her previous incarnation. Mambha smiled as she recognised the woman, or more particularly, "her eyes". Yes, Mambha knew those dark and soft eyes, as innocent now as those of a baby fawn, because she often saw them in her dreams...

When the woman saw her beloved resting on a grave, she ran towards him, her eyes wide with joy, until she realised that the grave was her own...

The large bronze cross at the head of her grave cast a dark shadow on her beloved's face, like death's cold hand.

For a moment, the woman was overwhelmed by confusion.

Should she beckon him or leave him be? But it wasn't her choice to make. The man's immortal soul was now slowly rising from his dead human body; then, like a large snake shedding an old skin, the soul was free; at last...

Mambha chanted again and sent the sweet comforting African melody to the poor black man to hush his primordial fears, but he didn't need her help for long; when he saw his beloved's soul calmly waiting for him, all sense of fear and disorientation suddenly dissipated, and he lovingly smiled...

The black priestess joyfully laughed, as she silently watched the man's dark eyes dart from his beloved's grave to his lovely young wife, who was now floating above him, lovingly smiling, while reaching her hand out to him. He seemed pleasantly surprised, but as soon as their fingers touched, the little cemetery below dissolved into billions of swirling grey particles; until an incredible surge of energy exploded within the man's soul, as forceful as an atomic bomb, in a blast containing all the emotions of his lifetime. A split second later, there was only "love" and the nurturing warmth of the primordial source of love peacefully surrounded the man; then, he instantly knew all the truth that he had been searching for all his life...

As the two lovingly souls reunited, the emotional chant that emanated from Mambha's throat became stronger and deeper. Riding on the wave of their sincere love, the black priestess' soul also began to vibrate at such a high frequency, that she was able to summon an archangel to guide the two happy souls into the glory of the source; into the place that the poor human sinners called "heaven".

Loving tears slowly fell down the proud black priestess' cheeks, and she lovingly smiled as she raised her hands and whispered, "Do not worry, my friends. Go in peace now. I will protect your beloved golden child."

Amen.

Chapter Thirty-Seven

"Milan"

En route to the "Principe de Savoia" hotel, after her last performance at "La Scala", Angela was sitting alone in the black of the dark blue Mercedes limousine, when her cell phone softly rang...

When Angela noticed that the Caller ID flagged the number as blocked, her body suddenly tensed and she felt like someone had suddenly snapped a rubber band on her neck...

"So, Angela, sweetie..." The sensual voice seemed to sing. "Have you found out what your handsome husband was really doing the night before he visited you, my darling?"

Angela's lips curled downward, forming now a deep frown.

"What exactly do you want from me?" She felt like weeping, but restrained herself, keeping her voice calm. There was no way that she was going to let that woman know that she had discovered her weak spot. She raised the black privacy window, so the limo driver wouldn't hear the conversation.

"What do I want from you? Well, nothing in particular, my friend," the woman sweetly replied. "As I mentioned in our earlier little discussion, I'm just concerned about your welfare... I'm a great fan of yours, you know. I think that no one dances as brilliantly as you, my dear, and I'd hate to see your art suffer on account of, well... emotional problems. I can't tell you how sincerely sorry I am that your stupid husband is taking you for granted... Why he would cheat on you is beyond me." Her tone turned fatalistic. "Then again, sweetie, men are just men, and their genetic inability to keep their dirty little dicks in their pants, is a curse they must live with..." She flatly said. "How would you feel if you were born with such a "nuisance" of a thing, hanging between your legs?" The woman softly asked with a little laugh. "Bad enough that it's so unbecoming, but it seems to keep them in a chronic state of... restlessness; unless, of course, they're busy plugging that thing into one hole or another..." She laughed again. "We, on the other hand, ought to bless the fact that we were born clear-thinking women; luckily for us, sweetie, we only have "one head" to contend with, instead of two... Still, with a cheating handsome husband like yours, it's quite dangerous... One of my closest friends contracted AIDS from her philandering husband," she slowly said, lowering her voice as if they were best friends sharing a secret. "The poor woman is dying because her pig of a husband couldn't control his compulsive need for extramarital sex; and now her children - all three of them - will be soon motherless!" She nervously exclaimed. "I know first-hand that your husband has been very careless; not to mention indiscreet..." She paused a little bit longer; as to let her words sink deep in Angela's brain. "I hope that you've the sense to use condoms if you still care to sleep with him; otherwise, you'll be playing "Russian roulette" with your life, sweetie, believe me! In my opinion, my dear, the world can't afford to lose a great talent like yours..." The woman finally said with a dash of admiration.

"Thank you for your great exposé, whoever you are," Angela icily stated, keeping her voice calm, even though her hands were now shaking. "It's all quite interesting, whoever you are, but I'm not really certain of the reason why you're telling me all this and I'm not really interested in hearing your sordid assumptions." She coldly said, while feeling her blood dangerously boiling.

"Assumptions? They're not assumptions, my dear, they're facts!" The woman nervously exclaimed, her voice suddenly high-pitched and surprised.

"Well, I don't believe you!" Angela icily exclaimed, before closing her eyes.

"It seems, my friend; that you're not only blind, but you're a fool as well!" The woman said, now raising her voice.

"First of all, I'm not your "friend" and you are certainly not mine! And second of all, I'm not a fool! What I'd like to know is what exactly you're getting out of all this. You must have something to gain; so the question is what? Please, tell me!"

"Well, you are a living proof that a high "IQ" doesn't equate with street smarts, my dear... I always wonder why intelligent women like you can't keep their men from straying... Maybe women of lesser intelligence are blessed with more sense when it comes to keeping their husbands in their beds? Perhaps it's a survival trait, a sort of strange phenomenon, indeed; but one that makes for interesting conversation," the woman nervously laughed, feeling now irritated by Angela's apparent calmness.

"This 'interesting conversation' as you said, was over before it even began!" Angela dryly said, while wishing for the mysterious woman to drop dead.

"Perhaps you're right, my friend... It really shouldn't have been necessary for me to contact you again. My good deed is done, but it's time to get you to work and dig up some dirt on a lovely gal named "Rose-Mary Bernhart"..." The woman paused for effect. "Miss Bernhart owns a rather nice antique shop in..."

"I know where Ms. Bernhart's shop is, thank you!" Angela's heart pounded now wildly and she was little by little losing control.

"Ohhh, you're still in the denial stage, aren't you sweetie? I know how it is... Happens to the best of us, my friend; but sooner or later, we must move on to the next stage. Do you remember the big difference between love and AIDS? No, don't bother scratching your lovely brain for the answer, my dear; I'll spell it out for you; "love" doesn't last a lifetime, but on the other hand, "AIDS", sweetie, lasts until the end... And you can be certain, my dear, that for better or worse, you'll die with it! Funny, that love isn't as consistent, no? Well, then, the next stage after denial is "acceptance" -" The woman coldly said. "But as you know, sweetie, your dear husband is -"

Angela didn't want to hear another poisonous syllable. Before the woman had the time to finish her phrase, she violently hung up; but she nervously continued to clutch her cellular phone in her trembling hand until she reached the hotel, thinking that if her husband was by her side, she certainly could kill him with her own hands.

Angela's world was in turmoil; again...

Chapter Thirty-Eight

"New Orleans"

"French Quarter"

By the middle of the week, André had finally found a private eye he trusted...

Bob Tanner had a reputation as the man to call when one needed to win a difficult palimony case, hunt down a dead beat dad, or find an ex-husband who'd left the country to avoid paying alimony; Tanner was something of a champion of "women in need"...

Tanner's mother had died from breast cancer when he was ten years old, then his father and his father's friends had raised him, so he never saw the point of complicating his life with a woman; not even when it came to satisfying his sexual needs...

Born and raised in New Orleans, Bob Tanner was a squat obese reddish blond man in his early fifties, with a mad craving for Southern deep fried foods and sweets. His thin lips curled into a real smile, when André Boivin mentioned on the phone that his famous adopted daughter was extremely interested in the ancestry of the extremely rich "Hoxworths and Mackenzies", so he arranged an immediate meeting.

That same afternoon, at a little downtown café, André painfully explained that his dear Angela was almost certain that "somewhere" in the Hoxworth-Mackenzie's family line, there was "a person of colour"...

After André had carefully explained in great details his adopted daughter's present situation, Bob Tanner practically began to tremble, because he hadn't heard such an intriguing case in all his years of digging through New Orleans' "rich and famous" dirty laundry...

Tanner perfectly knew who the famous "Angela Boivin-Haddington" was: he'd often been reading complimentary newspaper articles about her for quite some time; especially since she had jmarried the rich and handsome Pierce Haddington, the heir of one of the most prestigious business law firms in England.

Thinking about all this, Tanner could almost hear the sound of crisp hundred dollar bills being slapped into his palm; but on the other hand, he was quite worried about digging up information about the two most powerful families in New Orleans...

"So, Sir, if I understand the problem, your adopted daughter wants her due, then?" He calmly said, with an oily smile.

"No Sir, that's not really her goal. My daughter just wants to find the truth 'bout her family, that's all; so ya just do ya job!" André said awkwardly, feeling strangely embarrassed by the private eye's unpleasant insinuation. At this point of their meeting, André knew that it was time for him to leave...

'As soon as Tanner had cashed his first fat check, he rushed to the public library and a little more than an hour later, he'd found what he was looking for. It was an old article from the local newspaper describing the suicide of Jonathan Hoxworth, the son of the famous Reginald Henry Hoxworth, the former governor of Louisiana. It was a minor aside, a speculation on the part of the columnist that intrigued Tanner. If Jonathan Hoxworth had killed himself because his wife had given birth to a coloured girl, it meant that he either didn't know that there was a coloured gene in the family line, or that he didn't really want to know; thus preferred to believe that his wife was an adultress who had an affair with a Negro...

All of New Orleans believed that the powerful Hoxworth-Mackenzies are as white as freshly picked cotton, and always had been... But if they aren't, then this Angela Boivin would be entitled to inherit a big share of their vast fortune; half, in fact, which meant more than a billion dollars!... Tanner thought grinning.

If Angela Boivin-Haddington, as beautiful, talented and famous as she was, was a downtrodden mulatto woman, Tanner wouldn't have wasted his time on proving the validity of such a far-fetched claim; but in fact, she was a "world class act" and a worldwide celebrity...

If Angela Boivin were indeed the daughter of the extremely rich Jonathan Hoxworth, the news would ruffle a lot of important feathers; especially if she attempted to prove it in a local court of law...

During his three decades as a private investigator, Tanner followed New Orleans' high society enough to know that the haughty Eileen Mackenzie-Hoxworth would fight to the death, rather than publicly admit to having a "stained" bloodline. Tanner knew for certain that the "grand dame of New Orleans" would certainly not welcome with open arms the "exotic" Angela ...

As for the grand dame's grandson, the extremely arrogant Edmond Hoxworth, he wasn't really known for his "kindness". Only God knew what he would do, if he were forced to share the large family fortune, as well as his vast land and expensive properties, with his newly found mixed race "sister". Besides being one of the wealthiest real estate developers in Louisiana, Edmond Hoxworth was known to be Right Wing to the core; and it was even rumoured that he'd secretly financed an active branch of the "Ku Klux Klan"...

As a man born and raised in the south, Bob Tanner deeply shuddered when he thought of what kind of deranged scene might erupt. He also perfectly knew that; when one disturbs the thick mud at the bottom of the mighty Mississippi river, the water loses its clarity, and "things and spirits" then become extremely dangerous; as too many old family's secrets were buried there...

Angela might as well be tossing poisonous mud at everything the Hoxworth-Mackenzie families stood for during so many generations, staining the "purity" of their great Caucasian ancestry, as well as staining their highly respected name forever. Powerful people could kill someone for something like this; but not from their own hand, of course, Tanner fully knew...

Even if the famous "Angela Boivin-Haddington" could prove that she is the legitimate heir of the filthy rich Jonathan Hoxworth; she, as "a woman of colour", would never be accepted by the Hoxworth family, nor by their privileged Caucasian American friends.

No matter how hard this poor woman tries, she would always remain an outcast. Tanner deeply sighed. *She'd be a lot better off if she stayed with her own kind...*

Her own kind; coloured people, Negros and mulattos, of course...

The devil smiled again.

Chapter Thirty-Nine

"New Orleans"

"Mount Olivet Cemetery"

André tiredly gazed into the expanse of a luminous blue cerulean sky, then took a deep breath and smiled, feeling satisfied at having finally fulfilled his task...

His beloved golden child wanted the truth, no matter the emotional price she had to pay for it; and he wasn't going to deny her that last wish...

André calmly drove to the little cemetery, located fifteen minutes from his house; but for the first time since his poor Josephine was diagnosed with heart disease, André strangely felt in peace; something that he had never truly experienced during his entire life...

What a perfect day, André thought, staring into the bright sun without a single disturbing thought. A few minutes later, he slowly parked his old Dodge under the refreshing shade of a large Poinciana tree, then he carefully gathered the mixed flowers that he'd picked that morning in Josephine's garden; colourful flowers that he'd been careful to bundle in a clean plastic bag and water, so that they wouldn't wilt.

As André walked calmly towards Josephine's unpretentious gravestone, he swung his arms as if he were a young man again, simply because his mind was filled with happy memories of the days when they'd first met in Baton Rouge; the blessed day when their young eyes were full of love and passion, and every moment so sweet…

Today, Josephine's gravestone was gloriously bathed in light and warm to the touch. André carefully arranged the multicolour flowers and lovingly placed them in the brass vase that was attached to the tombstone. He then sat down and sighed. After looking up at the beautiful cloudless sky, as always, André lovingly wished his beloved wife a "good day" and then softly began to tell her about the unimportant events that had happened in the past twenty-four hours…

André slowly spoke, taking time to listen to the harmonious sound of the little light birds, as they hopped from one tree to the next, as well as the rustling of leaves in the afternoon soft breeze. As he spoke, André tenderly caressed Josephine's tombstone with his large hand, smiling.

An old skinny black woman with a black child in tow and a large white bouquet of flowers in her arms, stared at him as she passed by; but André didn't notice the pity in her eyes, because it wasn't the first time she'd seen him alone, sitting on that particular gravestone for hours, talking to himself.

The old woman slowly shook her head and tossed him a sad smile, as she took the hand of the child and quietly walked away, hoping not to disturb him, before she turned and hurried towards the grave of her own beloved one...

As soon as the old woman and the child were out of sight, André's eyes inexplicably filled with tears, as he finally realised that he would never see "his" beloved wife again. The sad reality that the sweet Josephine was gone forever, and would therefore never return, tore into his suffering heart with the force of a hurricane, and he was suddenly hit by a wave of total abandonment and despair.

My Josephine is gone... The great love of my life is gone; gone forever...

No matter how long the poor André waited, or how many sincere words of love he poured over his beloved's grave, he would never come home and see his beautiful Josephine sitting in her beloved rocker again; nor would he smell the wonderful scent of her succulent "jambalaya" simmering on the stove, or see her luminous ebony skin, moist and glowing, from hovering over the steaming pot for hours; never...

For a long time that seemed to be an eternity, André silently stayed beside Josephine's little grave, until the radiant sun slowly set over the old stonewall that circled the little cemetery; until the chirping of crickets filled the air; until the night would fall; until his tired heart would stop to beat...

André calmly watched the large opalescent mesmerising moon as it slowly rose in the dusky sky, then he silently watched the silvery stars slowly appearing, one by one, with their faint shimmering, until the figures of the constellations could be plainly seen by the naked eye; until he realised that the earth was a body in motion, and also that he was travelling alone now in the immensity of space; alone without "his Josephine"…

Little by little, a strange sense of peace softly enveloped him, while tender memories of his childhood flooded his mind, sending him spinning into the past; into his youth; into what his life had been…

André saw himself playing hide-and-seek with his siblings; then standing by his father's side, fly-fishing on the bank of the mighty Mississippi. André could almost taste now the wonderful spicy meals his mother made on Sundays; the crawfish stew; the deep-fried chicken; the sweet grilled golden corn; the delicious yams, as well as her delicious home baked biscuits. As they said in the South: "the darker the cook, the better the food". André lovingly remembered his mother's soft ebony skin; and above all, her heart of gold…

Seconds later, André saw himself kissing a beautiful young girl; his first love: the sweet Josephine…

How he'd passionately loved her then and still loved her now. She'd undeniably swept him off his feet; so much in fact, that less than a year later, they were married in Baton Rouge; and a year after that, John was born, rapidly followed by Blanche, then Aimée…

André lovingly remembered the special day when his dear Josephine came home from work, holding "something" wrapped in a little pink blanket - a very precious gift that he would never forget - and he lovingly recalled how he had marvelled, being struck by the pale skinned baby's stunning beauty. It was the first time he had set his eyes on their new found miraculous "golden child": the loving and generous Angela...

As the night air became cool, André slowly raised the lapels of his brown jacket. André suddenly felt tired and drained by too many emotions, and all he simply wanted to do now was sleep. He slowly curled up on the grass; laid his head on Josephine's grave, and closed his tired eyes, after looking for the last time at the magnificent moon. André rapidly felt as if his beloved Josephine was right next to him; as if she was there to comfort him; as if he wasn't alone in this terrible world anymore...

At this precise instant, André could smell Josephine's wonderful sweet perfumes of amber and violet, and he could clearly hear her lovely voice, and see her beautiful face again. Strangely enough, Josephine looked exactly as she did the first day that André had set his mesmerised eyes upon her; Josephine was seventeen years old again...

Smiling like an angel, but without a word, Josephine lovingly opened wide her arms and without hesitation André rushed towards her.

André Boivin was full of joy and anticipation now, as he clearly knew then that it was time to begin a new journey with his beloved Josephine, together again; a luminous journey for their immortal loving souls, forever and ever, and ever...

Amen!

Chapter Forty

"New Orleans"

As once again, Angela sadly crossed the Atlantic on her way to New Orleans - a classic black dress packed in her suitcase - she felt like she was reliving a very bad dream...

Her eyes swollen from crying, and with a bleeding heart, Angela was returning to her native city, with the task of burying her beloved André, the only father she'd ever known; the only father she had truly loved...

John was silently waiting at the airport alone. Little was said between them, as he drove through New Orleans and into the familiar black neighbourhood.

By the time Angela had climbed the old wooden stairs of her family home to pay her last respects to André's lifeless body that had been laid to rest on his bed, she couldn't recall a solitary detail of the previous day. She could not even remember packing in Milan, or sitting on the plane, simply because she had not slept in over twenty-four hours. Now she was so deeply drained and tired, that she could not really feel the pain; even though "pain" was not a strong enough word to describe what she was feeling within her broken heart...

At the moment, Angela looked more like a "beautiful zombie" than a human being; and if someone could have stuck her with a pin, she wouldn't have felt it, because her profound grief had completely anesthetised her from her head to her toes. Now and then, in a short moment of lucidity, she almost had an urge to scream; but she quickly reverted to the comfort that numbness provided...

André had been dressed in his favourite Sunday black suit and white shirt, his hands tied together with a white cotton scarf, a little rosary and a wooden cross tucked between his intertwined fingers. André looked strangely peaceful; death had softened the frown lines on his face, and he almost looked a decade younger; just like Josephine...

As Angela tiredly knelt beside his strange immobile body, she somehow heard her sisters crying from somewhere in the house, but it seemed to her that it was just a bad dream.

Angela softly laid her head on her father's chest; then she closed her eyes, and little by little, she added her own sobs to the on-going sad chorus. Angela was extremely drained; all she wanted now was to cast aside her tired body and simply follow her beloved parents to wherever they had gone, as to finally rest in peace...

As each of André's old friends walked in and out of the little bedroom to say their last goodbyes, Angela observed without really noticing. Her mind was so far away; far away and so lost...

The next morning, after a restless night, Angela was motionlessly sitting in the same pew of the same little church that she had sat in just months before; then again, she absently listened as the black choir sang the same liturgical songs, before the spectacular Reverend Brown vehemently spoke of "life and death"; "heaven and hell"; "good and evil"; again…

When André's shiny mahogany coffin was lowered into his cold grave, Angela finally collapsed in John's arms. The next thing she knew was that she was laying in her little bed, her white cotton pillow wet with tears. When she tiredly reopened her saddened eyes, she feared her wakeful life as much as she feared the terrifying nightmares that continued to plague her.

Angela was now feeling terribly alone; much more alone than ever before…

For another two terribly sad days, Angela stayed at her parents' home, trying her best to etch in her memory the happy times she'd spent there, when life was simpler and kinder; when the innocence of youth was still so tangible that even inanimate objects seemed imbued with a magical life. For hours at a time, she motionlessly sat in Josephine's favourite rocking chair by the living room window, and she vacantly looked at the ancient magnolia tree, watching silently as its branches softly brushed against the panes of glass.

Angela lovingly remembered the beautiful magnolia tree...

She remembered playing with her precious pale skinned porcelain dolls under its large umbrella of shade. She remembered the refreshing aroma that always emanated from its velvety ivory blossoms; sometimes so strong they almost made her dizzy. She also remembered how protective and generous the tree was.

What I would give now for my life to be so uncomplicated; to be so deeply grounded, so sturdy and yet reaching for the stars. Ohhh, I miss you so much, mama... I miss you so much, papa... She thought, while wiping her burning tears.

Numerous times, the phone rang in the living room, again and again, but Angela simply ignored it, as she had no desire to talk to anyone, since she could not even bear to hear the sound of her own voice anymore...

For two extremely long days and endless sleepless nights, Angela lived like a nun, cloistered in a cell of times past, her precious childhood memories drifting in and out of her deeply troubled mind.

During all that time, she didn't eat or sleep much, and was practically fasting; her monastic diet consisted of bread, water, and a few sips of wine. The only thing that she really longed for was her parents' constant nurturing love; and she often wondered how long it would be, before they were reunited again...

Three days after her father's funeral, the peaceful sanctuary Angela had created was finally disrupted. At the crack of dawn, her siblings and their noisy families... invaded her fragile privacy

Without warning, the "vultures" had descended, and the sacred family temple suddenly became an unpleasant marketplace. Her sisters, as well as the deeply unpleasant Marquesha were rapidly appraising every possession, even those with the most diminutive value. From the tiniest silver spoons, to each cup of fine China; even the hand-made patchwork quilts that Josephine loved to make...

Angela was profoundly disgusted, but she didn't feel entitled to speak her mind. After all, she wasn't a Boivin by either blood or marriage. She simply sadly realised that there was little for her to do at that place, so she quietly packed her things and silently left.

She had already told John that she would be forfeiting her share of the estate. There were only four little things she wanted, and she had slipped them into her suitcase when she'd first arrived.

In the middle of the day, Angela checked into a suite at the "Monteleone Hotel" in Royal Street; then she carefully placed her "precious family treasures" on her bedroom dresser. Her chosen inheritance simply consisted of Josephine's favourite hand-crocheted pale pink shawl and her Sunday white gloves, as well as her old blue crystal perfume atomizer that was still half full of the violet perfume she sometimes wore; and also André's favourite burgundy silk tie, as well as her beloved parents wedding portrait...

These four little items were now some of Angela's most priceless treasures.

Angela said a last prayer for her parents' souls, before she tiredly undressed, took two sleeping pills and crashed on the white king size bed, feeling terribly alone.

Artificial sleep was better than no sleep at all; this, Angela knew all too well by now...

Chapter Forty-One

"New Orleans"

"Monteleone Hotel"

The morning after, as Angela came off the elevator in the luxurious hotel's lobby, she couldn't take her eyes off the handsome couple that stood in front of her at the registration desk. There was something familiar about them; and a feeling of "déjà-vu" overwhelmed her...

When the beautiful young woman gracefully turned around, Angela felt like she was almost looking in a mirror. They shared the same pale golden skin, as well as the almond shaped golden eyes; the high cheekbones, the tall and slender silhouette, and the same exotic look. From afar, if they dressed in the same style, they could definitely be mistaken for twins, or as the same person...

The woman's consort was as elegant as any Italian, very tall, toned, and extremely handsome, with shiny and thick jet black hair. Although he could have passed for Caucasian, his skin was a bit reddish, and Angela guessed he might have some Polynesian ancestry as well. When he caught Angela staring, he elegantly took off his stylish 'Ray Ban' sunglasses, revealing dark and bright intelligent eyes; then he gave her a winning smile, showing perfect pearl white teeth...

"Well hello, Miss... We meet again!" He charmingly exclaimed; but when he noticed Angela's confused expression, he rapidly explained, "You were seated in front of us on the plane from New York."

Angela placed his slight pleasant accent as French Island, soothing and laced with a certain continental elegance.

"Ohhh," Angela said visibly confused, feeling her skin blush. "Yes indeed... I thought that your voices sounded familiar." She charmingly said, before she smiled back at him while discretely looking at his fascinating dark eyes.

"But, of course, your face is familiar to us," the woman interjected. "You're a prima ballerina from the London Royal Ballet, aren't you? Angela Boivin, I think, no?"

"Yes... Yes, I am," Angela modestly said, even more confused.

"Now I remembered... We saw you dance 'Petruska' in London a couple years back, and you were thrilling to watch." The man sincerely said, visibly delighted to meet her in person.

If the terribly handsome man weren't so well matched with the young and pretty woman, Angela would've thought that he was flirting with her...

"By the way, Miss Boivin, my name is Emmanuel Lambert, and this is my sister Jeanette," he said smiling again, with an elegant gesture of his hand.

Angela's smile grew as well. "Where are you from?" She softly asked, while looking into his intriguing eyes.

"Tahiti," Jeanette said before her brother opened his mouth. "Emmanuel is an artist - a painter - and we came to New Orleans to mix business and pleasure. Didn't we, Emmanuel?"

"Yes, indeed. And it would definitely be even a more pleasurable mix if you'd agree to be our guest for drinks and dinner, Miss Boivin."

"Well, that would be... lovely." Angela agreed after a slight hesitation, surprising herself.

"In that case, I'll ring your room, around seven p.m.," Emmanuel Lambert happily promised, before throwing her another ravishing smile. "Once again, it's been a great pleasure, Miss Boivin."

When Angela extended her right hand, Emmanuel slightly bowed, bent his head, and delighted her with a perfect French "baise-main"; his sensual lips lingering just a quarter-inch above her hand...

As Angela watched them leave the lobby, she somehow felt overwhelmed. Strangely enough, Emmanuel Lambert hardly seemed a stranger to her, but more like a ghost from her past. A deep cold shiver crawled up her spine. He too was perfumed with vetiver...

An hour later, when Angela returned to her suite, she called Bob Tanner and arranged to meet him at three p.m. Just after, she quickly removed her elegant pale blue jersey "BCBG" jogging suit, and took a hot, then cold shower. Ten minutes later, feeling more relaxed; she carefully applied her make-up, before she neatly tied her hair in a ponytail with a black velvet ribbon. She clothed herself in an elegant 'Armani' beige linen fitted pantsuit that she had recently purchased in Milan, and accessorised it with a large double strand of silvery grey Tahitian pearls – a recent gift from Pierce - as well as with a cream coloured 'Ferragamo' crocodile clutch with matching high heels pumps. After attentively looking at herself in the full-length mirror of her bedroom, she smiled at herself before she left her suite and firmly shut the door behind her...

Angela was physically, as well as emotionally ready for the important meeting with Bob Tanner; a meeting, she knew, that could definitely change her life...

Walking briskly, while leaving an exquisite perfumed trail of 'Eternity' in the path, Angela turned left on Poydras Street and made her way to Saint Charles Avenue, the central artery of the decadent Southern city. Even though she was a little anxious, she couldn't help but smile at the old majestic oak trees that softly lined the ancient French street, while admiring the beautiful antebellum mansions. For an instant, Angela felt as if she'd been thrown into a long lost time, so far from annoying modern technology. She also realised that no city in the world, even Paris, the eternal "city of light", the city of love, was as full of dear memories as her native New Orleans. Yes, indeed, New Orleans was the city where her roots were; this was the only place where her heart would always be...

Angela slowed her pace and took in as much as she could of the romantic scenery of her beloved city: its unique smells, happy noises, glorious light and quirky nonchalance; all the little things which made her beloved New Orleans so distinct. At that moment,

Angela softly smiled as she realised, that she was truly proud to be born in such a unique place; a place where some African slaves had been forced to blend with their Caucasian masters; a place where the coloured heirs of those two radically distinct races, those peculiar "mulattos" who now called themselves "African-American", had created a brand new world for themselves, as well as for their children. "New Orleans" was indeed such a place. And whether Angela wanted it, or not, she was in fact a "beautiful hybrid" of those two different races; a hybrid living now in the world of the "masters", even though a part of her came from an ancient African slave...

With this quite deranged jthought in mind, Angela glanced at her gold 'Bulgari' watch and she realised that she had plenty of time before her meeting with the private eye.

A few minutes later, Angela stopped at a classic little French café. It was full of habitués who seemed as if they hadn't a care in the world, and as she walked in; then looked around, she couldn't help wondering how all those noisy people made their living. As she sat down on a little wooden chair that was still warm from its previous occupant, she heard a familiar voice that made her heart beat even faster.

"So we meet again!" The man warmly said. "What an unexpected delight..."

"Emmanuel Lambert, isn't it?" Angela softly asked, feeling her face flush again.

"Good memory... Are you here alone, Miss Boivin?" He elegantly asked with a ravishing smile.

"Well, I'm quite early for a meeting. So, yes, I am," she said, somehow embarrassed.

"So, may I join you?" Emmanuel Lambert asked, before pulling out a chair as she nodded. "By the way, Miss Boivin, you look truly divine today..." He sincerely said, smiling. She blushed...

The handsome French man ordered two "café au lait" as well as a basket of freshly fried "beignets"...

"So, Mister Lambert, what brings you to New Orleans?" Angela asked, quite troubled by his eyes.

"I had to attend a few gallery meetings in New York and Miami... My sister always wanted to visit this lovely old French colonial city, so she convinced me to make a small detour, prior to returning home in Tahiti." He nonchalantly explained, while attentively looking at her eyes.

"I see... What style do you paint in?" She softly asked, before looking at his beautiful hands.

"Mostly large impressionist paintings of Tahiti, Bora Bora and other French islands; but I also work in all mediums." He casually said, while observing each detail of her lovely face; studying it, as if he wanted to paint her portrait.

For some strange reason, Angela couldn't really picture this extremely handsome man spending long hours in front of a canvas...

Although Emmanuel Lambert's hands were strong, his fingers were long and sensitive; something which mesmerised her. As the man brushed with a decisive gesture of his hand a heavy strand of straight jet-black hair from his handsome face, Angela discretely studied him.

"I wouldn't take you for a painter," she opined. "Perhaps a professional tennis player, or even a model." She smiled.

The French man heartily laughed. "Modelling is Jeanette's department, but my sister plays both sides of that field: she's a photographer, and a mighty good one at that, as well as an excellent tennis player!"

"What was it that drew you to painting?" Angela probed, still mesmerised by his fascinating artist's hands.

"What wouldn't draw one to the world of colour and real beauty?" He softly responded, his voice now soothing and calm. "When I was just a wee tot of five, my parents gave me a set of watercolours; and the rest is history... I'm truly blessed to make my living by capturing the colours and people of my islands..." He said, smiling, again. "Besides nature and its beauty, nothing gives me more pleasure than studying the expressions of the human face; its light, pride, love and sadness... No matter what befalls a person, there is always a glimmer of hope behind even the deepest despair." He softly said in a poetic manner, while looking deep into her eyes.

Angela couldn't help staring at this peculiar man. Kindness was etched on his dark irises, and calmness as well as peace, seemed to envelop him with an extreme grace; never before had she met a man so alluring, so different, so kind...

"Were you born in Tahiti?" She asked, hoping that he wouldn't notice the trembling in her voice.

"Yes, in "Papeete"... My father was born in Northern France, near the city of "Strasbourg". He was the son of a French father and

287

a Dutch mother, but my mother is a native Tahitian; although her mother was half Philippine and half Chinese... So you see, Miss Boivin, I am quite a mix!" He laughed again.

"Good Lord!" Angela exclaimed. "And I thought I had an exotic ancestry!" She laughed, while losing herself in his appealing black ink eyes.

"To tell you the truth, I simply see myself as a citizen of the world," Emmanuel Lambert proudly stated. "You must view yourself the same way, I suspect?"

Angela fell into a shamed silence. She'd never looked before at her mixed blood as something truly positive. "I... well, to tell you the truth, Mister Lambert; I'm not sure how I feel about the whole thing... Strange at it seems, I'm only right now on my way to discover my real roots." She nervously said, while slightly lowering her eyes, visibly embarrassed.

The French man saw the deep pain flash in her eyes. "Roots are as important as wings," he simply stated, before pensively taking a sip of his café au lait, while his artist eyes calmly continued to analyse her with kindness.

Angela was now feeling quite tense, but she tried to laugh, to push away the tears that were forming. "I'm going to be late," she quickly said, before nervously standing up. A perfect gentleman, the French man stood as well.

"I'd like to see what a great artist such as you thinks of my work," he warmly said, before elegantly kissing her hand once again.

"I... I'd like that," she agreed hesitantly, before she had a chance to think. His eyes, those dark, but luminous almond-shaped orbs, caught her off guard and she felt like an innocent little girl again; something which had not happened in a very long time...

Although Angela barely knew this intriguing man, one thing was certain; she truly liked him.

Happy and bewildered, Angela spun around with verve and danced away, feeling like a child again; a golden child...

Outside, enveloping New Orleans, the golden sun was brightly shining, and the entire universe seemed to love Angela again. Amen...

Chapter Forty-Two

"New Orleans"

"French Quarter"

At a quarter to three in the afternoon, Angela anxiously stood in front of a three-story building on St. Charles Avenue...

From the elegant Doric columns that flanked the entrance, she guessed that the building was at least two centuries old; however, it has been recently restored and repainted in stark white. The intricate large stucco mouldings looked brand new, but the craftsmanship told of its authenticity...

Angela took a deep breath before stepping into the spacious black and white marble lobby and ascending the imposing towering stairway. The sound of her heels strangely clacking echoed on the marbled steps. On the second floor, at the end of a long well lit corridor, a shiny brass plaque had been nailed to the door. As Angela read the name and before she had the chance to knock, Bob Tanner opened the door. As soon as she stepped inside, she felt as if she had fallen into a classic 1940 Humphrey Bogart film...

A tall wall-to-wall impressive bookshelf boasted hundreds of well-worn books, and a second wall was entirely reserved for black and white photographs of the private investigator with his visibly satisfied clients.

This is a good, good sign... Even in his grief-stricken state, daddy obviously picked a winner; or did mama's hand guide him?

Now Angela was the one believing in spirits...

Tanner nonchalantly sat behind a large French "art deco" desk. He wore a well-cut cream coloured linen suit with a pale pink shirt that lightened his jovial features. Without a word, he gestured towards a comfortable old brown leather armchair in front of him; then lit a Cuban cigarillo with a gold filter, not bothering to ask Angela if she minded the smoke.

Surprised at his nonchalance, Angela introduced herself.

"Madam, I perfectly know who you are," he suavely said with a little smile, before extending his stubby hand "Did you enjoy your stroll through our blessed city?"

"Yes, I did, Mister Tanner." She said, a bit uneasily. How did he know that she had walked?

"The scent of the city lingers, Miss Boivin," Tanner softly said, answering her unspoken question before smiling again. To her relief, after a few inhalations of the spicy tobacco, he extinguished the cigarillo, and plucked an 'Altoid' from a large silver tin.

He closed his little ferret eyes and noisily sucked on it, obviously enjoying its flavour; then, as if he was suddenly aware of time, he cracked it with his teeth, reopened his eyes, and finally picked up a thick file.

"As you are most likely aware, Miss Boivin, the Mormon Church's genealogical files rarely fail to please a client," he slowly said, marking each syllable with his charming accent from the South. "I think that you, as well as your mother, will be extremely pleased to know the results of my research..." He smiled again while discretely observing her eyes.

As the large wooden fan softly hummed above, Tanner's soft voice was almost hushed by the beat of Angela's heart. With his well-manicured little hands, he delicately opened the precious file and handed it to Angela. As he pointed to a hand-graphed family tree that revealed seven generations of the Hoxworth-Mackenzie family lines; he intertwined his little fingers and softly placed them neatly under his double chin, and then smiled, visibly satisfied of his work...

"The proof of your birth right lies on the Hoxworth line, madam... However, I don't think that Madam Eileen Mackenzie-Hoxworth will be pleased to know that she married the great, great, great, great-grandson of a Negro slave, known by the name of "Jenny"..." He politely said, grinning, while deeply looking into her eyes.

"Are you absolutely sure about this, Mister Tanner?" Angela nervously asked. He noticed that her hands were slightly shaking.

"There's no doubt about it, madam. The first and only son of Thomas Henry Hoxworth was the product of an indulgence with his father's favourite Negro slave girl. At that time, Miss Boivin, having sex with a Negro was seen by the church, as well as society at large, as a great sin and some people seriously thought that Africans as well as Australian aborigines were the "missing link" between the big apes and mankind..." Tanner seriously said visibly not embarrassed at all by this strange concept. Then he softly added; "racism, in fact, is just a by-product of our lovely species... Our first ancestors, as well as modern men always had the need to classify everything in terms of superiority and inferiority. This kind of behaviour started with their own kind; the strongest versus the weakest; but also men versus women." Tanner said with a little grin. "The latter seen as weaker by the former; thus inferior." He smiled again. "The fact is, Miss Boivin, that sexism and misogyny have always been the first signs of visible discrimination against another human being... And unfortunately for us "free spirits" even today in most male driven societies, for example in Arab and African countries, young girls, as well as women, do not have a better place in those societies than slaves had in the past centuries. Do you also know that today, as we speak, slavery hasn't ended with "globalisation"; the human rights organisations estimate that two hundred and fifty millions boys, girls and women are kept in a state of slavery today; something that most of us are not even interested in fighting against... Amazing, isn't it my dear Miss Boivin?" Tanner finally said with a condescending smile, while constantly scanning her eyes.

The man looked like a cat; a big fat cat...

Angela was appalled by his deranged monologue, as well as by his opinions about racism and sexism, since she had always being deeply interested in the two extremely delicate matters.

"Sir, did Thomas Hoxworth marry "Jenny"?"

"Of course not, Madam." He smiled. "It would've been a disgrace," he firmly said, his voice tinged with condescension, as he reached for another 'Altoid'.

"So, the mulatto baby was not only a bastard, but also a slave by birth right?" She nervously asked again, embarrassed, while lowering her eyes.

"Yes, yes, of course; but even in those days, Madam, money and power could turn many heads away from the truth..." He unctuously said. "And so that mulatto child, who in all likelihood was light-skinned almost like yourself, was given the Hoxworth's name by his paternal grandparents. If the two rightful heirs to the Hoxworth name - the boy's father and his brother - hadn't died before they wed and had childeren with a woman of their race, the whole thing would've been simply forgotten; but to the Hoxworths great disappointment, the mulatto kid was the sole survivor of their bloodline..." He calmly said with a little annoying grin. "When old Fitzgerald Hoxworth was on his deathbed, he and his wife, Martha, formally adopted the mulatto child, whom they also baptized and named "William" after his father, then they paid off the local judge to keep quiet... This will explain everything!" Tanner concluded before he tipped his head to the file and helped himself to another Altoid.

"It must've come as a surprise to the child," Angela nervously said, visibly embarrassed, while avoiding his eyes. "In those times, a mulatto slave claiming such a place in society would be unheard of, wouldn't it?" She nervously asked.

"More than that, madam; in fact, it was a big fat "no-no"... But as I said, money seems to remedy all sorts of awkwardness; and Fitzgerald Hoxworth had lots of it..." Tanner unctuously smiled again, while searching for her eyes.

Visibly horrified, Angela silently faced the ugly truth, while trying to stay calm.

Soon, she thought, her mother's name would be cleared of the abuse and the shame; even though she knew that the task before her was not as simple as it seemed...

"Now what? What can I do, Mister Tanner?" She calmly asked, while literally boiling inside.

"My advice, Madam, is first to contact the Hoxworths and see if they'll allow you to conduct a DNA test on Jonathan's body... I've also written down the telephone number of an excellent attorney in Baton Rouge, who has a bit of skill under his belt regarding such delicate matters..." He softly said, for the first time avoiding her eyes.

"But... But why should I hire a lawyer from Baton Rouge?" She asked with surprise.

"Well, it's quite simple, Madam." Tanner said slightly embarrassed. "For the simple reason that there isn't a good white or black lawyer in this town that will dare represent you in court in a battle against the Hoxworths. You see, Madam, with all the Hoxworth's powerful connections, it would certainly be career suicide..." He grinned while scanning her eyes again. "It's also safe to assume that Eileen and Edmond Hoxworth will fight tooth and nail to prove you wrong. Dame Eileen has quite a reputation as a maker, as well as a breaker, of the privileged classes... Not to mention that her grandson Edmond will soon be running for senator." He suavely said, before he elegantly handed her a card.

"Quinton Yardley? He sounds English." She said, while raising an eyebrow.

"Mister Yardley is a gentleman, madam; a trusted friend, as well as an excellent trial lawyer... He'll also be fascinated by your case," Tanner paused with an impertinent slight grin at the corner of his little mouth. "In the best possible scenario, of course, you won't need him. This is why, I suggest that you initially attempt to handle this in private; leave it between you and the Hoxworths... Their numbers are on the back of the card. Call Mister Edmond first. He should be more accessible; let's hope..." He smiled. "You may be able to strike a deal with him; particularly since he'd have to part with half of his inheritance, you being his father's daughter and all... There's quite a bit of money at stake." He grinned again. "Either way, Madam, you are bound to get enough to make you and your mother sleep easier until the end of your lives..." He unctuously smiled; evidently dreaming about the large fortune Angela might make off the deal.

Angela stood up as if a bee stung her. "Mister Tanner. This isn't about money!"

"Of course it's not, Madam," he purred like a fat cat, not bothering to hide a sarcastic lift of his trimmed eyebrow. "It's about declaring the truth; for what the truth is worth... The thing is, Madam, in most of these cases the truth seems to take a lesser seat, when up against a huge fortune that can change one's life..." He calmly said, smiling again...

"Not in my case, Mister Tanner!" Angela nervously exclaimed; feeling deeply insulted.

Tanner's smile did not fade as he slowly stood up and handed her a copy of the file, before gallantly opening the door. "It was a pleasure meeting you, Miss Boivin," he said with utmost sincerity, while having a lascivious look at her spectacular body.

Deeply troubled, Angela left without a word, her perfume sensually lingering in the room.

"That little lady is going to find that there are more wolves than grandmas out there..." Tanner said to himself before reaching for another Altoid. "Well, c'est la vie, mon chérie!" He loudly laughed, before taking a long suck of the curiously strong mints, while dreaming of Angela's beautiful little ass...

"This is life"; yes indeed...

Chapter Forty-Three

"New Orleans"

"The French Quarter"

As Angela briskly walked through Woldenberg Park, she nervously took a deep breath of fresh air, inhaling the woody scent of the tall ancient trees...

When Angela reached the wharf, she sadly watched as a group of fat American tourists embarked on the old 'Natchez' steamboat, for a leisure trip down the mighty Mississippi River. She tried to smile at an old obese blond woman who happily grinned at her, but inwardly, all she felt now was bitterness and a dash of jealousy...

What I would give to know peace and simplicity again... Why did Mama have to tell me about Elisabeth? Why? She deeply sighed.

Angela shivered in the warm afternoon air, when she suddenly realised that her battle had just begun. And what a battle it would be; for better or worse, Pandora's Box had been opened, and the fragile lid was now broken into bits...

Overcome with nerves, she sat down on a wood bench, feeling incredibly stupid and terribly naïve. Bob Tanner was right...

The Hoxworths aren't about to welcome Elisabeth or me with open arms... Jesus, what was I thinking? She sadly thought, refraining from shouting and panicking.

Eileen Mackenzie Hoxworth had put ten million dollars in a Swiss account, which was still awaiting Angela's signature, hoping that she would take the bait and keep quiet...

Angela fully realised now that her very existence was anathema to the Hoxworth-Mackenzie line. She had blamed Eileen's actions on ignorance, when it was clearly an act of choice; never before in her entire life had Angela felt so foolish, so dumb, and so worthless...

Along the riverbank, the water of the Mississippi seemed as opaque as her thoughts, her heart, and her near future. The alienation that she often felt when amongst her darker skinned childhood friends was nothing, compared to what she was feeling right now...

Angela felt truly alienated and terribly alone, and she knew that she couldn't even look to her husband for comfort anymore. Yet, she couldn't give up; it was almost as if something – a strange powerful force - was now encouraging her to prove her mother's innocence...

Later on, as the reddish large moon slowly rose above colourful ribbons of fiery little clouds, burning tears fell from her cheeks like drops of rain. Laughter echoed from the deck of a steamboat, but the lightness of the happy tourists aboard merely emphasised her profound pain. At this precise instant, Angela deeply hated herself for falling into such self-pity. Before her beloved Josephine told her the unpleasant truth, Angela always believed that she was good enough for society; but now, she doubted everything...

Trying not to cry, Angela walked back to her hotel as fast as she could. Once in her bedroom, she nervously stripped off her clothes, and curled up in the lonely bed, trying to find solace by imagining Pierce's protective arms around her; but all she could hear was the voice of the woman who had called her in Milan...

It is all too much to bear; all the questions, the not-knowing, the manipulations and lies... She sadly thought while refraining from crying.

As if stung by a bee, Angela jumped out of bed and called Pierce, but she hung up after the first ring. It was three in the morning in London, and she didn't want to know if her husband was home or not. If he wasn't, she could not bear it; but nonetheless she could not stop obsessing. Not knowing what else to do, she took two sleeping pills. Deep down, she just wanted to fade away...

Twenty extremely long minutes later, sleep finally beckoned with velvety fingers and the promise of a dreamless night; but not even strong sedatives could keep away the vicious ghosts of the past...

Angela awoke just before dawn, gasping for air, her own hands once again pressing the pillow over her face. When she angrily threw the large pillow towards the wall, she strangely caught a glimpse of the man of her nightmare; the man with the steely blue eyes...

The 'Rohypnol' left her groggy and cranky, so thinking about the difficult tasks that lie ahead didn't do much to brighten her sour mood. She ordered a carafe of strong Cuban coffee and two croissants, and then she reluctantly prepared herself for what must be done.

Edmond Hoxworth's butler answered the phone and told her that his "master" wouldn't be back until Monday; then Angela declined to leave a message. She considered calling her brother John, or one of her sisters, but deep down she honestly didn't know nwhat she would say to them; that she wasn't a blood relative? That they'd all been deceived? It was nonsense...

The fact was that Angela had no family anymore.

She showered and went for a long walk, as to clear her mind, hoping that the exercise would also relieve some of the extreme tension she'd accumulated over the past few days; at least, it would pass the time...

Angela headed towards the French Quarter. The sun was high in the sky and the sidewalks were already crowded with the same happy-go-lucky fat tourists. As she walked by them, many of them often stared at her, and she realised that she really was like a zebra in a living room. Her exceptional beauty, along with her great posture and poise, the elegant black 'Armani' pantsuit she wore, her mid-heeled emerald green designer shoes, as well as her refined European accessories, sharply contrasted with the terrible sloppiness of the people with whom she shared the sidewalk.

Many North Americans were borderline obese, and were dressed in baggy pants or shorts, with extra loose t-shirts. Even though it was not yet noon, a few of them were already staggering, carrying their pint sized umbrella drinks as they window-shopped. All around, the constant chattering and the laugher suddenly bothered her.

Angela felt a new disgust for the human species. Somehow, she was almost ashamed to be part of this decadent American society. All she wanted to do now was to get on a plane and return to London, or Ashington; but she couldn't forget that even in such an idyllic setting as Ashington, her genetic mother lived a life of constant sorrow and alienation.

Is there any cure for the pain of life? She sadly thought, feeling like crying again.

Passing by a little corner flower shop, Angela stopped to gaze at the colourful pails full of multicolour tulips, roses, carnations, and exotic orchids. She bent down to deeply inhale the scent of wisteria and lily, which reminded her of Josephine's garden.

How I wish I could turn back the clock... I miss mama and papa so much... She deeply sighed.

Had it only been weeks since the sweet Josephine and André died?

Angela made a mental note to buy some flowers for her parents' graves. She was determined to keep the tears from falling this time. If she were to win this battle, she realised that she would need to toughen her skin; and toughen her heart as well...

She walked, and walked with a heavy heart, until an incredibly sweet aroma - one of fresh dough and sugar - caused her to salivate. She could see the baker making 'Beignets', French delights that were similar to doughnuts - but much lighter - in the window of the quaint "Café du Monde". His face was red from the steam rising from the pot of boiling oil, but his expression was kind, reminiscent of an old world peasant. A feeling of safety permeated the place, and despite the long line of people waiting for tables, Angela gave the pretty young mulatto hostess her name.

Ten minutes passed, and there were still three names in front of hers on the list... Angela's stomach was growling, when a tall Caucasian man dressed in a dark blue suit and wearing dark glasses approached her.

"Miss, I suggest you forget the wait and take a seat at that table at the corner." His tone was more of an order than an offer. Barely smiling, he pointed towards a small corner table where the Texan that Angela had met on the plane, on her way to see Josephine, was seated...

The Texan was dressed in a stylish blue pastel suit, with a matching shirt, and ostensibly wore a heavy gold and diamond-studded "Rolex". Another goon with short dark hair- who could have been the twin of the man speaking to Angela - stood behind the Texan, his hands crossed behind his back.

"Thank you for the offer, Sir." Angela politely said, "but I can see that the table is already occupied..."

"Yes, Miss," the man said with a face void of expression. "But the gentleman who's sitting there requests your presence; so please, Miss, follow me." He firmly insisted.

The man was so arrogant that Angela almost laughed.

"And who are you, Sir, if I may ask?"

"His bodyguard, Miss," he flatly answered without cracking a smile.

"And why does this person need a bodyguard?" Angela dryly asked, almost amused now.

"That gentleman is an important man, Miss. Now, if you would please follow me." He insisted again.

"Him, a gentleman?" *That disgusting Texan is used to getting his way...* She nervously thought. "No thanks, Sir, but I prefer to wait for my own table!" She firmly said. The thought of conversing with the sleazy Texan again was too much for her to bear.

The bodyguard inched closer to Angela; a bit too close...

"Miss," he said; his voice becoming harsh, "the gentleman will be very disappointed if you refuse his invitation. So I advise you to follow me."

"Well, too bad. But I'm declining his invitation!"

The man frowned and his eyes flashed with menace. "I'd advise you not to decline, Miss." He coldly said.

"That's enough, now! Please, leave me alone," Angela calmly, but firmly said, although it was hard to contain her fury.

Without warning, the man grabbed her firmly by the arm. "I suggest you reconsider, Miss," he hissed. "This gentleman's not someone that you want as an enemy..."

Angela wriggled from his grip. "And I suggest you leave me alone, or I will call the police!" She firmly said again, this time raising her voice.

The man straightened his dark suit jacket and smiled coldly. "Once again, Miss, I suggest that you reconsider and sit down with the gentlemen for a short chat. That's all..."

This time he smiled, but it was just a trick of a smile. All Angela's pent up emotions from the past five weeks suddenly blew up to the surface. She was about to slap the man, when she heard a familiar voice coming from behind her back.

"Well hello, Miss Boivin... Is there a problem?" Emmanuel Lambert said before he threw a cold smile at the bodyguard.

"Yes, there is. This man won't take no for an answer!" She nervously said, rolling her eyes.

"Beat it, jerk!" The bodyguard hissed.

"Excuse me?" Emmanuel calmly said. "I think that the lady prefers that you beat it!"

Angela nervously watched as the second bodyguard rushed to the side of his twin and sneered at Emmanuel. "It's brave of you to defend the little lady, but I'd advise you to let her go, before I break your back, asshole!"

Emmanuel's expression dangerously tightened. "Don't threaten me, clown! I'm an expert in Tai Kwon Do. It'll be my pleasure to give you a free demonstration right now," he coldly said, before removing his jacket. Under his thin white cotton t-shirt was a torso as lean and muscular as a young Doberman's...

Both bodyguards laughed, then the first one said, "You don't scare me, asshole! If we get our hands on you, your own mother won't recognise you."

"Don't be so sure of that… How about we take it outside, Sir," Emmanuel coolly offered, while casually handing his cream coloured linen jacket to Angela.

The two men sneered, before turning to where their employer sat, watching. Angela saw the arrogant Texan gesture to his boys with a wave of his bejewelled hand.

"Guess this is your lucky day, Tarzan!" The first bodyguard said. "Your life has been spared; for the moment…" He viciously smiled.

"Well, needle head, I think it's the other way around," Emmanuel firmly rectified, before protectively taking Angela's arm. They watched in silence as the two men walked back to their boss like a couple of well-trained German shepherds. Then Emmanuel led Angela to a table on the other side of the café, where his sister was sitting.

"Christ! What was that all about?" Jeanette softly asked, putting a protective arm around Angela's shoulders.

"You don't want to know," Angela nervously said, before reaching for a hot beignet. "May I?"

"Please do," Jeanette responded with a lovely smile, while pushing the plate towards Angela.

"Who is the guy who owns the goons?" Emmanuel asked, his eyes still following the strange trio's every move.

"Just a rich obnoxious Texan," Angela explained. "I guess he's got some enemies, or perhaps he's plagued by demons." She nervously laughed.

"Do you know him?" Emmanuel asked, visibly intrigued.

"No, not really... I met him on a plane about two months ago. I don't think he gets the meaning of the word no."

"If you ask me, he looks more like a pimp," Jeanette added, while still observing the man.

A few minutes later, the three of them watched as the Texan and his unpleasant bodyguards stormed out of the café and got into a big white Cadillac limousine that was awaiting them outside.

As soon as the stretched limousine started, the Texan began ranting and raving.

"Who does that little ballerina cock teaser think she is?" He fumed. "She goes putting on big airs like she's some sort of lady, when in fact she's just a nigger lover! Dirty fucking cunt!" He finally screamed at the top of his lungs.

As he poured himself a glass of 'Three Roses' scotch, he nervously addressed the first bodyguard. "I want you to find out which hotel this 'Miss Angela Boivin' is staying at, ASAP, my boy; then send big Dick and little Dick over and tell them that she's expecting an intimate little "tête-a-tête" with those two sweet niggers... After all, that pretentious cunt seems to like Negros; so, those two over sexed niggers should be just what the doctor ordered!" He exclaimed, before he viciously laughed. "And let them know that this little tramp's a classical dancer. What a pity if her precious legs were broken; and what a pity if she couldn't dance anymore for the rest of her life…"

Inside the French café, Jeanette gaily laughed. "What a joke that man is!" She exclaimed before taking a delicious hot beignet.

Jeanette would not have laughed if she really knew who the Texan was.

Demons are known sometimes to put on the guise of a human face; yes indeed…

The devil smiled again.

Chapter Forty-Four

"New Orleans"

"The French Quarter"

Under a cerulean cloudless sky, as Angela briskly walked on Royal Street towards her hotel, her cell phone softly rang in her handbag...

At first, she didn't recognise the number; but deep down, she immediately knew who the person was, before the woman's high-pitched voice slithered through the atmosphere...

"Hello, sweetie. How have you been lately? Did you miss me?" The mysterious woman softly asked. "Ohhh, silly, me; of course you didn't. Not with your father dying and all!"

She's well informed, I'll grant her that. How can she know so much about my life? Angela thought, starting to feel panicked.

"By the way, sweetie, did you receive the little package I sent you yesterday?"

"What are you talking about? Which package?" Angela nervously asked.

"Just some, uh, artistic pictures... I think you will like the angles, my dear; I've never seen anyone so flexible... It's quite amazing!" She elegantly laughed. "And please, my dear Angela, don't thank me; it's just a small token of my appreciation... Simply enjoy those pictures, sweetie. I'm sure that they'll be a comfort in your great solitude." She laughed again.

"Whoever you are, you really are a real bitch!" Angela hissed, shaking now from her head to her toes.

"Oh pleeease, sweetie, that was uncalled for... I just want to help you, that's all, and it really hurts me to see how ungrateful you are... Oh well. Enjoy the photos, anyway." The woman dryly said, before she nervously hung up and threw away the little cotton handkerchief she'd placed over the public phone to protect her from disgusting human germs; then she left the red booth and hurried towards her top of the line luxurious limousine...

"Clive", her handsome Scottish private chauffeur, didn't dare to look at his "ladyship" when she nervously opened the door. Although it greatly piqued his curiosity to see his ladyship using a public phone, when she had one in her private limousine, and another in her crocodile purse, but the well trained Clive didn't dare ask any questions; after all, he was being paid extremely well for his lifelong discretion at her service...

As soon as the elegant Gail Haddington sat down on the plush burgundy back seat, she reached for the bar. She badly needed a drink. As she poured herself a double scotch on ice, Clive smoothly manoeuvred the spotless 'Rolls Royce" into the evening traffic.

What is the purpose of being so bloody wealthy, if I still have to put up with the annoyances of ordinary traffic? Where are all these people going anyway? Gail fumed.

She harshly surveyed the mixed crowds roaming London's sidewalks, trying to separate the true 'English people', from the mongrels...

How utterly depressing! Just look at all those coloured people; truly disgusting!

Along the sidewalk of the long busy artery, the cherubic pale rosy features that defined Gail's 'noble race' had become almost extinct lately...

While her elegant limousine passed in front of the "Royal Albert Hall", Gail took a swig of scotch and toasted to "the end of civilisation", cursing the bloody third-world immigrants, as well as all those annoying dirty Arabs who'd little by little invaded her beloved country during the last fifty years...

And to think that all those coloured people didn't even have to fight a decent war to get in... She fumed again, appalled.

Pure undiluted hatred filled Gail's heart, as she wondered if Britain had made a mistake when it chose to fight against Germany. *God forgive me!* She quickly muttered, her eyes rolling heavenward. *Still, it would be so nice to go back in time, to stroll down the streets of London and see nothing but pink cheeks and clear coloured eyes...* She sadly thought.

"I think that what we really need now is a good old-fashioned war! One that would allow most of these undesirable coloured immigrants to die for England!" She nervously said aloud, envisioning the beautiful Angela dressed in military duds, defending Gail's beloved motherland from the front lines; the first enemy bullet speeding straight into her head, of course...

Gail spat out a raucous laugh. "That's the spirit!" She joyfully exclaimed before she nervously laughed, feeling the alcohol's effect.

Clive sighed with relief, hoping that his ladyship's hellacious mood had finally passed; but Gail's pleasant fantasy popped as quickly as French champagne bubbles...

Even if there were a war, the annoying Angela wouldn't be drafted, because she's unfortunately too famous... Plus, she's not English; she's one of those retarded decadent Americans...

Still, the appealing idea of war brought Gail some hope, and she lifted her 'Water Ford' crystal glass in a toast to "World War III", giggling.

But a stray bullet could nonetheless kill Angela... She thought again, devilishly smiling.

At this instant Gail was too consumed by her batty fantasy to pay attention to the hotel on her side of the street; not that the building's façade of the 'Blake' was extremely remarkable, but the happy few clients who knew well this intimate "boutique hotel", knew full well that the service was always impeccable, and the rooms decorated with great taste...

In the intimate but decadently luxurious 'cardinal suite', a voluptuous young woman was languorously laying naked upon the spectacular crimson red baldachin bed.

The woman had her eyes half closed and she was softly moaning.

The dark golden skin of her complexion shone as if it were under a full tropical moonlight. Her pretty exotic face was framed by a mane of thick ebony hair, which sharply contrasted with the white satin pillow that she languorously rested upon. Her full voluptuous breasts fell slightly on each side of her chest, and her large brown nipples rose hard as unripen berries, as she slowly teased them with her long crimson red fingernails.

In one bold manoeuvre, the woman flung her legs apart; then a wide smile lit up the face of the cherub-like naked Caucasian man, who up to that moment, was silently watching her from a golden and red velvet chair, that he'd strategically placed in front of the bed for his sole pleasure...

Now, the woman's favourite and most generous client - a bi-weekly regular - stood up and poured a few precious drops of his favourite 'Macallan' scotch on the sacred temple between her soft legs; then he slowly dropped to his knees, as if he was ready to pray, before he eagerly lapped up the wonderful Scottish elixir, delighting in the musky flavour that the woman's strong fluids added to the aged scotch...

Soon, the voluptuous Anglo-Pakistani upscale whore was moaning loudly and convincingly, squeezing her firm melon sized breasts together, while the 'oh so proper' Sir "Stuart Eugene Edward Haddington", thrust his reddish reptilian tongue into her musky vagina, greedily drinking from her "font of pleasure"...

313

Stuart's thin pinkish penis was stiff as a bamboo stalk, when he lifted his heavily porky torso from between the whore's plump legs, finally taking his final position above her like a Spanish matador, before plunging himself with great delight deep inside her hot and moist vagina...

"Ohhh my God... That's sooo good!" Stuart ecstatically moaned, feeling the whore's intense heat spreading through his sensitive groin, not knowing that at the same moment, from the plush passenger seat of her luxurious limousine, his "beloved wife" uttered the exact same word; but that latter was referring to the double shot of exceptional 1973 scotch she had just poured herself; a 'Macallan' scotch, of course, since the extremely refined Gail Haddington - just like her "dear husband" - liked only the best things in life.

Ahhh, those little, but so important pleasures of life; ohhh, yes indeed...

"To the next bloody war!" She happily toasted.

To the next bloody war... The devil whispered again in her head, delighted...

Chapter Forty-Five

"New Orleans"

"Monteleone Hotel"

When Angela arrived at her hotel, two large 'FedEx' envelopes were awaiting for her at the front desk...

The first envelope was from the private detective agency she hired to follow Pierce when she was in Milan. Somehow, she felt ashamed that she had dropped to such drastic measures, but what other choice did she really have? After all, she was on a quest for the truth. The truth about her birth, as well as the truth about her private life; but so far, things hadn't always gone as she planned...

"A picture is certainly worth a thousand words", she sadly thought with great disgust, before nervously throwing the thirty or so photographs on the floor of her suite's spacious living room. To her total surprise, there wasn't just one woman involved with her husband; in fact there were three!

Angela felt as if a corkscrew was being twisted through her heart.

There must be a reason for it... She sadly thought, deeply shivering, feeling nauseous. Maybe the realisation that Angela was not exactly who her husband thought she was, caused him to go on some sort of "sexual binge", like an alcoholic?

I'm seeing ghosts and Pierce seems to be addicted to sex? Wonderful! She sadly thought, refraining from screaming.

When Angela had the courage to read the note that came with the photos, she found out she was deeply wrong. It seems that her dear husband had been seen with the pretty young blonde hairdresser, as well as the even younger brunette jazz dancer, much prior to Josephine's death; only his affair with the beautiful thirty-two year old Rose-Mary Bernhart, the sexy antique dealer who'd he'd said "was a client" of his law firm, when Angela had met her in the Italian restaurant, had begun only shortly after Angela returned from New Orleans from Josephine's funeral...

The little irritating voice in her head viciously shouted. *"You fool! Did you think that your handsome rich husband was faithful? Did you really think that any man could be faithful to you? Who exactly do you think you are? A diva? A goddess or what? You stupid coloured bitch!"*

Stupid! stupid! stupid! Angela stomped with rage on the photos, while a pain as sharp as a hot dagger twisted through her broken heart, before she shakily opened the second envelope.

As Angela threw the almost pornographic photos of Rose-Mary Bernhart and Pierce on the floor with the others, then she sadly looked at the precious 'Natalie Baroni' ring that she had always been wearing on the small finger of her right hand since her third weeding anniversary that they celebrated in "Carmel" after a romantic trip along the coast of California. The ring was a loving present from Pierce. It represented a cupid's face, which had been carved into a large piece of angel skin coral framed with solid gold. Cupid, the angel of love...

As Pierce gave her that beautiful ring, he looked into her eyes and said those loving words: "For you my love; to the love of my life. You made me the happiest man in the world. For my everlasting love for you..."

As burning tears blurred her vision, a disgusting acrid taste suddenly rose in her throat; then, weaving like a drunk, Angela ran into the bathroom and threw up.

Ten minutes later, she collapsed in her bed and wept.

An hour later, when her head had slightly cleared, Angela finally called her husband on his cellular phone.

After four rings that seemed an eternity, Pierce finally answered the phone.

She heard a din of voices and the sound of a woman laughing joyously in the background...

"It's me!" Angela exclaimed with a voice colder than the chilled vodka Pierce was drinking. "We need to talk…"

"Well, hello my daaarling. What's wrong? Hold on a bit, will you?" There was a hush, as if he'd put his hand over the receiver. "Daaarling, what's wrong?" He asked again.

"Wrong?" She coldly repeated, letting forth a short sarcastic laugh. *I've learned that my life has been one long lie, and he wants to know what's wrong? Amazing!*

Slowly, but surely, Angela narrated Pierce's past betrayals in full glorious detail, quoting the dates of each of his affairs, as well the ages, names, and professions of his three "paramours", as to demonstrate to him that she was extremely well informed...

Again, Angela heard Pierce's hand over the receiver, but this time the din was gone; all she could hear now was the sound of running water...

He must've retreated to the men's room. The bastard!

"Darling," Pierce slowly began. "I'm extremely sorry that you found out about my horrid behaviour... But a private investigator? Was that "really necessary"? Why didn't you simply ask me, darling?" He softly asked. "It was never my intention to hurt you. I hope that you know this... I truly love you, you know; perhaps if you'd come to me with your concerns... Perhaps if you –"

"Great!" Angela loudly interrupted him. "Now you're trying to blame me? Concerns? Do you want to talk about "my" concerns? You were terribly unfaithful, Pierce!" She finally shouted. "If that is "love", I don't need it! You totally disgust me!!!" She shouted again, this time beside herself.

"Calm down, Angela, pleeease calm down ... I'm truly, truly sorry." He softly said again, like an innocent young boy. "Deep down, you certainly know, my love; that those women are absolutely nothing to me... It was just sex! Try to take a look at it from my side. I simply didn't want to bother you, my darling, with all that's happening in your life lately… I'm only a man, you know!" He softly, but firmly said.

Like the excellent lawyer he was, Pierce was masterfully tap-dancing, turning the tables, making excuses and buying time; as always…

"You have to admit that you travel too much with the ballet," he calmly went on again. "And sometimes I get lonely… I was missing you; I miss us… I simply want to settle down, my darling, and have a family with you… I do love you so." He sincerely said. As Pierce said those simple, but so important words, Angela heard the sound of a toilet flushing and imagined her heart was swirling down into the sewer as well…

"So, my dear Pierce, you're the victimised husband now? And your latest fling; this Rose-Mary Bernhart? That refined slut came to help you bear "your heavy cross", as kindly as the sweet Mary-Magdalene? Who are you kidding? You jerk!!!" After shouting those words, at the very moment, Angela could have killed Pierce with her own hands.

"Oh, stop this Angela. Please just calm down! This is not you talking!" He dryly exclaimed, sounding truly annoyed. "Our marriage can survive this; we will survive this! You know what they say about us men. 'We're dogs', the lot of us, but we work hard, so sometimes we need to let off steam… It's in the genetic program, I guess. And of all people, you certainly know how "genetics" can play tricks, darling…" Pierce chuckled; but his attempt to make a joke about Angela's familial circumstances, made her even angrier and suddenly unlashed the ferocious demon living in her head...

"Pierce, you're not even sorry, are you? Proud to be a dog? Genetic tricks? Do you know who I really am? Do you have any comprehension of what exactly I've been going through lately? You haven't even bothered to ask me what I've found out about my family roots here! Do you even give a shit that lately I'm half losing my mind? That I'm really being haunted by ghosts! That my whole world has collapsed since my parents died?" She finally cried, while uncontrollably shaking from her head to her toes.

"Angela, pleeease! Are you losing your mind? And for the last time, my darling, there is no ghost! This is very hard on me as well, you know; and quite embarrassing... In fact, daaarling, you haven't been yourself the past few weeks and..."

That was it! Pierce had managed again to turn the tables; instead of being the accused, he was "the accuser"; the lawyer again...

Violently, Angela hung up. At this point of their conversation, she didn't want to hear his lame excuses; at this point of her life, she didn't care anymore...

Not knowing what else to do, she fell to her knees and fervently began to pray.

"Ave Maria," she whispered with a broken voice, trying her best to find a speck of peace in her tormented heart; but a knock on the door roused her from her supplication...

Her face fell when she opened the door.

"Ohhh," Jeanette said, surprised, realising that Angela had been crying. "I didn't mean to bother you... Maybe this is not a good time!"

"No, no it's fine," Angela tiredly replied, trying her best to keep her voice from shaking.

"Emmanuel and I are playing tourists tonight and we'd love your company..." Jeanette said, visibly embarrassed. "The agenda includes a lovely steamboat ride, dinner at one of the best restaurants in the French Quarter, and later on a fantastic classic jazz club. You in?" She softly asked, this time with a tender smile.

"I... I can't," Angela said a bit too quickly, before she took a deep breath and reconsidered. "Okay. Sure. Why not? I could use a night on the town, tonight." She sadly said. *Anywhere but here...*

"Wonderful! We'll be back in an hour to pick you up, then." Jeanette said with a big smile, before softly kissing her moist cheek.

As soon as she left, Angela ordered from room service a strong double Italian espresso, as well as some fresh cucumber slices, before taking a long hot shower to soothe her nerves. Although her tears still flowed mixing with the running water, she strangely felt a little bit less bitter than before. Pierce may have broken her heart, granted, but she would never allow him to harden it.

No! It's time to be gentle with myself. I love and respect myself, and I promise that I will never be weak; never! She thought, deeply revolted.

After her long rejuvenating shower, Angela slathered her skin with an English amber and vanilla scented nourishing lotion, placed the cucumber slices on her puffy eyes, then she lay down for fifteen minutes with her legs up against the white padded head of the large bed.

Later on, she put her hair up in an elegant "French twist", and carefully applied two heavy coats of black mascara, a dab of rich golden burgundy lipstick, as well as a light coat of powder, before she dared to smile again at herself in the mirror; then she clad herself in a spectacular 'Azzedine Alaïa' knee length black stretch jersey dress that was deeply cut in the back, and put on a pair of sexy high heeled strappy gold sandals that she'd picked up during the summer on a whim on Carnaby Street.

After spraying a few clouds of her beloved 'Calvin Klein' *Eternity* above her head, Angela was finally ready for the night. What she would make of it, was now up to her now…

A moment later, there was a soft knock on the door. Despite Angela's sour mood, she laughed along with Jeanette, as they eyed each other's outfits. Jeanette had her hair up as well, and she was wearing a white dress cut in a similar manner. As she graciously twirled around Angela, the scent of her wonderful *L'Air du Temps* 'Nina Ricci' perfume suddenly embalmed the air…

"You two could pass for sisters!" Emmanuel joyously remarked, before gallantly offering an arm to each of them. "Ladies, you are truly gorgeous; and that makes me an extremely lucky man!" He exclaimed with a big smile.

"You certainly are, brother!" Jeanette joked, as the three of them walked spritely towards the elevator. The company of her two new friends greatly lifted Angela's spirits and she realised that she'd never met anyone so charming before. She was deeply grateful for this.

Soon after, at the bar of the 'Creole Queen', the three of them drank exotic cocktails and enjoyed the drones and coos of a very pretty, middle aged black female vocalist whose voice was as smooth as the great "Billie Holiday's". The singer, elegantly clad in a black and white satin long evening dress, even looked a lot like the famous jazz legend...

The jazzy music, along with numerous delicious cocktails, made Angela quite receptive to the magic of the warm Louisiana night, as well as the haunting ambiance of the mysterious willow trees lit by a giant opalescent moon. When the stylish black singer paused, the nocturnal sounds of the bayou - frogs croaking and crickets chirping - soothed Angela's mind and somehow helped her forget; if only for a moment...

Much later on, Jeanette, Emmanuel, and Angela had dinner at "Antoine's", where they feasted on spicy 'Cajun' crawfish, delicious extra spicy jambalaya, creamy oysters 'Rockefeller' - Antoine's specialty – and, of course, the best French champagne. For dessert, they had an incredibly light 'Saint Honoré', a true French delight; as well as some freshly made chocolate profiteroles. Afterwards, they strolled through the busy French Quarter and club hopped...

This special evening, Angela fully gave herself to the music and languorously danced with her soul, until she completely merged with the hypnotic beat. Long after midnight, when the handsome

Emmanuel took her in his strong arms for a slow dance; she simply closed her eyes and imagined that she was floating upon the warm Caribbean Sea. If she had opened them, she would have seen the French artist gazing at her as though she were Botticelli's Venus…

Ever since the incident at the café with the annoying Texan, Emmanuel realised that he was possessed by a strange urge to protect her, as well as to take care of her; something that he never experienced with any woman before. But as they danced together, Angela kept her eyes closed and only the music was truly alive for her. Deep in her heart, she just wanted to escape from the gloominess of what her life had become lately. She just wanted to relax, to float, to fly; and above all, to forget…

By the time the three of them returned to the hotel, it was past four in the morning, and the opalescent moon was declining in the horizon.

"Thanks for coming, Angela. That's what I call a great evening out!" Jeanette sweetly said, before giving Angela a warm hug. "Maybe tomorrow?"

"I'm still wide awake," Emmanuel softly said. "What about a sunrise walk, Angela?" He winced when he saw his sister crack a smile. "Sleep well, Jeanette," he sweetly said, as he took Angela's hand in his. Strangely enough, without the slightest hesitation, she simply followed him, as if she were in a sort of trance…

The beautiful New Orleans was wonderfully quiet now. This was a rare moment; a moment of perfection...

When they reached the Mississippi's riverbank, Emmanuel gently took Angela's head in his hands, and then he deeply kissed her. Strangely enough, she didn't resist and an angel passed, smiling...

Much later on, the first golden rays of soft morning sunshine lazily slipped through the slats of the Venetian blinds of Angela's bedroom and softly played upon the white cotton sheets that were draped around her body. When Emmanuel opened his eyes, he wasn't sure whether to sketch Angela for his masterpiece, or passionately kiss her; but all he knew was that he could not summon the will to disentwine his limbs from hers, so he held on tightly, preciously; lovingly...

At some point, between the setting of the magical moon and the rising of the glorious sun, this beautiful woman who peacefully slept beside Emmanuelh had become essential to his well being, and to be separated from her now would feel like an amputation.

Emmanuel lovingly buried his face against Angela's neck and whispered, "I love you..." Then he silently watched as she sensually smiled at him, still half asleep...

In all his years of painting, Emmanuel Lambert had never seen such radiance.

He sensually followed the sinuous lines of her body; followed her slender arms, her elegant hands and her lovely fingers, as well as her long chiselled dancer's legs, sketching each minute detail in his artist's mind.

From her head to her toes, Angela was simply perfect...

The glare of the platinum and square diamond eternity ring she wore, shocked him out of his romantic revelry. Emmanuel had never dated a married woman before, simply because that was against his principles. As he sadly stared at the quite large 'Cartier' eternity ring, he sadly realised that it was more than just an expensive object; it was in fact a seal of property; and each facet was a wall of a fortress…

For an instant, Emmanuel tried to forget that Angela was married, so he held her tight, wishing only that they could fall back into the romantic cover of the night where dreams of eternal love felt like reality…

As Emmanuel closed his eyes, a few digitised notes of Beethoven's "Fifth" shrilly chimed from her cell phone, which was placed on the night table.

Slowly, Angela disentangled herself from his protective arms and tiredly glanced at the clock. It was almost 8 o'clock. Smiling, she realised that she had finally managed to sleep without being plagued by nightmares; and above all, without the help of pills. As the phone shrilly rang again, Angela froze, suddenly awake; suddenly anxious, guilty and extremely confused…

As she answered the call, she threw Emmanuel an apologetic look.

"Pierce," she nervously whispered, recognising the number, "I am listening…"

As she tightly held the little black phone to her ear, she watched helplessly as Emmanuel quickly threw on his clothes, before he silently left the room.

Fifteen minutes later, Angela stood in the shower, letting the hot water cascade over her body. In an instant of mental clarity, she thought she had made a decision; but now, she did not know what to do anymore; in fact, she was lost...

Could I be in love with Emmanuel? Or was last night just an afterthought, catalysed by hurt and anger? No, I didn't use Emmanuel... From the first moment I saw him, I wanted him. More than that; it's as if I've known him all my life. How strange... I have never felt this way before... She thought, shocked and deeply disturbed.

Angela energetically shook the water out of her hair, along with the idea that she could be so irrational out of her head. *It certainly was the alcohol... Alcohol combined with lust. There can be no other reason...* She thought again, trying her best to be rational.

Still, Pierce had to passionately court her for five long months, before Angela agreed to make love with him, simply because she had never been the easy type; she had too much self-esteem to automatically give men what they wanted, and God knew full well that they all wanted the same thing...

Angela fell into an excruciating irritating argument with herself.

This had nothing to do with alcohol, girl; you really wanted to feel him making love to you. Since the first moment he smiled to you, you wanted to fall into his arms... You know that. Don't lie! An annoying voice argued in her head.

No! It was just an escape... an escape from Pierce's despicable cheating; from Eileen Hoxworth; from manipulations, pain, deceit, and death... Grief sometimes makes people behave strangely; I wasn't - am not - myself. And I was tipsy; the cocktails and champagne; the cool jazz; the scent of the night, and... him! She thought, feeling now terribly guilty.

Emotionally drained by her intense internal argument, Angela fell back on the bed, feeling empty; feeling truly lost again...

The warm sheets smelled of their lovemaking; of Emmanuel's delicious vetiver scent; of his pleasant sweat...

Angela's world changed again in an instant. Could she be "in love", even when her entire life was lately falling apart? She lovingly recalled Emmanuel's passionate first kiss and immediately felt her genital muscles flutter; strangely enough, the very thought of him inside her, gave her a slight orgasm...

No, this can't be happening, it's just crazy! My husband had an affair, and I will be mature about it and forget about it!

But could Angela also forget about the unforgettable Emmanuel Lambert?

If it weren't for the damned Hoxworths, I'd pack my bags and catch the next flight to London. She thought, feeling lost and full of self-hatred.

Liar! You are a liar!!! A vicious voice shouted in her head.

Angela dangerously pointed her finger at her mirror reflection, before she nervously laughed, surprised by the loving expression of the strange beautiful woman looking back at her.

Angela hardly recognised herself; she was simply glowing! Glowing...

The beatific smile on her face was truly sincere...

The whole situation was so confusing, so hopeless, that Angela nervously laughed, and laughed, and laughed; she laughed until she cried...

No, I won't let myself! Never! I'm not this kind of woman. I have to stop it!

Angela quickly dressed, exited the hotel like someone on a mission. She walked straight to the little corner flower shop, purchased a large bunch of flowers, and took a cab to the cemetery.

Once there, as Angela sat between the graves of her beloved Josephine and André, she poured out her heart to them. For the first time, she forgave her beloved parents for keeping the truth a secret; then she fervently prayed; until, little by little, her burning tears ceased to fall...

By the time Angela returned totally drained to the hotel, it was almost five p.m.

Emmanuel had left a message...

Angela swallowed her intense desire to return his call. Three times, she picked up the phone; and three times, she slammed it down! She did not want to speak to Pierce either; she was still too angry with him. Yet, she didn't know what to do with herself, so she simply ordered a Turkey club sandwich and some 'Darjeling' tea to her suite; then she called the concierge and requested all calls to be intercepted.

Angela needed to think straight; yes indeed...

Things were complicated enough the way they were in her life now, without adding the unforgettable Emmanuel Lambert to the disturbing equation. Nevertheless, there he was, as real as her ghost; and almost as frightening…

Papa, mama; please, pleeease, help me! Angela sadly thought, feeling totally lost, before she started to cry; again…

Chapter Forty-Six

"New Orleans"

"Monteleone Hotel"

Cold with sweat, Angela awoke at dawn on Monday morning. She sadly watched the luminous numbers on the digital clock slowly transforming from one shape to the next; until they hit six am...

Angela rapidly got up fromh her bed; ordered a continental breakfast, took a long hot bath, and at exactly 8:59, she phoned Edmond Hoxworth's office. After she told the secretary her name, she was given an appointment for the beginning of the afternoon.

Even though the phone message light had been anxiously blinking for the past two hours, Angela did her best to ignore it, burying herself in a new 'Pat Conroy' novel she'd purchased in the hotel shop. But by noon, the walls of her suite were dangerously closing around her. *I've got to get out of here! I can't stand this place anymore...*

Fifteen minutes later, she ran into Jeanette in the lobby.

"Hello stranger," Jeanette sweetly said, before kissing Angela on the cheek. "We were looking all over for you yesterday. Where have you been hiding, my friend?"

"Well... I had things to do," Angela laconically said. "Sorry I didn't have time to play with you two." She said, embarrassedly, while avoiding her eyes, "but as I said before, I am in New Orleans for family affairs, so I'm quite busy..."

Jeanette rolled her eyes and dragged Angela to a nearby cosy sofa, where she made her sit down like a scolding mother. "My brother is very upset, you know," she said lowering her voice, but turning serious.

"Why?" Angela asked with innocent eyes. "I... I don't understand..."

"Oh, pleeease, Angela... Come on! Emmanuel left seven voicemail messages, and there's a giant bouquet of red roses being delivered to your room as we speak." Jeanette said, while searching her eyes.

Nervously, Angela looked up, and sure enough saw a long blond haired young man carrying a large expensive floral box to the front desk. "Oh no!" She quietly said. "I... I... well, I came in late last night and I was extremely tired..." She badly lied, feeling terribly sorry.

Jeanette gently took Angela's hands in hers and deeply looked into her tormented eyes.

"I'm your friend, Angela, and nothing's going to change that... We've got a bond; the three of us, but you've got to be honest with my brother and me... I saw the way you looked at him... I think you're in love, ma chérie, and I'm quite sure that he loves you." Jeanette softly said with a sincere smile.

"But... But I'm married, Jeanette!" *Married to a man who cheated on me, but nonetheless married...*

"I understand, Angela, and so does he; but you don't have to treat us as if we're lepers, just because of a slip..."

"Jeanette, let me finish, please... I'm not making excuses. Emmanuel is certainly the most delightful and decent man I've ever met, but what's good for the goose is not always good for the gander," she nervously said, lowering her eyes again.

"What? I don't follow you... Could you please explain?"

Angela quickly debriefed Jeanette on her recent marital troubles, along with the real reasons for being in New Orleans; something more than embarrassing to her...

"I know... It's not fair to Emmanuel," Angela nervously concluded. "I'm so terribly confused... I can't deny the real attraction that I feel for him, but I need to finish one thing before heading off to the next; don't you think so?" She asked with sad disarming eyes.

"Well, that's for you to decide, ma chérie," Jeanette calmly said. "All I can tell you is that Emmanuel's got something for you that he's never had for anyone else... I think he'd lay down on the railroad tracks and die for you, Angela; and this is a man who worships life!" She said sincerely, visibly not exaggerating.

"Yes, Emmanuel really does love life... He talks about it in wonder like a child. It's amazing," Angela emotionally said, before glancing at her platinum watch. "Oh God, it's so late… Jeanette, please tell Emmanuel I'm truly sorry; please, pleeease… I have to run now for my appointment!" Angela gave her a quick peck on the cheek before she scurried out of the lobby.

Smiling, Jeanette calmly sipped her Cuban coffee and waited for her brother, who joined her a few minutes later.

"Well?" He pensively asked.

"Don't worry bro. She's mad about you! Woman's intuition…" Jeanette assured, before lovingly caressing his handsome face.

Happy like a child, Emmanuel grinned, while thinking that his life was becoming even more wonderful having now found his soul mate; or so he thought…

Chapter Forty-Seven

"New Orleans"

As the taxi approached the imposing gate of Edmond Hoxworth's estate, Angela suddenly regretted drinking that second espresso...

While numerous security cameras whirred and rotated like little robots, their lenses discerning and inquisitive, an intense tension enveloped Angela like a shroud. She nervously wondered who was watching her...

"What a mansion!" The young mulatto cabdriver exclaimed, shrugging in amazement. "Must be important people, eh? Lots of money..." He said with a jealous grin.

"Wealth doesn't necessarily add up to importance," Angela flatly said. "Wait here, please."

"I've waited in worse places, Ma'am," he answered with another grin, before reaching into his pocket for a cigarette. He parked the cab in a shady spot, under three magnificent royal palm trees, and turned up the Reggae music he was listening to; then he settled back to enjoy the vastness of the incredibly luxurious emerald green courtyard.

Before Angela had a chance to step out of the car, an impeccably dressed middle aged black butler stepped from between two giant white Doric columns, and hurried down the large black marble stairs to open her door. He told the driver to park the car in the coach house, before making a graceful gesture to invite Angela to follow him. Somehow, the butler looked tense, and he never looked her directly in the eyes; not even once…

Although Angela tried her best not to be impressed by the grandiosity of the vast estate, she couldn't help herself. She had often danced in some of the finest opera houses in Europe and yet, they didn't hold a candle to the size and grandeur of this home.

This magnificent house was just Edmond Hoxworth's "humble abode", and was the same mansion that Jonathan and Elisabeth once shared; but the private detective told Angela on the phone that this vast estate was nothing, compared to Eileen Mackenzie-Hoxworth's superb French castle, located just outside of New Orleans…

A strange unpleasant feeling overcame Angela, as she suddenly realised that she'd spent the first two days of her life surrounded by such wealth; as strange as it seemed, somehow, this incredible estate was half hers…

Her high heels strangely echoed on the pristine white 'Carrera' marble floor, in marked contrast to the butler's silent footsteps, as he silently led her past three priceless 'Chagall' paintings. Somehow, the playful style and bright colours of the large and spectacular canvasses didn't really seem to fit with the ambiance of the great house, but Angela was certain that their strategic placement was indeed intended to impress. On that account, they greatly succeeded...

The stylish black butler slowly opened the massive mahogany double doors that led into a spectacular pentagonal office that could've passed for a room in the Metropolitan Museum; then he elegantly gestured for Angela to wait, before he silently took his leave.

The extremely spacious room was truly amazing. A mélange of ancient Greek and Roman artefacts had been carefully placed on massive black marble pedestals; and priceless paintings of 'Renoir', 'Cezanne' and 'Monet', lit from above, impressively hung on the mahogany panelled walls. Dozens of precious 'Fabergé' eggs, as well as a vast collection of exquisite solid gold and solid silver 19th and 20th century cigarette cases, were elegantly displayed in a large 18th century Italian curio cabinet; along with a rare collection of bronze, silver and gold antique Roman coins.

From floor to ceiling, two of the large walls were entirely covered with precious ancient books; most of them leather bound and gilded, and exceedingly rare...

It was quite difficult for anyone not to wonder what it would be like to live in such wealth, and to have the chance to have everyday access to such refined beauty; as well as to be surrounded by the works of such great artists. Although Angela didn't want to admit it, she was overwhelmed; but she also strangely and unpleasantly felt like an imposter in this place...

Even dressed as elegantly as Angela was today, in a perfectly cut celadon green 'Carolina Herrera' sleeveless silk dress, accessorised with superb ivory coloured python high heel pumps, and a matching clutch from the house of 'Dior', Angela was suddenly feeling strangely awkward, and ridiculous; almost cheap…

Behind the elegant and imposing presidential 'Regency' desk, two tall French doors theatrically draped with yellow silk brocade, graciously opened to a perfectly manicured garden full of blooming jasmine, honeysuckle and pale coloured roses. The view of the vast and perfectly manicured garden was breath taking, and from time to time, the wonderful flower fragrances rode a soft breeze into the room, adding their delicate sweet scent to the unmistakable aroma of a Cuban cigar.

Angela somehow felt as if she had fallen into a time warp. The entire décor spoke of a refined gentility. One unfortunately lost in a pre-industrial society…

There was no computer, no "iPhone", no television, as well as no unpleasant gadgets of modern technology anywhere to be seen. Except for a tiny surveillance camera in plain view; a warning, perhaps, to keep a guest or business acquaintance from sneaking away with a precious 'Fabergé' egg, or an antique Roman gold coin in his pocket…

Money can really buy one an escape from the stress of modern times, Angela supposed, feeling strangely nostalgic for times past. She was surrounded by things created before the idea of "built in obsolescence" had been invented; when permanence was greatly valued; when artisans made good and beautiful things to be handed down from generation to generation.

A time when a marriage vow meant something, and women like Rose-Mary Bernhart were scorned, not heralded as independent and savvy... She bitterly thought.

Angela's heart weighed heavy as she thought about a world that was lost forever; a world where honour truly meant something...

And yet, her genetic mother had been cast out of this impressive mansion, because of a tragic trick of nature, and also because "bigotry" was rampant; as a result, her genetic father had shot himself because he thought his wife had committed adultery with a Negro; thus, dishonoured...

Angela's nostalgia quickly passed...

To think that my father pulled the trigger in this study... In this very room and behind this very desk., she sadly thought feeling suddenly revolted.

A deadly chill ran down her spine, as Angela imagined her father sitting in the imposing black tufted leather chair, reviewing his options. Were his pale green eyes despairing? Apathetic? Remorseful? Regretful? Defeated? And did he really want to die?

A full size oil painted portrait of Jonathan Hoxworth hung regally above the large carved black fireplace mantel. Jonathan was clad in elegant equestrian clothing, and he nonchalantly stood in front of a spectacular white Arabian stallion. The background and details of the painting were simply magnificent, but it was Jonathan's eyes that really caught the attention; those eyes spoke of genuine kindness, as well as a noble heart...

At this precise instant, Angela strangely realised that she would have certainly loved this strange man; even adored him.

What would my life have been if I had been born white? She sadly thought, feeling strangely vulnerable.

The sound of the door jolted her from her thoughts. She rapidly turned her head, and found herself staring into a replica of her father's eyes; the only difference was that Edmond's eyes lacked kindness...

Her brother Edmond had beautiful, but capricious eyes; eyes that could change directions as quickly as the Northwest wind. Those eyes could affirm, deny, seduce, commiserate, endorse; or simply lie, Angela warned herself...

As if Edmond could read her thoughts, he narrowed his pale green eyes into small steel slits; then elegantly smiled...

Edmond Hoxworth was impeccably dressed in various shades of grey. The material of his suit was the colour of the sea just before a storm. His perfectly combed dark blond hair was thick and shone with a dash of silver grey; a "distinguished" colour that seemed to be the birth right of rich and powerful Caucasian men...

As Edmond silently took "his place" behind his father's imposing presidential desk, his precise mannerisms spoke a volume about him. It was quite obvious that the extremely wealthy Edmond Hoxworth had been bred to command, conquer and control; as well as quite obvious that he was not a man who would easily sway...

"Good afternoon, Miss Boivin." He said with a pleasant velvety voice. "I have to apologise for my tardiness, but I had a small business problem to resolve." He elegantly motioned for her to take a seat on a golden chair; but didn't wait on her before he sat down on the chair his father died upon...

"To tell you the honest truth, Miss Boivin, I'm quite surprised that you wanted to meet me... I'm flattered to make your acquaintance, of course, but I can't see how I can be of any help to you." He softly said, before raising a well-groomed eye brown. "If you're seeking "patronage" to commence some sort of new ballet company in our lovely city, you should know that my lovely grandmother is the one in charge of all our societal charities." His tone was full of condescension now; and somehow, he looked quite amused...

Angela took her seat and softly smiled, amazed at Edmond's chameleon-like qualities.

To think that this arrogant man is my brother! I hope that Jonathan was not like him...

Edmond opened his mouth to say something, but Angela won the race.

"Sir," she calmly said, trying her best to be polite, without seeming too soft, "I'm not seeking patronage. In fact, I do not need any kind of patronage". She icily said, before looking straight into his eyes.

"Then, Miss Boivin, I'm at a loss at why you're here..." Edmond softly said, while his eyes bore into her as he slightly leaned back in his imposing chair.

"Are you?" Angela flatly asked; then she raised an inquisitive brow before she glanced at their father's portrait. Slowly and deliberately, she gave Edmond an abbreviated version of how she had come to the conclusion that she was his genetic sister, while noticing that his facial muscles tensed with each passing word. By the time she'd finished telling him the strange story of the family wayward gene, Edmond's little smile had completely vanished, like a snowflake under the sun...

"Well, Miss Boivin," he calmly said, after he had carefully inspected the records which Bob Tanner had provided. "It seems you are a woman of many surprises... I can honestly say that I am simply taken aback, my dear; yes, taken aback..." He paused, neatly placing his hands palms down on the desk, while carefully examining her entire person. "I honestly don't know what to say, or what to make of this, uh... situation," he slowly continued, visibly buying time to think; then he stayed totally immobile for at least a minute, his strange eyes devoid of emotion, looking as cold as the Antarctica...

After a long embarrassing silence, Edmond Hoxworth was now pushing his palms into the desk with such force, that the bluish veins of his hands were protruding above his wrists.

For a moment, Angela was frightened...

Is he going to hit me? She worriedly thought, while trying to appear calm.

Edmond clasped his hands together and curled his fingers around his knuckles; all of them, except his index fingers, which he kept straight and pointed directly at her.

"No one will doubt that your little tale is a colourful one, my dear Miss Boivin," he calmly said, chuckling at his pun. "That being the case, let's get to the point, then. What exactly is it that you want from me?" He asked, while intensely scanning her eyes; this time Edmond coldly smiled...

Angela bit her tongue. *I want you to be on my side... I want you to admit to the truth; to acknowledge me as your sister, as well as to make amends to our mother; and above all, I want you to act like a real brother, and to say you are really sorry for what your grandmother did to me and our poor mother...* She sadly thought, feeling quite perturbed by his cold reaction.

"My dear Edmond, I was hoping that what I wanted from you would be quite obvious," she finally said, calmly looking now into his inquisitive eyes.

As if he were a little boy bored at the opera, Edmond leaned further back in his regal chair and simply rolled his eyes. "Well, my dear Miss Boivin, I'm afraid it's not obvious to me... Now, you will excuse me, Miss, but I have more important business to attend!" He firmly said. As if the game were over and won, and without looking at her anymore, Edmond Hoxworth slowly began to stand up.

"Then, let me make it very clear to you!" Angela icily exclaimed, settling into the chair. *If his eyes were guns, I'd be dead.* As Edmond eased back into his chair, she swallowed and continued.

"What I want today is for you to grant me permission to conduct a DNA test on our father's remains, so I might have solid proof that I'm indeed Jonathan's daughter; thus, your sister..."

Edmond let his annoyed pale green eyes rapidly brush over Angela's face and hands, before he coldly smiled.

"Well, Miss Boivin, I don't wish to insult the talented ballerina that you are, but I think you'll find the answer to that question by taking a good long look at yourself in the mirror... Unless I'm mistaken, that's not "a tan", I'm looking at; but the skin tone of a coloured woman... You can certainly see by that portrait, Miss, that my father and I are about as white as white can be; no offense to you "people of colour", of course..." Edmond unctuously said, while intending on lowering her "prima donna" ego.

At this precise instant, Angela could've slapped him.

"Right now, Edmond, I have enough proof in the papers you're holding, to get a court order! I was stupidly hoping that you might be a bit more helpful in this matter." She nervously said, slightly raising her voice.

"Really? I think that these papers won't mean much in any court around here, Miss Boivin; people often make mistakes... and the judges in this town are smart enough to know to trust what is as plain as the colour of grass, over some microfiche records kept by a bunch of Mormons," he arrogantly contested, disdainfully handing her back the papers as if they were dirty; but she noticed that his fingers were slightly shaking. "While it may be true that one of my ancestors had "an affair" with a pretty young slave, it certainly doesn't unequivocally prove that you're my father's product, Miss Boivin." Edmond said with a dash of repulsion.

"Precisely," Angela calmly said. "That is why I need the DNA sample. Don't you think it's a bit unfair to our mother?"

"My mother's a tramp, Miss Boivin; as well as a whore, and a nigger-loving liar!!!" Edmond finally shouted, his polished façade crumbling as easily as a sand castle hit by a large wave.

Angela kept her eyes level. "You really disappoint me, Edmond... Our mother has been suffering terribly ever since the day she was cast out of this very house by your dear grandmother; and since that day, the poor woman lives in hope that she'll be reunited with you, her only son, once again... I was sincerely hoping that you would help me; that you would help her. What a fool!" Angela finally said with a broken voice.

"Oh pleeease... You're a quite naïve bastard, then; aren't you? Who do you really think we are; the Kardashian family?" Edmond viciously sneered. "Did you truly expect to be welcomed into our life with open arms, you stupid nigger bitch?" He almost shouted with lethal looking eyes.

Utterly revolted, Angela nervously clutched her purse and firmly pushed her tears back, not knowing what to say.

"So you really did, didn't you?" Edmond viciously laughed. "I think it's time, Miss, that you leave my house and never return! You are totally out of your mind if you think that you're going to disinter my father's remains to satisfy your sick curiosity... I thought "your people" were into 'pride'; so, what's wrong with you?" His mouth dangerously tightened, as he felt a murderous anger mounting within himself. "Do you also think that, since we had a Negro family in the White House, a stupid mongrel like you and the rest of "your people", are really par with "us" now? Well, think again, you stupid nigger bitch!!!" He suddenly yelled, full of disdain, while instantly rising from his chair.

As Edmond Hoxworth dangerously circled Angela, his height ominous, pure hatred glinted in his tormented eyes; then, as he nervously flicked his perfectly manicured nails on the fine silk of her dress, Angela silently sat still as a frightened child.

"You stupid, stupid bitch! Behind those expensive clothes and "diva attitude", you are nothing but an upstart; a poor Negro bastard, and a greedy one at that! Let me tell you something about psychology, little coloured girl. No matter how famous you are now, the pain and shame that ails you will never be filled..." Edmond coldly said before he paused, looking truly disgusted by her. "Isn't it enough that my grandmother gave you ten fucking million? No, of course not! I am sure now that you wouldn't be happy, even with half my fortune... You stupid coloured bitch! Why don't you just go home now and get yourself a good therapist; I truly feel for you!" He violently exclaimed a few inches from her face.

The blood rushed to Angela's face. "Edmond! How dare you insult me? This has nothing to do with money! It's the principle. This is above else, about the truth!" She sincerely said, while her eyes were becoming misty.

"Lo and behold! The nigger bitch is a liar too!" Edmond viciously laughed, again.

Angela felt an ocean of burning tears in her eyes, but she would be damned before she would let her estranged brother know that he got under her skin; so she bit the inside of her cheek so hard, that she could now taste her blood...

"Perhaps I am naïve to expect a welcome from you, Edmond, "my brother"; or from our grandmother..." Angela bitterly said, refraining from crying. "I've certainly discovered that nurture and nature, are both powerful shapers of one's character; although I'm more inclined now to think that nurture is, in your case, the stronger factor... And you, my poor Edmond, are truly pitiful, and I don't envy you a bit; not your life, or your money..." She said with great disgust; then, with those harsh words, she regally rose to her feet. "My heart truly breaks for our poor mother... She still sees you as an "innocent boy"; a boy as kind as our poor father was..." She paused, while slowly shaking her head in disgust. "You're surrounded by so much great, precious beauty; and yet, my poor Edmond, none of it really touches your heart... In spite of your visible efforts to fill this impressive room with priceless art, this room simply stinks when you're in it..." Angela quietly said, as her eyes locked with his.

A large golden antique clock chimed the advent of a new hour, and Edmond Hoxworth began yelling insults again. As if deaf to the sound of his voice, Angela strangely stared at their father's life size portrait, suddenly paralysed by the reality of the composition; until a minute later, the clock chimed again...

Angela glanced at it and realised that it was three o'clock. Like an automaton, she returned her gaze to the portrait, then she blinked; suddenly, Jonathan's portrait seemed different, as if "alive"...

During that time, Edmond ranted on, but all Angela could hear now, was the strange resonance of the chime of the clock hanging in the still air; until an opaque bluish shadow - a strange shadow of light in the form of a human body - slowly emerged from the large painting, like a ghost…

It was Jonathan Hoxworth; it was her father…

Angela could smell now the sweet pipe tobacco and his fresh vetiver perfume…

At the beginning, Jonathan's ghost slowly floated downward, until his feet softly touched the shiny parquet floor. As they did, his ethereal body began to rapidly fill out, his features becoming more human; then the strange apparition silently crossed the large room and passed straight through Edmond, who was still shouting and flailing his arms about in a rage. Jonathan's ghost then sat behind his desk, while his soft gaze remained strangely focused on Angela.

Totally paralysed by fear, Angela watched as the ghost expression changed from peaceful to despairing…

What is he going to do? And why can't Edmond see him? She anxiously thought, feeling paralysed.

Angela was mesmerised and incapable now to say a single word.

Only now she realised that this ghost was definitely the same apparition that she had seen in her bedroom in London…

I'm not losing my mind. I can't be, can I? She thought while nervously blinking her eyes.

Edmond rapidly turned around to face the desk, wondering what had suddenly captured her gaze. Seeing nothing, he nervously shook his head. "I haven't got time for this... I'm a busy man; I want you out of here!" He shouted again, before he stormed out of the room like a madman.

But Angela didn't move. She simply watched Jonathan's ghost open the central drawer of the desk and pull out a little silver pistol. As he did so, several heavy books fell from the top shelves; then the room was suddenly filled with an unpleasant cacophony of strange noises, before Jonathan slowly lifted the nose of the gun to his temple, his gaze strangely fixed on her. Angela had never seen such sad eyes before, and she was deeply touched by a profound compassion that, somehow, overpowered her fear.

Today, another important truth had been revealed: Jonathan Hoxworth, "her father", had died of heartbreak...

Right before Jonathan pulled the trigger, Angela heard this ghost softly saying:

"Please, my dear Mary-Elisabeth; please forgive me, my child. I didn't know the truth..."

Then Angela heard the "bang" of the bullet inside her head, and everything became dark; extremely dark, then she fainted...

Amen.

Chapter Forty-Eight

"New Orleans"

"Monteleone Hotel"

Thirty minutes later, the cab driver parked on Royal Street in front of Angela's hotel and summoned the doorman with a rapid wave of his hand...

"Yeah man, I didn't even notice until I stopped," the cab driver nervously explained, pointing at the elegant young woman lying motionlessly in the back seat. "She seemed fine; I think she just fainted. I wasn't sure whether to take her to the hospital; you know how it is... I fetched her at the "Hoxworth mansion". Thought you might know something. She's something of a celebrity, ain't she? I think I recognise her..." He nervously said, visibly impressed by her beauty.

The doorman, a kind black man on the verge of retirement, rushed to Angela's side and rapidly opened the door. "Miss Boivin? Are you alright? Miss Boivin?"

Angela slowly opened her eyes. "Wha... What?"

"You fainted, Miss." Are you alright?" He asked again.

"I... I think... I'm fine," Angela mumbled, accepting the doorman's arm.

She slowly reached into her purse and gave the cab driver a few bills without bothering to count the sum. "I... I just need to... lie down," she awkwardly told the doorman, who tried his best to hold her steady.

"Angela! Are you alright, ma chérie? You look as if you've seen a ghost!" Jeanette nervously exclaimed, as she was stepping out of the hotel.

Angela blushed; if Jeanette only knew...

"I... I fainted," she whispered, feeling incredibly tired, before closing her eyes.

"But honey, you have quite a big bruise forming on your forehead," Jeanette said, alarmed, before placing her protective arm firmly around Angela's waist.

"Thank you for being so kind, Jeanette, but you're on... on your way out, aren't you? I... I don't want to spoil... your plans." Angela tiredly said, feeling terribly confused.

"Oh ma chérie, don't think anything of it," Jeanette said, frowning, as she firmly led Angela inside the hotel's lobby.

Back in the suite, she helped Angela into a white terry cloth robe; then she put her to bed, taking care to prop up a few pillows and straighten the sheets.

"You're a saint," Angela gratefully said, while closing her eyes.

Jeanette brushed aside the compliment, poured some 'Evian' water she had found in the mini-bar into a glass, and handed it to Angela.

"Sip it slowly, honey," Jeanette said. "And don't talk yet. Your nurse has one more task," she added, scurrying off to fetch a washcloth and some ice. She firmly held the ice pack to Angela's forehead, where the bruise was growing fast as a spring squash. "There now," she softly said, in a motherly way, while settling on the bed next to Angela. "The prognosis looks good, honey; at least from a medical standpoint." She tenderly smiled, before taking Angela's hand.

Soothed by a voice that held the warmth of the tropics, Angela felt the colour gradually return to her cheeks. "You're not going to believe me if I tell you what happened to me," she slowly began.

"You don't have to say anything if you don't want to, ma chérie." Jeanette assured. "But you should know that I would never doubt you, sweetheart. We're a bit beyond that, aren't we?" She softly said, before kissing her cheek.

Angela tiredly smiled, then she slowly told her strange story; including the reason why she had visited Edmond Hoxworth. She even told Jeanette that she had hired a private eye in London and discovered that her husband had betrayed her. With each syllable that painfully issued from her tongue, Angela felt as if a heavy weight had been lifted, little by little, from her shoulders.

Ahhh, the power of confession...

Strangely enough, Angela could breathe much better now, and even think more clearly; and she also felt less alone.

Jeanette's eyes brimmed with tears, then she delicately removed Angela's cold compress and squeezed out the excess moisture, before placing it back on the bruise, which was still considerably swollen.

"You are really something special, my friend." Jeanette finally said. "I can see why Emmanuel's smitten by you..." She paused, before adding, "just promise me that you'll never, ever, keep such terrible things inside yourself... The world doesn't have to be so lonely, you know." She softly said, tenderly smiling.

"So, you believe me?" Angela asked, visibly surprised at her friend's positive reaction.

"About the ghost, ma chérie; or the fact that your husband would be such a fool to cheat on a woman like you?"

Even though she didn't really want to, this time Angela laughed...

"Ma chérie, it's harder to believe that a man in his right mind would intentionally hurt you, than it is to believe that you saw an apparition... The manifestation of ghosts, or 'ancestors' as we generally call them, is quite common on our island, you know," Jeanette calmly said, her eyes lighting up again. "Your father is simply trying to tell you something; or perhaps he needs your help to free his soul from his earthly ties, so he can rest in peace..." Jeanette very seriously added before caressing her cheeks.

"But... But how can I help him?" Angela nervously asked, visibly confused. "How?"

"Well, you might not know it now, honey; but somehow, you're already helping him. And I would be surprised if your dad doesn't have something to do with your obsession to find out the truth behind your birth... There's an old Tahitian saying: 'when a ghost shows his face, there's always more to the story than what the living can see,'" Jeanette explained, grinning.

"Now you're teasing me," Angela said, trying to push herself out of bed; but she fell back on the pillows, totally exhausted.

"I think I should call a doctor. You might have a concussion," Jeanette worriedly said.

"No, please, don't! I don't think I could bear a stranger poking at me right now; particularly a man..." Angela nervously said, before closing her eyes again.

"Well then, have it your way... But I'm going to stay here and watch you for a while, ma chérie. You need someone to take care of you and make sure that you haven't injured yourself," Jeanette firmly added, as she picked up the phone to call her brother. "It's all set! I'm going to stay with you tonight, so no more nightmares, sweetie... And if your dear dad comes around trying to tell you something, he'll have to contend with both of us, my friend." She smiled, but her eyes seriously spoke.

"But I'm okay, Jeanette," Angela weakly protested, reopening her eyes.

"Yes, of course you are, my friend. But together, we'll be even more okay," she firmly said again, before patting her hand.

The next morning, when Angela awoke, she reluctantly admitted that she was grateful for Jeanette's company. "I don't know how to repay you," she said, feeling stupid.

"Shush! But if you insist, ma chérie, you can dance a little something for me... Maybe "Carmen" or "Sherezade"?" Jeanette sweetly joked, before opening the draperies.

Outside, the sky was solid blue and the sun was shining. Jeanette looked down to the street below, not noticing the dark blue 'Lincoln Continental' that was parked half a block or so down St. Charles...

The imposing man who waited and watched from inside that car was more frightening than any ghost that Angela might imagine or see. hGrande indeed was a patient man...

It was enough for Grande now to gaze up at the hotel from time to time, wondering which window led to Angela's bedroom; wondering how her beautiful naked body would feel to his cool touch, before he broke her fragile neck, while looking deep into her eyes just as he did so many times before...

This single exciting thought, by itself, was worth the wait; so Grande calmly waited...

Chapter Forty-Nine

"Hoxworth Castle"

Spectacularly bejewelled, and impeccably clad in a red organza 'Oscar De La Renta' stunning evening gown, the regal Eileen Mackenzie-Hoxworth was on her way out on her private suite, when her stylish black butler told her that "master Edmond" was on the phone...

Eileen nervously glanced at the massive Louis XV bronze doré clock that was displayed on the spectacular red marble fireplace mantel of her private salon, then she scowled. Eileen didn't like being late to any function; particularly charity affairs. She was opening her pretty painted mouth to make an excuse, when the butler interrupted her again.

"Master Edmond said that it is extremely urgent that he speaks to you now, Madam."

Reluctantly, Eileen took the call.

"Hello my darling," she softly said, emitting a small laugh. "Could you make it brief, my dear? I'm on my way to see my dear friend Adrienne Brodmoore... You know that I don't like to abuse the privilege of being fashionably late, my dear." She checked her impressive princess cut diamond-studded platinum 'Piaget' watch and mentally registered the time; she would give her grandson two minutes, no more...

Edmond felt his heart cringe. Even as a grown man, his well-mannered, but so aloof grandmother could still make him sometimes feel insignificant. Edmond knew full well that his grandmother was a rose from the south; an "iron rose" who had mastered the delicate art of saying "no" with an elegant smile. Edmond could not remember a single day in his life when the extremely busy Eileen placed his needs before those of whatever charity, cocktail party, or big social event fashionable in any given week.

"When you hear what I have to say, grand, I think you'll agree that your dear Adrienne Brodmoore and her cronies can wait," he firmly said, his resentment as thick as the fog that had settled on New Orleans for the past couple of days.

Eileen set her refined black satin evening bag on the priceless Louis XV gold-leaf console, then she nervously sat down on a red silk damask sofa; but even before Edmond began to explain, she already knew that Angela had contacted him...

Eileen cursed herself for not following the "tradition" of eliminating any infants that showed signs of their Negro heritage, but this particular baby girl seemed so special, she sadly recalled. Still, Eileen couldn't help wondering if there was some sort of 'curse' upon the family. Even though she had spared Angela from the "Hoxworth family tradition," blood had been spilled. Angela lived, but Eileen's only son – her beloved Jonathan - had killed himself in the wake of her exile...

What was she supposed to do now? Tell the truth? Explain to society that her mulatto granddaughter was stained by unspeakable "debauchery"; by the disgusting blood of African slaves, as well as seven generations of constant lies and infanticide?

If Angela was my own child, I would've certainly stood up and fought. Eileen sadly thought, while sadly remembering the past.

Eileen had lost her own daughter. The sweet "Angelica Maria Aurora" was snatched from her breast as if in a bad dream. Before she could notice, the Hoxworth's family doctor had stifled the baby's breath, and had suffocated her with a pristine white lace pillow that he placed over her tiny head. From within the Hoxworth castle birthing room, Eileen had cried out from her regal bed, her head fuzzy from the opiate wine that the doctor had given her to ease her labour, but no one had listened; no one...

Eileen had never been the same after that terrible day.

Most of the time, Eileen refused her husband's advances, in fear that she would get pregnant again. She also gave huge amounts of money to Christian charities, as to ease her conscience; then later on, she always surrounded herself in excessive luxury, as to also ease her constant emotional pain...

Eileen told herself that, throughout the ages, people had committed much worse sins to protect their names, their entitlements, and their societal status; and that it was not her choice, anyway. Still, for a long time after that terrible day, Eileen couldn't find happiness in life. Then, slowly, after decades of "luxurious misery", she finally managed to convince herself that she was simply content; that was, until that stupid Josephine opened her big Negro mouth and told the embarrassing truth to Angela about her birth...

On the phone, Edmond's voice rose to an almost unnatural pitch, straining to be heard, and the emotional distance between himself and his grandmother seemed to widen again with every syllable.

"Have you heard a single word that I've said, Grand?" He finally yelled, feeling like he could kill someone.

"Edmond, ohhh my dear boy, I'm truly sorry... Give an old woman a break," she sweetly apologised. "Please, my dear, could you calm down a little bit?"

"But why in hell did you deposit ten million dollars in an account in that woman's name?" He abruptly asked.

"Edmond? What are you doing eavesdropping on my personal affairs?" Eileen nervously asked, while covering the centre of her impressive 'Harry Winston' diamond necklace with her hand. "That certainly is not the way a gentleman acts, my dear. You were raised much better than that, my child! I'm severely disappointed in you," she dryly said, putting him on the defensive. "After all, my boy, it's "my" money, and I can do whatever I please with it!" She coldly added. Her grandson's impertinent demonstration of insolence suddenly infuriated her.

"Grand, you're evading my question!" Edmond harshly exclaimed, "Why did you give her this money? Why?" He coldly asked, raising his voice again.

"I am late, my dear!" Eileen coldly replied, deeply annoyed. If there was one thing that truly irritated her, it was justifying her actions to a man; she had enough of that when her husband was alive. God bless his wicked soul, but she was much happier since she had been widowed; happier, freer, and of course much richer...

Edmond realised that he'd gone too far. "Grandma, pleeease," he said, calming himself down. "Of course you have a right to do whatever you want with your money... But don't you think it's time to tell me what's going on with this coloured woman? Why didn't she take the money? Ten million wasn't enough? I want you to know if this woman is threatening you, or blackmailing you, then I'll put an end to it! You perfectly know that one phone call is all it will take... Grand, she is a fake, isn't she? Right?" As Edmond spoke the words, a glimmer of deranged doubt strangely crept up on him.

Eileen remained deadly silent, rapidly evaluating all her options...

"She can't be my father's daughter," he nervously asked again, feeling terribly tense while waiting for herj, as always, to reassure him. Edmond Hoxworth had not felt so alone since the day he realised that he was an orphan. After the incident, he developed a fear of ghosts and refused to enter his father's study. It took him fifteen years of intense psychoanalysis to exorcise most of his internal demons, and finally sit in the same golden chair that his father died in. "Those documents this woman gave me are forged, aren't they, Grand?" He nervously asked, suddenly feeling extremely vulnerable.

Feeling devastated, Eileen deeply sighed. Her grandson would surely find out that the papers were real; and sooner or later, Edmond would have children...

Eileen had wanted to put off telling him the unpleasant truth as long as possible, and she would have preferred to let him know by a post-mortem letter; but now, she was stuck between a rock and a hard place, and only the truth was a strong enough chisel to set herself free. Free; free at last...

"My darling, I am really, really sorry," Eileen slowly began, "but it is time you knew the truth..." She softly said, while her heart was breaking in a million pieces.

In the space of a mere nano-second, Edmond's great pride of being a "Hoxworth", and the core of his being, shattered like a fragile mirror dropped from a skyscraper...

The gold cornucopia that had always fed his extremely privileged world had been suddenly crushed into pulp. As for the name he so proudly enunciated each time he had introduced himself; this great name, his name, became now food for worms, as common as apples and cotton...

To think that the extremely rich and so refined "Edmond Louis Gabriel Hoxworth" was in fact related to a Negro slave was much more than that his giant ego could take; more than his brain could understand...

At this precise instant, Edmond wanted to phone a doctor; phone a shrink; take a pill; take a burning shower, and do anything possible that would cure him from this horrible truth that was, in his mind, worse than leprosy; right now, poor Edmond simply wanted to die...

"It's not the first time, my child," Eileen softly continued. "And it may not be the last... Angela's life was spared because I couldn't force your mother to follow the 'Hoxworth tradition', my child; and also, because I could not be a witness again to a monstrous act that I'd been forced into committing; a monstrous act which had severed me from my soul," Eileen painfully confessed, her voice finally cracking. The giant concrete dam that her iron will slowly had erected throughout the painful decades, suddenly threatened to break. So be it!!!

Her warm salty tears were so long overdue, that Eileen wouldn't be surprised if they were as murky and foul as a long-standing pool of stagnant water...

Attempting to hold her tears back, but totally ashamed, Eileen put her perfectly manicured hands to her face, and her always radiant and spotless skin suddenly felt like a tight mask. Now she felt terribly ancient, as if she had been mummified by a group of expert Egyptian morticians...

When Eileen tiredly glanced at the large Louis XV gilded mirror strategically placed above the imposing fireplace, she saw a reflection of herself that did not please her anymore...

"Yes, my dear child, it's true; Angela is your sister... Her real name was Mary Elisabeth," Eileen said, almost lovingly. Finally, the embarrassing truth was out.

Eileen silently watched as the image of the elegant ageless woman in the mirror seemed to genuinely smile; surprisingly, it seemed that the truth had a rejuvenating effect on her tormented soul...

With the weight of his grandmother's words, Edmond felt like a crushed worm, and for a moment, he didn't know what to say anymore...

"How long, Grand?" He feebly asked. "How long before we're free from this genetic curse?"

"I don't know, my darling... I suppose there's less of a chance with the passing of each generation; of course, my child, you must be careful to find out the exact genetic family background of the person you, or your future children, breed with. It's not as uncommon as you might think, my child... It's just that in most families not living in rural areas, especially among middle class and poor families, the mulatto child would've simply remained "a bastard" or an adopted child, in people's mind... But in our case, there was no other heir to the Hoxworth name, so when the mulatto boy became a teenager, he was forced by his Hoxworth grandparents to wear a wig, as well as pale make-up on every exposed area of his body to look like a Caucasian; and they also forbade him to go out in the sun... This poor boy was light-skinned enough but the Hoxworths knew that he tanned like a Negro boy... I have been told by one of our oldest servants who knew his story that the poor boy had become so terribly ashamed of his natural skin colour, that he almost lived like a vampire; sleeping during most of the day, and reading and working at night." Eileen sadly said, before crying.

Edmond felt his face flush with red-hot anger. "Grand, you stupid fool!" He almost shouted. "What made you rebel against our family tradition? Why didn't you think of me? If my wife gave birth to a... a freak mulatto, I'd have gotten rid of it without a thought!" He forcefully exclaimed, utterly revolted by her stupidity.

Eileen had never seen this side of her "dear Edmond" before...

"And your wife, my child; what about her? Don't you know, my boy, that after carrying a child in one's belly for nine months, a strong bond is created that's totally blind to colour..." She paused to softly wipe her tears. "I don't remember raising you to be so prejudiced, my dear Edmond." Eileen bitterly exclaimed, her voice trembling now.

"I am who I am, Grandma; so please, don't give me now this sudden talk of humanity! I learned everything that I know from you, anyway... Don't you remember what you drilled into my head since I was a child? If you make a mess, Grand, you clean it up! We're in this terrible mess now, simply because you didn't have what it takes to clean it up back then!" He viciously shouted, full of venom.

"And what exactly are you suggesting now, my dear Edmond?" Eileen coldly asked, while tiredly removing one of her 'Harry Winston' heavy diamond chandelier earrings. She was overcome now with an intense nausea and a profound disgust, so she suddenly had no more desire to attend Adrienne Brodmoore's elegant party anymore.

"Grand? Why not finish what should've been finished thirty-two years ago?" Edmond nervously asked with a voice as cold as a tombstone, while deep in his heart, he felt like killing both his Grandmother and Angela, the mulatto bastard.

Without another word, Eileen slowly placed the ivory phone on her precious rose wood desk; then she nervously walked away. Deep down, she was shivering. All she could see now in her tormented head was darkness; but then suddenly appeared the image of her new born baby, at the precise instant when Theresa Hoxworth, her inflexible mother-in-law, snatched her beautiful baby from her breast. Eileen saw the tender eyes of her beloved Angelica Aurora Maria, and deeply shivered; again...

The past has returned to harass me... Why couldn't I die that day? Why? Why?? Why??? She bitterly thought, feeling lost and terribly alone.

As always, no particular "divine answer" came from above; but at this precise instant, the devil himself was listening, smiling...

Amen!

Chapter Fifty

"New Orleans"

"Monteleone Hotel"

For several days, Angela floated in and out of a tormented sleep, grateful that whenever she awoke; either the sweet Jeanette or Emmanuel would be nearby...

I think it's time I get out of bed. She thought, while tiredly stretching her arms.

It was a particularly sunny morning in New Orleans.

Never in her life, had Angela remembered being laid up for so long, and now every muscle in her body claimed for movement.

Quiet as she could, she crept out of the bed and stepped into a pair of sweatpants, a sport bra and a white pair of 'Nike' running shoes. The morning air was cool, so she put on her well-worn ivory fleece jacket, her dancing jacket; the name "Royal Ballet School" was embroidered on the back...

Angela had told the manager of the ballet company that she needed some time off; and although Veronika had begged, argued, moaned and intensely pleaded, the Russian choreographer eventually succumbed to Angela's wishes; then reluctantly granted her a one month leave of absence.

As Angela ran her fingers over the ballet's insignia, she realised how much she missed the dance. In fact, she missed the constant discipline, the rigorous routine, because it had always kept her grounded. She rarely wore this particular jacket when she wasn't rehearsing, and she wondered why it was draped over the chair next to her bed. Her dear Jeanette must have placed it there to cheer her up, or to remind her of who she really was; an exceptional artist; one of the world best ballerinas.

Jeanette always loved ballet, and she told Angela that when she was a little girl, in Tahiti, she had dreamed of becoming a ballerina.

Angela stepped into the living room and tiptoed towards the rollaway bed, where Jeanette was soundly sleeping. She bent down, tenderly kissed her friend on the forehead, and then silently sneaked out the door.

Angela glided through the hotel's lobby, where strangely enough, not a soul acknowledged her presence… Somehow, she was relieved, enjoying the momentary absence of celebrity, as well as the absence of the relative charisma or beauty, that made one person much more noticeable than another.

This is what it must feel like to be a ghost… To move about rooms in complete freedom, invisibly; away from the constant judgment of the public eye… She happily thought, smiling like a child.

Marie-Madeleine MacLean

The moment Angela stepped out of the hotel's entry doors and onto the unusually calm street, she directly headed towards the park and began to run on the well-trodden dirt path.

The strange feeling that she was invisible lingered, and for a moment, Angela felt almost uneasy; but soon, the endorphins began to flow and she became one with the rhythm of her steps. After her muscles were worked, she slowed her gait and turned down a little alleyway, hoping to find a shortcut to the riverbank.

The sweet aroma of Cajun spices and jambalaya simmering; wafted from the back doors of restaurants and Angela paused to inhale the delicious familiar scent, reminding her of the sweet Josephine, then she suddenly became hungry; but the sound of a vehicle behind her caught her off guard...

A black Toyota van would have mowed her down, if she hadn't leapt so quickly to the right. Perhaps, she really was invisible, she nervously thought, deciding that it was time to go back to the hotel.

As Angela rapidly turned around, she saw the black van coming fast towards her again...

When the van screeched to a stop beside her, she jiggled the handle of the door that led into one of the restaurants, but it was locked. Frantically, she began to hit the door with her fists as hard as she could. From inside, she could hear the happy beat of Reggae music and the sound of people talking.

Why don't they open the door? Why does nobody hear me? Why??? She thought, suddenly frightened.

Angela pounded harder, feeling the sides of her hands becoming bruised, and when she turned around, she saw a short muscular black man wearing black sweat pants and a red t-shirt with a kung-fu logo on it, step from the driver's seat of the van; then she saw another black man, a larger one, in dark grey baggy clothing, who came from the passenger side of the vehicle. Looking straight at her, he violently grabbed her by the wrists and viciously smiled, showing a double row of gold teeth.

In total fear, Angela looked down the alley and saw a huge man staring straight at her. He must've been six foot five, she thought, as she opened her mouth and prepared to scream, hoping that he would come to her rescue.

"No one's gonna hear you scream, bitch!" The black man holding her sharply said, as he strongly stuffed a dirty cotton rag in her mouth. She recognised the smell of chloroform; then a short moment later, everything faded to nothingness...

Much later, when Angela reopened her eyes, she was lying naked on a dirty mattress placed upon the damp wooden floor of an old shack.

She could smell the fetid dank scent of stagnant water, and she realised that she was somewhere near the bayou; probably in one of the hundred clapboard houses that rimmed the swamp. The disgusting stink of stale wine, mingled with urine and the smell of the swamp inundated her nostrils, and she had to fight back the urge to vomit. As her eyes slowly adjusted to the light, Angela saw that a kerosene lamp dimly lighted the room; then she saw a big mosquito prick her arm.

Suddenly, the planks of half rotten wood that served as a door violently swung open, and the two black men who had assaulted her walked in with heavy feet. Ashamed to be naked, Angela tried to cover herself with her hands, before she realised that a coarse rope at the wrists had bound her. The two men viciously laughed, jostling one another, and hungrily eyeing her spectacular body. At that instant, Angela realised that there was no use in pleading with them; these thugs were of the sort that got off on a woman's fear. Instead of shouting, she tried to concentrate on the strange sound of a solitary owl hooting, and the strange melody of birds outside in the bayou...

How wonderful it should be to be free of the vicious forces that caused some men to fall into episodes of extreme violence towards women, Angela sadly thought before she closed her eyes, trying to will her consciousness to blend with that of nature...

The short black man let forth a guttural groan and menacingly walked towards her. As he placed a bony hand on her flank, Angela noticed that it began to rain. Drops that seemed too large to be natural, fell heavily upon the corrugated aluminium roof, drowning out the songs of the birds and crickets; but not her terrified screams...

Without reason, the short man viciously slapped Angela three times on the face, pausing just long enough between each strike, so that she could feel the sharp burning sting. The final slap was so brutal, that her vision suddenly blurred; at least, she was spared from seeing the vicious look on his face when he spat on her face...

"Ya little cock-teasing whore! Ya stupid little cunt shouldn't have said no to our boss, bitch! Ya thought ya were too good for him, didn't ya? Well, ya ain't too good for us, suga! Ya gonna get what ya want an be begging for more, sweetheart." Both men cackled, drunk on power, lust, and greed.

Angela tried to use her legs to kick the man away, but the other one firmly grabbed her by the ankles; then forcefully spread her thighs apart, totally exposing her.

The more Angela screamed, the more they viciously laughed; until she finally stopped, realising that no one around would hear her...

Totally frightened, Angela closed her eyes and braced herself for the worst. Cringing inside, she felt one of the man's bony knees on her thighs, immobilising her; then she heard the sound of a belt being unbuckled...

"Open an eye, sweetheart!" The big man exclaimed, still laughing, as he held his fat charcoal black penis in his hand, dangling it in front of her face as if it were a strange puppet on a string. Angela could smell the disgusting scent of acrid urine and musk, and she clamped her lips together, keeping her eyes focused on her ballet jacket, which strangely lay crumpled in a corner, like a dead animal.

"Come on, bitch!" The little black man yelled. "Ya should've known better than think ya're too good for the likes of our boss, suga! What'd ya think? That ya're too much "a fucking star" to be with ya own kind, sweet pussy? Prefer "white cock" to good black cock? Ya stupid cunt! A lill cock-sucker's a cock-sucker!" He shrugged. "Too bad, suga, ya didn't suck the right cock; yeap, now ya're stuck with sucking ours! Ain't she, big dick?" The thug laughed again, while rapidly masturbating now just in front of her face.

Angela was dumbstruck. *Could it be? Am I being raped because I refused that disgusting Texan's advance? How could anyone be so cruel?* The whole thing didn't make sense to her.

The fat black man violently pried her mouth open, holding firmly her jaws with fingers that tasted like sweat, urine, and cheap tobacco; while the other pushed his hard penis against her lips, hesitantly.

"Ya try to bite me an I'll kill ya, fucking bitch! Straight into the swamp, an to the alligators ya'll go, suga!" He menacingly said, while his skinny companion forced his disgusting bony fingers up her vagina.

Angela desperately tried to scream; but once she began screaming, she wouldn't stop. Then, from a strange opaque place that she could only imagine was hell, she heard a strange woman's voice calling her name from afar...

"Angela... Angela... Angela..."

Angela screamed again, wondering if the voice was death calling; then she clearly heard the sweet lullaby that her mother used to lovingly sing to her...

"Don't be afraid, my golden child. Don't be afraid of the thunder..."

At this instant, Angela felt so drained, so tired and so helpless, that she simply let go, surrendering herself to the Almighty and all his angels. Somehow, deep down she understood that she had no choice and that the men would rape her, maybe even kill her; so she simply relinquished her will.

She felt her soul taking leave of her body; then moving towards the pleasant voice that sweetly called her name.

"Angela... Angela... Angela..."

How familiar that voice sounded, she thought; wishing that maybe, she could awake from this horrible nightmare, as she did before with all the others. But when she reopened her eyes, she saw that the fat man was still on top of her, moving himself in and out of her, raping her, ripping her and viciously laughing, while enjoying his prey; his 'sweet', sweet victory...

"Angela!" He was slapping her now, but not as brutally as before. "Wake up! Wake up, honey!"

Startled, Angela opened her eyes.

Strangely enough, the clapboard shack had disappeared, and she was now in the luxurious bedroom of her suite. It was dawn and Jeanette sat on the bed next to her, her face red from worry.

Angela was sure that she was hallucinating, because the pain of the rape was way too much to bear, so that she'd turned off reality; but when Jeanette took Angela in her arms and lovingly rocked her as if she were a child, she let forth a sigh of relief.

The white cotton sheets were wet with her own sweat...

"You were dreaming, honey," Jeanette softly said. "That nightmare again? Your father?"

"No," Angela said, nervously laughing. "It was worse, Jeanette; much worse than that…" She looked up and saw her jacket, the gold embroidery of the Royal Ballet School gleaming. She deeply shivered.

Just a bad dream, a voice in her mind whispered.

Yes, 'just a bad dream'; again…

Chapter Fifty-One

"New Orleans"

"Hoxworth Residence"

Like a madman, Edmond Hoxworth paced back and forth in his vast study, phone in hand; nervously waiting for an answer...

Now and then, Edmond stopped his pacing and punched the richly panelled walls with his fist, not caring if one of the priceless artefacts threatened to fall off a shelf.

Two dozen rings and not even an answering machine. Fuck!

What kind of assassin is this asshole? He thought, revolted.

"Yeah, yeah," Grande finally said, his mouth full of food. "Gimme a second, boss, 'lkay?"

"For God's sake!" Edmond shouted. "Don't you tell me to wait, you idiot! I told you not to move; not even for a second!" He yelled, totally beside himself.

"Oh. Sorry, boss." Grande apologised, swallowing half of a large beef burrito in one bite. Edmond heard the sound of a toilet flushing.

"Where are you, you fucking jerk? And what are you doing? Are you watching her?" Edmond shouted, before punching the wall again.

"I said "I'm sorry", boss. Nature was calling, you know…"

It was the second time that week that Grande had an attack of the runs, after eating at a cheap Mexican take-out down the street; so he decided it was high time for a serious talk with the owner. Being half Mexican, he couldn't get over his addiction to their delicious burritos, even when he knew that the meat was bad; but his stomach never lied and he had to pay the price for his sweet indulgence…

"Fuck you, Grande! You told me you could hold it for a day if necessary; so, what's going on now? I knew I should've hired a professional for this job!" Edmond bitterly lamented, while wishing that he could kill the man.

"But I can, boss. I can!" Grande firmly explained. "Today, it's not my fault… You see, boss, the food's bad… In fact, I'm gonna go there tonight and search for evidence; and if I find as much as one 'cucaracha', I'm going to stuff it down the throat of that fat bastard Pakistani who owns that fucking Mexican place," he said before laughing.

"Grande, I don't give a shit what you do to get your rocks off; but from six in the morning to midnight, you're working for me, my man; remember? And you're paid to do one simple thing: to stay put and wait for that pretty coloured bitch to leave her room... I pay you enough, don't I?" Edmond icily asked.

"Yes, boss... But you know I always get the job well done for you. I got rid of that other beautiful coloured woman when you wanted me to; remember? The pregnant one? Smooth as my cock in my hand, if I don't say so myself..." Grande said, lowering his voice.

"Damn it, you stupid son of a Mexican bitch! Shut the fuck up and don't ever boast again of your work over the phone! Are you totally out of your fucking mind?" Edmond shouted, as Violette, one of his black young maids, silently entered the study, holding a large silver tray with a roast beef sandwich and a glass of Californian wine. As she put the silver tray on his desk, her hands started trembling; then, without a word, she quickly scurried out of the room, while shaking her head.

It's not like my master, to use such profane language... She nervously thought, truly alarmed.

The poor Violette wasn't sure whether to speak to Mister Princeton, the butler, about her master's strange behaviour; she hoped that the master wasn't developing Turret's syndrome, or simply losing his mind...

"Sorry boss," Grande awkwardly repeated. "I just want you to know that I always do a good job, Sir... Sometimes I think you forget that I am a professional. I'm a big man and I got a big pride, you know."

"If you don't shut up your big fat mouth, one day you'll be defending yourself in front of a judge and jury, you arrogant little fuck! And stop eating at those dives and go to 'Taco Bell', so I won't have to wait around for your fat ass to get back into your fucking car. Like I said, Grande, I pay you enough!" Edmond shouted out of control.

"It's not like anything's happening up there, Sir. She hasn't left her room for almost a week... She must be sick or something." Grande calmly said, while trying his best to control himself.

"She'll come out eventually," Edmond firmly said, before nervously glancing at his father's painted portrait. "I want this over before the end of the week; do you hear me?"

"Yeah, yeah... I know what you mean, boss... But I'm sick of this scenery; and my ass is aching from sitting all day." Absentmindedly, Grande massaged his sore buttocks, wishing that he could have a long relaxing walk along the bank of the Mississippi.

"If she doesn't come out soon, then you'll have to go in!"

"I don't think that's a good idea, boss... I don't look like the type of guest that belongs in that fancy place," Grande lamented; then he sadly stared at his exceptionally large hands, wishing that he could fit in. What he would give to be loved by a woman like Angela, who was so beautiful, so refined and so finely made; but he understood women well enough, to know for certain that the only way a gorgeous woman like Angela Boivin would stay by his side, was if she were quite cold and dead...

"Why didn't a guy as huge as you become a basketball player in the "N.B.A", anyway?" Edmond sarcastically asked.

"Not my gig, boss. I don't see myself in that fucking nigger basketball association; too many negritos." He laughed. "I'm into the deeper meaning of life... You know, that thing we can't talk about over the phone," Grande nervously said, stretching his long fingers before cracking his impressive knuckles. "I want to know what happens beyond this world... Don't you think sometimes about things like that, boss?" He softly asked, while trying to imagine the afterlife.

"I care about the "here and now", Grande. That's all there is! As soon as you figure that out, you'll understand that it's all about money and power, big boy! That being said, I don't want you to move your big ass from that car again, you understand? Just watch her! It's only a matter of hours, I can feel it now; and if you have to crap, shit in a bag!" Edmond yelled, beside himself.

"Yeah, yeah, yeah, boss," Grande said, feeling deeply annoyed, as he didn't like being told what to do by another man, specially a gringo, because it always made him angry. Now he just wanted to get off the phone, before anger interfered with his work. Grande had few ethics in life, but those he had, he adhered to strictly. The first and foremost, was "never to kill a person when angry". Grande murdered, simply because it soothed him; and also because he truly felt that he was helping his victims make the radical transition from a world of constant chaos, to a world of peace; a wonderful "world of quiet"...

Grande was an empathetic man and undiluted rage greatly disturbed his fragile and so precious "inner serenity"...

The bitter rage that flowed through Edmond's harsh voice was so palpable, that Grande would have killed that rich son of a white bitch, if they were in the same room; but in doing so, he unfortunately would be breaking his own code of ethics...

"Okay, okay, I get it boss... I have to go," he coldly said, while trying his best to hide his conflicting emotions; but making a note to never work for Edmond Hoxworth again. After all, this arrogant son of a bitch was only one of many clients, who also seemed not to really appreciate Grande's art as such; something that terribly annoyed him...

That rich bastard never even thanked me for killing his pregnant mulatto mistress... Now, that is a crime worthy of remembering! Grande sadly thought with a sudden profound hatred for the man.

The particular beautiful young woman was a New York top model. She had fallen in love with Edmond Hoxworth and had been his mistress for two years before she threatened to tell the newspapers if he didn't marry her. It was the second time Edmond had impregnated her, and she adamantly refused to have another abortion. Grande had cleaned up the 'whole mess', including any evidence that she might've collected, by setting fire to her house, after strangling her. It was an afterthought that his boss was not clever enough to think of. The arrogant Edmond Hoxworth would probably be in prison, if it wasn't for Grande's quick thinking...

"You should thank me for what I've done for you, boss... Everyone needs some appreciation, you know," he bitterly said, looking sad like a puppy dog, before hanging up. Then he rapidly reached for the glove compartment and extracted a large bag of 'Hershey' chocolate coated caramels, promising himself not to eat more than a hand full of the sinful extra sweet delicacy. But ten minutes later, the big bag lay empty at his feet, and Grande deeply sighed, terribly ashamed that he could not keep a simple promise to himself; again…

Chapter Fifty-Two

"New Orleans"

"Monteleone Hotel"

The message was written with a "Mont Blanc" fountain pen, in a royal shade of blue...

The handwriting was erratic and uncertain, as if an elderly person, or someone with an unsteady hand or unstable mind had written it, Angela decided.

"Dear Miss Boivin," it began.

My name is Princeton Harley, and I'm Mister Edmond Hoxworth's butler.

I was there when you visited him last week. I've attempted to contact you, but the clerks at the hotel registration had orders that you were not to be disturbed. My dear Miss Boivin, I must speak to you in person. I've been employed with the Hoxworth family during all my life. My parents were also employed by them, and I grew up in their service.

I suppose I should be grateful to have had steady employment. But I am growing old now, and there are certain matters that I may be able to clarify for you. Servants are often likened to shadows, and it is our duty to close our ears and eyes...

But sometimes, we must turn off our consciences and endure the actions of our employers. Anything less is seen as a betrayal of the trade; yet, in this particular matter, I must stand up, because I feel a duty towards you.

I am certain that my mother's spirit will rejoice once you know the truth.

My poor mother's spirit will finally be free, as will also be the spirit of her mother...

I must also warn you that, since you told Mister Hoxworth what you've discovered, your life is in great danger...

It's extremely important that we meet as soon as possible. So, my dear Miss Boivin, please call at: 555-2875 and leave a time when you can meet me.

I will be waiting for you at 139 Beaulieu Street.

Truly yours,

Princeton Harley.

Angela handed the letter to Emmanuel; then Jeannette read it over his shoulder.

"Call him," Emmanuel immediately said. "The sooner you get to the truth of this matter; the better for you, Angela."

The week before, Emmanuel had spent many hours in the public library, examining the archives, ferreting out some rather unsettling information about the Hoxworths. Either the Hoxworths were jinxed with bringing "bad luck" to their acquaintances or they were an unsavoury lot...

At least nine business associates of Edmond and Eileen Hoxworth had ended up victims of "unexplained deaths" that the coroner's office, after finding no evidence of foul play, simply filed as "accidental"...

Some died when their car's brakes mysteriously failed; and one man, who skied professionally, took a fall on an intermediate run in Aspen and "stupidly" broke his neck...

Another man that tamed wild horses as a hobby died, of another "broken neck" when he was out for a ride on his prized stallion; a horse known to have an even temper. But much more disturbing, was the "accidental death" of a well-known beautiful African-American model named 'Jessica Coldwell'. The local press had claimed this woman to be Edmond Hoxworth's mistress. Allegedly, the poor girl had been burned alive in her own home, victim of an accident; she was four months pregnant...

"In this town, it seems that money can always buy innocence," Emmanuel said, a rare cynicism affecting his normally cheerful tone.

Angela silently stared into space while sipping her coffee.

"You don't think they would go so far to kill me?" She calmly asked, not afraid.

The thought was absurd, but when she remembered the recent nightmare she had, the one in which she had been raped by the two vicious black thugs, she felt strangely vulnerable...

"Money has a strange power over people," Emmanuel knowingly said, before taking her hand.

"The root of all evil?" She softly asked, while looking deep into his eyes.

"Not all... But I can imagine that the fruit of the tree of good and evil was more likely a "gold coin" than an apple," he said, before handing Angela the phone.

She would meet Princeton Harley at three in the afternoon.

"Ma chérie, should we go with you?" Jeanette softly asked.

"No, I think I'll be okay."

"No way! I'm going with you, Angela. It's way too dangerous. So, call me when you're ready." Emmanuel firmly said, before rising from his chair.

"Okay, okay," Angela conceded. "If you don't mind."

"I insist!" He firmly said as he tenderly gazed into her eyes, before lovingly kissing her hand.

Once Angela was alone, she fervently began to pray...

Between each "Ave Maria", she asked for guidance and protection from her guardian angel, and begged the Almighty to give her the strength to follow the dangerous path that led to the truth; a truth, she hoped, that would finally bring her peace...

How many other horrible secrets could be there? How many more lies? How many more tears... She thought, shivering.

This, indeed, was the ultimate question; a question worth ten million dollars...

Chapter Fifty-Three

"New Orleans"

"The House of Angels"

The large ancient house at 139 Beaulieu Street was entirely built in the pure French colonial style, one extremely popular in Louisiana during the 18ᵗʰ century, when the elegant three-story structure was constructed...

The young black cab driver needed no instructions, as he knew the address by heart; it was the home of the beloved "Sister Light", the famous black voodoo priestess...

When Emmanuel had given the driver the address, the man grinned.

"Oh! So you're on your way to the 'House of Angels', my friends, aren't you? Nothing but good can come out of a trip there!" The cab driver exclaimed with a friendly smile.

Angela looked at Emmanuel and raised her eyebrows in surprise; but the cab driver's reassuring words somehow calmed her nerves...

"Why is it called the House of Angels?" Emmanuel asked, extremely intrigued.

The driver was happy to tell the story.

Two and a half centuries ago, a rich merchant named 'Jean-Christofe Lombard' and his beautiful wife 'Margaux'; along with their two young daughters, moved into the house. It was said that they came from France, from the original French city that New Orleans was named after: the city of 'Orleans'.

The master of the house was a well-known 'débauché', who was often dragged home by the local police in various states of drunkenness. Monsieur Lombard had a special love for the opium pipe as well. His wife was one of the great beauties of her native city of Orleans, with so fine skin that it was said that one could see the light of her heart shining through it; and yet, her ravishing pale blue eyes often spoke of sadness. Margaux's heart could not endure anymore of her husband's debaucheries; and so, after a decade of constant sorrow, she finally killed herself.

In order to spare her daughters the fate that had befallen her, the poor Margaux poisoned them before stabbing herself in the heart...

In a matter of months after losing his beautiful wife, as well as his beloved daughters, the French merchant completely lost his lust for women and wine, and became a recluse, as well as a religious fanatic. Some said that his wife's love was so strong that she and their daughters came to him every night, and kept him company until the sun rose.

Monsieur Lombard rapidly lost interest in luxuries and donated most of his wealth to the local Roman Catholic Church, keeping only enough money to maintain his house and pay for his new indulgence: a growing collection of precious life size statues of angels, in every shape and every skin colour...

Often, it was said that his black servants saw their sad master speaking to these angels.

On the day that Monsieur Lombard died, he was found lying at the foot of a large statue of Saint George, his hands clutching the sword that killed the dragon...

In his will, the French man left the "House of Angels", as it came to be known in New Orleans, to his closest black servants who, in turn, bequeathed it to their children.

Princeton Harley and his sister, the famous voodoo priestess, were the descendants of Jean Christophe Lombard's original black servants.

"I hope that the poor man reconciled with his wife and daughters after he died," the cab driver softly said. "For in leaving the big house to his servants, he left a legacy that continues to help and heal the faithful of New Orleans."

"I'm confused," Angela said. "Isn't this the home of Mister Princeton Harley?"

"Yes, yes, miss. A good man in his own right... Mister Harley works for Mister Edmond Hoxworth, you know... And his sister - Mambha - was born with the great gift of "sight". Most people here call her 'Sister Light'. This woman is a saint; a real live saint... You'll see," said the driver, before nervously glancing at his rear window. "Hmmm. Seems to me that we've got us a shadow," he said again. "You know anyone in a black van?" He worriedly asked.

Emmanuel sought Angela's eyes, but she averted them, before she nervously reached for his hand.

"It was only a dream," she whispered, visibly confused, but almost terrified.

Emmanuel suspiciously looked behind him. He could see that the van was occupied by two black men, but he also noticed something else; a more familiar vehicle and a more familiar strange man that he had often seen in their street, seated in that car during the past week. The man was a very large Samoan; the type of a man who could never escape an artist's eye...

"We are being followed," he nervously told Angela.

"You're paranoid," she said. "Please, Emmanuel. I'm nervous enough!"

Grande wondered whether to phone his boss or not; but he wasn't in the mood to deal with Edmond Hoxworth's natural abrasiveness. His heart was aching, and he was terribly jealous that the beautiful Angela was now with a man as handsome as Emmanuel. Grande would have gladly cut off three of his own fingers, in order to be as handsome as that man; as well as to be stared at for being beautiful, instead of being gawked at, because he was an overgrown freak...

What would it be like to be born so handsome? Grande sadly thought. *That man must be able to have any woman he wants: all he would have to do is summon her with a curl of his index finger.*

Grande imagined the handsome man kissing Angela, then passionately making love to her, as she pulled him towards her; inviting him to hold her, to take her, to entirely possess her body and soul. This thought was simply unbearable...

Suddenly, Grande was overwhelmed with a bitter rage.

How could God play such a trick on me, to give me a body that made me so repulsive to most women?

Grande didn't know whether to shoot Emmanuel, or shoot every good-looking man he saw; but survival, as almost always, simply wins over self-destruction...

"The handsome bastard is screwing that beautiful bitch!" Grande wildly yelled in his car, before banging the steering wheel with his enormous fists, throwing a tantrum like an out of control three-year-old. Grande would have loved to have Emmanuel's neck between his large hands; not for the pleasure of hearing it snap, but just to get a good hold on him, so he could smash his unbearable handsome face, then pulverise it into such a mangled mess of bone and cartilage, as to make him look like a monster; at last...

Emmanuel quickly paid the cab driver; then he put a protective arm around Angela's shoulders and hurried her towards the large massive antique front door of the "House of Angels".

A tall and slender black man in his twenties, with calming dark eyes, slowly opened the heavy dark wood doors and led them through the large peaceful courtyard, graciously weaving them through the intricate structure.

The architecture was typical of the time. Each of the main rooms was built around the large central courtyard and decorated with wrought black iron balustrades, entwined by thick vines. The extremely spacious verandas were wonderfully lush, where potted banana trees, white calla lilies and exotic tropical orchids bloomed in such profusion that Emmanuel felt as if he was in the garden of a master horticulturalist in his beloved island of Tahiti.

Whoever lives here, is blessed with a green thumb. What a peaceful place... Emmanuel thought with profound admiration.

In the centre of the lush courtyard, a large antique French stone fountain provided a soothing sound to the almost tropical atmosphere to the point that it was almost imperceptible to most that the house was in fact in the centre of such a noisy city. The luxurious fountain was surrounded by dwarf lemon trees potted within large Italian terra cotta pots. There was also a vast array of lavender, rosemary, thyme, verbena, mint, as well as other exotic herbs, with pungent scents that sensually stung the nostrils; all of them carefully tended to in large dark green boxwood planters.

Against the massive church-like stone columns that surrounded the verandas, large bronze wall brackets held antique gas chandeliers.

Angela imagined that the peaceful courtyard was as much a feast for the eyes at night as it was during the day. She imagined sitting down in one of the faded red velvet chaises that were elegantly displayed under the spacious verandas; then she wondered what it would be like to have lived three centuries ago, when life seemed so much simpler...

"It wasn't as romantic as it seems," Emmanuel said, as if reading her mind. "Humanity was still humanity; and cruelty, sorrow, bigotry and ignorance, were still the major themes of the day," he sadly added.

"At least, they weren't bothered by the constant noise of cell phones playing the national anthem!" Angela quipped, with a wry chuckle.

Emmanuel smiled. "It's nice to see you laugh, ma chérie," he softly remarked, before taking her hand.

The black young man graciously motioned for them to follow him into the large central corridor, which led into the heart of the house. Once there, they felt a strange presence surrounding them. It seemed as if they were in a crowded room, surrounded by people; but instead of feeling cramped, they felt caressed by an invisible gentle company...

The young man stopped at the fourth massive door on the hallway and knocked softly.

"Enter!" A man said.

As soon as the door was opened, Angela immediately recognised the black butler.

Princeton Harley graciously motioned to the young man. "Welcome to my humble home, Miss Boivin. This is my son, Daniel," he explained, his voice soft. "Would any of you care for a drink?" He graciously offered.

Angela shook her head, but Emmanuel accepted a lemonade from the pitcher of freshly squeezed juice sitting on a silver tray on Princeton's desk…

"I know that you must be wondering why I made such an urgent request to see you, Miss Boivin," Princeton slowly began. "Well, it is a long story, really; but I imagine that you're beginning to realise that you play a rather grand role in this century old tale of the Hoxworth family tree. And while I'm a stranger to you, please know that you are no stranger to me…" He paused while looking at her eyes. "I was there when you were born Miss, and I accompanied Madam Josephine when she took you home with her…" Princeton's eyes went soft as he recalled his youth. "My mother was one of Madam Eileen Mackenzie-Hoxworth's chambermaids; my mother also witnessed the birth of each of Madam Hoxworth's babies… When I was around twenty, my mother - God bless her loving soul - wanted me to know the facts, so I'd be able to choose my life…" Princeton paused for a long time, looking suddenly sad. "She told me what she had seen, many decades ago, in the castle's birthing room… At first, Miss, I thought about leaving, but I had a good position, and the family's viciousness seemed to have ended with poor Madam Eileen… You see, Miss Boivin, your grandmother Eileen was the first Hoxworth bride who had enough courage to speak up for herself, so I simply chose to let the past stay in the past; until now…" Princeton sadly said before he slowly wiped a bead of sweat from his brow.

"Black chambermaids are often prone to gossip and games." He said embarrassed, lowering his eyes. "The oldest chambermaid will often tell stories to the youngest, for their own amusement and maybe to frighten them off; or toughen them up... Who knows? Women have ways about them that, even at my age, I still have to understand..." He gently smiled. "My mother told me what she'd learned about the Hoxworth 'legend'; and I think that information might help you in your search, and finally put an end to this terrible tragedy." He sadly said again, before looking at her eyes; this time much deeper...

"You mean this nightmare, Mister Harley." Angela corrected, rolling her eyes. She took hold of herself, for she sensed a true sincerity in the man. His gentle brown eyes were filled with a compassion that reminded her of the eyes of the saints in the classical religious Christian paintings.

"Mister Harley, how do you know exactly what I'm searching for?" She bluntly asked.

"Well, Miss Boivin, it's not frequent to see Mister Hoxworth losing his temper, since he is a man with a great deal of self-control; but that day, when you visited him, my master was on the verge of erupting like a volcano, and I wasn't about to let things escalate into violence, Miss." Princeton said while lowering his eyes again; visibly embarrassed. "When Mister Hoxworth was shouting, and I couldn't help but hear; it was then when I realised that the frightened tales of the old chambermaids were true... You're the living proof of this, Miss Boivin... I realise now that the poor Madam Eileen spared your life because she couldn't live with another infanticide on her conscience; I also think that she also had a bit of time to love you as a granddaughter... It doesn't take long for the grand-maternal bond to thicken; and your skin, Miss Boivin, didn't begin to really darken until you were two days old..." He softly said, with a shadow of a smile upon his handsome face. "Madam Eileen's own daughter, who would've been much darker than you, the chambermaids said, began to show the signs of her colour within an hour of her birth." He concluded, while searching for her eyes.

Angela was aghast. "Are you saying that Eileen Hoxworth gave birth to a mulatto daughter as well, and that the baby was murdered because of her skin colour?"

"Unfortunately, yes, Miss Boivin," Princeton sadly said, lowering his eyes.

"So, I have my estranged grandmother to thank for the fact that my life was spared?"

"Yes, Miss Boivin. That is the truth... The Hoxworths were responsible for the death of many of such coloured children. It wasn't so unusual for rich white families to do so around here, when our people were viewed as little more than "livestock"..." Princeton sadly said, deep down feeling ashamed. "The white masters often slept with their young female slaves, and mulatto offspring were abundant then; but it was very unusual for a master to give his mulatto child his own name... More often than not, the coloured children and their mothers were rapidly sold by the master's Caucasian brides and then sent far, far away; as the wives didn't want to be constantly reminded of their husband's infidelity... For white people, Miss. Boivin, a "mixed race" child wasn't just a sign of adultery; it was a sign of unbridled lust... At this time, Miss, having sex with a black woman was a great sin on par with sodomy, or "bestiality"; or sex with the devil himself..." Princeton reluctantly said, feeling ashamed again.

"A mulatto child was indeed the "colour of shame"!" Angela exclaimed, utterly revolted, her lips trembling. "And things haven't changed that much lately, have they?" She nervously asked, feeling deeply insulted in the core of her being; ashamed!

"Well, Miss Boivin, the "high society" of New Orleans hasn't... Some of those white people seem to act as if the Civil War was little more than a fantasy; or so they'd like to think..." Princeton sadly said, looking sadly deep into her eyes.

"I'm realising that," Angela bitterly said, remembering her revolting discourse with Edmond, her "Caucasian brother".

"It's absolutely ridiculous the way people think here!" Emmanuel nervously added, before reaching for Angela's hand. He had never felt so confused by humanity; had never seen such evil. His eyes were dulled now by profound sorrow, and he wanted to take Angela away from all this; take her to his beloved Tahiti, where skin colour and race didn't seem to matter so much anymore...

"You see, Miss Boivin, because of your grandmother Eileen, and also the fact that she didn't have it in her heart to follow "the tradition", you now represent everything that the Hoxworths have always feared so much. You're a living stain on their white linen sheets, and the single stone that will shatter their glass house; you're, Miss Boivin, the "terrible truth"... You've got it within you to tear off the shroud that hides the unspeakable sins that are centuries old... My sister and I always knew you'd come back one day, Miss, because we knew that Madam Josephine wouldn't leave this world with such a lie in her heart; your Mama was too pure for that. She probably would've told you earlier, if it wasn't for Madam Eileen's interference... My poor mother remembers that one day, when the sweet Josephine came to the castle to call on Madam Eileen; and the next week, Miss, you were sent to London to study ballet..." Princeton said, while lowering his eyes, visibly embarrassed.

Angela's heart was now hurt. "Mister Harley, are you insinuating that I was invited to join the London Royal Ballet, because my extremely rich estranged white grandmother pulled some strings? My dance teacher in New Orleans said I'd won a scholarship only based on my merits and talent."

Princeton's smile slowly faded. "I think that it was a white lie to spare your feelings, Miss... One of many, I suppose, but Madam Josephine and Mister André Boivin never meant you any harm; neither did poor Madam Elisabeth, your genetic mother... Madam Elisabeth always thought that as soon as she found a way to take care of herself and you, she'd bring you to England to live with her; but the poor Madam Elisabeth didn't count on battling the will of a Hoxworth..." Princeton sadly said, visibly embarrassed again. "As long as you were part of the Boivin family, a decent 'African-American' family, Madam Eileen could make sure that you weren't taken seriously; not in her society, anyway... But she was wrong, Miss Boivin. My sister said that no matter where you lived, or where you were around the world, the truth, one day, was going to be told... Mambha says that the spirits of the dead don't rest well in beds made of lies; they're restless, you know..." Princeton softly said, looking into her eyes again.

Angela couldn't keep up. "Are you telling me, Sir, that my whole career was a farce? That talent had nothing to do with my scholarship?" She nervously asked, visibly revolted.

Princeton slowly shook his head. "Not at all, Miss Boivin. You can't do what you do without talent. I'm just saying that Madam Eileen pulled a few strings... You may have risen more slowly, if you'd been on your own. The fact is that your rich grandmother contributed a few million to the ballet, you know," Princeton uncomfortably said, this time nervously avoiding her eyes.

"So, Mister Harley, my whole life has simply been a lie!" Angela furiously exclaimed, tears swimming in her eyes. "One string of lies after another... It's... It's disgusting!" She almost shouted, visibly revolted.

"Well, unfortunately for you, Miss, too many lies have been told..." Princeton calmly said while sadly looking into her eyes again. "But it's not too late to start again; not too late to reclaim your birth right... Do you know that you were christened Mary-Elisabeth Hoxworth?" He softly added, while sadly remembering that day.

"What did you say?" Angela suddenly asked, before nervously wiping the tears.

"Yes, Miss Boivin; your real name was Mary-Elisabeth... That was the Christian name madam Elisabeth gave you..."

"Oh my God! That's the name that Jonathan's ghost keeps repeating… Was he talking to me?"

"Your father's spirit has been visiting you, Miss?" Princeton softly asked, his eyes suddenly lighting up.

"Yes." Angela trembled. "Do you believe me?"

Princeton smiled. "Yes, Miss Boivin; I believe in spirits, if that's what you mean… I've seen a few of them myself; but my sister lives much more in the world of the spirits than the world of the living." He gently smiled. "You see, Miss, neither this one nor the world of the dead, is more real than the other… In fact, it's a matter of opinion which world is the real one." Princeton quite seriously said. "For my sister, Mambha, who was born with the great gift of sight, the world of the spirits is eternal; and so it takes precedence; but again, Mambha can see things that others cannot…"

The sudden realisation hit Angela like a giant boulder. "Mister Harley, didn't you say that Eileen's mulatto daughter was named Angelica?"

"Yes, I did. Why do you ask, Miss?"

"If my birth name was Mary-Elisabeth, then why am I called Angela? Did Eileen ask Josephine and André to name me Angela?"

"Well, I'm almost certain of it, Miss; maybe in memory of her daughter… Perhaps poor Madam Eileen thought that the name would somehow bring her daughter back to life; but both names mean 'angel', you know…"

"Yes, I know. And sometimes I feel as if my life isn't really my own…" Angela said shivering. "In the past few months, Mister

Harley, I been feeling as if there was a strange force inside me, guiding me towards a path that I don't really want to take; and lately, I must say that this force is much stronger than me..."

"Ahhh," Princeton said. "That makes sense, Miss... also my sister has seen lately the souls of the murdered Hoxworth children rising to claim their truth... Mambha has seen them joining together, gathering strength in numbers, and becoming one entity... Perhaps this entity is using you as a conduit?" Princeton Harley was deadly serious...

Angela decided to tell the butler about her recurrent nightmares. "Since I was a child, Sir, I frequently awoke with a pillow over my head, as if I were suffocating myself; and lately, it's getting worse," she sadly admitted, looking terrorised, before nervously squeezing Emmanuel's hand.

Sorrowfully, Princeton cast his eyes to the wooden floor.

"Unfortunately Miss, it was the tradition," he sadly explained. "The Hoxworth family doctor would suffocate the mulatto child using a pillow, because there was no reason to suspect foul play that way... It was a gruesome sight, Miss Boivin." He sadly said with tears in his eyes. "I was only a child, but I was there when Madam Eileen's new-born baby girl was suffocated in cold blood; and I can still hear the echoes of Madam Eileen's screams... The poor woman was begging for her daughter's life, but Theresa Hoxworth, her mother-in-law, was adamant. When the poor Madam Eileen awoke, the awful legacy was explained to her by my own mother; God bless her soul." Princeton tried to restrain his emotions, but his hands were shaking now.

"And this doctor? Do you know his name?"

"Yes, Miss; it was Mister Aaron Stickley... The Hoxworths paid for the education of the first Mister Stickley, who, most probably, would never have made it into any medical school without their help... Then, from father to son, the Hoxworths generously paid their 'family' doctors." Princeton sadly said, while slowly shaking his head. "At that time, Miss, the Stickleys were active members of the local 'Ku Klux Klan', and were getting paid for what they saw as 'helping the world to get rid of undesirables'..." He painfully said, before tiredly closing her eyes.

Angela deeply shivered again. "So, if it weren't for Eileen's mercy, or her guilt, I would've been just another victim of these doctors? But I still don't understand, Sir. Are my nightmares visions of what might've happened to me?" She nervously asked him, visibly lost.

Princeton thought for a moment. "I think they're much more than that, Miss Boivin... And I think it's time that you meet my sister now." With an elegant wave of his arm, which reflected his great training as a butler, he gently motioned for Angela and Emmanuel to follow him.

After passing through a succession of large rooms overflowing with statues of angels, Princeton finally stopped in front of a high arched entry to a private chapel.

"Let me warn you," he firmly said. "My sister has no eyes, but she can see things that you and I cannot; and when it comes to the "world beyond", her vision is perfect..."

As he slowly opened the massive door, Angela was shocked to step into the very red room that she had so often dreamt about in detail...

Daylight softly filtered through the three large colour stained glass windows, which cast a fiery glow on everything it touched. Each window depicted a Christian scene: the Virgin Mary dressed in shades of blue, cradling the precious infant Jesus; the Nativity Scene where Jesus lay in his straw bed, surrounded by his mother, her husband Joseph, and the stable animals; then Jesus Christ being crucified, his mother crying out at the foot of the cross, along with the beautiful Mary-Magdalene beside her, with her long lustrous hair flowing down her back, as she lovingly gazed upon her Saviour...

Near the nave of the red chapel, in front of a life-size wooden crucifix, was a middle age ebony black woman dressed in immaculate white, praying on her knees.

As the proud black priestess heard them enter, she slowly turned around, smiling.

As Angela gazed into the strange empty sockets on the black priestess's face, she tried her best to control the natural fear that she felt in her heart; then she had to take a deep breath to ward off her profound repulsion.

Mambha sensed her fear, disgust, and embarrassment; but she lovingly smiled...

"Welcome," she softly said, her voice soothing and kind.

Her smile was so radiant, that within moments, her monstrous deformity had been suddenly replaced with an astonishing beauty. The beauty of a perfected soul; the beauty of holiness...

The black priestess' presence was a calming force; but a force to be reckoned with...

Mambha lovingly reached for Angela's hands and softly pressed them in hers.

As soon as she did so, Angela felt a rush of energy pass from the priestess's body into her own.

"I've been expecting you, my child," the black priestess softly said, before turning her head to face Emmanuel. "And you as well, my son... I see that you have come from far, far away; from a beautiful island... You have a great heart, I can tell, but you loved only once before in this life... Unlike most men born with such beautiful features, you don't abuse the power of beauty and you have an innate sense of justice." She calmly said, lovingly smiling.

"Thank you," Emmanuel answered, deeply troubled by what she sensed.

"Angela has loved only once as well," Mambha slowly continued, facing her now. "Although you gave your heart generously, my child, it was mishandled and broken by the man you gave it to... Even as we speak, I can feel your suffering; but you must let it go, as life goes on." She calmly said, pressing Angela's hands again.

Burning tears welled up in Angela's eyes. "You are so right." She painfully said, her lips trembling now.

"Sorrow is just another lesson of life," Mambha affirmed. "Often, it is a necessity... Pain, my child, can separate the dross from the gold... Have you ever asked yourself the real reason why you never had children with your husband, my child?" She softly asked while caressing Angela's hand.

Angela was taken aback by the black priestess' strange question. "My husband and I were talking about children before... I suppose I was selfish," she sadly said. "I suppose that I put my career first; and..." She painfully added, before wiping a tear.

"No, my dear child, that wasn't the reason," Mambha firmly said, still holding Angela's hands in hers. "It is the colour of your skin that innocently kept you from bearing children... Three times you were pregnant; and three times, you didn't tell your husband when you lost those babies... Do you know why?" She softly asked.

"I guess... I guess I should have quit dancing, but I didn't." Angela hesitantly said, suddenly blushing, while feeling strangely guilty.

"No, my child; it had nothing to do with that... Deep down, without admitting it, you didn't want the children to suffer as you did; you didn't want them to be called names." Mambha softly corrected. "There are no accidents..."

No accidents indeed... Angela sadly thought, truly amazed. Somehow she'd always felt that she wasn't good enough for Pierce, and that her mixed-race children would also feel inferior in their father's world; she also often wondered what would've happened if their children were unfortunately born with darker skin than herself. Would Pierce truly love them? Before Josephine revealed the truth, Angela greatly feared that she would give birth to a dark-skinned child, because she thought that her light colour skin was in fact an anomaly. More than likely, the Haddingtons would have seen a dark skinned child as a great stain on their pure Caucasian genealogical tree. Such a coloured child would surely have been ridiculed in an exclusive English boarding school because Pierce would certainly have insisted that his child be privileged to the best education his money could buy. For the first time in her life, Angela realised why she couldn't really hold any of her babies; why her tormented subconscious desire to protect her unborn offspring from the terrible weight of their bi-racial heritage, and had thus terminated each of her pregnancies...

Angela had unconsciously killed her own mixed-race babies, simply because she always thought that she was never good enough for the white society she lived in...

"Sister Light, why are you telling me these terrible things?" Angela nervously asked, terribly confused and almost angry now towards Mambha. At this instant, as irrational as it was, Angela was suddenly afraid that Emmanuel would run from her; that the wholeness and light she felt whenever she was with him, would disappear forever...

The black priestess' expression became sombre.

"My dear child, Emmanuel is not like any other man; and you, Angela, are not any woman either... Both of you are on this path together, and somehow, you have been for a very long time." She lovingly smiled while reaching for her hand again.

"But... But we just met two weeks ago," Angela mildly protested, more confused than ever.

"Yes, my child; in this life…" Mambha softly corrected. "Don't you believe in reincarnation?" The black priestess slowly turned to face Emmanuel. "And what about you, my son? Do you believe in reincarnation?"

"Yes, yes; of course, Sister Light," he calmly said, as easily as if she had asked him if the sun rises each day. "On my island of Tahiti, to believe that the soul simply vanishes upon death, is unheard of… What meaning would life have if it were so?"

Startled, Angela watched Emmanuel as he spoke, his eyes looking straight into Mambha's vacant sockets. She felt extreme pride; pride as well as undiluted love…

"You are a wise man, my son… People born in the islands are much closer to their roots, and it is easier for them to see that in fact, spirits are everywhere… Most men and women raised in this era of high technology are now so far from mother nature, that they have lost their natural ability to see; as well as, unfortunately, a big part of their humanity." Mambha sombrely said. "They constantly doubt everything; even themselves, and they respect no one anymore… Its very sad, my son; yes, very, very sad…" Mambha sadly said, bowing her head in prayer, before slowly continuing. "So, my son, you follow the golden rule: that the manner in which you live your life now will influence the next, then the one after that; for better or worse… It is my belief that the most important part of life is always to prepare oneself for the next one; as well as to free yourself of any vices and negativity, so you don't need to endlessly repeat the same tasks, as in a bad fairy tale… Unfortunately, some poor lost souls make the same mistakes for thousands of lives; but we all have the chance of purifying ourselves enough, my son, to free ourselves from the heavy cage of our poor human bodies..." She softly added, kindly smiling.

"Yes, Sister Light!" Emmanuel exclaimed, as he squeezed Angela's hand, before he lovingly looked into her eyes. "The first time I saw Angela, somehow, I strangely knew that I'd known her before... The attraction was so intense, but not just because she is a gorgeous woman; in fact, it was much deeper than that; as if we had known each other forever," he calmly explained. "My sister felt the same way; she's a bit clairvoyant herself, you know..." He proudly said, smiling like a child.

"To be clairvoyant, is unfortunately both "a gift and a curse", my son," Mambha said. "To be really receptive to the other world, you must keep your heart open to both good and evil... Some of us are born more sensitive than others; but even the most sensitive person must continue to train in the spiritual arts all life long." She seriously said while reaching for his hand. "It takes a great deal of focus, my son, to know the difference between a trick of the mind and the visions of the other world," the black priestess calmly said, slowly lifting her head up as if she could see the heavens.

Angela's expression suddenly softened. "Emmanuel, I must admit that I felt a kinship with both you and your sister; but now I strangely realise it was much more than that..." She said with a broken voice, feeling curiously exhausted.

Like a child, Emmanuel brightly grinned and placed a soft loving kiss on her lips.

"So, let me ask you again, Angela," Mambha said. "Do you believe in reincarnation?"

"I... well... maybe... I really can't say for sure, Sister Light; not absolutely... I wish I could say that I truly believe, but I'm still in the dark," she admitted, somehow ashamed, while lowering her gaze.

"Yes, indeed, my child. You're in the dark... But I am here to open your eyes and show you the glorious light," Mambha joyfully said, her voice stronger than before. "Tonight, my dear Angela, we must visit the place where you were "buried" in a former life. There, my dear child, you will find the answers to all your present questions; there, my child, you will find out who you truly are..."

Who I am truly... Angela sadly thought, deeply shivering, strangely excited and also terribly afraid at the same time; but so, so strangely alive...

Chapter Fifty-Four

"Hoxworth Crypt"

Regally facing a romantic five-acre man-made lake, which was always aglow at the sunset with fiery reds, purples, pinks, and magentas, the imposing white marble Hoxworth crypt resembled a majestic ancient Greek temple...

The regal crypt had been built long ago on the estate grounds, but was a half mile away from the French castle; and far, far away from the eyes of the prying security cameras...

Angela, Emmanuel, Mambha and Princeton cautiously stepped out from the back of the gardener's van from where they'd been hiding. Tom, the castle's head old black gardener, who was a long time devotee of Sister Light, had agreed to smuggle them inside. It was difficult for anyone to refuse the black priestess' rare requests. As fate would have it, the plan went smoothly. Fresh large bouquets of white flowers were brought to the crypt on Mondays and Fridays; today was Monday, thus the gardener's van wouldn't arouse any suspicions...

"Nothing happens by accident, my child," Mambha softly whispered into Angela's ear.

The gardener unlocked the massive golden bronze doors with his own key, before he punched in the seven digits of the security code.

"I feel like a cat burglar," Angela nervously said, while anxiously squeezing Emmanuel's hand.

The impressive enormous red marble ante room was mostly decorated with life size black marble statues befitting a grand house of the dead; some of them eccentric as in 'Anubis', the jackal-headed Egyptian god of the dead; others were beautiful and angelic; but each seemed to point the way to a massive golden doorway that led to a specific tomb, thus inviting the living to visit the dead...

As they carefully followed the gardener through the maze, Emmanuel tightly held Angela's hand. The only sound was the echoing of their footsteps, clapping on the shiny black marble floor. The first imposing large room was softly lit by Roman style golden bronze fixtures; that had been bracketed onto the massive stonewalls. Although the lights were electric, the bulbs flickered like candle flames; light played amongst the life-sized black marble statues, and their shadows seemed to strangely dance...

In silence, they carefully passed through six large red marble rooms, filled with princely mahogany coffins set upon impressive solid black marble platforms. Each precious coffin was surrounded by four massive five-foot 17th century Italian solid silver candelabras.

"This art is way too beautiful to be wasted on the dead," Emmanuel sadly said, "I really think that half the poor in my country could be fed for an entire year for what these things cost..."

Mambha sadly smiled. "Exactly what you are supposed to think, my son... Even in death, the Hoxworths prove that only the finest is acceptable to them..." She grinned. "The living take comfort in believing that they can bring their gold with them when they die; but the same riches they covet keep them dangerously attached to the past, and totally unable for them to move forward on the eternal wheel of life... It is a great pity, my son, that respect cannot be purchased." She dryly remarked, having faced this situation so many times before.

Above the head of each magnificent coffin, hung a golden framed life-size oil portrait of the deceased, painted when the occupant of the coffin was in the prime of his or her life...

The portraits of each and every Hoxworth were impressively bedecked with jewels worthy of royalty. Each of them also draped with the finest silk, velvet, brocade and taffeta intricately sewn, with handmade lace that was worth at the time its weight in gold... Some Hoxworths were elegantly wigged and powdered in accord with the fashion of the day; but the common point between all of them, was that their "pale pinkish skin", light-coloured eyes, and fine chiselled features, always spoke of their noble and pure "Aryan" race...

It seemed that all the Hoxworths were the result of "careful breeding", as if they were champion show dogs. Of course, the artists were clever enough to use the palest pigments when mixing the colours for the skin of their wealthy patrons; always staying away from "sienna" and "grey", in favour of blue tints...

It was extremely difficult for Angela to imagine that she was really related to such an arrogant and terribly racist family.

When they finally reached the large regal crypt that was dedicated to "Reginald Henry Hoxworth" and his family, they were immediately greeted by his imposing portrait, as well as the disdainful look on his face. One didn't have to be a psychologist to deduce that the man had been raised to always have his way, and also that the desires of others held little concern for him; if at all...

To the left of Reginald's portrait, hung the one of his son, Jonathan, whose jolly pale green eyes sharply contrasted with his father's domineering dark blue stare. It was easy to understand that Jonathan was everything that Reginald was not; and he was, as well, devastatingly handsome...

The photographs that Jillian showed Angela, when she was in Ashington, did not do justice to this painting; neither did the portrait in Edmond's study, for that matter...

Deeply impressed, Angela lovingly admired her father's image for a while. She was truly speechless.

Jonathan's elegant silhouette was backlit, softening his manly features. He was posing holding the edges of an old Bible. Underneath a well-cut black velvet jacket, he wore a crisp white shirt with an ascot grey tie that was fastened by a large black pearl pin. A white handkerchief, carefully folded into a triangle, had been placed in his chest pocket; Jonathan was simply regal...

"There's quite a resemblance," Emmanuel said, amazed. "You both have the same special light in your eyes, as well as the same bone structure and the same mark on your face," he added, before softly kissing the beauty mark above Angela's lip.

"Yes, it's true..." Angela couldn't help but remember that the last time she gazed on her father's portrait in Edmond's study, she had witnessed his ghost re-enacting his suicide. She trembled.

Princeton helped Mambha step up to the massive black marble platform, and once she was steady, she firmly placed her hand on Jonathan's precious coffin. The black priestess then took a deep breath, before calling out his name, intoning each syllable; preparing to summon his spirit. Visibly afraid, Angela moved closer to Emmanuel, wanting his protection.

"Jonathan Alexander Hoxworth, son of Reginald Henry Hoxworth and Eileen Rose Mackenzie," Mambha slowly began, placing her other hand on the shiny mahogany wood, while her long tapered fingers seemed to dance on the lid of the coffin, inscribing ancient symbols, or letters of some sort.

"In the name of our Lord and all the dark angels of death, I, Mambha, summon your spirit to come forth!" Each syllable she spoke took on a life of its own, echoing like waves between the massive stonewalls of the vast mortuary chamber...

When her father's portrait seemed to slightly light up, Angela feared that his ghost would emerge from the painting again, as it had in Edmond's study. At the beginning, a soft glow emanated from his coffin, reminding her of the way the opalescent moon looked when shrouded by a light fog; then, strangely, the temperature of the room suddenly dropped...

Forcefully, Mambha called out Jonathan's name again, repeating the simple chant, until a strange garbled voice could be finally heard; at first, the disembodied voice seemed to come from behind the painting, but it somehow sounded as if it was far, far away...

"Jonathan Alexander Hoxworth, I can feel your presence now," the black priestess firmly said, as the ethereal glow around the coffin softly pulsated, growing brighter and larger.

In that moment, Princeton stepped to Angela's side and whispered into her ear.

"Don't worry, Miss Angela. Your father's spirit will not harm you... He's appeared to my sister in private, and he is not to be feared. He simply wishes to make contact with us, that's all. So open your heart to him, and hear him out... My sister told me that Mister Jonathan desires the peace of his final rest; and you are the only one, Miss, who can truly free him from the heavy chains that bind him to his former life. The only one!" Princeton seriously said, while intensely looking into her eyes.

Calmly, but with palpable force, Mambha continued to chant Jonathan's name, each syllable echoing off the stonewalls again. After a few minutes, the pale bluish light seemed to enlarge, and was soon rising above Jonathan's coffin; then, a strange cacophony of sounds, the crying of children and the wailing of women, joined Mambha's chants. At the beginning they could not really tell where the sounds originated; they strangely seemed to emanate through the stonewalls. But one thing was certain; these were the sounds of sorrow: awful, powerful, terrible sorrow...

Tom, the old black gardener, who had been silent until this point, suddenly cried out, "That's enough! I can't stand this monstrosity anymore!"

He would've raced out of the chamber, if Princeton wouldn't have taken a firm hold of his arm.

"Not now, my friend. You must wait!" Mambha ordered. "No harm will come to you. Trust me!"

Tom stilled then, visibly mesmerised by the black priestess' words, then he ceased to move; even when, one by one, the massive silver candelabras that stood around Jonathan's coffin toppled over, crashing down as loudly as thunder onto the black marble floor...

Suddenly, and without any warning, the large room was filled with pure, undiluted rage, as if "Satan" himself had joined the party...

Completely panicked, Angela turned to run out of the freezing crypt, but she stopped in her tracks, somehow paralysed by a strong unseen force; then, within a second Jonathan's luminous bluish ghost firmly stood in front of her, barring her way...

"What... What do you want?" Angela almost screamed to her father's ghost. "Why are you haunting me? Please, pleeease, leave me alone! Go back where you came from. Let me be! I've had enough! Enoughhh!" She violently shouted, before she covered her face with her hands and nervously started to cry.

"Please, my child, don't shout at him!" Mambha scolded. "Can't you see that your father's spirit is in great torment? You must help him find peace, Angela. It's your duty! Don't you understand that you're the only one who can free him from his constant pain? That you're also the only one who can free him from his terrible guilt?"

Burning tears ran down Angela's cheeks. "But I can't!" She screamed. "I just can't! I'm too afraid." Angela could hardly breathe; her body was convulsing and heaving. "Let me out of this place! I can't bear it anymore! Please, please!" She cried out, panicked again.

When Emmanuel reached for her hand, he was violently pushed away by a strange invisible force. Mambha stepped down from the black marble platform and firmly took Angela's hand, steadying her, soothing her; until Jonathan's ghost softly spoke…

"Forgive me, Mary-Elisabeth… Please, forgive me for what I did," the ghost sadly said, while stepping closer to Angela. His strange disembodied voice filled the room with a palpable sadness; eliminating any sense of fear, rage, or anger…

Totally terrified, Angela moved slightly backwards, not wanting to be touched by the bluish apparition; but without hesitation, Mambha stretched out her arm and touched Jonathan's ghostly palm; then she firmly took Angela's hand in hers, working as a "conduit of energy", between father and daughter. As soon as she did, the sounds - the whimpering and the weeping – immediately ceased…

"Jonathan Alexander Hoxworth, tell your daughter what you need," the black priestess commanded. "What do you really want to say to Mary-Elisabeth? Tell her now!"

417

Jonathan's spirit became more defined and his words were becoming clear.

"Mary-Elisabeth, my poor child, your life is in great danger... A man is trying to kill you," the ghost said, locking his translucent pale eyes with hers.

"Who sent this man, Jonathan; and what is his reason for wanting to kill Mary-Elisabeth?" Mambha asked, while summoning all her strength.

Angela saw her father's ghostly face suddenly flush with shame. "This man is my own son... Edmond! He won't admit that I am Mary-Elisabeth's father... And he won't let me rest. He'll kill his sister, before he allows her to prove it..." The ghost painfully said.

Angela felt a great pity for her father's ghost; his voice was strange, defeated and helpless, but she could nonetheless feel his endless pain.

"Jonathan Alexander Hoxworth, you are indeed this woman's father?" Mambha asked, triumphantly smiling.

"Yes... Yes, I am. But I didn't know it when I took my life," he sadly said, then he hesitated a moment, before softly adding: "but you know that there is more to the truth than what Mary-Elisabeth knows now."

"And what is the truth, Jonathan? Speak now!" Mambha ordered, while looking deep into his strange eyes.

"Mary-Elisabeth needs to discover that on her own," the ghost said, before he pointed to a small doorway. "She must cross the threshold into the 'room of angels'... It is where the forgotten ones;

the forbidden ones, wait… It is where Mary-Elisabeth will find what she is seeking…"

Maybe it was a trick of her imagination, but Angela saw some tears in her father's eyes…

Could a ghost cry?

Chapter Fifty-Five

"Hoxworth Estate"

Deeply irritated and terribly hungry, Grande had been waiting in his car more than twenty minutes for the arrogant Edmond Hoxworth to return his call, when his cell phone finally rang...

"What do you want?" Edmond barked. "Haven't you taken care of her yet?"

Grande deeply sighed. Just once, he would've liked to hear a word of appreciation, but Edmond always treated him no better than a dog; or worse: like one of his black staff...

"I wish it was so, boss," Grande calmly replied. "But she hasn't been alone."

"What are you talking about? Who is she with? Her nigger family?" Edmond snarled. "I hope this mulatto cunt has finally realised where she belongs!" He viciously added.

"No boss. She's been with a man who isn't white, but he's not black either... He's a good looking man, a guest at her hotel.

420

From the looks of it, I'd say they were, uh, an item. You know what I mean?"

"An item? Speak in English, you Mexican idiot!" Edmond shouted, full of rage.

"You know. They're together, boss... like a couple. Maybe they're fucking... You should see the way this guy puts his arm around her waist; like he owns her, or something," Grande painfully explained, not bothering to hide his obvious jealousy. "Oh, he's no mongrel, boss. I tell you, this guy looks like he could be one of those models for Calvin Klein. I've never seen a man so good looking in my life." He sincerely said, while wishing that he could break Emmanuel's neck.

"Shut up, you giant idiot! Are you turning gay or something?" Edmond shouted again.

"No, boss, not me. I just tell it like it is. And I tell you that I wish I were that man."

"Screw you, Grande! So where did this gigolo and that coloured bitch go? I hope you followed them."

"I always do my job, boss," Grande firmly said, before hitting the steering wheel again. *Mister Hoxworth, you better start treating me right...* If Grande had a choice, he would rather kill the highly irritating Edmond than Angela, and if it wasn't for the fact that he was a professional who prided himself on getting a job "done right", he just might have; but he unfortunately thought of himself as an 'ethical businessman', through and through...

"They didn't go on any pleasure trip, boss; not this time. Nope! They took a cab into old town, to the 'House of Angels'. You know? Where does that famous New Orleans black voodoo priestess live? And they stayed there for almost three hours... Around dusk, I saw a green gardener's van pull up and park in the garage. They shut the garage door, so I don't know what happened; but ten minutes later, the van split, if you get my meaning, boss; but Grande - I'm a man with a mission - I was watching closely when they left, even had my binoculars, and you're not going to believe this, boss... He, he, he! Guess who was in the passenger seat? Guess?" He sweetly asked with a big childish smile.

"Get to the point, you fucking idiot!" Edmond impatiently shouted. "You are driving me crazy!

"Yeah, yeah, boss," Grande calmly said. He loved holding a trump card. "Sure you don't want to take a wild guess?" He asked, grinning, like a child.

"And you, asshole, do you want to keep your fucking job? Or do you want me to stick my foot up that big fat ass of yours?!" Edmond coldly said, visibly out of control.

"Not a sporting man, are you?" Grande bitterly laughed, before lowering his voice to a hushed whisper. "I hope you're sitting down for this one, boss... Well, in the passenger seat, right next to your grandmother's black chief gardener, was your very own butler; that Harley guy... And, get this, boss! There was also someone in the back... So I smoothly pulled up alongside of the van, real sneaky, and guess who I saw?" Grande waited a couple seconds, before landing the final punch. He was now as proud as a new father. "None other than the handsome guy, yeap! So my hunch is that this Miss Angela was in there too; but she was hiding, that one..." He smiled, while picturing the scene in his mind.

Edmond's expensive 'Davidoff' cigar almost fell out of his hand, as he didn't know what to make of the particular information. He always knew that Princeton was the famous "Sister Light's" brother; but what would his butler be doing riding around with his grandmother's old chief gardener? And what was Angela's new "boyfriend", or whatever he was, doing there with her?

Both Edmond and Eileen had always been more than generous with their staff; particularly Princeton, whom they trusted, because he had been with their family since he was a child. But if his butler betrayed him, without hesitation, Edmond would have his blood...

Ungrateful stupid nigger! Just wait and see... Edmond nervously thought, feeling that he could kill his ungrateful butler with his bare hands.

"Dumb ass! Where are you now?" Edmond shouted again.

"I followed them for almost forty minutes, boss. They stopped in front of an old gate, but I can't see much beyond that... I think that it's near your grandma's castle... It's off a small dirt road in the middle of nowhere, and there's no address or number... I climbed on the gate, so I could get a better view; but all I could see is trees... rows and rows of date palms as far as the eyes can see. Nothing but a little dirt road leading to nowhere and trees..."

Edmond's blood suddenly boiled. He perfectly knew that road. He was sure now that it was in fact the north entrance to his grandmother's estate; but unfortunately, the only area of the immense property that wasn't under the surveillance of cameras...

Edmond cursed himself for his frugality, thinking that it would've cost an extra half million to secure the palm grove with the entire property; but there was no way, he hoped, that they could get near the main property without being spotted. They couldn't even get near the acres of manicured French gardens, and lush groves that surrounded the imposing French castle; not with thirty armed guards on duty, twenty-four hours a day, along with three dozen trained-to-kill vicious Dobermans...

What are they thinking? Are they that stupid?

Then, it hit him hard as a 'Mac Truck': the family's crypt!!!

That little coloured bitch is planning to exhume my father's body, so she can get her damn DNA test! With the documents and our mother's testimony, the court would've certainly granted her permission. So why would this stupid bitch risk breaking the law and ruining her credibility? She had to be after something else, but what?

As much as Edmond deeply despised the beautiful and extremely talented Angela, she had already proven to him that she was no fool; no fool indeed...

"Grande, stay there until I call you back!" He suddenly yelled into the phone before violently hanging up.

"She wants to see our little family crypt; good for her… Let it be her final resting place then, before the night is through!" Edmond nervously said to himself, once he had called the castle's chief of security and given him precise orders, then he ran towards his car with a single idea in his head: death; Angela's death...

Chapter Fifty-Six

"The Hoxworth Crypt"

Angela, Emmanuel, Princeton and the black priestess silently followed the old gardener again, through the large cold corridors leading to the north side of the large Hoxworth mausoleum...

As they nervously walked, the sobbing that permeated the crypt suddenly seemed to intensify.

"I've never had a good feeling about this side of the crypt," Tom, the old gardener nervously said, rubbing his bony hands together. "I've seen things... And I don't drink, not a stitch. I'm clean as an arrow. But there are, uh, women... Terribly sad pale skinned women, with newborn babies in their arms... I don't change the flowers here as often as I'm supposed to," he said almost apologetically. "Because I don't like to come here. It's way too spooky; and it makes me depressed for days..." He sadly said, visibly being under an intense tension.

"We all hear the wailing, my friend; we all feel the sorrow... If the wheel of fate turns as it should, these poor lost souls will soon have their final rest." Mambha firmly said, visibly unafraid.

Two antique statues silently guarded the massive entrance to the northern chamber; life sized white marble carvings of weeping women, whose hands covered their eyes. Angela wondered if they were blind to the truth; or if their hands were raised as a warning not to look inside that particular chamber...

When the black old gardener nervously unlocked the intricately worked massive bronze door, the wailing rose to a pitch that was almost impossible to tolerate; then they all looked at each other, their eyes full of fear...

"I hear names," Angela nervously whispered, while shaking like a leaf.

Emmanuel squeezed her hand in affirmation. They'd entered a large circular room with a high domed ceiling, upon which an Eighteenth Century Italian mural, depicting dozens of angels cradling new-born Caucasian babies, had been masterfully painted; but the eyes of the "visitors" were quickly diverted to the strange and morbid display of tiny ivory coffins. The precious coffins - nearly twenty of them - had been set upon a five foot high black marble base that followed along the entire circumference of the room. Each coffin was a finely carved work of art; but displayed together, they almost resembled a rare collection of oversized music boxes...

As they approached, the wailing suddenly and madly echoed through the room.

"This is the children's chamber," the old gardener explained, while his little eyes searched the imposing circular room. Tom was full of fear, as if he were certain that great danger lurked all around him...

The strange room became hushed for an instant, as strange ethereal globs of opaque matter rapidly rose from the tiny coffins; then slowly took on the hazy form of infants. As one by one the globs rushed into the room, Jonathan's bluish ghost manifested again near one of the coffins; then he directly pointed at it.

Princeton guided Mambha towards that particular ivory coffin, and read the name on the silver plate that had been nailed at its foot. "Angelica Aurora Maria Hoxworth: 1944."

"Open it!" The black priestess commanded, facing the gardener; but the old man balked.

"What in hell's name would you want to do that for?" He almost shouted, visibly terrified.

"Do what Sister Light says, my friend, and open it now," Princeton firmly repeated. "Mambha knows what she's doing!"

"But... But I can't. This is sacrilege!" The old gardener protested. "If the Hoxworths find out, I'll lose my job; or be sent to jail!" He yelled, while intensely shaking from head to toes.

"Open this coffin now, Tom, before it's too late!" Mambha ordered, losing her patience.

Before the old gardener could touch the precious ivory lid of the coffin, Jonathan's ghost placed his hand on it; then, immediately, the silver screws unfastened themselves and scattered on the black marble floor...

Trembling and reluctantly, Princeton carefully lifted the lid. Inside the little coffin were the fragile remains of a baby, wearing a long white christening lace dress. A tiny lace bonnet was tied around the baby's skull.

Without hesitating, Mambha reached into the infant's coffin and placed her hand over the tiny head of the corpse; but the moment she touched it, her body heaved with intense convulsions.

"Angela, take quickly my hand," she ordered, before taking a deep breath.

Repulsed by the sight of the child's decaying body, Angela hesitated. Her troubled mind was immersed in the sound of the wailing women; their strange sad lament growing louder by the minute...

"Take my hand now!" Mambha violently repeated, her voice booming, before Princeton took Angela's hand by force and placed it on top of his sister's.

As if she was watching a "3D" show, and at the speed of light, Angela's entire life suddenly played before her eyes; each sequence encapsulating a memorable event...

Angela saw herself at her parents' funerals in the little church in New Orleans, then making love with Pierce on their wedding day; then dancing in London, Milan, Berlin, Madrid, Prague, San Francisco, Beijing, Istanbul, Sydney, Tokyo, New York and Paris; she also saw herself stepping off for the first time the plane in London, when she was just seventeen, being tutored by the talented Miss Lily Wing; then being taunted by her elementary school peers. She could also hear now the black children at her school in New Orleans, shouting, "Zebra! Zebra! She's a white nigger!" Then, Angela saw Elisabeth giving her a gift, an exquisite pale skinned porcelain doll, before new images of her past came faster and faster, as she spiralled further back into her memory, deep into her tormented subconscious, and deeper into her very being; deeper into her soul…

Now Angela was only three days old, and a tearful young and beautiful Elisabeth was reluctantly handing her to a young Josephine; then the brief intense vision dissipated and Angela saw herself being born, her tiny head pushing into the light of the birthing room of the Hoxworth castle, and each detail of that particular room was crystal clear now. The large room was full of people and her mother beamed for an instant, in spite of the fact that she had just endured the excruciating pains of labour. Elisabeth's lacy white nightgown was damp with sweat, and next to her, an old black female servant, a young Princeton and his mother, who was holding Elisabeth's hand, kindly looking down at her…

In a blinding flash of light, Angela went even further back. She saw herself floating now in her mother's womb, safe from the clanging of the dangerous world around her, at one with the universe and herself. At this precise moment, she was feeling so relaxed that she didn't want to leave that wonderful place, where peace and warmth were overwhelming; and so, so very secure…

"Angela, are you alright?" She heard a woman's voice asking; but she was feeling too happy at this instant to speak, and she was also afraid to break the magic spell. Then, as if she was suddenly sucked into the eye of a giant tornado again, Angela was rapidly taken further back in time…

This time, Angela silently witnessed her conception, as well as the intense passion of her parents' embrace, just before the calling forth of her soul, from where it had been waiting…

Unexpectedly, Angela found herself in a different body; and yet, she was in the same palatial room, with the same pastel walls and heavy draperies surrounding her.

A middle-aged black woman dressed in a maid's uniform, silently wept, while a young doctor with steel blue eyes, held Angela at arms' length, as if he were somehow disgusted by her; or feared her…

Strangely, Angela could clearly see her "past life" now, as if she were looking at a giant panoramic film screen. Now, there were two young black maids, as well as a white middle-aged nurse, and in command in the centre of the large room, she saw her paternal great grandmother, Theresa Eugenia Hoxworth… Theresa had a worried look crossing her face when she scrutinized the naked body of the new-born baby girl that was now wrapped in a soft pink blanket; while her son, Reginald, silently stood by the door, frowning and wide-eyed, looking horrified…

Completely exhausted from giving birth, a young and beautiful Eileen was frantically trying to push herself from the mattress.

"Please Theresa, no! It's not my child's fault. Pleeease, have mercy on her!" Eileen begged; her face was wet with tears and her expression full of fear.

"Give her something to calm her down!" Theresa Hoxworth told the doctor, before she rapidly walked to the bed and firmly spoke to her grief stricken daughter-in-law.

"Don't be foolish, my dear." Theresa's voice was pure ice. "If you keep this mulatto baby, it will be an indelible stain on all of us, my dear... To lose a child, Eileen, you must have a strong will... I know it is hard now, my dear Eileen, because I went through it myself; but as time passes, you'll realise that this is for the best; just as I did!" The elder woman said with a resigned expression. "But we, Hoxworths, cannot afford to have our name soiled by such a child. You must think of how this coloured baby will terribly affect the lives and reputation of all your other children, my child; as well as their children after that... No, my dear child, you cannot let your emotions get the best of you. You are a Hoxworth now!" Theresa nervously exclaimed, visibly not receptive to Eileen's heart breaking plea.

"Please, pleeease, Theresa, have mercy... Just have a look at her! Angelica is more beautiful than the summer sunrise. Please, Theresa, let my daughter live. Please, have mercy... We could give her away... Pleeease Theresa, have mercy!" Eileen endlessly begged, her beautiful lavender eyes streaming with burning tears; Eileen was barely seventeen...

Taking no heed of the mother's cries, and without a single word, the young doctor with the strange steel blue eyes, softly laid the poor Angelica down in the Hoxworth's regal crib. The next thing Angela saw, was a beautiful white lace pillow slowly hovering above her small body; then time suddenly froze, before she desperately screamed. It was the scream of someone who knows that it is the end; someone who is face-to-face with the dark angel of death...

"Sister Light, you must let her go! Stop it, please! It's way too much for her to bear!" Emmanuel strongly pleaded, placing now his arm protectively around Angela. But the black priestess held on tight. "It is necessary, my son," she firmly said.

In a fulgurate flash of light, Angela realised that the frightening nightmares that had plagued her since she was a child, were not dreams at all, but real flashbacks; in fact, she had been reliving her recent past life...

Now, the fragile Angelica Aurora Maria was about to be murdered, and her tiny body revolted and shook with intense convulsions; then Angela had no choice, but to relive the horror of her death again...

White as snow, and deadly as an avalanche, the lace pillow sank down!

As the softness of the down pillow warmly enveloped her face, the poor Angelica desperately struggled to free her tiny hands; suddenly, Angela couldn't breathe, nor could she scream anymore...

"She's suffocating!" Emmanuel shouted at the black priestess. He could not bear anymore to see Angela in such obvious pain. She was struggling to breathe and her limbs were violently flailing about. Emmanuel was about to pull Angela free from the baby skull, when he heard the sound of heavy footsteps and men shouting. The sounds were coming from the passage that led to the children's chamber...

Quickly, Princeton peeled Mambha's hand from the tiny corpse, suddenly breaking the trance; then, limp as a rag doll, Angela fell backward into Emmanuel's arms. He was holding her, when four armed guards rapidly entered the chamber.

"Put your hands up!" They menacingly shouted; their guns in hands.

Princeton and the old gardener did as they were told, but Mambha defiantly stood still, her hands firmly planted inside Angelica's coffin. Emmanuel held fast to Angela, who hadn't regained consciousness yet; then two guards rushed towards him, commanding him to raise his hands, while another grabbed Angela. As she slowly opened her eyes, not sure if she was still in a trance or not, the guard's expression changed to one of fear, then he violently slapped her face. When Angela recovered from the sting of the slap, she saw Eileen Mackenzie-Hoxworth standing immobile at the door, strangely staring at her...

"Let her go!" Eileen commanded. When the guard released Angela, she fell heavily to the black marble floor. Emmanuel bent down to help her up, but a guard hit him viciously with his gun on the back of the head. Seconds later, Emmanuel was lying unconscious over Angela's body...

"Stop this! You behave like animals!" The black priestess shouted, visibly revolted. "Stop it or I will curse all of you forever!" She menacingly added.

"Shut up, you old black witch!" A young white guard, yelled; but the other three, who were black, immediately recognised the famous black priestess; then they all froze in fear in their tracks...

"Man, don't fuck with that woman!" One of them remarked. "Don't you know who she is?" He said, with great fear in his eyes.

"An ugly eyeless freak!" The white guard shouted, before pointing his gun directly at the centre of her brow. Mambha slowly raised her left arm and firmly pointed her finger at him, while chanting now something in an old African dialect. Just as the white guard was about to viciously hit her on the face, one of his black companions intercepted the attack with a strong punch to his chin; then, like a brick, the young idiot heavily fell to the ground...

"Stop it now! All of you!" Eileen suddenly shouted, as she rapidly walked into the melee, visibly unafraid.

"What are all of you doing here?" She demanded, as she coldly surveyed the group of intruders, her expression full of revulsion. "Is that you, Tom? And Princeton? I'm highly disappointed to see you two here!" She sauntered up to the old gardener; then she violently slapped his face, and the large diamond ring she wore slashed the flesh of his cheek. Eileen was about to slap Princeton; but when she saw that Angelica's coffin had been opened, she suddenly blanched...

The wailing voices were now calling her name, before a baby's cry resonated throughout the room, like an insufferable lamentation from hell.

"Why must you torture me?" Eileen painfully asked, her eyes fixed upon the small ivory coffin of her beloved daughter.

"They are the souls of the mothers who cannot rest," Mambha firmly explained. "They will mourn until the truth is finally free… And when you die, dear Eileen, you will join them; unless you tell the truth before you die…" She coldly said, turning around now to face the famous "Grande Dame" of New Orleans.

Eileen painfully pressed her hands to her ears. "Stop it! Please, stop it! Shut them up! Please!" She almost screamed, before stretching her arms out; then, like a strange windmill, she slowly turned round and round. "Those voices are driving me crazy! I can't take it anymore!" She finally shouted through a stream of burning tears.

But the voices didn't stop; instead, they gained strength…

As if a strong wind was blowing from nowhere, the black silk velvet draperies that majestically flanked the crypt's entrance flapped violently against the walls, and the room filled with the scent of sweet tobacco and vetiver…

Jonathan's ghost suddenly manifested in front of his mother, causing her to lose her balance. Trying to stabilise herself, Eileen reached for the side of a coffin and pulled the small box off the pedestal; then, like a vision from hell, the tiny tangled bones, white silk and lace, slid out of the coffin and rolled onto the slick black marble floor…

What looked like a tiny arm rapidly rolled towards one of the black guards, before it touched his shoe. As if he were paralysed, his eyes widened with fear.

"Holly shit!" He nervously exclaimed. "Let's get out of here. This fucking place is haunted!"

But the guard couldn't move; his feet seemed to be glued to the floor...

"Mother..." Jonathan softly said. "Why didn't you tell me the truth?"

Jonathan's ghost stood so close to his mother that she could smell his breath; the cold exhalation of death. Repulsed, Eileen instinctively stepped back; but the ghost of her son inched closer, backing her up against the stonewall...

"Go away!" Eileen shouted out of fear. "Why are you tormenting me? Wasn't I a good mother to you, Jonathan? I didn't have a choice, my son. I had to lie! I had to, don't you understand?" She painfully exclaimed with a broken voice.

"No, it was you, mother, who was too weak to tell me the truth and save me, your own child... Your poor soul will never rest for your crime... Just like me, dear mother, you are bound to wander the world; neither dead, nor alive." Jonathan's translucent eyes expressed all the profound pain that his tormented soul felt; as well as all the agony that he had endured since he committed suicide...

Eileen scowled. "I've always done my best, Jonathan. I would've given my own life to spare yours, my son. You must know that; now you can see my soul! You can feel my heart! If I only knew that you couldn't handle the lie I told you, I would've told you the truth; I swear! Since the day you took your life, my son, I've prayed every day and every night that you would find peace, and I also often asked God's forgiveness." Somehow, Eileen's fear and repulsion had disappeared, and she spoke now to the ghost of her son as if he were truly alive...

"Peace is something that your fortune can't buy, mother," Jonathan's ghost sadly said, his voice strangely softening. The poor thing was visibly touched now by his mother's great suffering, and quite surprised at the ocean of tears in her beautiful blue lavender eyes, as he knew full well that Eileen was not a woman who cried easily; in fact, it was the first time that Jonathan saw his mother crying...

Then suddenly, Eileen tenderly smiled, as if all her fear had dissipated, and she lovingly reached out to her son, to his ghost, visibly wanting to take him in her arms; wanting to protect him as if he were still a defenceless child...

"No mother, please don't touch me! If you do, your spirit will enter the world of the dead... You will see your own death, mother; and you will see my tormented soul as well."

Eileen slightly hesitated for an instant; then she calmly said, "Well, I don't care anymore, my son... I'd gladly pay any price to feel you with my soul. Now God in His mercy is giving me a chance to demonstrate my love to you, as well as to your poor sister; my beloved Angelica Aurora Maria..." Eileen lovingly said; a tender smile for the first time crossing her face; then, without further hesitation, she draped her arms around her son's ghostly form. At the beginning, she felt his "flesh", but he was cold, so cold; like the stone statues of the wailing mothers...

"Please, forgive me, my beloved son," Eileen softly cried. "Please forgive me for what I have done to you, or didn't say..." She tiredly said while closing her eyes; but the joy of holding her beloved son again was so wonderful, that Eileen barely noticed when the chill of death passed from Jonathan's ghostly body into her bones, into her heart, and rapidly invaded her tormented mind; until it reached her very soul...

Around the two of them, ribbons of soft purple light emanated, and the room suddenly became strangely silent; deadly silent...

"Just stay a few moments longer, my son. Please, my darling, don't leave me again..." As Eileen desperately clung to her son's ghost, painful tears streamed down her face; tears of peace...

For a moment, Jonathan's spirit summoned all his strength, but he couldn't maintain his density; and soon after this, Eileen found herself holding onto nothing, but a cold, damp, amorphous opaque cloud; until terrible visions flooded her mind...

As Jonathan had warned, his mother instantly witnessed her own death; blood, so much blood, flowed from her head, then the entire room swirled around her, and her tormented soul was gone...

A black guard tried to pull Eileen away before she fainted, but the moment he touched her, he was also consumed by a vision of his own death. The guard shouted in fear, before an invisible force violently pushed him away; then he collapsed in a heap on the floor, blood running from his forehead, rapidly spreading on the marble floor...

Numbly, Eileen looked down and saw a dark crimson pool forming around her feet; but she held fast to Jonathan's ghost, as she did not want to lose her son again.

"Please, pleeease, forgive me, my son," she begged, crying again. "Please stay!" But her pleading fell on deaf ears. Little by little, Jonathan's ghost disintegrated into luminous particles of sparkling light, before he simply vanished; then the strange little lights dissipated like the remains of a firework show...

Like a somnambulist, Eileen stood with her arms wide spread, as if she were still holding her son; she was sobbing while softly chanting his name, again and again.

Her heart was wracked with intense pain, but Eileen lovingly kept calling his name. Even as she fell to her knees, spent and exhausted, she was not noticing that the guard's blood was seeping into her silken robes; not noticing that she was alone again...

Shortly after, the proud Dame Mackenzie-Hoxworth finally fainted; this was indeed her first foretaste of death...

Amen!

Chapter Fifty-Seven

"Hoxworth Castle"

Edmond Hoxworth was already furious when he stormed into his grandmother's bedroom; but the deranging sight of Angela seated on the bed, next to Eileen, tenderly holding her hand, was enough to throw him into a full-blown rage...

To make matters worse, the black eyeless voodoo priestess was softly chanting at the foot of the princely-canopied bed; while the family doctor and his assistant attended to the women's cuts and scratches.

"Fuck!" Edmond shouted. "Get that bitch out of here now! And take that black witch with her," he added, stomping over to the bed.

He roughly cupped Angela's chin in one hand and Mambha's chin in the other, forcing them both to face him, to feel his intense rage.

"If you try to trick my grandmother using highbrow diva tactics, or some kind of bullshit voodoo sorcery, I swear I'll kill both of you!" He screamed, his breath smelling acrid. Then, as if he were suddenly repulsed by the sight of them, he dropped their chins, turned on his heel, and began to pace like a madman, his steps heavy...

Before Angela came into his life, Edmond had managed to keep his emotions tightly capped; but now, constant hatred overruled his well-practiced self-control. And yet, Edmond didn't care anymore, as he was now beyond reasoning. The powerful rush of undiluted hatred that coursed through his blood, felt almost luscious and authentic; much more calming than love and more potent than lust...

"Please, sir," the young red head nurse urged. "Calm down! Can't you see that your grandmother is ill?"

"If you can't shut your fat mouth, bitch, which is what you're being paid for, then get the fuck out!" Edmond violently shouted, suddenly enjoying his folly. His eyes were clear as Patagonian ice, and as strange as the ones of a murderer before killing; and as frightening as well...

The doctor quickly came to his assistant's aid. "Mister Hoxworth, please Sir, you need to calm down. Perhaps I could give you a pill?"

"Yes, Sir; please, pleeease, for your grandmother's sake," the nurse begged, pointing towards Eileen, with a hand that was shaking as if she had a severe case of palsy. But Edmond viciously grinned and then, without warning, he violently pushed the nurse away and punched the doctor in the jaw; shortly after he was holding Angela by the throat. She desperately tried to fight back, but she was no match for a man entirely possessed by fury. Not even his grandmother's words could snap Edmond out of his extreme rage. The cool lucidness, the purity of hatred, was way too addictive now. Strangely, Edmond Hoxworth had never felt so "alive", never felt so strong; Edmond had never felt so completely himself…

He took a handful of Angela's hair in his fist, before snapping her head back and forth, like if she were a broken doll.

"You want our money, don't you, bitch? Ten million wasn't enough for your greedy nigger soul," he screamed to her face with a sardonic grin, visibly enjoying her pain.

Angela struggled to pry his fingers off of her fragile neck, but she could not breathe anymore, and the vision of the white pillow sinking down on her face became vivid again in her mind.

"So you think you can just prance in here with your fake family tree and dirty black voodoo witch, and bullshit my grandmother into believing all your dirty crap? What were you doing in our family crypt, bitch? Looking for evidence to prove your cockamamie story?" Edmond emitted a sound that was half grunt and half laugh, before violently shaking Angela again.

"Let her go, Edmond. Please, let her go!" Eileen begged. "You do not understand, my child; Angela is my daughter! I've always felt it in my heart, but now I know it's the truth!" She shouted, visibly afraid.

"Shut up, you stupid old woman! You've completely lost your mind! Your daughter is dead! Dead!!! Taken care of, in a civilized fashion; just like this upstart should've been!" He shouted to her face, enjoying his folly again.

In spite of the extreme anger that intensely raged around the room, Angela strangely ached for a deep sleep. She closed her tired eyes and saw her beloved Josephine, young, healthy and happy, her loving arms open and receptive; her tender brown eyes overflowing with pure love...

Why? Angela simply asked herself; then, for the first time, the answer came quickly: *love; love is the only real thing, my child... Love is more authentic than dance, or the drama of the afterlife, or marriage, or family; or even genetics, my child...*

'Love' was the only thing worth living for; love was the only thing that was real; the only escape. Certainly, death was no escape...

If Edmond only knew... Angela mused, before shaking herself back into the present. Perhaps she was also losing her mind, thinking about 'love' at a time like this...

Her only consolation now, was that tucked safely inside her handbag, was a hand-written letter that Eileen had given her; one that granted her permission to exhume her father's remains...

And yet, in the midst of the horror, the greed, the adultery, and the absurdity of all the events that had transpired since Josephine and André had died; there was Emmanuel.

When he entered the room, in spite of everything, his eyes were a beacon of light; then Angela suddenly felt like the luckiest woman in the world...

Attempting to regain her full attention, Edmond violently grabbed her torso, but she had slipped away into a mysterious world where only "love" ruled; a perfect place where white bell-shaped flowers grew in the snow, and where infinity of wonderful colours softly played in a northern sky. Angela was now in a perfect place, where new-borns cooed and joyously smiled because they felt totally loved; even during wartime…

At this precise instant, within herself, Angela had created a wonderful peaceful world, where love was everywhere; in the ugly and in the beautiful. *It is a lovely world…* She strangely thought, beatifically smiling; even as Edmond furiously squeezed her so tightly, that she could already feel the bruises forming. Before the room went dark and completely silent, Angela heard a loud crack and felt a thud on her skull; then, in a blink of an eye, Angela was gone…

Chapter Fifty-Eight

"Hoxworth Castle"

Like the painful stinger of a bee made of steel, the long hypodermic needle stabbed Edmond's upper arm and swiftly delivered ten ccs of 'Valium' into his boiling bloodstream...

Seconds later, his out of control body relaxed into the arms of the black security guard who'd been standing behind him, before he finally closed his eyes.

"Lay him down on the sofa," Doctor Stickley ordered, motioning to the anteroom. "And keep a good watch on him," he told his nurse. "If he stirs, give him another ten ccs. And be quick about it!" The furrows of his brow were deep with worry.

Eileen questioningly looked at him.

"He'll be alright, Madam," the doctor assured. "At least physically... It's your granddaughter who took the brunt of it. My technician is going to bring up the portable radiology machine, so I can check her lung... Hopefully, it's a simple fracture, but there's a possibility that the rib might've punctured her lung, Madam."

Her eyes closed, Angela lay motionless on her grandmother's regal red brocade canopied bed. Black and blue imprints of Edmond's fingers covered her torso and her breathing was strained; even with the oxygen mask…

Emmanuel sat on a French golden chair by the bed, lovingly holding her hand. He had never been so angry in his entire life, and his face showed it. He wanted to take Angela away from the Hoxworth castlen and out of Louisiana. His internal voice told him that she belonged with him on his island; that he will be spending the rest of his life making her happy there; now he finally knew that he could…

How Emmanuel wished he had someone he trusted to talk to. He tried to reach Jeanette at the hotel, but there was no answer. Half an hour later, he called again and worriedly listened as the phone rang and rang, wondering where his sister was; knowing that Jeanette should be in her room by now, since it was almost the end of the afternoon. He tenderly kissed Angela on the forehead and got up to find the black priestess. After the guard had subdued Edmond, Mambha went to the private chapel in the castle's north wing to pray for Jonathan's soul. Eileen had asked a chambermaid to escort her. As for Princeton, he left the moment he saw Edmond's limousine pull up. Tom, the old gardener drove him to Edmond's mansion, where Princeton rapidly packed his things into the gardener's van, never to return; knowing that it was time he quit his job…

As Emmanuel stood up, a man dressed in scrubs entered the room. He was pushing a cart laden with X-ray equipment and high tech paraphernalia. At least Angela would be well taken care of with the best that money could buy...

"It will only be a few minutes," the radiologist said. "Don't worry, Sir. The doctor said it's only a two star alarm."

Emmanuel realised that his face was wet with tears. The pain he felt in his heart was almost unbearable. What could be worse, he thought, than finding the love of his life only to lose her? It didn't make sense. He hurried pass in front of Edmond, who was snoring on a red damask sofa, without even looking at him. If he had seen that monster's face, he wouldn't have been able to restrain himself from punching it again. When Eileen saw Emmanuel leaving her bedroom, she sighed. "I just don't understand what overcame my grandson, Nathaniel," she apologetically said to the trusted family doctor, still trying to minimise her grandson's foolish actions.

Doctor Stickley frowned. "Mister Edmond always had a bad streak, madam... I remember now that he was the kind of boy that pulled the wings off of flies for no reason; and I don't think the years have changed him much... Your late husband had the same bad temper in him." The doctor calmly said while avoiding her eyes. "Your grandson needs some serious counselling and probably daily medication; otherwise, one day or another, he's going to end up in jail, madam." He firmly added.

"Nathaniel, how you dare imply such a thing?" Eileen harshly reproached. "My dear Edmond's just a bit high strung... After all, the poor boy lost his father quite tragically when he was at such a tender young age." She softly said while trying to smile.

Doctor Stickley rolled his eyes; he knew better than to argue with the authoritarian Dame Eileen. Long ago, when he was a young man, his father had told him that the Hoxworths would pay him much more than he could ever dream of, if he always followed their rules; but his father also said that they were not the type of people who took advice; especially when it came to their own behaviour...

"Doctor, it's just a small fracture," the technician said. "The lung is good as gold."

"So, just let her rest." Doctor Stickley nervously said, while rearranging his medical equipment.

Reassured, Eileen closed her eyes. The horrific events of the past hour; the encounter with her son's ghost, and the incredible revelation that Angela was indeed possessed by the soul of her beloved departed daughter Angelica; as well as the frightening vision of her own death, weighed heavy on Eileen's mind. More than ever, Eileen needed her grandson to be her rock now. If what she saw when she embraced Jonathan's ghost would really occur - and she was not so sure anymore - then she did not have long to live...

"My dear Nathaniel, Edmond does not need a psychiatrist, nor does he need drugs to keep him sane. I won't have it! You may take your leave now!" Eileen dryly ordered, with visible disdain.

No one, not even her trusted family doctor, could persuade the 'grand dame of New Orleans' that her beloved grandson was riddled with genetic defects...

Edmond was the last surviving male of the prestigious Hoxworth bloodline; a heavy legacy that constantly demanded that he maintain an image of absolute perfection.

If Edmond were physically or mentally ill in any way, Doctor Stickley would handle that condition with utmost discretion, Eileen firmly decided. In any case, it was imperative that her dear Edmond remain exempt from the "plagues of the masses"; posterity required such, and as far as Eileen was concerned, her dear Edmond Louis Gabriel Hoxworth, her only precious grandson, was among the finest of men.

Until the dead body of the great Eileen Rose Mackenzie-Hoxworth was in her regal crypt, the "Grand Dame of New Orleans" would not hear otherwise; never!

Chapter Fifty-Nine

"New Orleans"

"Monteleone Hotel"

Emmanuel carefully lifted Angela out of the wheelchair that Doctor Stickley had insisted she use, then lovingly carried her into the suite; but the moment they stepped inside, Emmanuel realised that they were not alone...

A handsome and elegant man with dark blue eyes sat on the sofa, leafing through a "Town and Country" magazine.

"Who are you?" Emmanuel asked, surprised and shocked by the man's poise.

"Well Sir, I think I'm the one who should be asking you the questions..." The man calmly responded, with a perfect Oxford accent. "That's my wife you're holding in your arms, my friend!" He coldly smiled.

Emmanuel blushed. "You're Angela's husband? I... I didn't expect to see you here."

"Obviously," Pierce suavely remarked, his intriguing eyes tumultuous as a storm-tossed sea...

Trying to buy time, Emmanuel nervously explained the day's events as best as he could; even though he realised how unbelievable his story must have sounded to an angry husband. While he was talking, he forgot to put Angela down.

"I see..." Pierce quite politely said, visibly trying to keep his cool. "Unfortunately for my wife, I wasn't around at the time; but now, Sir, your services are no longer needed..." He coldly added with a dash of disdain. Pierce would have loved to punch the handsome Emmanuel in the face; but being a professional lawyer, he did not want to risk a lawsuit, so he simply restrained himself. Pierce sought out Angela's eyes, but she somehow averted his gaze; then, in an instant, all of his "English reserve" melted away...

"Now Sir, give my wife to me!" He demanded.

"If you don't mind, I'll bring her to her bedroom so she can rest; she's ill, you know..." Emmanuel firmly said, before he walked to the bedroom, ignoring Pierce.

"Well, I have no doubt, Sir, that you have obviously done that before..." Pierce coldly remarked with a smirk, before snatching Angela from Emmanuel's arms.

"Are you crazy? You are hurting her! Angela has a fractured rib!" Emmanuel yelled, as she groaned with pain.

"Now get out!" Pierce nervously ordered, as he was helping Angela to the sofa. Then he silently stared at her, waiting for her to explain herself, to apologise; but she had closed her eyes...

"Whoever you are, thank you, Sir, but my wife and I are fine now!" He said to Emmanuel, employing the tone he often reserved for his servants.

Angela wanted to say something in Emmanuel's defence, but she was extremely confused, and hazy from the morphine that Dr. Stickley had injected. In fact, she was so drained, that she just wanted to sleep.

What is Pierce doing here? Why is he looking so mad?

Emmanuel pushed past Pierce and tenderly laid his hand on Angela's cheek. "I'll check on you later. Rest now," he softly said, visibly in love.

"That won't be necessary, Sir." Pierce harshly said. "If my wife needs some kind of attention, I'll phone a doctor!" He finally exclaimed, losing his patience.

"Your wife really needs support, Mister Haddington... She might need to talk to someone she trusts about what happened today. Do you even care?" Emmanuel nervously asked, while looking straight into Pierce's eyes.

Pierce's rosy face suddenly turned crimson with rage. "Angela *is* my wife; and I perfectly know what she needs, or what she doesn't need, Sir! My wife has been quite unstable ever since her mother died, and it's high time that she returns home with me now... to our home!" He stressed, his eyes now dangerously locked with Emmanuel's. "As far as I'm concerned, Sir," he nervously continued, "you're just nothing; but a con man who took advantage of a woman in a weakened state... In any case, Sir, you should be ashamed of yourself! And believe me when I say that you'll be forgotten as soon as we board the plane to London tomorrow!" Pierce exclaimed, while raising his voice.

"Tomorrow? Are you so selfish? Didn't you hear a word I said? This is Angela's life we're talking about!" Emmanuel retorted. It was obvious to him that the so refined Pierce Haddington cared nothing about Angela's history, or her real roots, or her family; nor he cared about his wife's profound feelings. "You cheating bastard!" Emmanuel shouted, visibly revolted.

Angela told this stranger that I'd cheated on her? Enraged, Pierce raised his fist, ready to fight. "You are really something, you bloody son of a bitch!" He shouted before he stepped back and sized up his competition. "What's your game? Are you some sort of an island gigolo? It's apparent that you're a "mongrel" of some sort; but if you think you're going to weasel your way into her heart, because you've got that in common, you're dead wrong, my friend!!!" Pierce finally shouted, enraged.

Emmanuel's martial arts instructor had often warned him that there would come a time, when restraining the urge to kill, would be more challenging than defending his own life. Power was neither "good nor bad", the master had often said; so Emmanuel took a deep breath and connected his tormented mind with his pure heart, while trying his best to cultivate real compassion for Pierce's profound ignorance.

Angela's eyes were now open; wide open…

The morphine was no match for the pain that her husband's harsh words had caused her.

"*Pierce called us mongrels...*" She sadly thought, suddenly feeling like crying again. "Go; please go..." She silently mouthed to Emmanuel.

When he saw her tears, Emmanuel transformed all the hatred he felt towards Pierce into nourishing love for Angela. Even though she was still overwhelmed with pain, Emmanuel knew that she had received the love that he had mentally sent her; Emmanuel had finally mastered his art...

"Goodbye, Mister Haddington," he calmly said to Pierce. "Have a pleasant flight back to London!"

"Thank you, Sir. We will!" Pierce arrogantly replied; but deep down, the irritating Pierce Haddington was not so sure anymore...

Chapter Sixty

"New Orleans"

"Monteleone Hotel"

Angela's ribs throbbed with each breath she took, but she didn't want to take any of the 'Vicodin' that the doctor had prescribed; nor did she take a pill to help her sleep, because she wanted her mind to say awake...

Her ribs were tightly bound with an ace bandage, and it was truly excruciating to lie in any position, other than flat on her back.

Angela was not afraid of pain anymore. She only feared not being able to think clearly in this particular situation. While Pierce slept beside her in the king size bed, his arms possessively resting on her thigh, she really needed to think clearly; and so she did...

Angela suddenly realised that she must have dosed off after Emmanuel left.

Pierce had dressed her in a simple white cotton nightgown. He had also put her diamond wedding ring back on her finger; she had not worn in it the past few days, not since she'd received the photographs and the private eye's report. Now and then, Pierce would awaken, softly kiss her hand, and play with the wedding ring on her tapered finger...

They were all endearing gestures, granted, but for Angela it was not enough anymore.

Before Josephine and André died, Angela might have been able to forgive Pierce's infidelities, but not anymore. She had taken her vows seriously; more seriously seemingly than most women in the new millennium. Angela was the kind of woman who certainly would not divorce her husband just because she might think she's "in love" with another man. She had learned long ago, that "love" is a very capricious animal, just like a ghost, it has a tendency to manifest or suddenly vanish, as if it had a will of its own; a will stronger than the flesh and blood it possessed, whether or not that flesh was dead or alive...

But now, how could Angela ever forgive Pierce for the words he spoke? Their harshness ran through her head again and again. *"It's apparent that you're a mongrel, but if you think you're going to weasel your way into her heart, just because you've got that in common..."* Those horrible words coiled around her heart like a boa constrictor, and she knew now that they would continue to suffocate her spirit, until she totally removed herself from Pierce, as well as all that defined him. In her husband's eyes, Angela sadly realised now that she was a mongrel; a mongrel he had redeemed...

Suddenly, it all made sense. Pierce certainly saw himself as Angela's saviour, 'her patron', and a man who'd given her a new lease on life; a great entitlement that came with the Haddington name. Angela remembered now how stunned he was when she decided to keep "Boivin" as her stage name. It had become quite obvious that Pierce wasn't interested in her recent quest to find her true heritage; in fact, he saw the truth as a threat. If Angela were indeed a Hoxworth, she would not just be Pierce's equal; she would be, in fact, superior...

Now, Angela finally understood that underneath the well-polished English façade, her dear husband, like most men, was nonetheless extremely insecure; and also, that unfortunately, there would always be other women; a lot of other women, who certainly would become much younger, as time passed while she became older by his side...

For Pierce, 'love' was not a prerequisite to sex; sex was just a sport! Good clean fun that had nothing to do with their marriage...

Silently, Angela watched her husband sleep. As handsome as Pierce Haddington was, he was simply an ordinary man; ordinary in his cheating, as well as ordinary in his selfishness...

If he weren't so handsome and rich, he might be a faithful husband... She sadly thought, refraining from crying again.

Pierce was so attractive, so charming, so elegant, and rich, that women of all ages would always throw themselves at him; and Angela sadly realised now that her dear husband could not resist their attentions, and even less their advances; like with this Miss Bernhart...

No, it was not an easy choice...

Angela reached over and softly squeezed his hand. She sincerely loved her husband and she knew him well enough to understand that he would not take her decision easily. Deep down, she would have liked to remain "friends", like some French divorced couples do; but she was almost sure that when he walked out the door the next morning, she would probably never see him again, except in a court of law ...

Angela knew for a fact that her dear Pierce was not the kind of man who did well without a woman - or many - in his life...

Pierce had only been divorced a year when he married Angela; and after their divorce, she was certain that he wouldn't be on the market long again. The moment the news of their separation hit the tabloids; the obviously "volage" Pierce Haddington would certainly reclaim his position as one of London's most eligible rich bachelors; and one of the most devastatingly handsome ones as well...

Angela spent most of the night nervously watching her husband soundly sleep.

How I wish I could pretend that I am still in love... I could still get on that plane tomorrow and leave those damned Hoxworths; along with their dirty family secrets and all their ghosts behind...

But Angela simply dismissed that tempting thought. Her soul, her mind, as well as her heart, had chosen a different path now; one that obviously didn't include Pierce anymore...

After this endless night, it was crystal clear to Angela that Pierce's world was not hers anymore; in fact, it never was. The way Pierce selected his friends; his snobbish and extremely elitist English family; everything that was "his", seemed now to make Angela's skin itch with constant irritation, as if she had suddenly developed a sudden allergic reaction; one that couldn't be cured by potions or drugs...

For better or worse, Angela's world had changed too much lately, and certain essential things couldn't be fixed or negotiated anymore...

Deep in her heart, Angela somehow knew that she would miss Pierce; but not enough to reconsider her final decision. Without hesitation, Angela sadly removed her large diamond wedding ring, then she tiredly closed her eyes, while thinking that dawn wasn't approaching quickly enough...

Chapter Sixty-One

"New Orleans"

"Monteleone Hotel"

Angela was fully awake when the wake-up call chimed at exactly 6:00 am; dusk had barely arrived...

Outside the window, a glimmer of red softly merged with the low fog that still hung in the air, and the eastern sky was painted with an ashen light; the exact colour of the dying embers of a fire...

When Pierce opened his eyes, he saw that Angela's answer was clearly written on her face...

Although Pierce knew that he'd lost the battle, his ego took precedence over his heart. He spoke his well-rehearsed words with as much passion as a door-to-door salesman, then decided that he had taken appropriate due diligence, and had fought for his marriage as much as he could.

After Pierce took a quick shower, Angela watched him dress, noticing that he had gained some weight; soon enough she thought, he would certainly begin to resemble his dear uncle Stuart, in more than one way...

When Pierce softly kissed Angela - small tender kisses - from her forehead to her toes, his mouth lingering at the small triangle of her pubis, Angela calmly remained as still as a doll, as if she felt nothing; neither repulsion nor attraction...

"I must tell you that I still love you, Angela," Pierce lovingly said for the last time. "I'm really sorry for what happened... Won't you forgive me, darling?" His eyes were sincere.

"Yes Pierce... I will forgive you," Angela flatly told him; but her unresponsive body said otherwise. "Just not in this lifetime..." She softly smiled.

At this point, Pierce did not dare press her, as he knew her well enough to know that she did not lie; and also that she could not live her life with a broken heart...

Not knowing why, Angela thought of the arrogant Gail Haddington, his uncle's dear wife, and a little voice told her that she'd indeed made the right choice; then she suddenly thought of the sweet Emmanuel, and an unwitting smile brightened her face...

"Darling?" Pierce said again, her loving smile giving him hope.

"No... I am sorry," Angela softly said. "Goodbye Pierce," she calmly said, as she softly put her diamond eternity ring inside the chest pocket of his well tailored green tweed jacket. She caught a fleeting glance of pain in the tormented blue sea of his eyes, before the natural cloud of English reserve crossed over him again; then, his irises suddenly became darker, like the cold deep of the ocean...

Pierce calmly adjusted his burgundy striped silk tie, and the wonderful husband that Angela had so sincerely loved during so many years, suddenly just disappeared...

The man who faced Angela now, was not smiling anymore, and almost unfamiliar. That strange man simply looked like a distinguished English business lawyer; something he truly was and the rapid change was truly frightening...

As Angela expected, her dear husband left without saying "goodbye".

Pierce Haddington's last unspoken words were the cruellest: silence; stone cold silence...

Amen.

Chapter Sixty-Two

"New Orleans"

"Monteleone Hotel"

At the precise moment Pierce Haddington closed the bedroom's door behind him, the phone rang again...

"Hello?" Angela tiredly said, feeling her ribs ached.

"I'm sorry to wake you, Angela, but there's something wrong," Emmanuel said, with a trembling voice.

"What's wrong?"

"It's Jeanette! She didn't return to the hotel last night. Has she called you? Have you seen her?" Emmanuel's voice shook with fear.

"No, I haven't."

"When's the last time you saw her?"

"I think you were there," Angela said. "She was going for a jog, and I gave her my ballet jacket to wear, remember?"

"Do you think I should call the police?" Emmanuel nervously asked. "Angela?" He took her silence as a sign that Pierce was still there. "I'm sorry. Your husband's there," he apologetically said.

"No, no. He's gone," she finally said. *His sister was wearing my jacket...* She tried to keep the disturbing thought from her mind. "Don't panic, Emmanuel. Everything will be all right. We are going to find Jeanette."

"Something's wrong. I can feel it... I should've called the police last night."

"Why didn't you tell me sooner?"

Emmanuel sadly laughed. "With everything else that was happening, I lost track of time. Now it may be too late!" He said while looking at the clock. It was 6:30 am.

"Please, pleeease calm down," Angela softly said. "Come up to my room and we'll wait for Jeanette together."

"Thanks. I need you," he said, feeling strangely lost, for the first time in his life.

"I know... I need you too, you know," Angela reluctantly admitted, before she hung up. Her body shook with apprehension, as she recalled in vivid detail the terrible nightmare she had about the two black thugs. *Jeanette is in trouble, and it's my fault...I am sure of it.* She thought, frightened.

Angela gathered her strength and pushed herself out of bed, brushed her fears away, and slowly walked to the door. She led Emmanuel into the bedroom and surmised, by the painful expression on his face, that he feared that the worst had happened to his sister. During the last hours, he'd phoned every hospital and police station in New Orleans with no success. Exhausted and lost, he finally laid his head on Angela's chest and she comforted him the best she could; like a friend; like a mother; like a woman in love...

Angela felt Emmanuel's profound pain like her own; each beat of his tormented heart in her own, while each broken word he uttered seared her flesh. When he regained some of his self-control, he looked deep into her eyes, and asked her the question she didn't want to answer.

"I need you Angela, and I don't want any secrets between us," he sincerely said. "So tell me what happened."

"Pierce left," she flatly said, strangely feeling no pain.

"Yes, I know; somehow I thought that it would happen this way... But the crypt, what did you see there?" His eyes were dark and serious. Her voice quivering, Angela described what she had seen in the crypt, when the black priestess was holding her hand, while touching Angelica's skull; how she saw with her own eyes, that she was in fact the reincarnation of Eileen's child, and how she was then suffocated by a pillow because she was a mulatto. She also told him about all the innocent mulatto babies that were murdered, just after their birth, in the castle, throughout the last centuries, because they were seen as "a stain" on the glorious Hoxworth name. After understanding all this, she would never be the same again, Angela sadly confessed.

The hideous knowledge of those terrible infanticides was like a deep wound infected by deadly bacteria; a wound that would never heal, she knew. The lingering pain would remain buried in her heart until the day she died, unless she did something...

It was now up to Angela to end the terrible Hoxworth legacy and therefore make public what had been done. She, "the human stain", must take the insufferable Edmond Hoxworth, her brother, to court and win the case. She would prove to the world, without the shadow of a doubt, that Negro blood also flowed through his veins; and as a result, his wife - present or future - would know the terrible truth and would never be forced, if they had a coloured child, to accept the unacceptable...

With each word that Angela spoke, more tumult grew within her being.

Emmanuel could feel her pain, which was palpable, as real as the ghosts they had encountered; as real as his profound love for her.

"I feel truly sorry for Elisabeth, my mother; and even sorrier for the poor Eileen..." Angela said, wiping her tears away. "Now, I know that when Eileen lay in that bed, helplessly watching as the doctor began to suffocate me, "Angelica", just after I was born, I truly felt her love. And since that terrible day, I know now that her love for me never died; in fact, it only grew stronger with time... I think that somewhere, deep in her heart, Eileen somehow knew that I was the reincarnated soul of her beloved Angelica Aurora Maria," Angela calmly explained, while suddenly realising how strange this whole situation was.

"It's quite possible..." Emmanuel agreed, before he lovingly caressed her face. "It's strange to think that this domineering woman is not only your grandmother; but also your mother in a previous life... There are certainly deep ties, like an invisible umbilical cord, which link you to each other... Maybe if we have a girl, the poor Eileen will choose to be reincarnated as your daughter..." He softly added, visibly not afraid of the thought.

Angela's heart skipped a beat. *If "we" have a girl...* As if the logical conclusion to their relationship would naturally be children. Then she remembered the words of the black priestess, when they were in the gardener's van en route to the Hoxworth crypt. "Two boys and a girl," she'd prophesied. "The beautiful island where Emmanuel lives is where you'll find peace, my child." *Peace... Babies... Two boys and a girl...*

Appealing as it was for Angela, the thought of such normalcy, at this point of her life, was as hard to imagine as living on the moon...

Angela lovingly looked at Emmanuel, and for a second that seemed to be an eternity, she lost her soul in his reassuring eyes. To think that this man was a complete stranger only ten days ago...

If strange circumstances hadn't brought Angela to New Orleans again, and to that particular hotel, she would have never met that exceptional human being; and that, by itself, now seemed totally impossible. It had to be destiny. Neither she, nor he, were the masters of their own lives; but somewhere, deep within her heart, it was already written: "peace on his island... two boys and a girl..."

All Angela knew now was that it was up to her to break the chain of guilt and sorrow in order to free the wailing mothers from their ordeal, and finally let the essence of love flow. Yes, it was up to

Angela now, simply because she was the only one who held such a power in her heart; in the core of her soul...

Destiny waited for everyone, granted; but it was a personal choice to follow the eternal nurturing light, and to let love - not envy, greed and lust - in...

As Angela deeply looked into Emmanuel's loving eyes, she could see the end of the dark tunnel. There, deep within his exceptional being, was the glimpse of light she had been desperately searching for, since her long living nightmare began.

At this particular instant, Angela utterly understood that if she decided to climb the highest mountain, and also that each time she took a dangerous step, Emmanuel would be there besidej her, kindly offering his strong but gentle hand. The "high peaks", Angela knew, might be quite difficult to reach, but they would reach them together from now on; always together; forever and ever...

Angela suddenly thought of Jeanette. In the horrible nightmare she had, she'd only seen the woman from the back, and had assumed that it was herself, because she was wearing her ballet jacket; but in fact, if it was a premonition; if it was not herself, but Jeanette whom had been raped? She thought terrified, while she deeply shuddered...

For many long hours, Emmanuel and Angela lay in each other's arms, dozing and worrying, waiting for enough time to pass, so that he could file a police report; but by sundown, there were still no news about the sweet Jeanette, and Angela's internal demons came back to terrorise her; again...

Chapter Sixty-Three

"New Orleans"

Feeling hungry as a wolf and extremely happy to escape the mosquito-infested swamps, Grande sped back to town...

The impressive Mexican-Samoan had never liked the Bayou, but he was a professional and he fully knew that a good killer had to be flexible enough to deal with "impromptu situations" of any kind, no matter how distasteful; but since his job was done, all he wanted to do now, was to celebrate his victory with a delicious triple beef burger with the works from Johnny's Diner...

Grande was happy to be done, and if he had to, he would certainly have somehow killed again, just for a good cup of hot java...

The rain had finally let up, but the heavy wet clouds still hung low, almost touching the fetid swamp, and Grande had the feeling that he was inhaling water with each breath. Now his sensitive lungs felt dirty and cold, like black snow melting in a gutter.

Earlier that morning, Grande had thought he'd hit the jackpot. After seven days of waiting, Angela was finally leaving her hotel alone. Even in her jogging clothes, she was more beautiful than any good-looking whore he'd ever seen. He'd discretely followed her as she ran around the park, until he noticed that, when she got to a little alley, someone else was tailing her: two black thugs in a van...

Terribly surprised, Grande silently watched as one of the black guys stuck a rag in her mouth, before he threw her into the back of the van. Then Grande discretely followed the van for almost forty minutes, until it took a small path at the end of a little dirt road leading into the pit of the bayou; into the mosquito infested 'Chacahoulas' swamp...

The van finally parked in front of an old dilapidated shack, and the tallest of the thugs carried Angela in his arms. She was limp and unconscious. Grande discretely waited from a prudent distance in his car and watched the black men sit for a while in front of the shack; each of them downing several beers, before they went back inside.

Grande had looked up at the sky, hoping that the rain would stop soon.

The impressive Mexican-Samoan truly hated the rain; and that particular day, it was pouring buckets...

When Grande was a child, 'Lupe', his Mexican mother, often locked him in the bathroom to punish him. During the rainy season, all he would hear was the sound of the rain pounding against the corrugated tin roof and the window, and his young heart was racing in fear. Since that time, Grande had developed a terrible phobia and never got over it; but he didn't like to admit his only fear to anyone...

To his delight, after waiting for almost an hour, a small patch of pale blue sky seemed to be moving his way. Five minutes later, the rain had diminished to a slight sprinkle, and Grande got out of the car and sprinted towards the shack; smiling...

It was time for business; it was time to kill...

The two black thugs were easy marks. Even the big one's neck broke as quickly as a rooster's, but the woman was a disappointment; she wasn't Angela...

The beautiful young woman was already half-dead, her nose and jaw, as well as her long golden legs, savagely broken...

What a waste! She must've been drop dead gorgeous, before those fucking niggers got to her; not as beautiful as Miss Angela, but too pretty to be hit in the face, Grande sadly thought. He wondered if the thugs had hit her, before, or after they raped her; blood and semen ran from her vagina...

Grande took great pity on the poor young woman, whose beautiful honey green eyes pleaded for mercy; so he "kindly" strangled her, before leaving the shack...

Grande was just about to bite into his juicy triple burger, when his cell phone suddenly rang.

"Damn!" He shouted when he saw the Hoxworth's name on the caller ID.

Every time he was ready for a good meal, the rich arrogant jerk interrupted him.

"Where are you?" Edmond barked instead of "hello".

"I'm having my breakfast at a burger joint, boss; then, in half an hour, I'll take my spot in Royal Street, in front of the ballerina's hotel and wait below her window again… I'm beginning to feel like that guy, "Romeo". You know the one? But I'm not a young boy anymore, and I'm getting bored of sitting on my sore ass all day…" Grande quite nervously said. "I need some action, boss, and soon!" He lamented, while thinking that there was no reason he should tell the terribly irritating Edmond Hoxworthn about his "little excursion" in the fetid Chacahoulas' swamp, the night before…

"Of course you do, big boy," Edmond sneered. "And that's exactly why I'm calling you… There's been a slight change in our plans; thanks to that nosey bitch you've been watching."

"You know I'm up for anything, boss… What ya have in mind?"

All excited, Grande rapidly shoved the rest of his large burger into his big mouth, chasing it down with a thick, extra sweet, vanilla milkshake; just the thought of murder made him terribly hungry again…

"I want you to pay a "little visit" to my son of a bitch butler, Princeton; as well as his black voodoo sister tonight."

"Your butler and his sister? But why, boss? I don't understand."

"Don't ask questions, dumb ass! Just make sure that when you leave their place, "the House of Angels", or whatever these superstitious niggers like to call their heathen houses; that both him and the fucking voodoo bitch are dead, okay?"

"You mean that "Sister Light"?" Grande nervously asked. He could not differentiate now if the sudden rush of blood that lightened his head was a product of his fear, or his excitement...

"Bingo, big boy. That's the one! And make sure to cover your tracks. A fire might be nice... That old house should be condemned, anyway; both by God and the Department of Safety..." Edmond viciously grinned, while imaging a spectacular big fire.

Grande hesitated. "I'm not so sure about killing a witch, boss... I mean, what if she's the real thing?" He asked with a dash of fear in the voice.

"Shut the fuck up and simply do your job, you idiot!" Edmond coldly hissed. "That black cunt of a witch deserves worse than hell; so feel free to kill her slowly and painfully..." At this instant, Edmond wished he could kill Mambha himself. It was certainly her fault that his grandmother's head was now full of "mumbo-jumbo" and that she was suddenly stricken with an absurd generosity towards Angela. Edmond would not be surprised if the thick-headed Eileen changed her will, and left half her fortune to 'his coloured sister'. As soon as he'd taken care of this terrible mess, Edmond decided that he would try to have his grandmother committed; Eileen was obviously not of sound mind anymore...

"And don't forget about that Boivin bitch. She's still your priority," Edmond added, before nervously glancing at his Platinum 'Rolex' watch.

"Sure, boss, sure," Grande mumbled.

"I can't hear you, freak. Speak louder!" Edmond barked.

"I said okay, boss." The rain started up again. "Bad connection..." Grande blew into the cell phone; then he hung up, hoping that the highly irritating Edmond Hoxworth would assume that they were disconnected.

His highly demanding boss was giving him the creeps lately...

Rain and black witches... No matter how Grande looked at it now, it stank of bad news; so bad indeed that he didn't feel like having another juicy burger.

Edmond Hoxworth's strange sadistic behaviour was really bothering Grande now. The man was not himself anymore, that's for sure. Lately, that filthy rich son of a bitch was cussing like a truck driver; and now, he also wanted his own butler and his famous sister dead...

Grande deeply wished that he could phone his loving Lupe and rest his tired head on her soft, and so comforting large pillow breast.

Yup, there's something wrong... Professional assassins don't cry, Grande sadly told himself, thinking about the poor girl in the shack. *No, professional assassins don't cry,* he sadly thought again, deeply annoyed, before suddenly changing his mind and joyously ordering another double beef burger...

Yeap; that's the spirit, man!

Chapter Sixty-Four

"New Orleans"

Like a patient giant boa constrictor, and while digesting his excellent meal, the Mexican-Samoan giant had been calmly waiting in his car, in Royal Street, for less than two hours, when he finally saw Angela and Emmanuel exiting the lobby of the elegant Monteleone Hotel...

When she stepped into the street, Angela was looking so beautiful, that Grande smiled, while thinking that she was worth waiting for.

Killing that woman of exception would be the high point of his life, Grande knew; so he decided to savour each moment when she would finally be defenceless in his large powerful hands...

Grande rapidly turned the ignition key of his old black 'Cadillac' and discretely tailed the cab, as it headed downtown. After making two lights in the nick of time, a motorcycle cut in front of him and he was forced to step on the brakes. *Good reflexes, my man...One more second and that "hijo de puta" would've been hit.*

"Mother-fucker!" The young man on the Japanese bike shouted, while he gave him the finger.

"Ungrateful son-of-a-bitch!" Grande screamed back. "People just don't care anymore..." He sighed, realising that he had almost lost the beautiful Angela.

Grande wanted to keep a safe distance from his target, so he wouldn't be noticed. He put on dark sunglasses, slid down in his seat, so he would look like an average-sized man, and stayed one car's length behind the old cab; even so, from time to time, the handsome man with Angela kept looking behind him suspiciously...

Fifteen minutes later, the cab pulled up in front of the back entrance of the New Orleans county hospital, where the morgue was located. Grande nervously watched as Angela and the handsome Emmanuel got out and walked through the revolving doors of the main entrance. This time, they weren't wearing the smiles of lovers. Their expressions were much more sombre, and they looked as if they hadn't slept. The man's eyes were puffy and red; so it wasn't hard for Grande to put two and two together.

The handsome pussy had been crying... He smiled, deeply satisfied.

Grande manoeuvred his Cadillac into the employee parking. Luckily, the space that he used to park in many years ago when he worked there, was free; this was a good omen, he decided...

He waited outside, behind the glass doors, and discretely watched as a middle aged white man, who looked like a detective, approached Emmanuel and Angela. After a few words, he led them towards the door of the morgue. The second they turned the corner, Grande slipped into the building and tipped his head to the security guard at the reception desk; an elderly skinny black man with not much teeth, who seemed to have somehow forgotten, that it had been almost four years since Grande had quit his job...

An elderly black couple and a middle-aged obese mulatto woman were leaving the morgue. The elder woman was crying, while the younger one was hysterically shouting. Angela and Emmanuel backed up against the wall and let the family pass.

"I told Ramon not to get involved in that shit!" the obese woman shouted. "We didn't need a fancy car, and all that fancy crap Ramon wanted." She cried, before she ripped a diamond earring from her lobe and angrily threw it on the floor. "For this shit he died! For a fucking stone!" The old black woman hobbled down the corridor and fetched the expensive earring; it would certainly pay for the funeral...

"What am I supposed to do without him? I loved that asshole!" The obese woman lamented, looking truly devastated.

"Ramon was a good man, honey," the old man said while lowering his eyes.

"I hope whatever fucking nigger killed my man, gets the electric chair!" She hollered, before putting a protective arm around the old man's shoulders. Carried by hatred, the sound of her harsh words strangely echoed through the long silent corridor...

In the waiting area, the detective opened the heavy door to the morgue; then, a sudden rush of cold acrid air burst out. He motioned for Angela and Emmanuel to sit down on one of the few orange plastic chairs, which had been placed against the dirty mint-green wall. Angela swallowed the bile that rose in her throat, while nearby Grande took a deep breath and smiled, feeling calmer; he truly loved that smell...

For a moment, like an Egyptian cat, Grande motionlessly stood around a corner, fairly certain that they couldn't see him. Angela's pretty face was now hidden behind Emmanuel's tall and lean body; a good thing. Even though Emmanuel's face was quite puffy from crying, Grande found him disturbingly handsome; in fact, this man was driving him completely crazy with constant jealousy...

A few minutes later, the detective returned, along with the medical examiner, and Grande strained to hear the conversation.

"Sir, the preliminary findings indicate that your sister died of strangulation... The same person who killed her, apparently also killed two African-American men; both who had prior criminal records... But I have a reason to believe that her killer wasn't the same one who raped her and broke her legs," the detective explained without a dash of compassion in his monochord tone of voice.

"Jeanette's legs were broken?" Angela asked meekly. She could barely hold back her intense nausea; and the medication that she had taken that morning to ease the pain of her fractured rib, wasn't working anymore.

"A better word might be 'mangled', Miss Boivin... Her legs were broken in over a hundred places; and now the real question is why?" The detective paused, visibly disturbed, while avoiding eye contact.

"They might've not been found for a long time, if it weren't for a vagrant who used the abandoned shack to escape the rain this morning," the detective flatly added.

"My sister was raped?" Emmanuel rhetorically asked, clenching his fists tightly. Angela put her hand on his arm, hoping to soothe him; but he brusquely moved away from her. His breathing was short and his face was red with anger, with beads of sweat appearing on his forehead.

"Yes Sir. There were traces of two types of semen... I sent the samples to the lab to do a match with the DNA of the two black males."

"The two black men were hired thugs, and not very professional," the detective added again. "A 'Toyota' van registered in one of their names is still parked at the shack... We suspect that they picked up the victim, brought her to the shack, got drunk, raped her; and then broke her legs... Both of the dead men had high levels of alcohol in their bloodstream; and one of them used crack." The detective flatly said, avoiding their eyes again.

Grande cursed the rain...

"Sir, the responsible person for strangling your sister and the two black men was pro all the way," the detective calmly explained. "Forensics is still working at the murder scene; but from the size of his foot prints, this man is a veritable giant and a master at breaking necks!" The medical examiner added, before he shook his head in amazement. "I've been doing autopsies in this town for twenty-five years and I've seen a lot of strangle victims; but I've only seen a break this clean one other time in my life... About four years ago. I remember that she was an extremely beautiful young mulatto woman; a model..."

Grande blanched. He didn't know whether to be proud that he'd finally "mastered his art"; or simply ashamed, that out of the scores of people he'd killed in the past years, only this one had been perfect enough to have earned the respect of the chief medical examiner...

"It would be helpful, sir, if you could think about your sister's friends," the detective said to Emmanuel. "Did she have any enemies? Anyone who hated her enough to break both her legs in such a vicious way? Someone else, Sir, who hated her enough to want her dead?"

Angela almost blurted out that it was "her legs" that someone wanted broken; but her profound shame kept her deadly silent...

"Mister Lambert, we'll need to complete some paperwork," the medical examiner added as kindly as he could.

Emmanuel nervously looked at Angela. "Let me go alone," he softly said, visibly bracing himself for the worst, before he gently kissed her on the temple.

Grande carefully watched as Emmanuel slowly got up and followed the two other men down the long pale green corridor; then Grande smiled, while feeling his blood suddenly rushing to his groin.

Finally, Angela was alone now; helplessly alone...

The devil smiled again.

Chapter Sixty-Five

"New Orleans City Morgue"

Petrified and deeply saddened, Angela motionlessly sat on an orange plastic chair, nervously waiting for her dear Emmanuel to return...

The strong, unpleasant smell of formaldehyde, blood and death, hung heavy in the cold hallway; and every breath painfully reminded Angela that it should be "her body", the one lying lifeless and atrociously broken-limbed on an autopsy's cold steel table. Death, Angela knew, had made a grave error this time and taken the wrong victim. In fact, it was a human error that took Jeanette's life; just as it was a terrifying human error that had destroyed the life of her genetic parents, because of an unforgettable "human stain"; the same one that stole the lives of so many mulatto children in the Hoxworth Castle...

Angela sadly thought again about the Hoxworth's terrible legacy and the bone-chilling secret behind the majesty; all of this for what? Honour? A great name? A place in "high society"?

Unfortunately, such terrible things were nothing new in mankind's long and painful history...

Many ancient history books were full of tales of terrible family bloodshed.

For mankind, life wasn't simply sacred enough - they had proved this in the indecent way they treated poor animals - but what was paramount was one's social position...

Angela was simply petrified, not knowing where to cast the blame anymore.

The tormented spirits of the wailing mothers who were too weak to stand up for the lives of their mulatto infants? Then whom? The Hoxworth patriarchs? Poor Eileen? The arrogant Edmond? What if Josephine had died with the terrible secret held intact? Perhaps, the negro's wayward gene would eventually have subsided into nothingness; and the sweet Jeanette would be alive today.

So much pain; so much guilt; so much constant hatred and manipulation...

Such a heavy cross to bear; and all this for what? A few shades of darker skin?

Totally immersed in her deeply disturbing thoughts, Angela didn't even notice the janitor silently entering the room, until she heard the swashing of the coarse broom on the floor.

Angela had no desire to make eye contact with anyone, so she sadly looked downward and without a word she stared at her legs; her exceptional ballerina legs that were insured for 3 million dollars each; the beautiful legs that two vicious black thugs believed they'd broken into shards of worthless bones...

As if the janitor understood her need for silence, he kept his distance, redundantly sweeping the same area of the hallway. Somehow, the sound of the swashing broom strangely soothed Angela's nerves. It reminded her of the end of summer, when her beloved André slowly swept the first leaves off the veranda, while the sweet Josephine sat on her favourite rocking chair near Angela, as she lazily curled on the rattan sofa, feigning sleep, content, happy, and loved; those were safe and happy days...

The sound of the door opening suddenly startled her. The lulling sound of the sweeping stopped, and when she looked up again, the janitor was gone, but was replaced by the detective. His face was solemn as he handed Angela a large black plastic bag...

"Miss Lambert was wearing those," the detective flatly said. "The jacket - the one in the bag that your friend was wearing, it is yours; isn't it, Miss Boivin?" He flatly asked while searching her eyes.

With plastic gloves, the detective, as not to contaminate the evidence gently removed a pair of grey cotton jogging pants, and a stained white t-shirt that had been torn around the collar; as well as a white sport bra and a pair of pale pink panties, which looked as if they'd been sliced off with a knife...

Angela uncontrollably trembled, as the detective carefully folded the clothing on an orange plastic chair beside her. When he removed her ballet jacket, her hands were shaking so much, that she could barely control herself. Underneath the jacket, a pair of broken

'Ray Ban' sunglasses and Jeanette's brand new white 'Nike' trainers, spotted with dried blood, lie at the bottom of the bag...

In vivid detail, Angela's terrifying nightmare of her rape slowly replayed itself in her tormented mind.

Angela saw quite clearly inside her head the two black men, one large and the other small and skinny; as well as a large heavy crowbar leaning against the wall, strangely glinting in the moonlight that shone through the decayed wood of the shack...

Now it occurred to Angela that, during the entire nightmare, she never saw her own face. In fact, she had only seen her ballet jacket and had assumed that she was the victim. If she would've only paid more attention to that premonitory dream, maybe Jeanette would still be alive...

"Yes, Sir, the jacket is mine," she almost murmured to the detective, while her eyes rapidly sank to the white tiled floor, because she was feeling terribly guilty now.

"Do you know of anyone who might've wanted to harm you, Miss Boivin?" The detective asked; his tone neutral, while carefully observing her.

Angela slowly shook her head, then told him about the incident she had in the French café with the strange Texan and his two unpleasant bodyguards. Besides this particular man, she could not think of anyone else who would want to kill her; yet, deep down, she was certain now that when she gave the poor Jeanette her ballet jacket to wear, she had as well signed her death sentence...

"We'll need to ask you some more questions, then," the detective told her. "Your, uh, friend, will be out in a few minutes... He's okay, but it's rough in there." He said, referring to Emmanuel's identification of the body of his sister. "It's a cruel world, Miss Boivin," he unemotionally added, before rapidly going back into the morgue.

As soon as the detective had left, the janitor approached Angela, his hands fumbling in the pocket of his white overalls; then he pulled out some hard fruit candy and he softly said: "you're looking a bit pale... You want some, Miss? Sugar will help the queasiness," he gently offered, smiling like a child.

The janitor was a huge man. His jet black hair was neatly pulled back in a thick ponytail, and the effect made his forehead look too massive for his head; almost deformed. His impressive features were so awkwardly shaped, that his face resembled a strange jigsaw puzzle that someone had somehow forced together; but his big dark eyes were extremely soft as he gently gazed down at her, smiling, as he generously held the little fruit candy out in his enormous palm.

"The sugar will make you feel better, Miss," he softly repeated.

Hesitantly, Angela took three pieces, and the janitor shoved the rest back into his pocket; then he kindly smiled and he amicably put his large hand on her left shoulder. His cool touch startled her so much that she dropped the candy. When she bent down to pick it up, she noticed that he was wearing black cowboy boots with three roses nicely embroidered on each side...

What kind of a janitor wears leather soled cowboy boots? She thought, intrigued.

As if the man were searching for something, he silently stared into Angela's eyes. "Please, let me help you, Miss," he softly said again, before bending down to pick up the last piece of candy.

Suddenly, Angela remembered that the medical examiner had told her that the hands of the killer were certainly very large, and extremely powerful. As a cold shiver of fear rapidly coursed through her spine, she tried to toss the terrifying thought from her head.

The killer wouldn't work in the county morgue; she thought, panicked; *and he certainly wouldn't be giving out candy to strangers...*

Feeling quite stupid, Angela didn't want the janitor to think she was panicking, but she urgently wanted to get away from him. She slowly grabbed her purse and prepared to get up.

"You shouldn't do that, Miss," the janitor softly said, smiling, before placing his huge hands on her shoulder again. His smile revealed a shiny gold tooth, like a wild animal. Angela suddenly felt trapped, so she froze...

Now Angela could hear the sound of her heartbeat grow louder and louder...

With his large cool palms still pushing down her shoulders, the strange janitor began to slowly caress the nape of her neck with two of his long fingers.

"You're still pale, Miss," he kindly said. "I wouldn't want you to faint... People pass out all the time in this hallway," he almost whispered now, as his huge hands slowly moved like a strange animal, closer and closer, to the middle of her fragile neck...

Totally terrified, Angela met his gaze. His dark pupils were strangely dilated and his eyes deeply bored into hers. She opened her mouth, as if to scream; but no sound came out.

Angela was totally paralysed by fear, and it seemed as if she were in the midst of a horrible nightmare again...

Perhaps it's just a dream... God, pleeease let me awaken!

"Hush, hush; calm down, Miss," the man hissed, as his hands now formed a large circle round her neck, like snakes; snakes which felt cold and vicious...

"Don't be afraid, Miss, I'm not going to hurt you... Just look into my eyes, now... Yes, just like this..." He calmly suggested; his voice as smooth as a hypnotist's; then his large pupils rapidly dilated, like a big cat's in the dark...

Am I really dreaming?

As his cold fingers slowly tightened around her neck; little by little suffocating her, her vision finally blurred. In state of total shock, Angela closed her eyes, hoping that when she opened them again, the frightening nightmare would be over.

"No, pleeease, Miss, don't close your eyes yet," the man softly begged; but Angela couldn't breathe, and she didn't have the strength to open them anymore.

Angela was about to faint, when she heard the sound of heavy footsteps echoing down the hallway; then seconds later, like a violent wind, a rush of oxygen entered her lungs.

"That woman is not feeling well," she heard the janitor explain. "I'm going to get her some water," he added, before high-tailing it out of the room.

When Angela finally reopened her eyes, she saw a group of people curiously eyeing her. Less than a minute later, Emmanuel appeared. His eyes were red-rimmed, and his face was stern; then he was strangely looking at her.

When Angela finally looked around, the janitor was nowhere in sight...

Chapter Sixty-Six

"New Orleans City Morgue"

When Emmanuel saw Angela, her eyes were wide open and full of fear, and incoherent mumblings were falling from her tongue; it seemed as if she was wandering in another world...

"Angela?" Emmanuel worriedly asked, taking her by the shoulders, before gently shaking her. But she did not respond and her eyes were still strangely fixed on the hallway; as if the devil himself stood there...

"Sir, what happened?" The detective asked.

One of the strangers who lingered around Angela explained, "a janitor, a big guy, told us that this woman here might need help; he said he'd be right back with some water."

Emmanuel and the detective quizzically eyed each other, since there was a water dispenser, as well as paper cups, just a few feet away from where Angela sat...

"You say he was a large man?" The detective asked the witness.

"Huge!" The man exclaimed. "Well over six feet, if he was an inch."

Angela nervously shook her head as if she were coming out of a deep trance, then she said with a little voice: "I saw his hands... his eyes... I had an ominous feeling. They were death, Sir. Death!" She deeply shivered, before she nervously clutched Emmanuel's arm.

"Have you seen him before, Miss Boivin?" The detective asked.

"No, Sir; but I know that it was him... The one who killed Jeanette," she quietly said, stunned by the certainty of her statement.

"But how can you be so sure, Miss?"

"I know. I just know... When this man put his hands around my throat, then when he looked at me, his eyes grew wide with anticipation; almost joy... I knew that he wanted to kill me; he would've if these people hadn't surprised him... I am certain now, that if I hadn't given Jeanette my ballet jacket; and if she didn't resemble me so much, she would still be alive... Ohhh Emmanuel, I'm so sorry." Angela said with a broken voice, and then she finally broke down in tears, while her body shook with violent convulsions.

"But why would this man want to kill you?" Emmanuel asked, while protectively holding her as she uncontrollably wept.

"My brother... I mean Edmond Hoxworth." Again, her voice was as sturdy and certain as a judge.

"Your brother is *the* Edmond Hoxworth?" The detective repeated, raising his thick eyebrows; it was the first time his face had shown expression.

"Why would Mister Hoxworth want you dead, Miss Boivin?" He suspiciously asked.

Visibly ashamed, Angela buried her face in Emmanuel's chest.

"It's a long story, Sir," Emmanuel calmly explained, "but Mister Hoxworth certainly has his reasons..."

"Do you have proof, Sir?" The detective asked, visibly interested.

Angela nervously looked up. "No, not yet; Sir, but I'd bet my life on it... That is, if I'm still alive to win the bet..." She sadly added, looking straight into the detective's hazel eyes. "I know that it sounds strange, but few days ago, I dreamed of Jeanette's death in vivid detail... You have to arrest Edmond Hoxworth!" She finally exclaimed, visibly revolted.

"Look, Miss Boivin, with all due respect, I can't go arresting people without cause; especially not the likes of Edmond Hoxworth," the detective said, apologetically, before he handed her his card. "Call me if you have something "tangible" that we can use; because "dreams" don't hold up in court, Miss Boivin." He firmly said, while looking straight into her eyes.

"But wait! Wait! I know exactly how it happened, Sir. In my dream…

"I'm really sorry, Miss Boivin," the detective cut her off mid-sentence. "As I said, a dream is not enough to warrant an arrest; but we'll look into it." He firmly said again before he sharply turned, then rapidly walked away.

"Emmanuel, you believe me, don't you? Do you forgive me?" Angela asked with a broken voice, while wiping her tears with her hand.

Emmanuel took a deep breath. "Yes, I believe you, Angela... And I know that it wasn't your fault," he tenderly assured her. His eyes were full of pain, but his voice was calm and soothing; then he lovingly held Angela, as she sobbed again.

While Emmanuel was trying to reassure Angela, he heard a woman scream from down the corridor; and then he raced down the hall.

A young black nurse had found a dead man in the janitorial closet; he had been stripped of his uniform; and from the unnatural way in which his head was positioned, it was obvious that his neck had been broken; neatly broken...

Chapter Sixty-Seven

"New Orleans"

Like a hawk firmly holding its prey, Grande's huge hands tightly clutched the old Cadillac's steering wheel...

Turning left down Beaulieu Street, where the famous "House of Angels" stood, Grande was still hunting, the muscles of his hands just warming up for his next assignment. Grande was extremely angry; it was a strange emotion that he rarely experienced. Even the half bottle of tequila that he had used to wash down a dozen cream donuts, did not seem to work to calm him anymore, simply because he thought that he had fucked up; he wasn't used to 'fucking up', and he didn't like it at all...

Grande liked to think of himself as a sort of scientist; a "professional man" whose desire to kill arose from an incessant curiosity to discover where life really goes, when the body dies. Always in the past, Grande has thought that the 'key' to his lifelong quest, would be found in the eyes of the "perfect victim"; but when he sadly realised that the young woman he had strangled in the shack wasn't the beautiful Angela, somehow, he had lost his concentration...

Although this victim's soft golden eyes seemed to plead for an escape from her misery, by way of death, Grande was too irritated by his recent mistake, to see the "nuances" of her soul...

Grande wouldn't deny that he'd received some kind of pleasure killing Jeanette; especially after he lovingly held her superb naked body in his powerful arms, and gently rocked her for a long hour, just like a baby, until the first light of dawn broke through the sky; until the strange sounds of bayou animals filled the air again; until he decided that it was time for Jeanette to die...

At this point of his life, Angela was Grande's Holy Grail; and for a moment of unspeakable joy, he had thought that he had finally found her.

For ten interminable days, Grande had anticipated seeing that last precious glimpse of life in Angela's beautiful eyes, before he could voluptuously break her elegant neck; and with each passing day, his excitement had grown to an insufferable level.

To think that he had been so close, was unbearable now...

When Grande saw Angela waiting at the county morgue, he suddenly felt like the luckiest man in the world. It was as if the entire universe was finally "in sync" with him. But when he realised that his beautiful prey was so preoccupied in grieving, he suddenly understood that she would fear him and death; even though he could feel that Angela almost sought death's relief, its "peace", as her final release from life's constant miseries...

Never had he been so close to fulfilling his lifelong dream; and never had he failed so miserably! Now, Grande sadly realised that as soon as he would approach the beautiful Angela, she would certainly run like a nervous mouse from a cat; thus, intense fear would cover the windows to her soul, like a thick fog above the bayou...

The large quantity of sugar and alcohol he'd consumed, combined with the high levels of stress hormones, was adversely affecting him; Grande was now a time bomb ready to explode...

For the first time in his life, Grande suddenly realised that he looked forward to killing for the sheer pleasure of it. He also sadly realised that he was no longer "a scientist", but a cheap mercenary and a common murderer; something that he despised...

That lingering disturbing thought filled his entire being with intense self-disgust. He also didn't like the idea of killing the famous black voodoo priestess; especially when he heard that she'd lost her eyes...

What would he look at when he strangled her?

Grande sadly parked two blocks away from the famous "House of Angels".

The sidewalks were practically empty. Two couples - one silent and morose, the other arguing - were walking in opposite directions; and a white elderly woman with purplish mossy hair, stood waiting, while her two little white French poodles stopped to do their business at a nearby magnolia tree. The old woman stooped to pick up her dog's excrement, before she smiled at him while keeping her inquisitive piercing blue eyes fixed on him; then, nervously, she and her dogs scrambled along...

Without witnesses, Grande took three steps at a time.

The massive wood door of the House of Angels was locked, so he used the ancient knocker. The look of the heavy brass knocker disturbed him; it was a quite strange angel's face with an uninviting expression, and two strange wilted wings that had been dusted with red paint, the colour of dry blood...

"May I help you?" The young black man who answered the door politely asked.

"Yeah. I have to see Sister Light. I have an extremely important message to give her." Grande said with a big, friendly smile.

"Well, I'm sorry, Sir," the young man apologised. "But my aunt doesn't receive visitors after five p.m. You'll have to come back tomorrow morning, Sir."

"That won't do. Gotta see her now! It's a life and death matter," Grande insisted; then he brushed his cheek as if he were brushing a tear away.

The young black man - really a boy - hesitated. It was always a matter of 'life and death'; but he finally felt pity for the sad exotic giant.

"So wait in the courtyard. I'll see if my aunt can make an exception... You can sit there," he calmly said, pointing towards a stone bench that stood near the large peaceful stone fountain. "What's your name, Sir?"

"Huh?" Grande said, surprised. "Uh, Greg... Greg Gimener. Sister Light doesn't know me, though. My..." Again he brushed his cheek. "Paquita, my beloved, well, she wrote me a letter advising me to come here today... She wrote it before she died." He painfully said while lowering his strange eyes. "She mentioned a man named "Princeton" as well..."

"You know my dad?" The boy excitedly said.

"No, but Paquita knew him, and what I have to say concerns him as well."

"A matter of life and death? Is my father alright?" The boy asked, now worried.

"I need to speak to Sister Light; and then to your father," Grande softly stated. *The kid is getting annoying*, he thought, as he suddenly stared at the boy's neck...

"I'll get my aunt, Sir," the boy said, before disappearing into the big house.

Shortly after, Grande discretely slipped in...

The lower level of the ancient house was all hallways and rooms, and Grande felt like he was in a strange labyrinth.

Like a big cat, Grande strode quickly and quietly, following the hallways that were lit, until he finally found a door that was ajar and peered into the room. A middle age black man sat behind a desk, looking at some papers that he was holding in his hands. When the phone rang, he answered it.

"Oh, it's you... Well, thank you, Miss Boivin... No, no, I'm alright," he softly said while closing his eyes. "As the brother of Sister

498

Light, I lost my fear of the otherworld a long time ago, Miss." He calmly said, before he laughed. "I believe that Mister Hoxworth will be at his grandmother's castle for dinner tonight around 8 p.m. If you want to meet with Madam Eileen again, try to go to the castle around 6 or 7 p.m.; and make sure that you leave before Mister Edmond arrives... I've resigned, you know... I should have, a long time ago, but it's easy to deny the truth when you're being threatened... But be extremely careful, Miss Boivin. I know for certain now that Mister Hoxworth is a dangerous man." Silence. "Please be careful, Miss. My son and I are leaving New Orleans at the end of the week... I know now for certain that Mister Hoxworth's the kind of man who could kill his own mother." The butler sadly smiled, reopening his eyes. "I'm truly ashamed to have served this arrogant man for so long; but at least my son is now able to go to college... He's the first in our family to have had such a chance." He paused again, as if thinking about the Faustian trade he'd made for his son's benefit. "So, good luck, Miss Boivin; and please, be careful!" He stressed again, before hanging up.

Small world... Perhaps I'm still in sync with the universe. Grande almost chuckled. If he could get, he thought, Princeton and Mambha quickly out of the way, he could get to Angela's hotel in time, and he would wait until she went to the castle; and then hopefully finish his task...

Grande peeked into the room and saw Princeton rustling through his desk, before filing documents in a large manila envelope;

then he turned off the overhead light, leaving the room dimly lit by a small green desk lamp.

Grande stared at the butler's skinny old neck; then he studied his fearful eyes, recalling the conversation that he had just overheard. If he stripped away his good manners, Grande thought, Princeton Harley was just an ordinary black man. It was obvious now that the stylish butler truly hated his work, but always lived in hope that his only son would not have to spend the rest of his life bowing to a "white master", as he had done during his entire life. Now Princeton was fleeing the confines, wishfully thinking that he might have a few good years of rest and relaxation, somewhere far, far away, in a place where no one could give him orders anymore; especially not a white man...

Princeton Harley is just an old tired man, whose death would stir the universe about as much as an ant... Grande snorted in disgust. To kill such a man would be worthless, he knew; in fact, Princeton was not even worth the energy. Grande deeply sighed before he silently walked past the door, unnoticed; then he decided that he would take care of Princeton after Mambha; or simply let the old black ant burn when he set the old house on fire...

Right now, Grande was hungry for "action" and poor Princeton wasn't even a crumb. Perhaps the so famous "black priestess" of New Orleans would feed his lust; thinking of it, Grande suddenly became very excited at the pleasant thought of killing a woman whom so many adored...

Chapter Sixty-Eight

"Hoxworth Castle"

Behind her regal Louis XV desk, the always-elegant Eileen Mackenzie Hoxworth sat rigid as an antique Greek statue, her will as inflexible as her spine; as she carefully observed her attorney's face suddenly shrivel with shock...

James Cloverdale's left eye nervously twitched as he carefully read again the hand-written will that the Grande Dame of New Orleans had composed just an hour before she summoned him to her magnificent French castle. For the entire forty-five years that James Cloverdale had been employed by the Hoxworth, he had never expected something as drastic as this to occur one day...

"My dear James, I took the precaution of having an affidavit signed by my personal doctor, assuring that I am completely sound of mind and body," Eileen calmly said, while elegantly handing him a document that she'd just received by fax. "So there will be no disputes around my word in this matter..." Indeed, the shrewd Dame Hoxworth had hired the most esteemed psychoanalyst in New

Orleans to cite her "sanity", as she obviously no longer trusted her beloved grandson; her only heir...

"But... But I don't understand, Madam," the well-mannered man politely argued. At seventy years of age, the attorney's heavy lids almost eclipsed the silvery grey of his eyes. "You don't even know this woman!" Cloverdale exclaimed, showing a dash of stress, before taking off his gold-rimmed spectacles to scrutinise his client's impassive face. For the first time in his life, the brilliant man was truly confused; never before had he failed to anticipate the needs of one of his extremely rich clients.

"To tell you the truth, madam, I am simply flabbergasted by your strange decision," he quite nervously said, while deeply questioning Eileen's sanity, despite the doctor's affidavit. "Has your grandson lately done something to displease you? I doubt that Mister Edmond will take this matter lightly, Madam... Half of his inheritance to a mulatto woman whom you've never mentioned before? Don't you think he'll find it quite bizarre?" The attorney firmly asked while daring to look straight into Eileen's eyes.

"Well, my dear James. If my grandson displeased me, I would simply give him nothing!" She calmly said with a little smile. "Half of my large fortune is more than enough, anyway... But I think that you should know the truth, my dear James, just in case "something" happens to me..." Eileen calmly said again, this time not smiling at all while nervously adjusting a superb emerald and diamond earring, from 'Cartier', that she bought for herself the preceding day, as to lift her spirit...

The old attorney slid up to the edge of his seat, and his jaw dropped slightly open.

"As for the recipient of the other half of my fortune – my dear Angela Boivin-Haddington – she is no stranger to me... You see, my dear James, this young woman is, in fact, my granddaughter..." Eileen seriously said with a little Giaconda's smile, while watching her attorney's expression move from confusion to shock. "I've also given her permission to obtain a DNA sample from my son's remains; in case my dear Edmond contests my will... My granddaughter will be also entitled now to change her family name to Hoxworth; then, when her time comes, she will also be entitled to be buried in our family crypt, as a Hoxworth; as was, and is, her birth right... As for Elisabeth, my daughter in law, when her time comes too, she shall also be buried by my dear Jonathan's side in our family crypt; and her name is to be reinstated as well..." As Eileen calmly spoke, her beautiful face strangely illuminated, as if her tormented soul finally could shine through. "If nothing else, my dear, I firmly intend to reunite "my dear family" before I go; it's the least I can do..." She softly smiled. "As you can see, my dear James, I am also giving a portion of my fortune to my daughter-in-law, who, I hope, will forgive me for any suffering I have involuntary caused her... Yes, I've been a fool, I know that now; and I deeply regret the past," Eileen sadly said, sorrow and guilt flavouring her words. "It's unfortunately way too late to undo what has been done, my dear James; but it's not too late to try to make amends..." She softly said while lowering her eyes. "I've often acted foolishly in my life; but I'll not be a fool in my death... Despite what the world thinks of me, I don't have a heart of stone, my dear James." Eileen finally said, slightly blushing like a little girl.

"But, Madam, your granddaughter is not Caucasian," the attorney politely protested, as an intense look of confusion and doubt slid over his face.

Slowly, but efficiently, Eileen explained the theory of the "wayward gene"; but she did not tell him about the numerous infanticides that had only ceased with the birth of Angela...

The attorney discretely cleared his throat before speaking, wishing he had a tissue to spit the phlegm in his throat, but instead he swallowed it down; the demands of a polite society...

"Well, then, Madam," he slowly began, visibly shocked. "I truly think that you've always acted in your family's best interests, and your courage is frankly admirable!" He courteously smiled, even though he thought that Eileen was making the wrong decision.

"Thank you my dear... You see, when Angela was born, I thought I was acting in my family's best interests; but unfortunately, I realise now that I was not, James... The truth is that I didn't have then the courage to face such a terrible scandal... If I would have had it, my son would now be alive," Eileen finally confessed, tears blurring her vision.

Reluctantly, the attorney gently took Eileen's bejewelled hand.

"Please, Madam. You couldn't predict the consequence of your actions... The past is the past," he politely lied, while still thinking that she took the right decision then...

Eileen snatched her hand away from his, feeling that she didn't deserve his compassion.

"The past is eating me like a cancer, James; so please, register these papers immediately. Another day and it may be too late…" Eileen nervously said, wiping her tears with an embroidered handkerchief. Her tears felt strangely cleansing, but she was not a woman prone to crying; especially in front of a stranger.

While Eileen firmly signed the documents, the attorney witnessed in silence before replacing his spectacles on his long nose; then he silently worried about how he would deal with the arrogant Edmond Hoxworth, when he heard about all this…

"I can't say that I'm not worried about your grandson's reaction, Madam," he nervously said as he carefully placed the documents in his 'Gold-Phiel' attaché case. "Mister Edmond won't be pleased, you certainly know that, Madam; and at your age, forgive me for saying this, he will undoubtedly question your sanity… He may even take you to court." He said again, before nervously scanning her eyes.

Just as the attorney finished his last sentence, a man's voice boomed from across Eileen's vast study.

"Sanity? "Who" are we speaking about, my dear James? Has the "great Dame Hoxworth" lost her mind, lately?" Edmond's voice was terrible hostile, violence seeping from every pore, and his tormented eyes were strangely bulging from the sockets, causing him to look almost freakish…

"Ohhh, my darling… I wasn't expecting you for another half an hour," Eileen calmly said, slowly rising from her golden chair.

"Well, good thing I'm early, Grand... The "early bird" catches his worm, doesn't he? Pity the late bird that loses out... The meek will never inherit the earth!" Edmond flung his bitter words violently across the room; they were as heavy as rocks. "What business does your dear lawyer have here?" He dryly asked, as he dangerously approached her regal desk.

"Oh, nothing of importance; Sir..." The attorney lied, hurrying to close his attaché case, "I just need your grandmother's 'Henry Adams' on a few documents," Cloverdale lied, nervously smiling.

Quick as a snake, Edmond stuck his hand in the attorney's briefcase.

"Not so fast, my dear James!" He coldly exclaimed, before removing the papers; then, as he quickly scanned the words, his jaw dangerously tightened...

"What do you know? It's nothing of importance..." Edmond viciously grinned. "Just Grand's new 'Will and Last Testament' dated today... Not "important", eh?" The tone of Edmond's voice immediately cooled the air.

The attorney tried to snatch the will from Edmond's hands, but the latter raised his arm, clutching the papers, playing a game of cat and mouse with the man.

"Come on, old man! Come and get it!" Edmond said with a vicious grin.

"But it's just a slight update, Sir," the attorney nervously explained, as his grey eyes nervously twitched.

"My dear Edmond," Eileen firmly said, raising her voice for the first time. "Please, my boy, return the documents to Mister Cloverdale. You're acting now like a child, Edmond! Do you hear me?" She exclaimed, before slapping the palm of her hands against her desk.

"I will, Grand, I will..." Edmond smirked. "Just as soon as I get a good look at them!" He leapt on Eileen's desk and firmly held the will up to the ceiling light. "Minute details? Eh!" He spat, his strange eyes glinting as he bent his knees, so he could look his grandmother in the eye. "How could you do this to me, Grand? How? How??? What the fuck is going on in your fucking nigger-loving head!" He finally screamed, the large vein on his neck ready to blow.

Eileen carefully slid away from her desk. "Edmond, my daaarling, this is a very, very expensive desk; so get down from there now!' she ordered, trying her best to appear in control of the situation.

"Certainly, Grand; certainly..." Edmond sweetly said, with a crazy smile crossing his face; then, like a panther, he jumped down with a thump and moved forward. Eileen's back was now to the wall and she was cornered; but she strangely did not look afraid.

"Grand, how could you give half of your money to that bastard nigger! How? I'm your only grandson, and this woman is nothing to you! Nothing!!!" He shouted before he violently grabbed Eileen's fragile shoulders, dropping the will in his madness. As if being guided by "invisible hands", the will floated under the large desk...

"I trusted you, Grand! I always loved you more than my mother!" Edmond shouted again, visibly out of control, his eyes quickly darting from side to side, like a madman.

Discretely, the attorney quickly bent down, picked up the precious documents, and slid them into his attaché; then Eileen rose and nodded. James Cloverdale could read the message in her eyes…

"James, I need to speak to my grandson alone… Will you leave us, please?" Eileen softly asked.

Then, to the attorney's surprise, Eileen firmly pushed Edmond aside and sat back in her chair; reassuming control…

"Are you certain, Madam?" The attorney nervously asked, not knowing what to do anymore.

"Do as you're told, and get lost!" Edmond barked to his face. "Get the fuck out of here now, James! Grand's right!" We need to have a serious talk…" He coldly said, looking lethal.

"Then I'll talk to you shortly, Madam… Please call me if you need me. It was a pleasure, as…"

"Get the fuck out!" Edmond yelled, before bending down to pick up the will. "Where the fuck is that damned will?" Edmond was frazzled. Now his vision was slightly blurred, and all he could see was red; blood red…

Meanwhile, the attorney dashed out the door. The old man knew madness when he saw it, and was not about to risk his life; not even for his best client.

James Cloverdale decided that he would notify the security guards on his way out; at least, Dame Mackenzie-Hoxworth could count on that…

Chapter Sixty-Nine

"New Orleans"

"House of Angels"

Without a sound, Grande stepped into the large red walled room, but the black eyeless priestess immediately felt the chill of his strong presence...

As Mambha concentrated, Grande's image became increasingly clear, until she was able to see him as easily as someone with 20-20 vision. She could see that the man in the room was tall and lethal; and also that his only true relationship, was a life-long love affair with "death" and its minions...

Mambha instinctively brought her hands to her long Nubian neck, protectively wrapping her tapered fingers around her cool flesh. As the Mexican-Samoan giant silently approached, her temples began to throb and her heart rate immediately accelerated. Even though the black priestess knew that "death", was merely a passage to another dimension, and a simple progression of the soul towards a new adventure; Mambha was still a human animal and was suddenly overwhelmed by the primordial fear of losing one's mortal body...

Mambha tried her best to calm herself; to simply tell herself that the "will to survive" was only natural, because it was a necessary genetic imprint designed by the great "Creator" of all universal beings. Without the essential fear of death, she knew, the numerous pains of life would be too much for most to bear; thus the immortal soul would never progress. Humans, in particular, would be prone to take the coward's way out, and more often commit suicide...

Still, even for a superior soul as herself, the primordial fear was extremely uncomfortable; to the point that it paralysed every muscle of her body. Mambha suddenly felt as if she were anesthetised, but still conscious. Breathing was now extremely difficult...

Summoning all her strength of spirit, the black priestess fought hard to take total control of her body, as to shake off her natural terror. Mambha wanted to die in peace; a difficult task, considering that she always knew that her death would be brought on by violence, instead of natural causes. The only solution now was to fervently pray; and so she did...

Soon, the numerous protective spirits that the black priestess had so often invoked during her long life as friends and "allies", came to her rescue; and they swept her fears away with one strong blow of their breath. Her strong life force finally rushed through her veins; then suddenly, the black priestess felt more alive than she had in her entire life.

Mambha firmly stood up; then she slowly turned around smiling, and raised her slender arms to "the light", before she calmly surrendered her immortal soul to the great force that drove the universe; to the ultimate power...

"Dear Sweet Lord," she softly intoned. "Have mercy on the tainted soul of my assassin and pity him, for this man has never seen your magnificent light, my Lord, nor felt the pure love and endless joys of the eternal world beyond; a world this poor man will never know..." She sadly said.

Like a breath of fresh air, Mambha's words echoed powerfully through the large room.

Grande was about five feet away from her, when he suddenly stopped. Smiling, beatifically, the proud black priestess calmly turned to face him; turned to face her death...

For a moment, Grande hesitated, feeling deeply disgusted by her deformity, the hideous black sunken holes that had replaced her eyes; and yet, he couldn't stop looking at those empty sockets as if a strange light, maybe a "soul", had residence in them. As Grande nervously stared, he began to hallucinate, for he saw what seemed to be now two magnificent translucent eyeballs, rapidly looking back at him, deep into his heart; deep into his dark soul...

Without knowing why, his powerful hands suddenly trembled, and his lips became parched and dry. Cautiously, like a cat, he approached the black priestess, his eyes still fixed on the strange luminous cavities where her eyes should have been. Grande was now strangely hypnotised and felt as if he were looking into a mirror; into his own eyes; into his own life...

"Why do you hesitate, my friend?" Mambha softly asked, her face incredibly serene. "A man who kills like you do, cannot be afraid of an defenceless old woman, can he? What is it that you see in my eyes, my friend? They are merely pools of water... a mirror to your own soul." She calmly said with a radiant smile.

Visibly empowered now, the black priestess stood erect and tall, and Grande suddenly felt decimated by the frail eyeless woman...

"You're a crazy old witch!" He exclaimed. "You don't scare me! You don't scare me at all! I see nothing in your eyes! You don't even have eyes, you ugly black witch! You know that!" He finally shouted, feeling terribly inhsecure and strangely vulnerable, before he stepped closer, refusing to give in to his fear; but from deep within Mambha's empty sockets, came a strange soft light that he didn't understand, and that light was probing him now...

"Why can't you look away from my eyes, Cuauhtémoc? I can see fear in your face now... You cannot hide, my son; not from the blind. For the blind can see what the sighted cannot... My inner eye can see into the depths of life; into the depths of death..." Mambha beatifically smiled again, her beautiful face glowing now with undiluted faith.

"Shut up, you fucking black witch! You don't know me! You can't even see me!" Grande shouted again, deeply perturbed, before nervously reaching for her slender neck. As soon as he touched her skin, his whole body began to tremble; then sweat soaked through his shirt, his pants, his socks, and his strange face reddened with profound shame; had he wet himself? Mambha's skin was cool and soothing, and so soft to the touch...

Now the black priestess' eyes were fully formed and intensely looked at him. At first, they seemed to be mirroring Grande's own eyes; but then, they delved deeper, boring into the very depths of his tormented tainted soul. Desperately, Grande tried as hard as he could to turn away, to look anywhere else; but he could not. In total fear, he closed his eyes, but Mambha's intense gaze - a sorceress's looking-glass – rapidly broke through the thin barrier of his heavy eyelids, and there was no escape; there was no place to hide...

"Stop it, you old black witch!" He screamed, panicked, before trying to get a grip on her neck again. But it was no good; his large palms were now too slippery, and he was shaking with an intense irrepressible fear...

The black priestess's eyes grew huge, almost filling the room, like a giant screen in a movie theatre; and on them Grande strangely saw his entire life playing out at an accelerated pace.

"Cuauhtémoc" saw himself as a boy, a lonely child growing up in the poor Mexican barrio; then he saw his mother 'Lupe', placing him lovingly in a small coffin, while grotesquely cackling, her large firm buttocks voluptuously swaying; and the bodies of the dead everywhere... Then Grande saw Lupe washing the cadavers limp limbs, before applying stage make-up to their motionless faces, preparing them with care for their "final display"; the "last theatrical scene" of their miserable lives, where, from an open casket, the dead would silently say their final goodbyes to their loved ones, before being buried into the cold ground; before being, most of the time, rapidly forgotten forever...

Then Grande saw the girl. His first innocent victim was only six years old...

Accusingly, the girl stared at him from the other world, her little brown eyes brimming with anger, before she was suddenly surrounded by all of his other victims.

All of them now stared at him in silence, eyes blazing. Everywhere he turned, Grande saw the accusing eyes of someone he had killed, and he could intensely feel their profound anger reaching out to him; deeper and deeper...

"Demonio! Demonio!" They all shouted at him, their voices howling now.

"No! You are the demons!" Grande violently shouted back. *It's the black witch doing this to me!*

Grande had to kill the witch; he had to make the strange frightening eyes go away; but the black priestess' slender neck kept slipping from his grasp...

Summoning all his strength, Grande tightened his large hands as strongly as he could; until finally, Mambha went limp. When her neck was broken, Grande shouted with triumph, before he violently tossed her frail body onto the wooden floor; but even dead, he didn't dare to look at the black priestess...

At last it was finally done, finished, and all he needed to do now was retrieve the gasoline from his car, then burn the old damned house down, with Princeton in it; but one thing was for sure, he really needed to get out from that frightening haunted place as fast as he could.

When Grande tried to leave the red room, he was suddenly frozen by intense fear.

Even though the black priestess was dead, Grande was not alone anymore; all around him there were ghosts; so many frightening ghosts...

The angelic statues had now also turned their strange lifeless gazes accusingly towards Grande. The angels were pursuing him, judging him; weighing his entire life on the scale of good and evil. Grande was chilled to the bone and the sweat that poured down his massive body was like ice. Even though the windows were shut and the air was still, the large burning candles flickered and the room suddenly smelled like death; his death!

In a state of total fear, Grande heard voices whispering, laughing, and strangely calling his name. In total panic, desperately searching for a way out, he began to run; but he lost his balance and slipped onto the floor...

As the first frightening ghost appeared to his left, its face distorted by hatred, Grande jumped out of the reach of its bony hands; but another ghost immediately appeared at his right. Within seconds, the large red room was full of dead entities, each manifesting in front of an angel; each one calling out Grande's name, like a strange litany. Then they menacingly marched towards him, until they totally surrounded him, while still calling his name; while grasping for his dark soul...

When Grande closed his eyes in fear, a putrefying stench filled his nostrils, and he instinctively knew that he had to get out of that haunted place, or he would certainly be dead within minutes.

In an ultimate burst of energy, Grande leapt up; then ran like a madman through the long silent corridor. What he would give at this instant for wings or a horse, something that would help him escape the curse that the black priestess had certainly put on him; but his large feet felt as heavy as sand bags and he stumbled; then heavily fell on his face, painfully breaking his fat big nose. The metallic taste of blood touched his tongue. No matter what, he had to get out! When he pushed himself up, the sad little girl, his first victim, stood before him, blocking his way, her strange eyes boring through him, questioning.

"Why did you do this to me? Why? I had my whole life before me, but you stole it, Cuauhtémoc!" She sadly smiled, before reaching for his hand, as the hoard of hellish apparitions rapidly joined her. The ghosts were parading themselves, cackling; death was now embracing him, wanting him like a vicious lover...

"Let me go!" Grande screamed at the ghosts, uncontrollably shaking, before he finally found the way out of the frightening labyrinth. The invigorating fresh air of the peaceful courtyard never felt so welcome. Once outside the massive front door, he blindly ran towards his car, shouting like a madman, totally oblivious of oncoming traffic. Grande was so overwhelmed with total fear, that he hardly felt the impact of the motorcycle. His large Mexican belt had become tangled within the spokes of its wheels and he was being rapidly dragged, madly screaming through the street; then into the intersection. Suddenly, a massive black 'Cadillac' SUV swerved from the right, ploughing into him; and seconds later, another car swerved from the left, its large bumper smashing into his ribs. Flanked now by two cars and totally paralysed, Grande motionlessly lay on the cold pavement, staring sadly into the night sky...

Minutes later, a hand full of people came running towards the scene of the accident. Some of them had witnessed the accident; but most of them were asking questions, or sadly shaking their heads. The middle age white driver of the Cadillac SUV was sobbing hysterically, standing above the body of the dead motorcyclist, a young Asian man; blood was pouring out of his open mouth...

A moment later, Grande heard strange sirens approaching from the distance, cutting into the sounds of the cool night; but they weren't loud enough to drown out the ghostly cackling. His victims were now surrounding him again, glaring, visibly waiting for his wicked heart to stop beating; waiting for his dark wicked soul to finally join them...

Grande sadly looked into the ghosts lifeless eyes and finally saw death; his death.

Death's cold black shadow hovered for a moment above the sidewalk on which he motionlessly lay, and its frightening laughter rose above the wailing, howling and pain of his victims. But Death was not a ghost; it was a sentence!

Cuauhtémoc understood that he would spend eternity accused by the innocent souls, whose lives he had selfishly stolen; and his own death would be nothing less than an endless living hell, all torment and pain.

For Grande's life work, the tormented Mexican-Samoan would receive nothing, but an eternity of pain; constant, delicious, excruciating pain…

Amen!

Chapter Seventy

"Hoxworth Castle"

Three black security guards ran past James Cloverdale, and began to pound on the impressively carved double doors of Eileen's study...

"What's happening?" Angela worriedly asked the attorney. They had met briefly when Cloverdale had first arrived; but Eileen had been quick to whisk him into her study to talk business and had told Emmanuel, as well as Angela, to wait downstairs in the castle's grand salon.

Breathlessly, the old attorney rapidly explained the frightening situation; but just talking about it, made his blood pressure dangerously rise...

"Madam Mackenzie-Hoxworth's new will pushed her grandson over the edge, Miss Boivin. Not only was she giving you half her fortune, but she also insisted that you take the Hoxworth name; and also that your mother be reinstated as a Hoxworth as well... I believe, Miss Boivin, that this was the proverbial straw that broke the camel's back, as they say..." The attorney nervously said, before he removed a neatly pressed white handkerchief from his well tailored vest pocket, and nervously wiped the sweat from his bushy silver brow. As Angela listened to the attorney, she could hear the security guards pounding on the massive doors of Eileen's study; without much luck...

Emmanuel frowned and gestured to the butler. "Besides those doors, is there any other access into Madam's study?" He asked, while trying his best to think about a solution.

'Windsor' the stylish middle age black butler, succinctly and calmly explained that Dame Eileen's private salon led to the study; but also, that earlier that evening, 'Madam' had instructed him to bolt it...

"And what about windows? Balconies?" Emmanuel pressed.

"Oh, yes, Sir; there is a large balcony; both in the salon and the study," the butler preciously said, elegantly raising his well-defined eyebrows. Windsor was a great fan of old swashbuckling Hollywood movies, so he quickly caught on.

"They're about five to six feet apart, Sir." He calmly said again, while clearly picturing the exciting scene in his fertile mind...

"Lead the way, my man!" Emmanuel gently ordered, with a constricted smile while raising his eyebrows.

Realising what he really intended to do, Angela followed him nervously, fretting. "You're not actually thinking of jumping from one stone balcony to another? This isn't a movie, Emmanuel! You could really break your neck!" She exclaimed, alarmed.

"Please, don't worry, ma chérie; I'm a world class climber!"
He seriously said with a quite reassuring smile, before giving her a
soft kiss on her lovely lips.

Angela gently patted his large chest, her heart wildly beating.

"Please, Emmanuel; please darling... Just be careful," she
emotionally called after him; but he was already gone...

With his long muscular legs, taking the steps three at a time
and painfully followed by a rather excited butler, who was breathing
as loudly as an old locomotive, the handsome Emmanuel Lambert
truly looked like a real action hero.

Another guard rushed passed them, wielding a crow bar.

Angela rapidly followed the black guard up the monumental
white marble stairs, while praying that the guards would break
through the massive doors before her beloved Emmanuel attempted
something truly crazy. From inside Eileen's large study, Angela could
hear Edmond yelling, as well as sometimes, the sound of crystal
breaking...

While one of the guards was trying to pry the crowbar
between the doors, Angela pushed passed him and pounded on the
thick wood.

"Please Edmond, pleeease! Leave grandmother alone!"
Angela shouted through the door, before realising that it felt quite
strange to refer to Eileen as her "grandmother"; and yet, Angela
would be damned if she let her genetic brother treat the 'Grande
Dame of New Orleans' as if she were a vulgar piece of dirt...

"You fucking coloured cunt!" Edmond's voice boomed through the door. "What the fuck are you doing here, anyway? This isn't your family, you fucking bitch! You're not my equal and you will never be! I am the master! Get that through your stupid Negro head! You're from the dirty blood of slaves and always will be! I hate you, bitch!!!" Edmond viciously shouted, before he violently kicked the door to show his terrible anger, his deep hatred, and his undiluted rage; but Angela calmly stood her ground…

"My poor Edmond, you're terribly insulting for a gentleman; and what you're saying really makes no sense… I'm from the same blood as you, little man, and you will just have to accept that!" Angela suddenly yelled. "If I'm the daughter of slaves then so are you, my dear "brother"; so just try to put that idea once and for all in your sick head!!!"

"Fuck you, bitch!" Edmond screamed again like a madman, before violently kicking the massive door again. "Fuck you, dirty black cunt! Yes, fuck you and fuck your dirty Negro loving mother; and fuck Granny over here!!!" He finally shouted out of his lungs.

"Edmond; just leave grandmother alone!" Angela yelled again, feeling now her blood boiling. "She truly loves you. You know she does! She has always done the best she could for you, Edmond," she firmly added, thinking that it was time to change strategies; pleading was obviously not working, and Eileen's life was at stake now…

"Edmond, if you want, you can keep my share of the inheritance," Angela offered. "I don't want the money, believe me;

so please, open the door, and I'll sign whatever you want. But please, Edmond, pleeease, don't hurt her!"

"I don't trust you!" Edmond shouted. "I don't trust any of you! Not Grand; not my mother... I know that you all want to rob me what is rightfully mine; I'm not going to let any of you manipulate me anymore. You're all fucking bitches, and you should all go to hell!!!"

"Stop it now, Edmond!" Eileen finally shouted. "Your sister is speaking the truth, my boy!"

Suddenly the sound of flesh against flesh was loud and violent.

Angela's ear was now to the massive door, nervously listening, while Edmond viciously slapped his grandmother again, hard and repetitively; then she heard a body fall to the floor with a grunt, and the sound of a woman moaning...

"Can't you hurry?" Angela yelled at the guards, who continued to work at the deadbolt with the crowbar. *Where is Emmanuel? Please, God, please protect him.* She thought; feeling panicked.

The sound of the first gunshot was louder than a sonic boom, and the one that followed shortly after seemed even louder; then everyone froze...

"Edmond! Ohhh, Edmond, you fool; what have you done, my child? What have you done?" Eileen was screaming in between her heart breaking sobs.

A third shot reverberated through the thick walls of the study, and Angela heard the sound of furniture and crystal crashing again to the floor; then, a moment later, the lock gave way and the massive doors finally opened...

Horrified, Angela witnessed the scene as if in slow motion; then she suddenly froze in fear.

Eileen was laying on the floor by her desk, while a few feet away, on a bed of broken crystal, Edmond was struggling with Emmanuel; the latter trying to keep the former from reaching for his gun, which dangerously laid at Eileen's feet...

Emmanuel firmly straddled Edmond, forcing his back to the floor, before hammering his chest and stomach with powerful punches. Blood covered each of the men's faces; but it was not enough to hide the hatred that shone now from Emmanuel's eyes.

Today, Emmanuel knew he would not respect the "pious promise" that he had made, long time ago, to his beloved martial arts master. Today, it would be a fight of vengeance; a fight to death...

But Edmond's total madness seemed to have rendered him immune to the pain of Emmanuel's expert blows; his eyes were strangely fixed on a middle size bronze statue of a ballet dancer by "Richard MacDonald", which stood upon a golden end table, next to a red brocade sofa...

Emmanuel was about to deliver a final punch to Edmond's face, when the heavy statue violently smacked against his skull; strangely sounding as if someone had dropped a large watermelon...

Horrified, Angela screamed; then she rushed to Emmanuel's side and knelt by him, visibly unafraid.

Edmond viciously grinned at her, before he violently grabbed her hair and lifted her into the air with one hand; then he firmly placed his other hand on her throat, and his long fingers clutched her fragile neck; they were as cold as an iron gate. This time, it was clear that Edmond would not let her go...

Angela could read the message in her brother's eyes: *I want to kill you now!*

She could not breathe, nor move anymore. Her feet were off the floor and she strangely hovered in the air, like a fragile puppet on a string, quickly losing consciousness...

Angela did not see that each guard had a gun trained on Edmond now; nor that as he walked towards the desk, he was using her body as a living shield. Edmond released Angela's hair; then he picked up a large silver letter-opener shaped like a dagger. His eyes insanely glinted and he viciously smiled at the black guards, taunting them while aiming the sharp dagger at Angela's heart...

Angela heard voices shouting and arguing, but the lack of oxygen was rapidly affecting her nervous system, and she could no longer comprehend what was being said.

Totally resigned, she closed her eyes and prepared to surrender to death; but instead of the quiet of death, another gunshot blasted her eardrum...

Edmond's grip lost enough, so that she could gulp down some air, but he still held on fast; then a second shot was fired, and Angela felt a warm liquid wet the front of her legs. When she looked down, horrified, the pristine white marble floor slowly became red...

Edmond loudly cursed, and then he put his hand firmly on his upper thigh, trying to stop the blood flow. Angela was about to escape, when he lowered the letter opener towards her back; then a third shot was fired...

As if in a slow motion movie, Angela turned around and saw her grandmother, who was now standing behind her desk, holding the gun which had just shot a bullet into Edmond's left shoulder blade; a single lethal bullet lodging itself deep into his wicked heart...

Stunned and without a sound, Edmond strangely looked at Angela, before he fell to her feet, like a rock.

As the little silver gun fell from her hand, Eileen's eyes brimmed with tears.

"Edmond, my darling," she mumbled. "Ohhh Edmond... what a fool... You gave me no choice, my poor child. I never wanted it to be like this..." She painfully cried. "I love you so much, my darling. I love you more than myself. I always did... Edmond, my dear child, do you understand me?" Eileen knelt by his side, softly talking to him as if he were still a child. "But I just couldn't let you kill your sister... I couldn't let you kill my baby; not again... No my child, I couldn't let you kill Angelica..." She cried out with a broken voice.

Angela was overcome with a chaotic mix of intense emotion; and yet, deep inside her heart, she felt a strange sense of peace and freedom.

This was not Angela's present, but the past awakening. Her old soul, that same soul which had waited so long for revenge and justice, had been finally avenged...

Eileen, her mother from her previous incarnation, had finally made amends for her sin towards Jonathan and Elisabeth, and she had made the necessary sacrifice to redeem herself.

Against her will, the Grande Dame of New Orleans had killed her beloved grandson in order to save the precious soul of her daughter, the sweet Angelica Aurora Maria.

The constant painful lies, the profound guilt, as well as the excruciating shame of the past, were now finally cleansed and purified with blood; Hoxworth blood...

The long infernal circle was finally closed. Amen.

"Only blood can wash away the stains of blood," Angela said, mesmerised by the tragic scene.

"What?" Emmanuel asked. "What are you saying, Angela? More blood has never solved anything!" He was almost angry that she could think such a terrible thing.

Angela slowly shook her head, coming back to her senses; her present reality.

"I don't know why I said that... It wasn't me, Emmanuel," she softly assured him.

Yes, it was you, my child; it simply was your soul speaking... The black priestess' voice resonated in her mind.

Emmanuel sadly nodded, before wrapping his arms around Angela, while he looked at Eileen who sobbed, as she gently placed her grandson's head on her lap. Edmond's eyes were pinned to some indecipherable point of the beautiful painted frescoed ceiling, representing a romantic cloudy sky with rosy cherubs and colourful birds. Edmond's expression was strangely peaceful and his facial muscles were now relaxed. In death, there was not a speck of hatred or envy colouring his eyes anymore...

For the first time since the terrible day in which his father had committed suicide, the extremely arrogant Edmond Louis Gabriel Hoxworth looked completely at peace...

As Angela silently watched her grandmother sobbing, suddenly a strange feeling enveloped her entire body.

To think that only a few months ago, Angela was bereaving the loss of the woman she thought was her mother; totally unaware that the incredible drama of her life had yet to unfold, was quite mind blowing now...

A whole new world, "another world", had strangely opened for Angela, and she was now blessed to have three mothers; the sweet Josephine, Elisabeth and Eileen; three great women; three amazing mothers...

For the first time, Angela lovingly looked at Eileen, before she tenderly smiled.

When Eileen caught that particular look in Angela's eyes, she softly curved her carmine lips and her cerulean eyes twinkled with a bountiful love that seemed to suddenly embrace the entire room. At that instant, a gentle peace prevailed; as if the ghosts that had inhabited the old castle, those broken-hearted mothers who had wailed and moaned for centuries, had finally been released...

"Please, forgive me, my darling Angelica; please forgive me, Angela." Eileen emotionally said, her lips slightly trembling as she slowly rose up, her eyes never leaving the ones of her beloved Angela. "Ohhh, my child, I missed you so much every day of my life..." She said with a broken voice, her eyes full of tears. "Please, my darling, pray for my poor soul, dear blessed child of mine... I love you so much." Eileen softly smiled again and an intense feeling of love emanated from her; a pure, motherly love that seemed to touch and enlighten each cell in Angela's body, until it finally reached her soul; Angelica's soul...

This was truly a magical moment. But suddenly, the extraordinary bubble of tranquillity broke again.

In a blink of an eye, Angela understood what Eileen really meant to do, but it was unfortunately too late...

While lovingly looking into Angela's eyes; into her very soul, Eileen already held the little silver gun in her bejewelled hand and smiled.

As Angela helplessly watched Eileen lift the gun towards her own head, her eyes still lovingly gazing into Angela, her lips still curled, her smile as tender and beautiful as a young woman in love; time strangely slowed down...

Eileen's mesmerising gaze became fixed on what seemed to be an empty point in the middle of the study, but what she really saw was more there than not; Jonathan's ghost stood in front of the large red marble fireplace, lovingly smiling at her...

"Yes my love... I am coming!" Eileen sweetly said, as if she were talking to a child again. "Dear Lord, please forgive me for the sin I'm about to commit, but we both know that this is my time!" As Eileen negotiated with the Almighty - a businesswoman to the end - at the speed of light, the little silver bullet snaked through her exceptionally intelligent brain, killing her painlessly; lovingly...

During her entire miserable life, Eileen had borne the great burden of the Hoxworth curse, of the blood on their hands; of the terrible shame and the constant sorrow that had built up over five generations. No matter how much charity work she did, Eileen couldn't cast off the poisoning heavy weight of guilt that she carried since she had lost her beloved Angelica and Jonathan; now the terrible spell was finally broken, and her poor tormented soul was finally liberated...

Before Eileen lost consciousness, she saw her beloved Jonathan, his arms welcoming, standing now between herself and Edmond, who lay close to her upon the floor.

As Jonathan watched his mother's liberated soul pass from the world of the living, to "his world", he lovingly smiled. His face became peaceful, before he slowly turned to face Angela; to face his daughter...

"Forgive me, my dear Mary-Elisabeth; my darling Angelica... Please bless our poor tormented souls in your prayers, my child; and may God bless you, as well as your children..." Jonathan lovingly said, while his eyes seemed at peace now.

For the last time, Jonathan Hoxworth lovingly looked at his daughter, then he let forth a hearty laugh; before he finally vanished, never to return...

Amen.

Epilogue

After almost twenty long hours, an 'Air New Zealand' Boeing 744, like a majestic bird, slowly approached the fabled coastline of the French island of Tahiti, revealing a precious emerald green pearl, magically floating upon a blue liquid canvas...

Smiling, Angela gazed down at the calm peacock blue water that was languorously caressing the sandy shoreline. She was relieved to see the golden sun illuminating the beautiful exotic island, with all its embracing glorious light; a light that was so different and so far from the misty islands of England...

A loving tender smile brightened Angela's face, and she deeply sighed with contentment.

In the past year, her life had transformed her in so many ways that she would have never imagined. Despite her many painful losses, Angela was extremely grateful to God and all the angels of the universe; grateful for the sorrows that had made her into the person she was today, simply because she could finally see herself more clearly, and as a result, her world was more beautiful than ever before...

The words that the black priestess prophesied while they were in the van, softly lingered in Angela's mind. "The island where Emmanuel lives will be the place where you will find peace, my child... There you will have a family; two boys and a girl... There, you will be truly blessed and no longer isolated from your kindred; your neighbours..."

How strange it was to think that, while Angela was in the midst of a dark mental labyrinth so convoluted, she never thought about the eyeless black priestess having such a lucid vision. Now Angela finally realised that during all this time, there was an invisible thread in her life; a thread that simply led her "home"...

Life could be hell, Angela perfectly knew, because she had journeyed there herself; but life could also be paradise. Perhaps to fully experience happiness, one had to experience hell as well...

Today, Angela deeply believed in the life of the soul, even though she had always thought that religions were invented to help poor humans cope with the meaninglessness of their lives; but what an incomparable comfort for her to have true faith, now...

Angela had also learned that, if one person was lucky enough to achieve happiness, it was to be fully enjoyed without guilt nor remorse; because happiness never lasted long enough, since a human life was so terribly short...

Now, with her beloved Emmanuel by her side, Angela felt that the words of the mystics and saints were true; but she also knew the past still lurked behind her. Sometimes, she could still hear the wailing of the bereaved mothers, whose babies were suffocated in order to protect the Hoxworth name.

Had such evil actually existed? *Yes, evil exists; and so does good...* A voice said in her head.

As the plane circled the paradisiacal island below, the ocean languorously lapping its gleaming shore, Angela tenderly kissed Emmanuel on the cheek. He had dozed off, but when she looked into his eyes, she could feel his intense love, like the glorious sunlight that softly poured through the plane's windows. Emmanuel's love was, as warm as the island's waters; deep, nurturing and supportive. His love was Angela's sun, reliable and all embracing; and if clouds covered her sun one day, the next day, it would surely shine; and if not, the day after, she knew...

As Angela looked peacefully outside the window, she noticed that the shadows on the breath-taking island seemed outlined with silver.

It's incredible how lucky I am. God has been truly good to me... She thought, lovingly smiling.

For the first time in her life, Angela realised that she could be truly herself now; not "black or white"; "African-American or English"; but simply a wonderful human being. A human being finally free of the pretences that cause barriers of fear to separate one person from the next.

Angela also realised that Emmanuel loved her for herself, not for who she was in society, or for how well she danced; he simply loved her being, and just that was a relief...

There was an easy harmony in their relationship and each day, they simply and wonderfully nourished each other. As much as Angela loved Pierce, she always felt a sort of strange gap between them; and sometimes it grew as deep as the Grand Canyon. It was true that they shared an intense attraction; but this attraction was only skin deep, on both of sides.

Besides Angela's beauty, Pierce had loved her because he was extremely proud of her artistic achievements; as for Angela, she would be lying if she said that she would have loved him as much, if Pierce Haddington hadn't possessed the accoutrements and the undeniable charm of his upper class upbringing. To be honest, as handsome as he was, Angela probably would not have married Pierce if he were an ordinary man...

But now, her life was totally different with Emmanuel. As the years passed and age, little by little, wrinkled their skins and slowed their minds, Angela was now certain that their love would only grow, like Josephine's and André's. Love, when it was decent and pure, was the ultimate reward of life and the only way to truly live; the only decent way to truly experience one's humanity...

For the first time in her life, Angela was strangely aware of something else, too; something extremely important in fact...

Angela realised that she totally accepted herself; respected herself; even loved herself! Yes, she finally realised that she had the right to live, breathe and move about the vast world without any fear; and above all, without thinking that she had to constantly prove her worthiness...

Now Angela was indeed Mrs. Boivin-Lambert; and the simple gold eternity ring around her finger, seemed more beautiful to her than all the flawless diamonds in the world.

Angela had not removed this so precious eternity ring, since the day her dear Emmanuel lovingly placed it on her finger, two months ago, in a little stone church, near their island's lovely home by the sea. Deep down, Angela was certain now that this "blessed ring" would remain on her finger even when she would be in her grave; and she did not need a black voodoo priestess anymore to tell her this...

If one thing was certain now, it was that her future near her beloved Emmanuel would always be full of respectful love; full of constant nurturing love...

As the plane approached the magical island, Angela softly squeezed Emmanuel's hand. Today was a brand new day, and it was finally time to leave the painful past behind, including the city of her birth, the beautiful New Orleans; along with "its ghosts" and painful memories...

Goodbye, my dear New Orleans; goodbye ghosts...

Eileen and Edmond had been placed to rest by Jonathan's side in the Hoxworth family crypt; and every night now Angela fervently prayed that their souls had found some kind of peace in the other world. As for her newfound vast fortune, since she had inherited the entire Hoxworth estate, she would use most of it to create two foundations. The first foundation would offer abused children and women a way out of their hells, as well as enough therapy, so they could heal themselves, and above all; learn to love themselves again...

The second foundation would be a scholarship fund; one that would provide children from low-income families the opportunity to study classical music and ballet...

Angela also decided to let the Hoxworth name die with Edmond.

Angela didn't want to carry their name anymore, nor their tormented bloodline; besides, the simple thought of her body spending eternity in that frightening crypt sent shivers down her spine...

As for 'La Rêveuse" the magnificent Hoxworth French castle; along with Edmond's regal mansion in New Orleans, they were turned into museums opened now to the public.

The proud Dame Eileen Rose Mackenzie-Hoxworth would have certainly approved; the regal stones themselves would keep the Hoxworth name gloriously alive...

On the other hand, Angela's divorce had not been a quiet affair; although she was told by some of her London friends, that the Haddingtons had somehow celebrated and rejoiced when they heard the news from Pierce... That is, until they found out that their dear Pierce was dating a young model from South Africa; a model who had quickly and undoubtedly become pregnant with his child...

There were wedding bells in the air again; but ironically, Pierce's new exciting flame wasn't Caucasian like he was; nor was she a light skinned mulatto, similar to the beautiful and gifted Angela. Pierce's new flame was black; black as a moonless night...

As for the sweet Annabelle Haddington, she had decided to break her engagement with the extremely wealthy Philip Bainsbury, calling the big wedding off only two days before the date, so she could elope instead with a young and terribly handsome English middle class stableman...

This was much more than Annabelle's parents could bear. Shortly after the young lady ran off, Stuart Haddington peacefully died in the bed of his pretty Pakistani whore; whereas Gail's trials had just begun...

The English tabloids had a field day, of course; so Gail left her beloved city of London, to find refuge in their 17th Scottish large country house. There, she spent countless days in her bedroom, doing nothing, but staring out the tall leaded windows at the white sheep peacefully grazing in the vast emerald green meadows below. The gentle woolly animals seemed to have a calming effect on Gail's fragile nervous system; gin, on the other hand, sufficed to numb her rebellious spirit...

Although Angela felt that Gail never really liked her, she sent her sincere condolences, along with a large basket of cheerful exotic flowers, from her beautiful island.

To enjoy another's sorrows - no matter whether they were due justice or not - was not in Angela's nature, so she made a promise to keep in touch with the 'poor Gail'; and if she could, she hoped to be a friend to the lonely bitter woman, because deep down in her being, Angela always suspected that the terribly pretentious Gail Haddington never truly knew what real friendship or simple love felt like...

While the plane was circling 'Papeete Faaa' International airport, awaiting clearance to land, the softness and warmth of

Elisabeth's hand touching her cheek brought Angela back to the present.

"Are you alright, love?" Elisabeth's voice was sweet as honey.

"Yes, mother. Why do you ask?" Angela asked, surprised.

"Oh, I just thought I saw you look a bit sad, my darling," Elisabeth softly said, before taking Angela's hand.

"Don't worry, mother. I'm fine... I was just thinking about the past."

"Well then, put on your seat belt and prepare for the present, my darling." She smiled. "We'll be landing any moment. Are you happy to be home?" Elisabeth asked, lovingly looking into her daughter's honey green eyes.

"Yes, mother. Yes, I am... Gratefully so." Angela deeply sighed; she truly meant it.

"I am too, my love," Elisabeth softly said, smiling again, before she looked down at the spectacular emerald green island. She could see now a few small cars below, the drivers relaxed as they went about their day...

"Do you know, love, that our dear Emmanuel did a wonderful job with the house. I truly adore my bedroom and the gorgeous view I have of the gardens... I wonder if the English roses that I planted six months ago, have started to bloom yet," Elisabeth mused, happy as a child.

"If they haven't, mother, I'm sure they will burst into flower the moment they see you," Angela sweetly joked, before giving her a soft tender kiss on her rosy cheek.

"Speaking of blooming, love; have you been having any more nausea today?" While she asked this strange question, Elisabeth's eyes were lit up like a child holding on to a precious secret.

"Yes, mother," Angela worriedly said. "I was feeling a bit nauseous this morning, again... I suppose I've become so used to the pace of Tahiti, that the stress of civilisation makes me sick... Mother, do you think I should see a doctor?"

"Perhaps, my dearest, you should make an appointment with your gynaecologist. You are glowing..." Elisabeth broadly smiled, before placing a protective hand upon Angela's tummy.

Two boys and a girl... The black priestess's prophecy softly resonated in Angela's mind again.

"I think I'm ready to be a grandmother, my darling. Yes love, it's high time! The title perfectly suits me, don't you think?" Elisabeth laughed, and her mirth made her appear two decades younger.

Ahhh, the simple power of looove...

Angela was taken aback. "Mother! Do you really think? Can it be?" She said visibly surprised, while opening wide her lovely eyes.

"What else, my love, what else? It's as clear as the blue Tahitian sky, my sweet little bee," Elisabeth knowingly said; then she joyfully laughed again, before she lovingly wrapped her arm around her "golden child"...

As the plane slowly began its final descent, both mother and daughter looked out of the round window, totally entranced by the multitudinous luminous shades of blue and green; totally entranced by the calm limpid sea, and the incredibly lush vegetation under the luminous sky. Then, like a magical balm, the warmth of the tropical sun softly caressed their faces; caressed their heart...

As the plane touched down the black tarmac, mother and daughter were finally reunited. They were ready now to embark on a new adventure, on a nurturing and beautiful land that they would now call "home sweet home", until the last days of their lives...

Angela breathed deeply, and warm tears of joy slowly started rolling down her glowing cheeks; cheeks that were rosy from the precious life that grew within her.

"Two boys and a girl..." an angelic voice echoed in her mind. Three wonderful seeds from three of the human races, and a loving bridge between all the children of a new world... Three... the sacred number of the divine universe. Hope, Adam and Eve; a loving trinity...

Pure primordial love suddenly surged through her heart like she never felt it before; then her lips tenderly curved into a crescent moon smile.

I am home... Home!

Closing her misty eyes, Angela whispered the simplest of phrases, "Thank you my Lord for this precious gift... God, it is so good to be alive..."

"Yes, indeed..." Her guardian angel whispered in her hears, while spreading his pure, undiluted love, deep into her human heart.

"Yes indeed, my child; it is good to be alive..."

Amen!

THE END

Biography of Marie-Madeleine MacLean

Marie-Madeleine MacLean is the daughter of a French Air Force General and a descendant of the De Mees family ennobled in Rotterdam in 1630, who held some of the oldest private banks in Europe. Her great uncle was Monsieur Pierre Roussel of the French Academy.

She was born in Africa and grew up in Switzerland where she graduated with degrees in History and Art.

In addition to French, she speaks English, Italian, Spanish and Portuguese.

At the age of 17, she began a career in high fashion modeling in Paris.

At 25, in London, she married Mr. Michael MacLean, the son of the famed international novelist Alistair MacLean, author of the world famous "The Guns of Navarone", among others.

At age 26, Mrs. MacLean opened an interior design firm in Geneva, Switzerland. Her works have been featured numerous times in international interior design magazines.

She recently sold her business to devote herself exclusively to writing, finishing her first novel, "Race. The Colour of Shame" in the Fall of 2012. She is currently working on her second novel, "Act of Intention" which will be the first part of an exciting trilogy.

She spends her time between California, Switzerland and the South of France.

CPSIA information can be obtained
at www.ICGtesting.com
Printed in the USA
BVHW032359300522
638434BV00001BA/1